# MADELINE BAKER

## *Wolf Shadow*

SIGNET

SIGNET

**$5.99  U.S.**
**$8.99  CAN.**

ISBN 0-451-20916-8

9 780451 209160

50599

S > EAN

## Other Books by Madeline Baker

Hawk's Woman

Apache Flame

Lakota Love Song

# WOLF SHADOW

## Madeline Baker

A SIGNET BOOK

SIGNET
Published by New American Library, a division of
Penguin Group (USA) Inc., 375 Hudson Street,
New York, New York 10014, U.S.A.
Penguin Books Ltd, 80 Strand,
London WC2R 0RL, England
Penguin Books Australia Ltd, 250 Camberwell Road,
Camberwell, Victoria 3124, Australia
Penguin Books Canada Ltd, 10 Alcorn Avenue,
Toronto, Ontario, Canada M4V 3B2
Penguin Books (N.Z.) Ltd, Cnr Rosedale and Airborne Roads,
Albany, Auckland 1310, New Zealand

Penguin Books Ltd, Registered Offices:
80 Strand, London WC2R 0RL, England

First Published by Signet, an imprint of New American Library,
a division of Penguin Group (USA) Inc.

First Printing, July 2003
10  9  8  7  6  5  4  3  2  1

PUBLISHER'S NOTE
This is a work of fiction. Names, characters, places, and incidents either are
the product of the author's imagination or are used fictitiously, and any resemblance to actual persons, living or dead, business establishments, events, or
locales is entirely coincidental.

*Much love to
Alyssa and Marissa,
the newest members of our family*

# Prologue

The Indians came boiling out of the timbered hills like angry ants whose nest had been disturbed. Teressa Bryant stared at them out of the window of the stagecoach, her eyes wide with delight. Mama had said they might see Indians on their way to San Francisco, but Teressa hadn't expected anything like this.

As the Indians drew closer, she saw that they wore pretty feathers in their long black hair. There were streaks of paint smeared on their faces and chests. Some of the Indians carried bows and had quivers filled with arrows slung over their shoulders; some carried long lances with feathers tied to the shaft. A few of them waved rifles in the air. She noticed that the Indians painted their horses, too. One had a red handprint painted on its rump; another had white circles painted around its eyes; still another had zigzagging lines painted on its legs.

She felt a shiver of unease as some of the Indians drew alongside the coach. She could see their faces now, hear their cries, and they didn't sound friendly.

As more Indians surrounded the coach, Teressa turned to look at her mama for reassurance, but her mama looked as scared as Teressa felt.

*"Venuto qui, bambina,"* Mama said, and Teressa scooted into her mother's lap.

Papa patted Teressa on her arm. "Don't worry, Teressa *mia,*" he said in his big booming voice. "Everything will be all right."

She nodded, her heart pounding with fear.

Mama pressed Teressa's head against her shoulder. She could hear Mama praying, asking the blessed Virgin to protect them, could hear the sounds of arrows whizzing around the coach like angry hornets.

Teressa heard the driver shout at the horses, heard the crack of his whip. The coach picked up speed and for a moment she thought they might get away. And then, to her horror, the coach began to tilt to one side.

With a shriek of fear, Teressa threw her arms around her mother's neck. The coach balanced precariously on two wheels for what seemed like a very long time before it slowly toppled over onto its side.

Teressa cried out as she was thrown off the seat along with Mama and Papa. Stars exploded in front of her eyes as her head hit the side of the coach. She heard Mama groan softly, heard Papa swear as they tumbled inside the coach, arms and legs flailing. Hearing Papa swear scared her almost more than anything else because her papa never said those words in front of her or Mama.

The coach skidded to a stop in a choking cloud of dust. Outside, the Indians were shouting to each other. Moments later, the door, which was now where the roof should have been, was wrenched open and an Indian peered down at them.

"Teressa," Papa said, "get behind me."

Teressa stared at the gun in her father's hand and covered her ears with her hands when he fired at the Indian and missed. With a low cry, the Indian shot two arrows at Papa. One arrow pierced his right shoulder, the other his left thigh. With a cry of pain, her father fell backward. Teressa stared in openmouthed horror at the arrows quivering in her father's flesh.

Mama screamed Papa's name as she pulled him into her lap and cradled him in her arms.

Teressa stared up at the Indian, her eyes filling with tears. "I hate you!" she shrieked. "You killed my papa!"

The Indian looked at her through narrowed eyes, then dropped lightly inside the coach. Teressa tried to duck out of his way, but he grabbed hold of her with one big hand and pushed her up through the doorway and into the arms of another Indian. She saw three other Indians cutting the horses free of the broken traces and leading them away. The driver lay face-down a few yards away. She wondered if he was dead.

*"No! No! La non mia ragazza piccola! Non prendere la mia ragazza piccola! Teressa!"*

Teressa heard Mama screaming her name as the Indian lifted her onto the back of his horse and vaulted up behind her, one arm settling around her waist.

"Mama! Mama!"

Teressa scratched the Indian's arm, trying to get free, and when that didn't work, she bit him as hard as she could, but he only laughed and urged his horse into a trot.

"Mama . . ."

Sobbing and hiccuping, she stared over the Indian's shoulder, crying for Mama and Papa, but the Indian ignored her and kept riding.

With tears rolling down her cheeks, Teressa stared at the coach, watching it get smaller and smaller until it was out of sight.

# Chapter 1

Sitting back in his chair, Chance McCloud regarded the cards in his hand, his face impassive. A full house, aces over jacks. He laid his cards facedown on the table and tossed five dollars into the pot.

He glanced around the room while he was waiting for the other players to decide whether to stay or fold. The Red Dog Saloon was large and square and pretty much like every other saloon he had ever seen, from the picture of the voluptuous nude hanging behind the bar to the sawdust on the floor and the heavy layer of blue-gray smoke that hung in the air. A wizened man wearing a black derby hat sat at the piano in the corner, plinking out a tune on the yellowed keys.

Returning his attention to the game at hand, Chance glanced at the men sharing the table with him. Joe Remington sat to his left. Remington published the local newspaper. He was a tall man with thinning gray hair and a thick gray mustache. Pete Wright was one of the local ranchers and a longtime resident of Buffalo Springs. He sat at Chance's right, his stubby fingers drumming on the tabletop. He was an average-looking man in his early twenties, unremarkable except for a shock of white hair. Vince Salazar, the town blacksmith, sat across from Chance, his slouch hat pushed back on his head, his shirtsleeves rolled up, revealing arms as thick as tree trunks.

Remington regarded Chance through narrowed

brown eyes, nodded to himself, and tossed five dollars into the pot.

"Did you see that new rig over at the mortuary?" Wright remarked. He tossed his cards facedown into the center of the table. "I hear tell it cost old man Jensen near eight hundred dollars over in Dodge City."

"Right fancy for our town, I'd say," Salazar replied. "I'm out." He tossed his cards onto the table.

"Bought himself a new team to pull it," Wright added.

Remington grunted softly. "Business must be good. When I'm dead and gone, I don't imagine I'll be caring one way or another what they use to carry me away. All right, McCloud, let's see what you've got."

Chance turned his cards over one at a time.

Remington muttered an oath as he tossed his own cards onto the table—a pair of kings, a pair of nines, and the fourth ace.

Chance raked in the pot, then sat back while a new hand was dealt. Lady Luck had smiled on him. He figured he was ahead by about three hundred dollars. Another hand or two, and he'd go check on his horse and call it quits for the night.

He was picking up his cards when he felt a shiver down his spine. Someone was watching him. He pushed his chair back from the table and dropped his right hand onto his thigh, close to the butt of his Colt, and casually glanced around the room.

He frowned as his gaze settled on a man standing at the bar. The gent didn't look like trouble—quite the opposite, actually. He wore a natty blue pinstripe suit, a boiled shirt, and a black bowler hat. A neatly folded white handkerchief peeked out of his jacket pocket; a diamond stickpin winked in his cravat. His hair was brown with a heavy sprinkling of gray, his eyes a deep dark blue.

The man's gaze met his, and then he pushed away from the bar. He leaned heavily on a stout wooden cane as he threaded his way between the tables.

"McCloud, are you in?"

Chance glanced at his cards and tossed five dollars into the pot. "I'm in."

"Mr. McCloud?"

Chance looked up at the man with the cane and wondered what a gent of such obvious wealth and good breeding was doing in a backwater town like Buffalo Springs. "Who wants to know?"

"My name is Edward Bryant. I would very much like to have a few moments of your time, if I might." The man's voice betrayed a slight New York accent.

"I'm busy."

"Yes," Bryant said dryly. "I can see that." He reached into his pocket, withdrew five crisp hundred-dollar bills, and laid them, one by one, on the table in front of Chance. "Do you think that might buy me twenty minutes of your time?"

Chance regarded the money coolly for a moment. Rising, he tossed his cards facedown on the table. "Deal me out." He picked up his winnings and the five hundred-dollar bills and shoved them into his pants pocket. "Let's talk."

He followed Edward Bryant across the dusty street and into the plush lobby of the Windsor, the town's finest hotel.

Bryant gestured at a sofa covered in a dark green damask print. "Please, make yourself comfortable."

Chance sat down, his gaze moving around the lobby. He didn't have much call to frequent the place, but it was every bit as fancy as he remembered, with spindly legged furniture that didn't look strong enough to hold anyone who weighed more than fifty pounds. There were a dozen or so fancy lamps with fringed shades, and a sparkling crystal chandelier. Potted palms provided a touch of greenery in the corners. There were low tables of shining mahogany in front of the sofas, thick carpets on the floor, and a number of discreetly placed brass spittoons. A clerk in a dark brown coat and starched collar stood behind the desk, idly thumbing through a copy of the local paper.

Chance turned his attention back to Bryant. "So, what's this all about?"

"I was told that you sometimes go into Indian territory to search for people, that you"—he ran a finger inside his collar—"that you have a certain . . . ah . . . inside track with the Indians."

Chance lifted one brow. "Is that right?" It was true, but only a few people knew that he occasionally went looking for whites believed to have been captured by the Indians. It was something he preferred to keep to himself.

"I did not mean to offend you," Bryant said quickly.

Chance grinned. Apparently Bryant feared he had somehow insulted him by referring to his obvious Indian heritage. "I'm not offended. If I was, I'd be on my way out the door. Let's cut to the chase. What is it you want?"

Bryant laid aside his cane and pulled a folded piece of paper out of his coat pocket. He unfolded it and handed it to Chance.

It was a flyer, similar in size and shape to a wanted poster. His gaze skimmed over the words:

> *Fifteen-thousand-dollar reward*
> *for the return of*
> *Teressa Elizabeth Bryant,*
> *kidnapped by Indians.*
> *The same reward will be paid for*
> *information that leads to Teressa's recovery,*
> *Teressa, now 17 years old,*
> *has blue eyes and dark brown hair*
> *Contact Edward Bryant c/o Wells Fargo*

Chance grunted softly as he studied the pen-and-ink drawing above the description. It showed a pretty little girl with large light-colored eyes and long dark curls. But it was the reward that held his attention. Fifteen thousand dollars. That was mighty sweet, and he could sure as hell use the money.

"My family and I were on our way to San Francisco when our coach was attacked by Indians. They left us alive, though I don't know why. The men who rescued us said the Indians were probably Sioux." Bryant regarded Chance curiously. "Why didn't they kill us?"

"Most likely they were just after the horses. If it had been a war party, you'd be dead now."

"If all they wanted was horses, why did they take my daughter?"

Chance shrugged. "Indians have a soft spot for kids. Any kids. A lot of theirs die young."

Bryant stared at him a moment, then went on. "Be that as it may, they took my Teressa. I have hired several men to find her over the years. They have all given up."

"Go on."

"Teressa was—*is*—our only child. My wife has been understandably heartbroken. We have been told our daughter is most likely dead. If that is true, then I want—" His voice broke and he took a deep, steadying breath. "I want to know for sure. I need to know for sure."

Chance glanced at the flyer again. "How long ago did this happen?"

"Ten years."

Chance whistled under his breath. "Ten years and no one's found her? How old was she when they took her?"

"Seven."

Chance shook his head. "You're wasting your time and your money."

"It is my time, Mr. McCloud, and my money. Will you help me?"

"If she's still alive, she's one of them by now. You'll never find her, and if you do, she won't want to leave."

"I don't believe that."

"Doesn't much matter what you believe. That's how it is."

Bryant started to reply, and then gained his feet, his expression softening.

Chance looked over his shoulder to see a slender woman clad in a modest dark gray dress, a matching hat, and white gloves walking toward them. She had dark brown hair, an olive complexion, and a figure that was slender but well-rounded. But it was her eyes that caught his attention. They were dark brown, fringed with thick dark lashes—and filled with so much sorrow he felt it like an ache in his own soul.

Bryant smiled at the woman. "My dear."

"Eduardo, I am sorry I am late. The dressmaker . . ." She made a vague gesture with her hand.

"Mr. McCloud, this is my wife, Rosalia. Rosalia, this is Mr. McCloud."

She graciously offered Chance her hand. "I am pleased to meet you, Signore McCloud."

"Ma'am." She had a thick accent. Italian, perhaps.

Rosalia Bryant sat down, spreading her skirts around her. Edward Bryant sat beside his wife, and Chance took the chair vacated by Bryant.

"I was just telling Mr. McCloud about our problem," Bryant told his wife. He took her hand in his and held it tight.

Mrs. Bryant turned dark luminous eyes toward Chance. "Will you help us?"

"Does your daughter look like you, Mrs. Bryant?"

"She did as a child, yes, very much, except for her

eyes. Teressa has Eduardo's eyes. Of course, I do not know how she looks now . . . if the resemblance is still there." She took a deep breath, her free hand worrying a fold in her skirt. "You will help us, will you not? Please, signore, you must help us."

Chance stared at the woman. Was it possible? Could he be that lucky? Damn, if he was right, the rest of that fifteen grand was as good as his. "I can't promise you anything, ma'am," he said. "But I'll scout around some and see what I can find out."

Hope flared in Rosalia Bryant's eyes, spilling over in a sprinkling of tears. *"Grazie! Grazie! Dio Di Elogio."* Thank you! Thank you! Praise God.

"I will draw a bank draft for you in the morning," Bryant said. "Five thousand dollars now, and another ten thousand when you return with our daughter. Is that acceptable?"

Chance nodded. "Just deposit the money to my account over at the bank." Five grand would go a long way to keeping that weasel Harry Conreid off his back, at least for a little while. He held up the flyer. "Can I keep this?"

"Of course."

Chance folded the paper and slid it in his back pocket. "Where should I get in touch with you?"

"Right here. My wife and I will be staying in your town until we hear from you."

"As long as you don't expect to hear from me right away."

"I understand. But . . . do you have any idea how long it might take? We are understandably anxious."

"I don't know. Could be a couple of weeks. Could be a couple of months. Depends on how long it takes me to find the Lakota Sioux, and whether or not your daughter is willing to leave."

"Why should she not want to leave?" Rosalia

glanced from her husband to Chance and back again. "Surely she is as anxious to return to us as we are to have her with us once again."

Bryant patted his wife's hand. "Mr. McCloud seems to think that Teressa might not want to leave the Indians."

"Not wish to leave?" Her eyes widened in disbelief. "But that is, how do you say . . . *ridicolo!*"

Bryant smiled soothingly at his wife. "Of course it is. I fear we have taken up enough of Mr. McCloud's time, my dear. No doubt he has business elsewhere."

Bryant stood up and Chance rose with him.

"We shall expect to hear from you as soon as possible," Bryant said as he walked Chance to the door. "Godspeed."

The two men shook hands and Chance left the hotel. Outside, he stretched the kinks out of his back and shoulders. For a moment he considered returning to the game over at the saloon and then decided against it. He'd be leaving for the Lakota's summer camp first thing in the morning. Best to turn in early and enjoy sleeping in a real bed while he could.

He stepped off the boardwalk, heading for the livery to check on his horse. The stable was dark save for the lantern burning out front. Chance rapped on one of the big double doors.

A moment later, Burt Sorenson, the owner of the stable, opened the door. "Oh," he said, scratching under his armpit. "It's you."

Chance didn't reply as he walked past the man toward a stall in the back. His horse, a bay Quarter-Morgan mix, made a soft snuffling sound at his approach.

Reaching over the stall door, he scratched the mare's neck. "Hey, girl. They takin' good care of you in here?"

The mare rubbed her head against his shoulder,

then nosed his coat pocket. Grinning, Chance reached into his pocket and withdrew an apple. The mare gobbled it down, her head bobbing in approval. Smoke wasn't the prettiest horse he'd ever owned, but she was far and away the best. She was fast and quick, with enough staying power and heart to keep going long after another horse would have folded up and quit. That extra speed and bottom had saved his life on more than one occasion.

Chance gave the mare a final pat, nodded at Sorenson, and left the stable.

Pulling the flyer from his pocket, he read the description again, then, whistling softly, he turned down the street toward his hotel. Bryant's fifteen thousand dollars would not only pay off the mortgage on the ranch, but also allow him to buy the section of land adjoining the east pasture, repair the roof on the barn, and buy that new bull he had his eye on.

He glanced up and down the darkened street. Bryant's offer had come at just the right time. Chance ran a hand over his jaw. He'd been filled with an old restlessness lately. Spending some time with his mother's people might be just what he needed. And if what he suspected was true, it would be time well spent.

# Chapter 2

Winter Rain sat outside her mother's lodge, tanning a deer hide her father had given her that afternoon. As she scraped the flesher over the hide, her thoughts wandered to a certain young warrior. Strong Elk.

She had met him that morning when she went walking through the forest to gather firewood. Having collected an armful of wood, she was almost back at the village when she heard the soft call of a dove. She had felt a thrill of excitement as she glanced to her right and then to her left, then smiled when Strong Elk stepped out from behind a tree. He was a handsome young man, held in high esteem by the elders of the tribe. The maidens in the village spoke of him often, for he was a daring hunter and a brave warrior, one who had counted many coups. One who had not yet taken a wife.

"Good morning," he said.

Winter Rain had smiled shyly. A maiden was not to be alone in the company of an unmarried warrior, but it was acceptable to meet "by accident."

"I was just gathering wood." Such a foolish comment, she thought, when he could easily see that that was what she had been doing.

Strong Elk had nodded, then glanced up and down the trail, making sure they were still alone. "I might be walking by your lodge this evening," he remarked.

She had felt a rush of color sweep into her cheeks.

"I might be outside this evening," she had replied and then, hugging the firewood to her chest, she had hurried up the path to her mother's lodge.

Now, she felt her cheeks warm at the thought of seeing him again.

Wiping a wisp of hair from her brow, Winter Rain chided herself. She would never complete her task if her thoughts were on Strong Elk. Sitting back on her heels, she stretched her back.

It was then that she saw the stranger ride into camp. He wore black trousers, a dark gray shirt, and a long black duster that was pushed back behind the gun he wore on his hip.

At first she thought he was a *wasichu*, and she felt a quick surge of fear. Dawn Song's older brother had been killed in battle by the Long Knives. Almost everyone Winter Rain knew had lost a loved one at the hands of the *wasichu*. She stood there, her heart beating wildly. Should she raise an alarm? Was the village in danger of attack? And then she noticed his long black hair, his dark skin, the way he rode boldly into the camp, as though assured of a welcome, and she realized that, though he was a stranger to her, he must be one of the People to have made it this far into the village unchallenged.

Her gaze moved over him again, more closely this time. He had broad shoulders, high cheekbones, a nose that was slightly crooked, a strong jaw, a generous mouth. There were fine lines at his eyes, lines that were caused by squinting into the sun, she thought, and not from smiling, though she couldn't say why she thought that. Perhaps it was his expression, which seemed closed and bitter. There was an air of danger about him that wasn't entirely due to the pistol riding on his hip.

He turned as though aware of her perusal. Their gazes met and she saw that his eyes were a cool gray under straight black brows. An odd flutter erupted in the pit of her stomach when his gaze met hers. Flustered, she dropped her fleshing tool on the ground and ducked into her mother's lodge.

Chance stared after the girl. Unless he missed his guess, she was the Bryants' long-lost daughter. He had seen her a time or two when he had come to visit his cousin in years past, but he had never paid her any mind. She had been too young to spark his interest before, but she had done some growing up since he had last seen her. She had been a girl before, but she was a young woman now. And quite a looker at that.

He glanced around the village as he rode toward his cousin's lodge, nodding to men he recognized. As always happened when he returned here, he felt a sense of coming home, and he sat there a moment, watching the activity around him.

As usual, there were dogs everywhere. Large dogs for working, small dogs for eating. Most were black or brown with pointed faces and sharp ears that resembled those of a coyote. Chance remembered a large dog his mother had had when he'd been a young boy. She had hooked the dog up to a travois whenever she went to pick fruit. As she filled bags with berries or plums or cherries, she had piled them on the travois.

Dismounting, he gave Smoke a pat on the shoulder, then handed the mare's reins to Kills-Like-a-Hawk's nine-year-old son, Bear Chaser.

"Take good care of her for me," he said, ruffling the boy's hair.

With a nod, Bear Chaser took the reins. *"Ai, leksi,"* he replied.

"Is your father inside?"

*"Ai.* Go on in," Bear Chaser said, smiling. "He will be happy to see you."

*"Pilamaya."*

After removing his hat, Chance ran a hand through his hair, then ducked into his cousin's lodge. Kills-Like-a-Hawk was the tribal medicine man. Their mothers had been sisters. Kills-Like-a-Hawk's mother, Laughing Dove, lived in the village. Chance was still looking for the last of the four men who had killed his.

Kills-Like-a-Hawk was sitting cross-legged on a robe, wrapping layers of rawhide around the handle of a skinning knife, when Chance entered the lodge.

It was a large tipi, made from seventeen or eighteen buffalo hides. The beds were folded near the rear. The place of honor was opposite the door at the back of the lodge. There were backrests made of willow poles. Parfleches containing food and clothing were stacked out of the way. A water bag hung from a forked pole near the door. Kills-Like-a-Hawk's shield hung from another pole at the rear of the lodge. A small altar was located behind the fire pit. Buffalo robes, hairside up, covered the floor. As always, the lodge was clean and neat.

Kills-Like-a-Hawk was almost ten years older than Chance, and wise beyond his years. He was a tall man, with a strong blade of a nose, prominent cheekbones, and piercing black eyes. It was said he could foretell the future, that he could command the wind and harness the whirlwind. There were times when Chance believed it.

Kills-Like-a-Hawk looked up, a smile of welcome lighting his face when he saw Chance. His wife, Dancing Crane, covered her mouth with her hand to hide her surprise. She was a pretty woman, a little on the plump side, with wide black eyes and a ready smile.

*"Hau, ciye,* welcome to my lodge." Kills-Like-a-Hawk rose lithely to his feet and embraced his cousin. "It has been too long since we saw you here. Come sit."

Dancing Crane gave him a shy smile. "Will you eat?"

Chance nodded. "Sounds good. *Pilamaya.*"

Dancing Crane went outside. Like many of the women, she did most of her cooking outside during the warm summer months.

Kills-Like-a-Hawk resumed his seat and Chance dropped down across from him.

"So, my brother," Kills-Like-a-Hawk said. "Have you come home to stay?"

Chance shook his head. "No."

Kills-Like-a-Hawk regarded his cousin through knowing eyes. "You are still looking for the one who wronged you."

Chance nodded.

"You will never find the peace you are seeking until you put your hatred behind you."

Chance met his cousin's gaze. "There can be no peace for me while he lives."

"He is not here," Kills-Like-a-Hawk said. "Why have you come?"

"I'm looking for a woman."

A slow smile spread over Kills-Like-a-Hawk's face. "You seek a wife here, among our people?"

"I told you before—I'm not the marryin' kind. This woman was captured by the People when she was a child."

Comprehension dawned in Kills-Like-a-Hawk's eyes. "You speak of Winter Rain."

"I think so. She's the right age, and she fits the description."

"Mountain Sage and Eagle Lance will not let her go. She is their daughter now."

"She has other parents who are anxious to see her. They have been looking for her for ten years."

Kills-Like-a-Hawk laid his weapon aside. "She is

one of us. You will not take Winter Rain away from the People unless she is willing to go."

Chance nodded. He had known he wouldn't be able to just ride in, grab the girl, and make a run for it. Not if he wanted to be welcomed in the village again. Not if he wanted to keep his cousin's respect. He would just have to convince the girl to go with him, bribe her somehow if necessary, maybe promise that he would bring her back here if she didn't want to stay with the Bryants. Hell, there was ten thousand dollars at stake, and he needed that money.

Later that night, lying on his back on a pile of furs, Chance stared up at the slice of sky visible through the smoke hole of his lodge. Before leaving town, he had sent word to Dave Dreesen, foreman of the Double C, that he would be gone for a while.

He blew out a deep breath. It was good to be among his mother's people again. He loved the ranch and what he had accomplished there, but this was home. His best memories, and his worst, were tied to this place, this land.

He smiled faintly as the lilting notes of a *siyotanka*, the courting flute, were carried to him on the night wind. Somewhere in the dark, a warrior sat near the lodge of his beloved, pouring out his heart through the Lakota instrument. And somewhere in a dark lodge, a maiden smiled.

Lakota courtship was, of necessity, carried out within the confines of the village, though couples often managed to meet "by accident" when the girl was gathering wood or water. Still, it was not safe for a couple to venture far from the protection of the tribe, nor did most mothers allow their daughters to wander away without a chaperone. To that end, when a young man went courting, he took a big blanket with him.

Standing beside the girl of his choice, he lifted the blanket over their heads, cocooning them in a cloth world away from prying eyes. If a girl were very popular, there might be as many as a dozen young men waiting to spend a few minutes alone with her.

He wondered if anyone was courting the Bryants' daughter. He closed his eyes and her image came quickly to mind—a body as slender as a willow, brown hair so dark it was almost black, eyes as blue as a robin's egg beneath delicately arched brows, a fine straight nose, lips that were pink and—

A sharp stab of desire twisted through him. Muttering an oath, he shoved her image aside. Pretty or ugly, it didn't matter. He had ten thousand good reasons to get her back home as soon as possible. Bryant's offer couldn't have come at a better time.

Winter Rain smiled into the darkness as the notes of Strong Elk's flute wafted through the night air. She had met him earlier that evening in front of her mother's lodge and they had stood together under a big red courting blanket. Huddled together, the blanket had given them a measure of privacy, though Winter Rain was well aware that her mother was nearby.

Now, lying in her bed, she felt a little thrill of excitement. He had been courting her openly for several months. In time, he would bring her father many horses. If she fed them, it would mean she agreed to be his wife. She found it odd that the thought of being courted was more exciting than the idea of being married to Strong Elk, and she wondered if all maidens felt that way. She thought of the stranger she had seen ride into the village that afternoon. His stark image swept all thought of Strong Elk from her mind. There was something about the stranger, something that called to her. She had never spoken to him, did not know his name, yet just thinking of him made her heart beat fast, made her wonder what it would be like to be held in his arms. . . .

She frowned, confused by her chaotic emotions. She was fond of Strong Elk. She had imagined herself falling in love with him, but he did not stir any deep feelings within her.

She rolled over onto her stomach and closed her eyes. Unbidden, the stranger's image again sprang to the forefront of her mind. He was a tall man, perhaps even taller than her father. And more handsome than Strong Elk. He moved with a fluid grace that made her think of a mountain lion hunting its prey. She didn't remember seeing him before and she wondered who he was and why he was here. He had gone to visit Kills-Like-a-Hawk. Were they friends? Relatives, perhaps? How long would he be here? Perhaps Strong Elk or her father would know who the stranger was and where he came from.

She was still thinking of him when she fell asleep.

# Chapter 3

Winter Rain rose early the following morning. Her first waking thought was of the stranger, which was not surprising, she mused, since she had dreamed of him all night long—horribly immodest dreams that had awakened her, breathless and warm all over, several times in the night. She had dreamed of standing with him in the sheltering folds of a courting blanket, dreamed of his hands touching her face, his body pressed close to hers. Remembering those dreams brought a wave of heat to her face.

Padding quietly out of the lodge, she made her way down to the river, thinking she would bathe and then fill the waterskin with fresh water. She walked upriver to her favorite place, a clear blue pool screened by young cottonwoods and tangled berry bushes. At the sound of splashing, she frowned, dismayed that someone else had reached the pool before her. A doe flicked its tail and bounded across her path as she drew near the water.

Peering through the brush, Winter Rain saw the stranger standing in the waist-deep water. His back was toward her—a broad copper-hued back marred by a thick spiderweb of faint white scars.

He rinsed the soap from his body, then turned and started toward the shore. She was no stranger to the sight of a man's bare chest, but she found herself staring at him, admiring the width of his shoulders, the finely sculpted muscles in his arms and chest, his hard, flat stomach, the way the sunlight glistened on his wet skin.

She wasn't aware of making any noise, but he paused abruptly, his eyes narrowing as he scanned the shoreline.

Winter Rain froze, not wanting to be caught staring, but she felt his gaze search her out.

"What do you want?" He put the question to her in flawless Lakota.

"I did not mean to intrude," she said, stepping out from behind the brush. "I just came to bathe."

He glanced around. "You picked a nice place for it."

She nodded, unable to draw her gaze away from such masculine perfection. Her mouth went dry as he took a step forward, apparently unconcerned by his nudity or the thought of her seeing him that way. Water dripped down his chest. He took another step, and she realized that very soon the water would no longer cover his private parts. She had seen naked men before. There was no shame in it, and couples often bathed and swam together. But the thought of seeing this man naked was most unsettling, and she quickly turned her back to him.

His soft chuckle brought a flush of heat to her cheeks. She stood there, her heart pounding as she listened to the soft whisper of cloth being pulled over wet male skin.

"You can turn around now," he said, a smile evident in his tone.

Instead of the white man's clothing he had worn the day before, he now wore a wolfskin clout and moccasins. He had long muscular legs. A knife was sheathed in a beaded belt at his waist. A small medicine bag dangled from a rawhide thong around his neck.

"You are Winter Rain?"

She nodded, suddenly aware that she was far from the village, alone with a stranger. If she called for help, no one would hear her.

"I am Wolf Shadow," he said. "Cousin to Kills-Like-a-Hawk."

She nodded in acknowledgment, felt her cheeks grow warm once more as his gaze moved over her in a long lingering glance.

Chance watched the color bloom in Winter Rain's cheeks. There was no doubt in his mind that this was the Bryants' daughter. Her resemblance to Rosalia Bryant was unmistakable. She had her mother's olive skin, dark hair, and delicate bone structure, and her father's deep blue eyes. His gaze moved to her lips— smooth pink lips that she moistened with the tip of her tongue.

Like a doe poised to take flight, she stood there watching him, her eyes wide and uncertain. Did she feel it, too, the attraction that sizzled between them like summer lightning? What would she do if he closed the distance between them, if he took her in his arms and slanted his mouth over hers, tasting her lips to see if they were as soft, as warm, as sweet, as they appeared? Clad in a simple doeskin tunic, her hair falling over her shoulders in twin braids, she looked young and vulnerable. He could see the pulse throbbing rapidly in her throat. One kiss. What could it hurt?

As though divining his thoughts, she crossed her arms over her breasts and took a step backward.

With a wry grin, he picked up his rifle and rested the barrel on his shoulder. "Enjoy your bath, *chikala.*"

She watched him walk away. Only when he was out of sight did her heart stop its wild pounding and her breathing return to normal.

When she was certain she was alone, she slipped out of her dress and moccasins and waded into the water. She unbraided her hair and combed her fingers through it. And as she washed her hair, she thought of the way his had looked, long and blue-black, in the sunlight. She soaped her arms and thought of his. Were they as strong as they looked? What would it be like to feel his arms around her, to run her hands over his biceps? She washed her breasts and thought of his broad shoulders and chest. She washed her legs and pictured his, long and well muscled. She reached around to wash her back and thought of his. How had he gotten those awful scars? Had someone whipped him? Who would do such a terrible thing?

With a shake of her head, she stepped out of the water, dried herself off with a piece of soft trade cloth, and slipped her dress over her head. Sitting on a rock, she put on her moccasins. She was spending far too much time thinking about a man she didn't even know, yet she couldn't seem to stop herself.

She thought about him while she gathered wood, while she cut out a new pair of moccasins for her mother, while she roasted a cut of buffalo meat for dinner. She wondered who he was and where he lived and why he didn't live in the village all year. And that night, as she crawled into bed, she wondered if he had a wife waiting for him somewhere.

Later that night, Chance stood at the river's edge, his thoughts far away. The full moon overhead was reflected on the face of the slow-moving water, shining silver against midnight blue. A faint breeze stirred the leaves of the trees. A coyote howled in the distance, its lonely lament echoing the pain he carried deep in his soul. A muscle twitched in his back. It had been on a quiet midsummer night like this a little more than nine years ago that outlaws had killed his mother and left him for dead.

Since then, he had found two of the others, but the

third man, the leader of the gang, continued to elude him. He had stuck to the trail like a burr to a saddle blanket until three years ago, when his father got sick. Though Chance hated to quit his search, he'd had no other choice and returned home to care for his old man. Six months later, his father passed away. Shortly after that, Chance had been contacted by the bank and learned, for the first time, about the huge mortgage on the ranch. As much as Chance had longed to resume the hunt for the man who had killed his mother, there had been no time. He had gone over his father's books, paid off the debts he could, and managed to come up with enough cash to keep the bank from foreclosing. From time to time he had been hired to search for men, women, and children who had been captured or lost in Indian territory. Most of the time, he had managed to find those who had been taken captive by the Lakota and the Cheyenne. In most cases, he had been able to buy the captives from the warriors who held them prisoner. Occasionally, he'd had only bad news to give to the parents or husband or wife who was looking for lost loved ones.

Picking up a stone, he sent it skipping across the water. He would not be able to buy Teressa Elizabeth Bryant's freedom from Mountain Sage and Eagle Lance. She was not their prisoner or their slave, but their daughter. They would not willingly let her go.

Feeling suddenly restless, he began walking along the shore. He wondered how much Teressa remembered of her former life. Did she secretly yearn to return to her rightful parents, or had she blocked all memory of Edward and Rosalia and her life with them from her mind? And what would he do if she refused to go back with him?

He was pondering several possibilities when he rounded a bend of the river and ran into the object of his musings.

A wordless cry erupted from her throat as she lashed out at him with her fists.

"Quit that!" He grabbed her in a bear hug, pinning her arms to her sides. His breath went out of him in a whoosh of pain as she drove her knee into his groin. Agony exploded through him.

"Dammit, Teressa," he said, gasping for air. "I'm not going to hurt you."

She stopped struggling and he let her go, doubling over in an effort to ease the ache in his groin. After a moment, he looked up to find her staring at him, a shocked expression on her face.

"I am sorry," she said, her voice shaky. "I thought . . ." She shrugged. "I did not recognize you. I thought you might be Crow."

Chance grunted.

"What are you doing out here so late anyway?" He tried breathing through his mouth to ease the pain. That didn't help, either.

"I could not sleep." She regarded him through narrowed, thoughtful eyes. "Who are you?"

"You know who I am," he said, lapsing into English.

"Teressa." Her voice was little more than a whisper. "You . . ." She spoke in English haltingly, as though trying to recall the words. "You called me Teressa."

"That's your name, isn't it?"

"No." She shook her head vigorously. "I am Winter Rain."

"You know that's not true. You're Teressa Elizabeth Bryant."

"No! I am Winter Rain. My mother is Mountain Sage—"

"Your mother's name is Rosalia Bryant."

"And my father is Eagle Lance. He is a great warrior—"

"Your father is Edward Bryant," Chance went on

doggedly. "He's a wealthy man, and he wants you back."

*"Heyah, heyah, heyah!"* she said. No, no, no!

Turning her back to him, she put her hands over her ears.

Chance drew in a deep breath and let it out in a long shuddering sigh. One more breath, and he slowly straightened up. Damn, she'd got him right where it hurt.

"Teressa?"

She shook her head. "I will not listen! I will not!"

He swore under his breath as he realized she was crying and trying not to let him know.

"Why did you have to come here?" she asked, sniffling.

He stared at her back. Her shoulders were shaking. "Your parents sent me to find you."

"How did you know I was here?"

"I remembered seeing you when I was here year before last. You look exactly like your mother. Except for your eyes," he said, recalling Rosalia's words. "You have your father's eyes."

She started to deny it, then realized he wasn't talking about Mountain Sage and Eagle Lance, but her *wasichu* parents, Edward and Rosalia.

"I do not believe you."

"I'm surprised you remember English so well after such a long time."

She turned to face him, her eyes widening a little. "I often interpret for the *wasichu* traders who come here. They cannot cheat my people if they know I understand what they are saying."

"And where did you learn to speak English, if not from your *wasichu* mother and father?"

She didn't answer, but he saw the confusion in her eyes. Maybe she didn't remember where she had come from or who her real parents were.

His gaze moved over her face. In the light of the full moon, he could see the tears shining in her eyes. Answering some inner need, he drew her into his arms again, careful to turn his body to the side in case she tried to knee him again.

She stood rigid in his embrace for several moments and then, with a sob, she leaned in to him, her face buried in the hollow of his shoulder, her body racked by sobs.

He held her close, one hand lightly stroking her back while she cried. He had always been a sucker for a woman's tears. Sympathy for her plight gradually turned to his awareness of her as a woman. Her breasts were soft and warm against his chest, her hair and skin smelled faintly of the soap she had bathed with earlier that day.

When she looked up at him, he cupped her face in his hands and wiped the tears from her cheeks with his thumbs. She looked lost and forlorn and more beautiful than anything he had ever seen. Unable to help himself, he lowered his head and kissed her. *Just a taste,* he thought, *one quick kiss to see if she is as sweet as she looks. One kiss to comfort her.*

Bending down, he covered her lips with his.

She immediately drew back, her eyes wide. "What are you doing?"

"I was going to kiss you," he muttered.

"Kiss?"

Of course, he thought, she wouldn't know what it was. Living with the Lakota, she had probably never been kissed before, would have no frame of reference other than the kisses she had received from her parents when she was a child.

"Let me show you," he said, and tilting her head to one side, he covered her lips with his own.

He drew back when she didn't do anything, simply stood there, her eyes wide and staring into his own.

Chance ran a hand through his hair. How the devil did you teach someone to kiss? "Close your eyes."

"Why?"

"Just do it."

She looked at him suspiciously for a moment, then did as he asked.

Cupping the back of her head in one hand, he slanted his mouth over hers and kissed her lightly.

She didn't move, just stood there with her eyes closed.

"It's better if you kiss me back."

"I do not know how."

"Press your lips against mine."

She was a quick study. When their lips met this time, it was like touching a flame to gunpowder. He felt the explosion down to the soles of his moccasins.

When he could breathe again, he drew back a little to look into her eyes. She was staring up at him, looking as dazed as he felt.

Not trusting himself to keep his hands off her, he backed away. He was there to collect a reward, he reminded himself, not to seduce her.

"Come on," he said, his voice none too steady. "I'll walk you back."

She didn't sleep at all that night. She tried to shut out the words of Wolf Shadow, but they were seared into her mind. Could it be true? Could her parents be white? She choked back a sob. No, it couldn't be true. He was lying.

"Teressa Elizabeth Bryant." She whispered the words into the darkness. The name sounded vaguely familiar, like something forgotten from her childhood.

And yet . . . what if it *was* true? It would explain why she had no memories of growing up with her parents, why her hair and skin were lighter than that of the other Lakota, why her eyes were blue, why she understood the white man's language. Why had she never wondered about such things before?

She glanced over at Mountain Sage and Eagle Lance sleeping soundly on the other side of the lodge. They were her parents! No mother could be kinder, sweeter, or love her more. No father could be braver.

She rolled over onto her stomach and forced her troublesome thoughts from her mind. Sleep. She needed to sleep, but the minute she closed her eyes, the face of Wolf Shadow rose in her mind and with it the memory of his arms around her, his touch as he wiped away her tears, the heat of his mouth on hers. Kissing. She liked it very much, she thought. Just thinking of his kiss sent little shivers of excitement coursing through her. She ran the tip of her tongue over her lips. Was it possible that she could still taste him there, or was it just her imagination?

She smiled into the darkness, wondering if she would see him tomorrow. Wondering if he would kiss her again.

# Chapter 4

Mountain Sage frowned as she studied her daughter's face. Winter Rain, who was usually lighthearted and smiling, seemed distracted and subdued.

"Daughter?" Mountain Sage tapped Winter Rain on the shoulder. "Are you feeling well?"

Winter Rain looked up, surprised by the question.

"Is something troubling you? Has Strong Elk done something to upset you?"

"No, nothing." Winter Rain hesitated a moment. "Do you know the stranger who came to the village yesterday?"

"Wolf Shadow? Yes. He is cousin to Kills-Like-a-Hawk." Mountain Sage laid the shirt she had been mending aside. "Did he hurt you in some way?"

"No. No, nothing like that. But he . . ."

"Should I call your father?"

"No!"

"My daughter, if you do not tell me what is bothering you, I cannot help."

Winter Rain folded her hands in her lap, the doubts that had haunted her the night before running through her mind. Should she confide in her mother? Should she ask the questions that had kept her tossing and turning all through the night?

"Winter Rain?"

"Are you my mother? Is Eagle Lance my father? Was I born here?"

Mountain Sage sat back on her heels. A sigh that seemed to come from the very depths of her soul slowly escaped her lips.

Seeing the expression on her mother's face, Winter Rain felt a sudden coldness in the pit of her stomach. "It is true, then, what he told me? You are not my true mother, are you?"

"Winter Rain . . ."

"How did I get here? Who brought me?"

"Eagle Lance brought you to me. Our daughter had died only a few moons before he found you. She was our fourth child. The first three had been born dead. After our daughter died, I wanted to die, too. I could not sleep or eat. I was sick"—Mountain Sage tapped her breast over her heart—"in here. Your father . . ." She paused and looked away. "Eagle Lance was worried about me. He went on a raid with some of the other men. They attacked some white men and stole their horses. Eagle Lance brought you home to me."

"How old was I?"

"You were seven summers. The same age as the daughter we had lost."

Winter Rain shook her head. Why didn't she remember? Ten years was a long time, but even so, she should be able to remember something. Had the attack been so awful she had somehow blocked it from her mind? Perhaps she had hated living with her *wasichu* parents and that was why she could not recall her past.

"I welcomed you into our lodge," Mountain Sage said. "You have been my daughter ever since that day."

Wordlessly, Winter Rain rose to her feet and left the lodge. Standing outside, she looked around the village. There was old Three Crows nodding in the shade. Children and dogs chased each other through the camp. A group of little girls were playing with dolls. In the distance, she saw a handful of elders watching a group of young boys shoot arrows at a target. The horse herd grazed across the river. Women were caring for their children, tanning hides, drying meat, laughing together as they watched White Doe's baby take its first steps. Men were gambling, or dozing in the sun, or repairing their weapons. They were sights she had seen a hundred times, a thousand, and yet on this day she felt as though she were seeing it all for the first time.

With a shake of her head, she walked down to the river, nodding to those who called her name.

At the water's edge, she walked along the shore until she found a quiet pool and then she dropped down to her hands and knees and studied her reflection. Wolf Shadow had said she looked like her mother. Her *wasichu* mother.

Leaning forward, she stirred the water with her hand, shattering her reflection.

Who was she? If she was not the daughter of Mountain Sage and Eagle Lance, then who was she? Would Strong Elk still wish to marry her if he knew she was not Lakota? But he must know. Everyone must know. Why had no one ever told her she was different?

With a toss of her head, she stood up. She might have the blood of the *wasichu* in her veins, but she was Lakota in her heart and soul. Nothing could change that. She belonged here with Mountain Sage and Eagle Lance, and here she would stay.

Smiling, she turned away from the river's edge and came face-to-face with Wolf Shadow.

"So," he said, "we meet again."

Her smile faded and her heart began to beat faster. "Are you following me?"

"Maybe."

"Why?" she asked, her voice thick with suspicion.

"Why not?" One corner of his mouth lifted in a

smile. "Lakota men often follow pretty women to the river in hopes of catching them alone." And she was pretty, with her sky-blue eyes and pouty pink lips. And her hair . . . It fell to her waist like a mantle of dark brown silk, a brown so deep it was almost black.

"Why would you want to be alone with me?" she asked suspiciously. "You do not even know me."

"Maybe I would like to know you better." He had a sudden image of her lying on top of him in his lodge, her hair tickling his skin. He swore under his breath. Where had *that* come from?

She stared up at him, stunned by his words. "I . . . That is . . . Strong Elk and I . . . We are . . ."

He frowned, and then nodded. "He is courting you."

"Yes," she said proudly. "He will bring horses to my father one day soon, and we will be married."

Chance muttered a short, pithy oath. That complicated matters. He would never get her away from here once she was married. Somehow, he had to woo her away from the People, and away from Strong Elk.

His gaze moved over her. Wooing her wouldn't be any trouble for him at all.

Later that night, long after Mountain Sage and Eagle Lance were asleep, Winter Rain lay awake in her blankets, her thoughts troubled. Strong Elk had come courting that evening. They had stood side by side under his courting blanket, but it was Wolf Shadow who had been in her thoughts. Strong Elk had told her of his plans to go hunting. There were two types of hunts: the *wani-sapa*, which was a tribal hunt and was shrouded in custom and ritual, and *tate*, which was a family hunt undertaken whenever a warrior wished to add to his food supply. This time, Strong Elk was going with his two best friends, Two Beavers and Pony Boy. They were leaving in the morning. She had nodded, all the while wondering where Wolf Shadow was and what he was doing.

Now, listening to the sweet notes of Strong Elk's *siyotanka*, Winter Rain found herself again thinking of Wolf Shadow. What was there about him that he occupied so much of her thoughts? He was tall and handsome, yes, but so was Strong Elk. Wolf Shadow wanted only to take her away from here; Strong Elk wanted to make her his wife. He was a brave warrior and hunter; he would make her a good husband.

Clinging to that thought, she turned on her side and pillowed her cheek on her hand. The music faded and she closed her eyes, seeking sleep. Instead, she found herself trying to remember her life among the *wasichu*. Had she been happy there? Why couldn't she remember anything of her life before she came to this place?

Why couldn't she put Wolf Shadow out of her mind?

Chance sat in front of Kills-Like-a-Hawk's lodge. Overhead, the full moon hung low in the sky. Everyone else in the village had gone to bed long ago, but sleep had eluded him. His thoughts turned briefly to the ranch, but he had nothing to worry about. His cowhands were competent and loyal; his foreman knew as much about running the place as he did.

The bittersweet notes of a courting flute were borne to him on the night wind. Hearing it brought the woman to mind. He had nothing to worry about at home, he mused with a shake of his head. But the woman . . . She worried him. She was too young, too pretty, too tempting.

He cocked his head to the side, listening to the music of the flute. Was it Strong Elk sitting out there in the dark, pouring out his heart in the haunting melody that filled the air? Was Winter Rain lying inside her mother's lodge, smiling a secret smile?

He cursed softly. The girl's happiness meant nothing to him. Once he returned Winter Rain to her rightful parents, she could stay in San Francisco and live a life of ease, or she could run back here and marry Strong Elk. Either way, he would have the money he needed to pay off the loan at the bank. Nothing else mattered.

He swore softly as a muscle twitched in his back. One other thing mattered, he thought bitterly. Finding the last of the men who had raped and killed his mother. Hands clenched, he let himself remember that day. Rage and pain flowed through him like a flash flood, stirring up old hurts, old memories, washing the dust of years off the horror that was never far from his mind. . . .

It was a summer he would never forget. He had been sixteen at the time, old enough to be considered a man by the People. His mother, Summer Moon, had expressed a desire to go and visit her cousin, who lived with the Cheyenne. Chance's father had been away from the village, attending to ranch business at the time, so Chance had volunteered to accompany his mother.

Chance and his mother had been a day's journey from the village when the white men found them. Four white men who had been Army deserters, though Chance hadn't realized that at the time. He had known they meant trouble, though. He had known it from the moment the men rode up to their campfire just after dusk. Too late, he had reached for his bow. One of the men struck him over the head with a rifle butt. Stunned, he had dropped to the ground. One of the men tossed his bow into the fire. He had tried to fight them while they tied his hands and feet, but he had been no match for four men. His head had throbbed so badly it was hard to think, hard to focus.

He had watched the men surround his mother. She had screamed in defiance and fear, her fists and feet

flailing as they reached for her. One of the men struck
her hard across the face. She stumbled backward and
they were on her like coyotes after a wounded doe.
In the wavering light of the fire, the scene had looked
like a horrible nightmare. Three of the men had wres-
tled his mother down to the ground, held her there
while the fourth unbuckled his belt and dropped his
trousers.

Chance had felt the bitter taste of bile rise in his
throat as he realized what they were doing to her. He
had tugged against the rope that bound his wrists,
hardly aware of the pain as the rough hemp cut into
his skin.

The sounds of his mother's cries and the grunts and
lewd remarks of the four men spurred him on. In des-
peration, he struggled harder against his bonds. Blood
oozed from his lacerated skin, trickled down the side
of his neck from the gash in his head.

The fourth man was lowering himself over Summer
Moon by the time Chance managed to free his hands
and feet. Crawling snakelike across the ground, he had
grabbed a knife that one of the men had left stuck in
a log. Chance rose to his knees and sprang at the
nearest *wasichu.* clutching the weapon in his fist. He
had grabbed a fistful of the man's greasy hair and
pulled his head back, slitting his throat.

Blood gushed from the wound and sprayed over
the other three. They scrambled to their feet, cursing
viciously. One of them pulled a gun and aimed it at
Summer Moon.

"Drop the knife!" he hissed. "Drop it or she's
dead."

Chance believed him. As soon as he dropped the
knife, two of the men had grabbed him and tied him
to a tree. And then they had taken turns whipping
him until his back was a bloody mess and he was
unconscious.

When he came to, his mother was on her knees behind him, fumbling with the rope. She managed to loosen the knots enough so that he could free himself, and then she fainted.

Tears had blurred his eyes as he knelt at her side. She had put up a fight when they raped her and the white men had not been gentle with her. Her face was swollen from their blows, one eye was black, and there was a cut on one cheek.

*"Ina."*

She groaned softly as he gathered her into his arms.

*"Cinks."* With an effort, she lifted one hand and stroked his cheek, and then her hand fell weakly to her side and she closed her eyes.

He had looked at her helplessly, at the dark red blood that stained her thighs. They had hurt her badly. Her breathing was shallow, as if every breath she drew caused her pain.

He had to get her back to the village, he thought frantically, but he was afraid to move her and afraid to leave her unprotected while he went for help. Their horses and supplies had been stolen by the *wasichu*. He was badly hurt. There was no way he could carry her back to the village.

*"Ina,* what should I do?"

Her eyelids fluttered open and she shook her head. "There is . . . nothing . . . to be done."

The finality of her words chilled him to the marrow of his bones.

She was shivering now. He glanced around, looking for something to cover her with, but there was nothing. As gently as he could, he moved her closer to the fire. He left her for a moment to gather more wood, then knelt beside her once more. It was then, in the light of the flames, that he saw the blood leaking from a wound in her side. When had they stabbed her? Not while they were raping her. He would have seen them, would have heard her cry out. It could only have happened while they were whipping him, he thought. Hurt and weak as she had been, she must have tried to stop them and they had stabbed her for it.

He closed his eyes as an agony of guilt and regret washed through him. He bent over her, wanting to hold her but afraid to cause her more pain. "I'm sorry," he murmured. *"Ina,* I'm so sorry. Forgive me."

"Take care . . . of your father," she whispered. "You are all he has . . . now."

Chance had nodded, unmindful of the tears that dripped down his cheeks, the blood that dripped like thick red rain down his lacerated back. He was cold inside. So cold. The fire did nothing to warm him.

Toward dawn, she had reached for him. As gently as he could, he cradled her in his arms, hardly aware of the pain of his own wounds.

Her breathing grew labored. Gasping for every breath, she whispered, "Be happy . . . my son." A moment later, her breathing stilled, and he knew she was dead.

He had held her close until the sun cleared the horizon, and then he had found a sturdy piece of wood and dug her grave. Every movement had sent fresh slivers of agony burning through his back.

He had buried her, then covered the grave with rocks to keep the scavengers away. Standing there, he had raised his arms over his head as he prayed for Wakan Tanka to take his mother safely along the spirit path to the Land of Many Lodges.

"I will avenge you, my mother. By my blood, I swear it!"

Kneeling beside her grave, he had smeared some of his own blood on one of the rocks, and then he had passed out.

When he regained consciousness, he was in the lodge of his mother's cousin. They had nursed him back to health. When he was strong enough to ride, they gave him a horse and food for his journey, and sent him on his way.

He would have gone after the men who had killed his mother as soon as he was able, but the news of what had happened to Summer Moon hit his father hard. Luke McCloud had lost interest in the ranch, in his son, and in everything else. From time to time, he drank himself into a stupor, and when he sobered up, it was like the news of her death hit him all over again.

When his old man finally recovered enough that he could be left alone, Chance had gone in search of the men who had killed his mother. He had found two of them and now only one remained: Jack Finch.

As soon as he returned Winter Rain to her parents and paid off the loan at the bank, he would try yet again to find the last man, though he knew that after so many years the odds of finding his quarry were slim.

Hands clenched, he stared into the darkness. "I will yet avenge you, my mother," he whispered fervently.

And in the stillness of the night, he heard his words echo on the voice of the wind.

# Chapter 5

In the days that followed, Winter Rain had little time to miss Strong Elk, who had gone hunting as planned with Two Beavers and Pony Boy. Every time she turned around, it seemed that Wolf Shadow was there. She met him on the trail when she went to gather wood. She met him by the river when she went to fill her waterskin. When she went in search of wild onions or berries with the other maidens or with her mother, he managed to seek her out.

His presence was disconcerting. She was going to marry Strong Elk. Everyone in the village knew it. Why, then, did she find herself looking for Wolf Shadow as soon as she left her lodge? Why was it his face that invaded her dreams, his voice that echoed in her mind?

He was constantly in her thoughts. When they were apart, she told herself he could not be as handsome or as exciting as she remembered; then, when she saw him again, he was more handsome, more exciting. More desirable than ever.

This morning was no different. She awoke from dreaming of him and wondered if he was awake. Rising, she judged the time, and then, with a word to her mother, she picked up a clean tunic and went down to her favorite place to bathe, knowing that it was his favorite place as well, and hoping, to her shame, that she would find him there. And she had. Seeing him, she had quickly ducked behind a tree, content to admire him from afar.

He was in the water, his back to her as it had been the first time she had seen him. Once again, she felt a quiver of excitement deep within her, felt her cheeks grow warm, felt herself smile at the sheer beauty of him, a perfection that was marred only by the hideous scars on his back. She wondered again who had whipped him so cruelly, and why.

"You could join me."

His voice startled her out of her reverie. How had he known she was there? She hadn't made a sound.

"You could wash my back for me," he said. "And I could wash yours."

The image of his hands moving over her body sent a flood of heat through every fiber of her being. Her mouth went dry, making a reply impossible. She stared at his broad shoulders, imagining her hands gliding over his skin, and her mouth went drier still.

Like a mouse trapped in the gaze of a coyote, she couldn't move, could only stand there as he slowly turned toward the shore. She was certain he could hear the rapid beating of her heart.

"You might as well come out," he said. "I know you're there."

On legs that felt as heavy as tree trunks, she walked down to the water's edge.

He looked up at her, his gaze warmer than the heat of the sun on her back. "Sure you won't join me?"

The thought was far too tempting. He was far too tempting. Why did she find him so exciting? He was just a man like any other, but even as the words crossed her mind, she knew they were a lie. There was something about this man, something in the deep sadness in his eyes that called to her in ways she did not understand.

He took a step toward the shore, and then another.

She stood her ground until the last moment, then quickly turned her back to him. She had inadvertently seen naked boys and even men from time to time, had laughed with Dawn Song about it. But she knew on some deeper level that seeing Wolf Shadow naked would not be cause for amusement.

She heard the swish of water as he moved through it. All her senses came swiftly to life as she imagined him standing naked behind her. Close enough to touch.

She closed her eyes, swallowing hard and listening to the sound of cloth being pulled over damp flesh.

"What brings you down here so early?" he asked. "Could it be you hoped to find me here?"

"Of course not! I always come here in the morning to bathe. This is *my* place and you know it."

Suddenly angry, she whirled around to find him grinning at her.

She was surprised to realize that a little part of her, way down deep inside, was disappointed that he was fully clothed. And if that wasn't bad enough, she had the feeling that he knew it, too.

"Tomorrow morning I'll try to get here earlier." His gaze moved over her, as intimate as a caress. "Or maybe I'll come a little later and see what I can see."

The idea of having him watch her while she bathed made her blush from head to foot.

"One of these days," he predicted, "I'll ask you to bathe with me and you won't refuse."

Before she could think of a suitable reply, he was gone.

Winter Rain wasn't sure how she got through the rest of the day. She helped her mother clean the lodge and prepare the meals, but at the end of the day, she had no clear memory of doing so. Dawn Song came to visit, but later, Winter Rain could not recall what they talked about.

At dusk, she went outside, hoping to clear her head.

And he was there, waiting for her, a blanket draped over his arm.

"You!" she exclaimed softly. "What are you doing here?"

He tapped one finger on the blanket. "I have come to court you."

She blinked at him. "Court me? You? But . . . but Strong Elk and I . . ."

"Strong Elk is not here."

She felt a quickening deep inside her as Wolf Shadow unfolded the blanket and held it up, waiting for her to join him. Almost without conscious thought, she moved toward him, her heart pounding wildly as he enveloped them in the folds of the blanket.

She shouldn't be here, yet even as the thought crossed her mind, she was taking pleasure in his near-ness, in the press of his hard-muscled thigh against hers, the scent of horse and sage and smoke that clung to him.

"How long will you be staying here?" she asked, needing to break the heavy silence between them.

"I haven't decided." She felt his gaze move over her face. "Maybe I'll stick around long enough to see you get hitched."

"Hitched?"

"Married."

Her eyes widened. She did not want Wolf Shadow to be there that day, refused to consider why she found the thought of his presence at her wedding so unsettling.

His amused chuckle filled the air between them. "Do you want me to go?"

"Yes."

"Why?" The question was a soft whisper.

She felt the warmth of his breath against her ear, and she took a step away from him. "I do not know."

"I think you do."

His reply, and the truth in it, sent a shiver down her spine.

He came courting the next night, and the next. She knew she should refuse to stand under the blanket with him, but there was something about him she could not resist, something in his voice that captured her imagination, something in his eyes that held secrets she longed to know.

It seemed she could think of nothing else, no one else.

And then Strong Elk returned to the village.

She saw him ride in with Two Beavers and Pony Boy. All three men led packhorses heavily laden with deer and elk. Strong Elk smiled at her as he drew near. He reined his horse to a halt and looked down at her.

"Will you be outside this evening?" he asked.

Winter Rain nodded, her heart pounding. What would she do if Strong Elk stopped by her lodge at the same time that Wolf Shadow came by?

With a nod, Strong Elk moved on. She watched him ride to his mother's lodge, where he unloaded a part of his kill before moving on to his own lodge.

Winter Rain looked up at the sky. It would be dark all too soon.

She took special care with her appearance that night. She dressed in her prettiest tunic, the one with the red and yellow beading on the yoke. She brushed her hair until it was soft and shiny, spread a thin layer of red paint in the part. She pulled on her best moccasins.

Mountain Sage regarded her preparations with a smile. "Strong Elk will be pleased," she said.

Winter Rain nodded. Strong Elk. Of course she was dressing to please Strong Elk.

It was full dark when she stepped out of her lodge. No sooner had she done so than Wolf Shadow appeared. It was in her mind to tell him that Strong Elk had returned and he could not come courting anymore. It was a speech she had rehearsed carefully, but when she looked at Wolf Shadow the words would not come. And when he opened his blanket, she moved to stand beside him.

"I have waited all day for this moment." He draped the blanket over their heads and shoulders, cocooning them in world all their own.

She could feel his heat beside her, the brush of his arm against her breast. Now, she thought. She had to tell him now.

She was trying to form the words when he kissed her. His touch went through her like lightning. It seemed to draw all the air from her lungs, the strength from her legs, leaving her breathless and weak. She knew she would have fallen had it not been for his arms around her. It frightened her, the power of that kiss, the knowledge that she wanted more.

"Why?" she gasped. "Why did you do that?"

"Didn't you like it?"

"I am going to marry Strong Elk."

"I know."

She wished she could see his face, and at the same time she was glad she couldn't. It was most confusing!

And then, at the sound of Strong Elk's voice, she froze. Flushed with guilt, she pushed away from Wolf Shadow. He lowered the blanket and Winter Rain found herself face-to-face with Strong Elk. She was taken aback by the anger she saw glinting in his eyes.

Strong Elk's gaze narrowed, moving from her face

to Wolf Shadow's and back to hers again. "I thought you would be waiting for me," he said.

She looked away from his probing gaze.

"Winter Rain? We are to marry soon. Why do I find you with another man?"

She looked up, her cheeks burning with shame. "Forgive me," she said.

Wordlessly, Wolf Shadow folded his blanket over his arm. He looked at her impassively for a long moment, and then he turned his back to her and walked away.

Strong Elk put his arm around Winter Rain's shoulders. "Tomorrow I will go to the land of the Crow."

"But you just returned home," Winter Rain exclaimed. "Must you leave again so soon?"

"I must steal horses to give to your father," he said. "With your father's permission, I think we should marry when I return."

She nodded, her gaze on Wolf Shadow's back. "My father will be pleased."

Strong Elk unfolded his blanket and draped it over them. "And will you also be pleased?" he asked, his voice seeming muffled by the heavy cloth.

Through a narrow slit in the folds of the blanket, she watched Wolf Shadow walk away, noting the confident, easy way he moved, the width of his shoulders. She lifted a finger to her lips, remembering his kiss. She felt bereft when he disappeared from sight.

"Winter Rain?"

She blinked up at Strong Elk as he lowered the blanket. "What?"

"I asked if you would also be pleased."

Pleased? She stared at him. What had they been talking about? Oh, yes, talking to her father. "I think we should marry soon." The sooner the better, she thought. When she was Strong Elk's woman, she would no longer have to worry about Wolf Shadow coming to court her. She looked up at Strong Elk and forced a smile. "I am eager to be your wife."

She thought of those words later that night. Lying in her bed, she tried to imagine herself married to Strong Elk, but it was Wolf Shadow's image that teased her dreams, Wolf Shadow who shared her lodge, and her bed.

Chance muttered an oath as he walked away from Winter Rain's lodge. Strong Elk's timing couldn't have been worse. If the warrior had only stayed away another week, Chance mused, he might have won Winter Rain away from Strong Elk, and away from here.

Leaving the village behind, he made his way down to the river. Shafts of yellow moonlight danced on the face of the black water. *There might still be time,* he thought. The attraction between himself and Winter Rain was real. With a little luck, he might still find a way to use that to his advantage.

He stood there for a long while, listening to the soft whisper of the wind sighing through the trees, the gentle gurgle of the water skipping over rocks, the faint chirr of the crickets, the low bellow of a bullfrog, the distant lament of a lonely coyote. They were sounds as familiar to him as the beat of his own heart. Sounds associated with his childhood.

He had grown up here with the Lakota. When he was old enough to leave his mother's lodge, he had spent a part of each year living with his father, who had been known as Snow Wolf among the People. Chance had not understood why his father was different from other fathers, or why his parents did not live together all year long. He had wondered about it until he was five or six, and then he had asked his mother why his father went away so often. She had explained to him that his father had a lodge of his own among the *wasichu* and that he had to return there from time to time to take care of it.

Snow Wolf had come to visit them several times each year, always bringing presents for his Indian wife and his son.

And then Summer Moon had been killed and Chance had gone to live in his father's world. It had not been easy, being a half-breed in a white world. At first, the people of Buffalo Springs had looked at him with suspicion, but they had gradually come to accept him. In time, he had learned a new way of life, but he never forgot his vow to avenge his mother's death. He had learned to shoot, practicing with a Colt and a rifle until he could use both with the same skill and accuracy that he enjoyed with bow and lance. When he turned seventeen, he had gone in search of the remaining three men who had violated and killed his mother. He had nothing to go on but their names. Surprisingly, less than a month later he had found one of the men in a saloon in a small town not far from the ranch.

He had followed the man until he got him alone, then called him by name.

*L. J. Weston had stopped and glanced over his shoulder. "Who's there?"*

*Chance stepped out of the shadows. "Remember me?"*

*"No, should I?"*

*"You killed my mother a year ago."*

*Remembrance and recognition flared in Weston's eyes. "You!"*

*Chance nodded, his hand hovering over the butt of his gun. "Make your play."*

*Weston took a step backward. "I got no quarrel with you," he said, and even as he spoke the words he was reaching for his gun, pulling it from the leather.*

*Too late. Chance's Colt was in his hand before Weston's gun cleared his holster.*

*Chance had stared down at Weston's body while he punched the spent cartridge from his gun, but in his mind's eye, it had been his mother's body he had seen.*

*He had found the next man in a fancy whorehouse in Kansas City a year later. Chance wasn't sure who was more surprised, Luther Hicks or the woman he was with, when Chance burst into the room.*

*The woman had screamed and dived under the covers. Hicks had stared at Chance for stretched seconds, and then, as recognition dawned in his eyes, Hicks had made a mad grab for the holstered gun hanging from the bedpost.*

*His gun had never cleared leather.*

*Chance was replacing his Colt's spent cartridge when the woman peeked out of the blankets. Her eyes went wide when she saw he was still standing at the foot of the bed.*

*Chance had holstered his weapon, then withdrew a double eagle from his pocket and tossed it at her. She had caught it deftly in one hand, bit down on it, and smiled her thanks.*

*"Sorry about the mess," he had said, and turning his back on the woman, he left the room.*

Now, as he turned away from the river, he wished he could as easily turn his back on the past.

# Chapter 6

When Winter Rain woke the following morning, she wondered if Strong Elk had already left for the land of the Crow. He was a brave warrior, well respected among the People. She smiled inwardly. She knew he would return with many horses to offer her father, perhaps as many as ten. And hard on the heels of that thought she found herself wondering if Wolf Shadow would come courting while Strong Elk was away.

Rising, she greeted her mother, who was preparing the morning meal. It was one of Winter Rain's favorites, gooseberry mush.

Mountain Sage nodded in return, her expression troubled. "Strong Elk came by early this morning. He wished to see you before he left, but you were still sleeping. He was displeased to find you with another warrior last night."

Winter Rain nodded. "I have told Wolf Shadow that I am to marry Strong Elk, but"—she shrugged—"he does not seem to care. I did not mean to upset Strong Elk."

"It is good for a man to be jealous from time to time," Mountain Sage replied. She looked at her daughter thoughtfully. "Does it matter to you that Wolf Shadow does not care?"

"No, of course not," Winter Rain said quickly.

"Strong Elk wishes for us to marry when he returns from the land of the Crow."

"So soon?"

"Yes. You do not approve?"

Mountain Sage looked pensive for a moment, and then nodded. "I had thought of waiting until the spring, but I do not think it is wise to wait."

Winter Rain didn't think so either until later, when she went down to the river to bathe and saw Wolf Shadow standing on the bank, his back toward her, his arms raised over his head in prayer.

She had not thought of him as a man who greeted the new day in prayer to Wakan Tanka. She had not thought of him as being one of the People in his heart. Hadn't he come here to take her back to her *wasichu* parents? Though he had said no more on the subject, she didn't think he had forgotten about it. It was another reason to marry Strong Elk as soon as possible.

She knew she should leave. A man deserved privacy when he said his prayers, yet she found herself taking a step closer, her curiosity overwhelming. What did he pray for?

Her gaze moved over him, noting again the width of his shoulders, the way his back tapered to a tight waist, narrow hips, and long legs. She stopped wondering what it was he prayed for and wondered instead what it would be like to run her hands over the muscles in his arms, to feel his skin beneath her fingertips. . . .

She froze as a leaf crackled beneath her foot. Had she been paying more attention to where she was going and less to the man before her, he would never have known she was there.

Drawing the knife from the sheath at his side, Wolf Shadow whirled around, every muscle taut. He relaxed visibly when he saw her.

"We meet here far too often to blame it on coincidence," he remarked, sheathing his knife. "If I didn't know better, I'd think you were following me."

"I am not! This is my place. I told you that."

"Then maybe I'm following you," he replied with a teasing smile.

"You are wasting your time if you are," she replied with a toss of her head. "I am to marry Strong Elk. He is strong and brave and will make me a fine husband."

"So you said."

"He has gone to the land of our enemy to steal horses. We will marry when he returns."

"Is that right?"

"Yes. I did not mean to interrupt your prayers," she said, and turned to leave.

She hadn't gone more than a few steps when she felt his hand close around her arm. His touch sent a shiver down her spine, made her heart race in anticipation.

"Don't go," he said, and turned her around to face him.

"What do you want of me?" she asked.

"What do you think I want?"

"To take me back to the land of the *wasichu,* but I will not go, and you cannot make me."

His hand tightened on her arm. "That's only part of it."

She gasped as he drew her up against him.

"This is the other part," he said, his voice husky, and then he lowered his head and kissed her.

As it had before, the first touch of his lips on hers stole the strength from her legs, the breath from her lungs. She clutched his shoulders, wondering what magic he possessed, what power he had over her that made her react so strangely. His lips moved over hers, eliciting myriad sensations in her body and sensual images of the two of them in her mind.

Chance swore softly as he let her go. If he wasn't careful, he was going to seduce her right here, right now, and then where would he be? He wasn't looking for a wife, didn't have the time or the inclination to settle down. All he wanted to do was collect the reward for returning Winter Rain to the Bryants, pay off the loan at the bank, and find the last of the men who had killed his mother. Until then, there was no place in his life for a woman, even if she had a cloud of rich brown hair, eyes as blue as the sky overhead, and a way of kissing that set his blood on fire.

"The water's yours," he said curtly, and turning his back on her, he headed upstream. If he was lucky, the water would be cold enough to put the out the flames.

When he got back to Kills-Like-a-Hawk's lodge an hour later, he found his cousin sitting outside, surrounded by a group of young boys and girls, all listening in rapt silence as Kills-Like-a-Hawk told how the Lakota came to be.

Having nothing else to do, Chance sat down to listen.

"It was in the long ago time," Kills-Like-a-Hawk was saying, "when the world was new, that the Lakota came out from the middle of the earth. They were all one People then. They made one winter camp. They had but one council fire. Many years passed. After a time, some of the People did not return to the winter camp and when they did join with the original camp, they kept their own council fire. They were called *ton-wan* because they wanted to be separate from the others.

"As time went on, others decided they, too, wished to be separate, until there were seven council fires. While each *tonwan* was separate, they remained friends, so they called themselves Lakota, and they were allies against all other peoples.

"When all the Lakota come together, each *tonwan*

placed its lodges together and built their own camp-fire. But the original *tonwan* was given the place of honor. Over time, the Tetons became very powerful and warlike and they usurped the place of honor that had been given to the original *tonwan*, and that is why the Tetons now have the place of honor in our camp circles."

Kills-Like-a-Hawk nodded once, indicating that the story was over.

It was a story Chance had heard often growing up and it had, for the moment, taken his mind off Winter Rain. But only for a moment.

With a shake of his head, he went out to the herd to check on his horse.

Winter Rain sat in the shade with Dawn Song, keeping her best friend company while she looked after her four-year-old sister who was asleep inside the lodge. Dawn Song was slightly taller than Winter Rain. She was a pretty girl with a wide generous mouth, heavily lashed black eyes, and a fine straight nose. She was a year younger than Winter Rain.

"Have you seen the stranger?" Dawn Song asked.

"Yes," Winter Rain answered. "I have seen him." The thought of how she had seen him brought a flush to her cheeks.

"He is a handsome warrior," Dawn Song remarked.

"Do you think so?" Winter Rain asked.

"You do not think so?" Dawn Song asked, aston-ished.

"I have not thought about it," Winter Rain said, though, in truth, she had thought of little else since Wolf Shadow had arrived.

"I think he is even more handsome than Strong Elk," Dawn Song said.

Winter Rain thought so, too, but said nothing.

"The Brave Hearts are having a dance tonight," Dawn Song remarked.

Winter Rain nodded, grateful that her friend had changed the subject. Only she hadn't.

"I wonder if the stranger will be there. You are coming, are you not?"

"Yes, of course," Winter Rain said. Strong Elk belonged to the Brave Hearts. It was one of the warrior societies. Her father belonged to the Kit Fox society. There were other societies, like the Naca Ominicias, who were often referred to as the Big Bellies. The Naca Ominicias was made up of retired hunters and distinguished elderly shamans.

She wondered if Wolf Shadow was a member of the Brave Hearts. If so, would he be at the dance?

Afraid that Dawn Song might question her further about Wolf Shadow and discover her interest in the stranger, Winter Rain changed the subject.

She dressed with care that night, her heart pounding with mingled anticipation and trepidation at the thought of seeing him again. She put on the new moccasins her mother had made for her. Soft and pliable, their tops were covered with tiny yellow, blue, and red beads. She brushed her hair until it fairly crackled, then applied a bit of red paint to the part. She fastened a blue and yellow beaded bracelet around her wrist, smoothed a hand over the skirt of her tunic.

Mountain Sage smiled at her as she stepped out of the lodge. "Have a good time, daughter."

"Thank you for the moccasins."

After hugging her mother, Winter Rain followed the other young men and women who had been invited to the dance, which was being held in a large tipi near the center of camp.

Upon entering the lodge, Winter Rain sat on the

south side with the other women. The men sat on the north side. A fire had been built in the center of the lodge. Two paunch kettles were located near the fire, filled with meat provided by the hostesses.

Dawn Song entered the lodge. She paused, her gaze moving over the guests until she saw Winter Rain. Walking behind those already seated, she headed toward Winter Rain and sat down beside her.

"Is he here?" she asked.

"Who?" Winter Rain asked, though she knew perfectly well who her friend was talking about.

"Wolf Shadow, of course. Is he here?"

Winter Rain's heart skipped a beat as the object of their discussion entered the lodge. He wore a wolfskin clout, fringed leggings, moccasins, an elkskin vest with a wolf's head painted on one side and a bolt of yellow lightning on the other. A single white eagle feather was tied in his long black hair; a wide copper band spanned his right biceps.

His gaze found hers immediately and something hot and alive passed between them before he sat down. He spoke to the warriors who sat on either side of him, but his gaze never left hers.

When everyone had arrived, the girls rose. Walking across the lodge, they each chose a partner by kicking the sole of his moccasin. Winter Rain was not surprised when Dawn Song chose Wolf Shadow. Tamping down a rush of jealousy, Winter Rain chose Strong Elk's older brother, Buffalo Bear, for her partner.

When the singing began, the dancers each grasped their partner by the belt, and with their knees slightly bent, began two-stepping sideways, going clockwise around the fire to the rhythmic beat of the drums.

Winter Rain's gaze strayed time and again to Dawn Song and Wolf Shadow. He danced with an effortless grace. Dawn Song stared at him in a most unmaidenly way, giggling behind her hand at something he said.

After they had danced awhile, the singers stopped for a few moments and then started up again. As four was a sacred number to the Lakota, there were four parts to the songs. When the fourth section had been sung, the men and women went back to their places and there was a short intermission.

Dawn Song, Winter Rain noted, was all smiles.

Dawn Song was bubbling over. She went on and on about Wolf Shadow, how tall he was, how handsome, how well he danced, until Winter Rain wanted to shake her and tell her to be quiet.

Just when she thought she would do just that, the singers called for the Circling the Kettle dance. Two of the men rose and danced before the girls and then each of the men picked a partner. Now the four formed a line, with the last girl chosen standing on the right. The four of them danced around the fire and then the girl on the right chose a partner as she passed the men's side of the lodge. On and on it went, with the last dancer chosen picking a partner. Each time a new dancer was chosen, the singers sang a different song, whereupon the dancers all swung around and danced in the opposite direction.

Winter Rain's heart was pounding as the line moved toward her. Wolf Shadow had been the last dancer chosen and now she waited, wondering if he would choose to dance with Dawn Song. She slid a glance at her friend. Dawn Song had eyes only for Wolf Shadow. There was an expectant smile on her face as Wolf Shadow drew closer, a smile that quickly faded as Wolf Shadow reached for Winter Rain's hand and pulled her to her feet to join in the line.

The song changed as she joined the line, and then changed again when everyone was dancing.

Winter Rain was acutely aware of Wolf Shadow's hand holding hers as they danced. Strange that it took no more than the touch of his hand to send shivers of excitement coursing through her.

She was sorry when the singing stopped and the men and women separated yet again. During this intermission, food was served. All during the meal, she was aware of Wolf Shadow watching her. Feeling self-conscious, she kept her head down and tried to enjoy what she was eating, but she hardly tasted a bite. Dawn Song sat beside her, a sour expression on her face.

When everyone had finished eating, the warriors stood and each one chose a girl. Once again, Wolf Shadow picked her to be his partner and they stood facing each other. Winter Rain felt her cheeks warm under his blatant regard and wondered, briefly, if Dawn Song would ever speak to her again.

When the singers began to chant, the couples moved toward each other, met in the center, and then danced back. As they moved forward, the dancers sang while the singers only drummed. As the dancers moved backward, they were silent while the singers sang and drummed. They did this four times and when the fourth part was completed, Crooked Lance, who was one of the Brave Hearts, asked the drummer to hit the drum so that he might count a coup. Crooked Lance then told of his bravery in a battle against the Blue Coats and how he had counted coup on two of them and killed a third in hand-to-hand combat. When he was finished, he offered a gift to the hostess.

Dancing shadows cast by the light of the fire flickered over the lodgeskins and the faces of each of the warriors as they stood and spoke of one of their exploits in battle and then offered a gift to someone in the crowd.

Winter Rain paid little attention to the tales of bravery, many of which she had heard before, until it was Wolf Shadow's turn to speak.

Rising, he stood in the center of the floor. There was something about him that made her heart beat a little faster. He reminded her of the wolf for which he had been named, lithe and dangerous but gentle with those he loved. His gaze moved slowly over the crowd and then settled on Winter Rain's face.

"This is a tale that began many moons ago," he said, his voice low and compelling. "I was a young warrior then, one who had sworn a blood oath of vengeance. Because it was necessary, I left the land of my ancestors and traveled to the land of the *wasichu.* I saw many strange things but my heart was set on vengeance. Years passed and my enemy foolishly thought himself safe. I did not take his life until he remembered who I was and what he had done. And when he was dead, I took his scalp and then I dipped my hands in his blood."

There were murmurs of approval as Wolf Shadow finished his story.

Shivering, Winter Rain folded her arms over her breasts. She was not repelled by the tale, only by the cold look that had settled in his eyes as he spoke of the blooding.

Wolf Shadow pulled a pouch of tobacco from inside his breechclout and offered it to one of the warriors, then resumed his seat.

After the last warrior had taken his turn, the singers took their places again and the dancing resumed. When the hour grew late, the couple acting as chaperones rose and after dancing with the other couples for a short time, they made their way to the door and danced themselves out of the lodge. This was the signal that the dance was over.

Winter Rain stood and followed the other girls as they filed out of the doorway. Mountain Sage stood outside with the other mothers who were waiting for their daughters. Winter Rain knew the young men would not immediately return to their lodges. Given the freedom of men, they would wander around the camp for a time before going home.

"Dawn Song did not bid you good night," Mountain Sage remarked as they made their way home.

Winter Rain shrugged. "I think she may be angry with me."

"Angry? What have you done?"

"I did nothing. She has soft eyes for the stranger in our village. She chose him as her partner, and she did not like it when he chose me instead of her."

"Ah." A single word, but it said all there was to say.

Winter Rain bid her parents good night and went to bed, only to lie awake wondering if the enemy Wolf Shadow had followed to the land of the *wasichu* was the one responsible for the scars on his back.

# Chapter 7

Strong Elk returned late in the afternoon two days later. An hour after he returned to camp, his best friend, Two Beavers, approached Winter Rain's lodge leading eleven Crow ponies.

Eagle Lance listened solemnly as Two Beavers spoke.

"The warrior Strong Elk desires to take your daughter, Winter Rain, as his wife. To show his respect, he offers you these ten ponies, which he has stolen from our enemies the Crow. This horse"—he gestured at a pretty buckskin mare with foxlike ears—"is a gift for Winter Rain."

Eagle Lance nodded. "Tell Strong Elk I accept his offer. Tell him to prepare a feast tomorrow and we will bring Winter Rain to his family's lodge."

Two Beavers passed the lead ropes of the horses to Eagle Lance. "My friend will be pleased."

Winter Rain stood inside the lodge, listening to the exchange between her father and Two Beavers. So, it was done. She was to marry Strong Elk. Now that it was arranged, she was beset by doubts. She had had little opportunity to be alone with Strong Elk. Most of what she knew of him she had learned from friends and from meeting him "by accident." In the last year, they had managed to meet dozens of times. When she had come of age, many of the young men had come courting. Some nights there had been half a dozen young men waiting outside her lodge. Gradually she had refused all the others until only Strong Elk remained. Still, courting beneath a blanket was not the best way for a couple to get acquainted, not when there were curious children running around nearby, not when she was ever aware that her mother was not far away.

And now it was done. Her father had accepted Strong Elk's gift. Tomorrow she would take her place as his wife. She was already past the age when most girls married. Her mother had taught her all she needed to know. She could cook, she was virtuous, honest, and a hard worker. She had a fine hand when it came to sewing and beading. She was also accomplished at quillwork, which was considered one of the most desirable of female arts. Tanning a hide required a good deal of strength, but quilling demanded a gentle hand and dexterity. Her mother was one of those who taught others. Mountain Sage had dreamed of the Deer Woman. Such women were noted for their ability to do quillwork. Mountain Sage had told Winter Rain that the first Lakota woman who had dreamed of the Deer Woman had learned the art of quilling in a vision while she dreamed. On waking, she had set up a new lodge. Over time, she had sorted and dyed the quills of a porcupine, and then she had passed her skills to another.

Winter Rain sighed. Tomorrow she would leave her mother's lodge and begin her new life as Strong Elk's wife. She would do the things she had seen her mother do: She would tend the fire, do the cooking and sewing and mending, keep the lodge tidy, gather wood and water, and entertain Strong Elk's friends. If Strong Elk was not pleased with her as a wife, he would divorce her. Among the Lakota, it was a simple thing. All he need do was publicly announce that he had "thrown her away" and she would return to her mother's lodge in disgrace.

Winter Rain frowned at the turn of her thoughts. Not even married yet, and she was thinking of divorce.

A moment later, her mother hurried into the lodge and there was no more time for worry or doubt, only time to make plans for the morrow. Mountain Sage laid out the dress and moccasins she had prepared for the occasion. In addition to the new clothing, Mountain Sage gave her daughter new robes for sleeping, a sewing kit of her own, and a pair of willow backrests.

"You have chosen wisely," she remarked later that night while brushing Winter Rain's hair. "Strong Elk will make you a good husband. He is wise and brave. He is a good hunter. You will always have meat in your lodge."

Winter Rain nodded. She would gain honor and prestige in being married to a warrior such as Strong Elk.

She went to bed early that night, yet sleep eluded her. She was to be married tomorrow. Why did the thought fill her with trepidation instead of excitement?

Long after her mother was asleep and her father was snoring softly, she lay awake, staring at the sky through the smoke hole of the lodge. And when sleep came, it was not her future husband she dreamed of, but a tall man with a scarred back and storm-colored eyes.

Chance sat outside his cousin's lodge, a cigarette dangling between his lips. So, she was getting married tomorrow. She would don her best tunic and moccasins and her father and mother would escort her to Strong Elk's lodge. There would be a feast, presents would be exchanged, and Winter Rain would become Strong Elk's bride. She would build a new lodge for the two of them, bear his children, warm him on cold winter nights.

Damn.

Taking a last drag on his cigarette, Chance tossed the butt away, watching the faint red glow as it arced through the darkness, then winked out in the dirt. His hopes of collecting the reward were in the dirt, too, he thought glumly. Maybe he should have just grabbed her and made a run for it. He considered that a moment, then shook his head. As much as he wanted to pay off the mortgage held by the bank, it wasn't worth losing his cousin's respect, or jeopardizing his standing with the People. In a choice between the two, he would give up the ranch. The Double C might be all that his father had left him, but it was just a few thousand acres of land. The Lakota were his people. Though he had not made his home here in years, his heart and soul were here, in the land where he had been born. His ancestors had lived and died here. His mother's blood had watered the ground.

Tomorrow he would go back to the ranch. Maybe, if he was lucky, he could talk the bank into an extension on the loan. As a last resort, he might be able to sell enough cattle to make up the difference between the five thousand Bryant had paid him and what he owed the bank. If not . . .

He gazed out into the darkness. There was no point in worrying about that now.

He glanced at Winter Rain's lodge. Was she sleeping soundly, dreaming of tomorrow? And tomorrow night?

He scowled at the thought of her sharing Strong Elk's lodge. What was it about the Bryants' daughter that had him tied in knots? Hell, he hardly knew the girl. She wasn't even his type. He liked his women tall and blond and experienced. Yet none of the women he had known stirred him the way she did, or kept him up nights just thinking about her.

Muttering an oath, he went into his cousin's lodge and crawled into his lonely bed.

Winter Rain woke early after a restless night. Sitting up, she saw that her mother and father were still sleeping. She snuggled back under her blankets, closing her eyes and trying to go back to sleep, but she was too agitated by her upcoming marriage to rest, too nervous to stay in bed.

Rising, she dressed quietly and slipped out of the lodge.

Only a few people were outside. She glanced toward Strong Elk's tipi, wondering if he was as nervous and uncertain as she was, and then, as if pulled by an invisible string, her gaze moved toward Kills-Like-a-Hawk's lodge. Would Wolf Shadow come to the feast?

Needing something to keep her mind from paths better off not taken, she walked toward the timberline, thinking to gather some wood for the morning fire. Tonight she would be building a fire for her husband. The thought did not please her as it should have and the next thing she knew, she was walking toward the river.

And he was there. Clad in clout and moccasins, his skin like burnished copper in the early-morning light, his arms raised above his head. Wolf Shadow. His hair fell past his shoulders, thick and black. The scars on his back shone like a fine silver web in the pale sunshine. Her heart quickened at the sight of him and she knew in that moment that she would never be happy with Strong Elk, or with any other man.

As though sensing her presence, Wolf Shadow slowly lowered his arms and turned to face her.

His gaze met hers, intense, unwavering. "Today is

your wedding day." His voice was soft, but she heard the hard edge beneath it. "Shouldn't you be getting ready?"

"There will be no wedding."

His eyes narrowed. "Why not?"

She placed one hand over her heart. "It does not feel right. In here."

He took a step toward her. "Is that the only reason?"

She felt her heart begin to pound as he took another step toward her. "I . . ." She made a vague gesture with her hand. "I think you know the reason."

One more step, and he was near enough to touch. "Tell me."

She looked up at him, feeling as though her heart were trapped in her throat. What if she poured out her heart to him and he didn't feel the same? How could he, when she wasn't sure what it was she was feeling?

"Tell me, Rain. Why can't you marry him?"

"Because when I lay in my bed, it is you that I think of when I should be thinking of him," she said, the words pouring out of her in a rush. "Because I cannot stop thinking of you, dreaming of you. Because—"

He didn't let her finish. His hands curled around her upper arms and he drew her up against him. When he spoke, his voice was low and husky.

"Because he doesn't make you feel like this," he said. And he kissed her.

Her eyelids fluttered down as she gave herself up to his kisses. Warmth flowed through her. Millions of butterflies seemed to be dancing in the pit of her stomach. She pressed herself against him, her breasts crushed against his chest, her arms locked around his waist. A low moan filled her ears. She was embarrassed when she realized it was coming from her own throat.

She was dazed, disoriented, when he put her away from him. "What . . . what's wrong?"

She stared at him a moment, only then realizing he was not looking at her. She followed his gaze, gasped when she saw they were surrounded by a group of mounted warriors armed and painted for war.

"Don't move," Wolf Shadow said quietly. "They might take you alive."

"What about you?" she asked.

He stared at the warrior riding toward him, war club raised above his head. "I'm a dead man," he muttered. "Remember what I said. Don't fight them."

The words had barely left Wolf Shadow's mouth when a warrior struck him along the side of the head. Wolf Shadow dropped to the ground, a splash of bright red blood spreading across his temple.

She would have screamed if another warrior hadn't grabbed her from behind and covered her mouth with his hand. She stared at Wolf Shadow, at the blood dripping down the side of his face.

She tried to go to him, to see if he was dead, but the warrior behind her refused to let her go. Moments later, her arms and legs were tightly bound and she was lying facedown over the withers of one of the Crow horses, her hands and feet tied beneath the horse's belly.

She heard the sound of hoofbeats and knew with dreadful certainty that the Crow were going to attack the village. There was silence for what seemed a very long while and then a bloodcurdling war cry rent the stillness of the early morning. The sound seemed to vibrate within her and she closed her eyes. From deep within her memory she heard a voice crying, *No! No! La non mia ragazza piccola! Non prendere la mia ragazza piccola! Teressa!*

Teressa! She opened her eyes and the memory faded. Though faint, she could hear an occasional scream, a gunshot, the terrified wailing of a child. She tried to block out the sounds of the battle but to no avail. Her thoughts turned to Mountain Sage and Eagle Lance. Hot tears stung her eyes. Even if her parents survived the battle, she might never see them again. If the Crow were victorious, she would be their prisoner. They would take her to their village where she would be killed or forced to be a slave.

She looked over at Wolf Shadow. She could see him lying where he had fallen. Fear wrapped around her heart. He lay so still. Was he dead?

She lost track of time. Her wrists and ankles ached. Her back ached. She closed her eyes again and her mind flooded with images of paint-streaked warriors swooping down on her, of golden brown eyes filled with fear and concern. Confused, she opened her eyes. Spots danced before them. She was trying to work her hands free when she realized the sounds of battle had ceased. It occurred to her that it had been quiet for some time.

She felt her blood run cold when she heard a high-pitched cry of victory.

The Crow had won the battle.

Chance groaned softly as consciousness returned, bringing a wave of pain and nausea. He opened his eyes and quickly closed them again. Where was he?

Rough hands grabbed him and hauled him to his feet. The world spun out of focus and he groaned again as pain slashed through the side of his head. A Crow warrior jerked his arms behind his back and bound his wrists together, then dropped a noose over his head and pulled it tight.

What the hell had happened? Squinting against the sunlight, Chance slowly looked around. At first, nothing made sense. Not the warriors painted for war. Not the bloody scalps tied to their horses. Not the thick black smoke spreading like ink across the sky. And then it all came back to him. The Crow war party. The club swinging at his head.

Gradually, he realized the battle was over and the Crow had won. Where was Winter Rain? Had they killed her? And what of Kills-Like-a-Hawk and Dancing Crane? What of Bear Chaser? Were they all dead?

He took a step toward the village, grief welling up within him, only to come to an abrupt halt as one of the warrior's gave a jerk on the rope around his neck, nearly knocking Chance off his feet. Muttering an oath, he stumbled, barely managing to keep his feet as the warrior urged his horse to a walk. He shuffled along in the horse's wake, every step sending shards of pain lancing through his skull.

By midafternoon his head was throbbing incessantly. Sweat stung his eyes, ran down his back, his chest. His shoulders ached from having his arms drawn tightly behind his back.

A short time later, the war party stopped near a shallow stream to rest and water their horses. Chance stared at the water. He moved toward the stream. Just one drink, he thought. He hadn't taken more than half a dozen steps when the rope brought him up short, the rough hemp cutting into his throat.

He heard the sound of laughter behind him. Slowly, he turned to find a trio of warriors watching him. One of them spoke in a guttural tongue, gesturing for Chance to get down on his knees. He caught the word "dog" and knew they wanted him to beg for a drink.

Fighting off the urge to do so, he turned his back on them and closed his eyes, quietly cursing himself for his show of pride. He couldn't go on much longer without water. Why not beg for it now? He would have to, sooner or later. Why suffer any more than

he had to? But some inner wellspring of pride refused
to let him abase himself while he still had the strength
to resist.

All too soon, the rope around his neck grew taut.
Reaching deep down inside himself, he found the
strength and the will to put one foot in front of the
other.

He lost track of time. One hour blurred into the
next. Every step sent new slivers of pain knifing
through his skull. Time and again he thought of giving
up. If he'd been certain they would shoot him and put
him out of his misery, he might have surrendered to
the pain and given up, but the thought of being
dragged was more than he could bear.

At dusk, the Crow made camp.

Chance dropped to the ground the minute the horse
ahead of him came to a stop. Closing his eyes, he
tried to pretend the pounding in his head belonged to
someone else.

He was on the brink of unconsciousness when a few
drops of cool water fell over his face. With an effort,
he opened his eyes to find Winter Rain kneeling beside him.

"Here." She helped him sit up, then held a waterskin to his lips. "Drink this."

He gulped the cold water greedily. He'd never
tasted anything better in his life, he thought, not even
his old man's bonded bourbon.

"Drink it slowly," Winter Rain admonished.

The warning came too late. Turning on his side, he
retched, then lay there panting, thinking he had never
felt more miserable in his whole life.

Winter Rain brushed his hair away from his face,
then offered him another drink.

Chance rinsed his mouth, then took several slow
sips. "Are you all right?" he asked.

She nodded. "Will they kill us, do you think?"

He took a deep breath, let it out in a long, slow sigh. "I don't know." There were worse things than death, he thought. Prisoners not killed out of hand usually faced one of three fates: They were tortured, they were forced to become slaves, or they were traded to another tribe for goods. Winter Rain knew the consequences of being captured as well as he did. No doubt she was looking for reassurance from him, but he had none to give.

Winter Rain gazed into the distance, her lower lip trembling. "They are dead, aren't they? My mother and father. Strong Elk. Dawn Song and her family. All of them."

Chance looked at her, wondering if a lie would be better than the truth, but before he could answer, a tall warrior wearing black and white war paint strode up to them. He kicked Chance in the side, then grabbed Winter Rain by the arm and hauled her to her feet.

Chance swore as he doubled over, the pain lancing through his ribs rivaling the ache in his head. Curled up on the ground, he watched the warrior push Winter Rain toward a flat stretch of ground, gesturing that she should build a fire.

With a sigh, Chance closed his eyes and slid into oblivion.

# Chapter 8

"Wolf Shadow? Wolf Shadow, wake up!"

He climbed up out of the darkness through layers of pain, drawn by the sound of her voice and the gentle touch of her hand on his cheek.

He opened his eyes to find Winter Rain staring down at him.

"You are still alive!" she exclaimed, the worry in her eyes quickly turning to relief.

He had to be alive, he thought. He couldn't be dead and hurt this bad. His head ached. His ribs ached. His arms were numb.

"Can you sit up?" she asked. "I brought you something to eat."

"Water." He forced the word through a throat that felt as dry as the Arizona desert.

"All right." She helped him to a sitting position, then offered him a drink. Remembering his earlier experience, he sipped it slowly, felt the coolness revive him.

Glancing around, he saw the Crow warriors gathered around several small fires. Though he couldn't understand much of their language, it was obvious that they were bragging about their victory over the Lakota. His thoughts turned toward his cousin's family again. Were they all dead?

"Here." Winter Rain offered him a chunk of meat. "You must eat something."

He ate it from her hand, surprised to find that he

was ravenous. Sitting there, eating from her hand as if he were a heel hound, took a hefty slice out of his pride, but there was no help for it. And he had a nasty feeling that things would get a lot worse before they got better.

A short time later, the warrior who had claimed Winter Rain as his prisoner came after her. Jerking her to her feet, he dragged her over to his blankets and pushed her down. He quickly tied her hands and feet together, then stretched out beside her.

One by one, the warriors turned in for the night, save for the two armed men who stood beside the nearest fire, keeping watch.

Neither of them seemed to be paying him any mind, and after a few minutes, he scooted backward a little, and then a little more, and then a little more. With any luck, he could lose himself in the shadows and work his hands free. And then . . .

He swore softly as the taller of the two warriors turned to look in his direction. The man spoke to his companion, then walked toward Chance. Grabbing Chance by the arm, he pulled him to his feet and freed his hands, gesturing for him to relieve himself.

Chance stifled a groan as feeling returned to his hands and arms. Jaw clenched, he stretched his arms and shoulders. All too soon, his hands were tied behind his back again.

Lying on his side, he stared up at the sky. It was going to be a long, long night.

Winter Rain lay rigid beside the Crow warrior, afraid to move, afraid, almost, to breathe for fear of waking him. What did he intend to do with her? He had not touched her tonight, but what of tomorrow? Was she to be violated? Made a slave? Killed? Though she had no wish to die, she thought she would prefer death to being raped or enslaved by the enemy.

She stared up at the sky. Had her parents been killed? Tears burned her eyes. She should be lying dead beside them, she thought, blinking back her tears. She would be dead if she hadn't gone down to the river. And what of Strong Elk? And Dawn Song? They had not spoken to each other since the night of the dance at the Strong Heart lodge.

Winter Rain closed her eyes, overcome with a sense of guilt. Tears trickled down her cheeks. She didn't want to live if everyone she knew and loved was dead.

But not everyone she knew was dead. Wolf Shadow was still alive. What would his fate be? Did they mean to take him back to their village and torture him for the amusement of the Crow people? If they killed him, she would truly be alone.

It was that depressing prospect that followed her to sleep.

Chance woke with a low groan. Every muscle in his body ached from sleeping on the hard, cold ground. His ribs ached. His head throbbed monotonously. He knew he should be glad to be alive, but at the moment it was hard to remember why.

One of the warriors freed his hands and gestured for him to get up. Feeling like he was a hundred years old, Chance gained his feet. He lifted a hand to his head, wincing as his fingers touched a lump the size of a goose egg. There was blood matted in his hair.

With a grunt, the warrior pushed him toward a stand of timber, indicating he should relieve himself. Chance did so gratefully. For a moment, he considered trying to overpower the Crow warrior and making a run for it even though he wasn't sure how far he'd get on foot in his present condition. Still, he might have tried it if not for Winter Rain. He couldn't leave her behind.

With that in mind, he didn't offer any resistance

when the Crow bound his hands behind his back once again.

Returning to the campsite, Chance saw that the warriors were getting ready to leave. He spied Winter Rain standing off by herself. Since no one seemed to be paying any attention to him, he walked over to her.

"You okay?" he asked.

She nodded, her gaze moving over him. "Are you?"

"My head hurts. Other than that, I'm fine, all things considered."

"Here." She offered him a bite of the pemmican one of the warriors had given her.

Chance took a bite and chewed it slowly, only then realizing how hungry he really was.

Winter Rain took another bite, and then gave him the rest. "How long do you think it will be before we get to their village?" she asked.

Before Chance could reply, one of the warriors came striding toward them. Lashing Winter Rain's hands together, the Crow lifted her onto the back of a horse. The warrior then grabbed Chance by the arm and helped him onto the back of another horse. Though he was only guessing, Chance figured he'd been slowing them down. Now that he was mounted, they could make better time. Minutes later, the rest of the war party was mounted and they were on their way.

Chance closed his eyes and willed the hours to pass.

When they stopped to water the horses at midday, Chance knelt beside the stream. Stretching out on his belly, he took a drink, then dipped the side of his head into the water. The cold water numbed the pain in his head even as it rinsed the blood from his hair. He stayed there for several minutes before levering upright. Cold water dripped onto his shoulder and back.

A short time later, they were on the move again.

Chance glanced at the surrounding countryside. If he recollected right, the Crow village was about an hour away. He'd be glad to get off the back of this horse, he mused, and yet he couldn't stifle a sense of growing unease as he wondered what his fate would be when they reached their destination. And what of Winter Rain? Would she be passed from warrior to warrior? Or would the Crow who had captured her make her his slave?

Dammit, he had to get away from here, had to find a way to get Winter Rain back to her parents so he could collect the rest of the reward, hopefully in time to pay off the mortgage on the ranch.

Lost in thoughts of escape, he was hardly aware of the passage of time until he looked up and saw the Crow camp. Dozens of lodges were spread in a shallow valley. The Crow horse herd grazed alongside a winding river. It was a peaceful scene, he thought, reminiscent of what the Lakota village had looked like before the Crow attack. He hated to think of how it must look now.

For the first time, he wondered what had provoked the Crow attack. Had it been in retaliation for the horses stolen by Strong Elk? Chance grunted softly. Neither the Crow nor the Lakota needed a reason. They were enemies and that was reason enough.

As they neared the village, a number of dogs came running toward them, barking furiously. Men, women, and children stopped what they were doing and surged toward the returning war party. The warriors dismounted and tossed the reins of their horses to their wives or children. A few women and young girls moved through the throng, obviously searching for their husbands or fathers. Soon after, a high keening wail broke the still afternoon air as the bereaved gave voice to their grief.

One of the warriors pulled Chance off the back of

his horse and dragged him toward a tree. A noose dangled from a limb. The warrior tugged the loop over Chance's head and snugged it tight, then hurried toward his lodge.

There was just enough play in the rope to allow Chance to sit down and he did so, resting his back against the trunk.

He saw Winter Rain standing between the warrior who had claimed her and a very pregnant woman. Speaking rapidly, the woman gestured at Winter Rain and shook her head, apparently not at all happy that her husband had brought home a slave. Chance couldn't blame her. The Crow woman was as homely as a horse. Little wonder that she didn't want a pretty young slave to share her lodge.

The conversation went on for several minutes. Then, with an air of defeat, the warrior nodded. Indicating that Winter Rain should follow him, he walked toward a small lodge and rapped on the door flap. A wrinkled old woman with gray hair stepped out of the lodge. He spoke to the old woman for several minutes. She nodded and the warrior untied Winter Rain's hands. The old woman motioned for Winter Rain to enter the lodge. She spoke to the warrior and then followed Winter Rain inside. The warrior stood there for a moment, then turned and went back to his own dwelling.

Chance grunted softly, pleased that Winter Rain would be living with the old woman. At least he wouldn't have to worry about some randy young buck stealing into her bed late at night. And stealing her away from an old woman would be a sight easier than trying to spirit her away from a warrior's lodge, assuming he could find a way before they killed him.

With that grim thought in mind, he rested his head against the trunk of the tree and closed his eyes. Rest was what he needed now. He had to regain his

strength, had to be ready to make a break for it should
the opportunity arise.

Winter Rain stepped inside the old woman's lodge
and glanced around. There were a few cooking pots
stacked on one side of the doorway, and several stor-
age containers along the other side. A backrest made
of willow branches and covered by a warm robe was
located alongside the fire pit. A bedroll was situated
against the back wall of the lodge.

She stood in the center of the lodge, wondering
what would be expected of her. She didn't speak
Crow; it was doubtful the old woman spoke Lakota.

The old woman solved the problem of speech with
sign language.

*What is your name?*

*Winter Rain.*

Murmuring, *"Itche,"* the old woman nodded, then
went on signing. *I am called Blackbird-in-the-Morning.
You will keep my lodge clean, gather wood and water.
If you try to escape, you will be whipped. You
understand?*

*Yes.*

*"Itche,"* the old woman said again.

Winter Rain repeated the word in her mind, decid-
ing it must be the word for "good" in the Crow
language.

The old woman gestured at the door. *Go. Get wood
for fire.* She pointed at a small pile of twigs and
branches. *"Bale,"* she said, then, pointing at the fire
pit, *"Bilee."*

Winter Rain nodded. *"Bale. Bilee."*

*"Itche."* Blackbird-in-the-Morning said. She gestured at the doorway. *Go now.*

Winter Rain stepped out of the lodge. Things could
be worse, she thought. She could be the slave of that
warrior and his wife. Given her choice, she would

much rather be Blackbird-in-the-Morning's slave, she thought, and then frowned. Given her choice, she'd rather be back home. Home. Would she ever see Mountain Sage and Eagle Lance again?

With a sigh, she started toward a stand of timber when she spied Chance sitting against a tree. Changing course, she walked toward him, wondering what his fate would be.

As she drew closer, she saw that his eyes were closed. Thinking he was asleep, she turned away, only to do an about-face when he called her name.

"I thought you were sleeping."

"Just dozing a little." He winced as he sat up straighter. "Everything all right?"

"I guess so. I am to be a slave for an old woman. Her name is Blackbird-in-the-Morning."

Chance nodded. "I reckon you'll be fine as long as you don't give her any excuse to beat you."

"What will they do with you?"

He grunted softly. "Nothing good, I'm sure of that."

Her eyes widened. "They won't . . ." She bit down on her lip, reluctant to put the thought into words.

"Kill me? I'm pretty sure that's what they have in mind."

"No! What can I do?"

"Nothing," he said sharply.

"But—"

"Winter Rain, listen to me. If you interfere, you'll just make more trouble for yourself. Do you understand?"

She nodded. She understood, but she didn't have to like it. "I must go," she said with regret. "Blackbird-in-the-Morning told me to gather wood."

"Take care of yourself."

With a nod, she headed toward the timber. She couldn't just sit idly by while they killed him. Tonight, after the village was asleep, she would sneak

out of Blackbird-in-the-Morning's lodge and cut Wolf
Shadow loose. If she didn't get caught, they could escape. Together. Smiling inwardly, she began gathering
wood for Blackbird-in-the-Morning. Tonight, she
thought. And then her optimism vanished.

What if he was dead by tonight?

# Chapter 9

Winter Rain's first day as a slave passed quietly enough. After she gathered wood for Blackbird-in-the-Morning's fire, she straightened the old woman's lodge. A short time after that, the old woman's son, Elk Moon, stopped by to drop off a deer that he had killed. Like the Lakota, the Crow apparently looked after their aged parents by providing them with meat. Along with the meat, he had brought the heart, liver, kidney, and pancreas bundled in the paunch, which had first been turned inside out and cleaned.

Naturally, it was left to Winter Rain to butcher the carcass. First she cut off the front legs close to the ribs and set them aside. The rear legs came next, and then she removed the *takoan,* or great sinew, that ran over the backbone from the rump to the shoulder, which was considered a delicacy to the Lakota. Setting the *takoan* aside, she split the carcass along one side of the backbone and then cut each half in half just below the rib cage, so that she had four large pieces. The neck and head were the last to be removed. She hung one hindquarter of the meat from a pole near the lodge. Tomorrow she would prepare it for drying. If she was still here.

She cut a chunk of meat into small pieces and dropped them into Blackbird-in-the-Morning's kettle for the evening meal. She added some water, a few wild onions, and a pinch of sage. She lit a fire beneath the kettle and when she was sure it was burning evenly, she wrapped the remainder of the meat in a piece of hide, then went down to the river to wash her hands.

She saw a few of the Crow women at the river. Some were filling water pots, others were washing clothes or bathing their children. The women stared at her suspiciously, their expressions unfriendly. The children eyed her with curiosity. One little boy smiled shyly, ducked behind his mother, then peeked at her from behind his mother's back.

Winter Rain grinned at him, then knelt on the bank to rinse off her hands. She sat there for a time, watching the swirling water. Now and then a fish swam by. She saw a turtle climb up on the far bank and disappear into the cattails. Somewhere in the distance she heard the deep croak of a bullfrog.

The other women left one by one. Winter Rain sat there a little while longer, watching the sky turn to flame as the sun went down behind the mountains.

By the time she made it back to Blackbird-in-the-Morning's lodge, it was full dark.

Blackbird-in-the-Morning was waiting for her outside the lodge. With an impatient gesture, she handed Winter Rain two bowls. Winter Rain filled one with stew and handed it to the old woman, who went back inside her lodge to eat.

After filling a bowl for herself, Winter Rain sat down with her back to the lodge. She could see Wolf Shadow across the way and wondered if anyone had given him anything to eat or drink. When she finished eating, she filled the bowl again and carried it over to him.

Several men and women stared at her as she made her way toward him, but no one tried to stop her.

"I brought you something to eat," she said, kneeling down beside him.

"Thanks."

She dipped her spoon into the bowl and offered him a bite. "Does your head still hurt?"

"A little."

She offered him another bite and then another, noticing, as she did so, that several warriors were adding wood to the fire burning near the center of the village. Gradually, a crowd gathered around the fire.

When she offered Wolf Shadow another bite, he refused.

"You cannot be full already," she said, frowning.

He shook his head, his gaze on the crackling flames.

"What is it?"

"I think the entertainment is about to start. And I'm it."

She looked at him blankly a moment and then, as comprehension dawned, her eyes widened in horror.

Chance nodded. "Go on back to the old woman's lodge and stay inside until it's over."

Winter Rain stared at him. He didn't look afraid. He didn't sound afraid. But surely he must be. The Crow wouldn't just kill him. They would torture him first.

"Go on," he said gruffly. "Get out of here." He didn't want her to watch or to be there if his courage ran out.

Slowly, she rose to her feet. She stared down at him for a long moment, and then she hurried back to Blackbird-in-the-Morning's lodge and ducked inside.

Chance sucked in a deep breath when he saw two men striding purposefully toward him. He held it for several moments, then blew it out in a long shuddering sigh.

Dammit, he didn't want to die like this, trussed up like a Christmas turkey! His gaze slid toward Blackbird-in-the-Morning's lodge. He'd had a pretty good life. Looking back, he only had two regrets: that he hadn't brought the last of his mother's killers to justice, and that he wouldn't get to hold Winter Rain in his arms again.

One of the warriors untied Chance and jerked him to his feet; then the warriors took hold of his arms and dragged him toward the fire, where they shoved him down to the ground and spread-eagled him between four stout wooden stakes driven into the hard-packed earth.

He swore under his breath as the warriors who had attacked the village paraded around him. Most of them were armed with skinning knives. One carried a war lance from which dangled a long black scalp. Another brandished a torch.

Chance glanced at the men and women gathered around the fire. They watched him avidly, their expressions filled with hatred. The very air seemed to crackle with anticipation.

The armed warriors began to dance. Watching them, Chance realized it was a victory dance. He sucked in a deep breath as one of the warriors drew a knife and waved it over his head. The crowd shouted the warrior's name as the warrior danced around Chance.

"Short Buffalo Horn! Short Buffalo Horn!"

Chance grimaced as the blade slashed downward, slicing into his thigh. Blood trailed in the wake of the blade, looking black and shiny in the firelight.

Hands clenched, his body rigid, Chance tried to concentrate on something other than the pain. A movement to his left caught his eye and when he looked up, he saw Winter Rain staring back at him. The old woman was standing beside her.

Dammit, what was she doing here? Chance's body convulsed as another warrior stepped forward and dragged the blade of his knife over his chest. A third warrior drove his knife into Chance's left shoulder.

With each show of blood, the Crow hollered their approval.

And now the warrior with the torch moved forward, swinging the torch above his head as he spoke to the crowd. Chance stared at the flame, his stomach churning, the taste of bile rising in his throat.

He looked up at Winter Rain again, willing her to go before it was too late. He wasn't sure how much longer he could hold out before the pain became too great, before he started sniveling like a baby, before he begged the Crow for mercy they didn't have.

The warrior holding the torch moved closer, each swing of his arm bringing the flame closer to Chance's body. He could feel the heat of it now and he broke out in a cold sweat as he waited for the touch of the flame against his skin. . . .

*"Oochia!"* Blackbird-in-the-Morning's quavery voice rose above the shouts of the crowd.

The man with the torch fell silent as the old woman stepped forward.

Chance sucked in a deep breath, his eyes narrowing as the old woman spoke. He didn't know much of the Crow language, but he caught the word *chilee,* husband, and the word *baanistaache,* slave.

The man who had captured Chance strode forward and there was a rapid exchange between the warrior and the old woman. The warrior looked thoughtful for a moment and then he nodded. He spoke to the crowd and they gradually dispersed until only Winter Rain and Blackbird-in-the-Morning remained.

The old woman spoke to Winter Rain. Withdrawing a knife from her belt, the old woman handed it to Winter Rain, then turned and made her way back to her lodge.

Winter Rain knelt beside Chance and began cutting his hands and feet free.

"What was that all about?" he asked.

"I told Blackbird-in-the-Morning that you were my husband, that you were a brave warrior among the Lakota, and that you did not deserve to die without a chance to defend your honor."

"And they let me live on her say-so?"

Winter Rain paused, wondering how much to tell him. "She is a medicine woman. Very holy. Come." She slid her arm under his shoulder. "We must tend your wounds."

His gaze probed hers. "What aren't you telling me?"

"You will be her slave until you have recovered your strength."

"And then?"

"You will fight the warrior who captured you. If you win, you will be his slave."

"And if I lose?"

"If you lose, the warriors will finish what they started."

"Guess I'd better win, then," he muttered.

With her help, he managed to gain his feet. Blood ran down his thigh from the gash in his leg, dripped from the wounds in his shoulder and chest.

Winter Rain slipped her arm around his waist and they walked toward the old woman's lodge.

Blackbird-in-the-Morning was waiting for them inside. She had a fire going in the pit; the scent of sage filled the air. She gestured at the robe spread in the rear of the lodge. With a weary sigh, Chance sank down onto the warm fur. Winter Rain hovered at his side while Blackbird-in-the-Morning tended his wounds.

The old woman's gnarled hands were surprisingly gentle as she washed and dressed the cuts. Then, chanting softly, she picked up a small tortoise-shell rattle that she shook over him four times. Still chanting softly, she put the rattle aside and passed her hands through the sage-scented smoke, drawing it toward him while Winter Rain stroked his brow, her eyes filled with concern.

The chanting, the smoke, and Winter Rain's gentle touch soothed him to sleep.

Winter Rain looked at Blackbird-in-the-Morning. *Will he be all right?*

The old woman nodded. *He is not bad hurt. Sleep now.*

It was then that Winter Rain realized Wolf Shadow was stretched out on her sleeping robes, and that as his "wife," she was expected to lie beside him.

A short time later, Blackbird-in-the-Morning signed that it was time for bed.

There was nothing for Winter Rain to do but obey. Sitting down, she removed her moccasins, then lifted a corner of the robe and slid under it, careful not to touch Wolf Shadow, who was sleeping soundly.

The fire burned down low. Winter Rain stared into the darkness, acutely aware of the man who lay beside her clad in nothing but a breechclout. Closing her eyes, she was careful to keep as much space as possible between them.

She didn't remember falling asleep, but she woke with a start, instantly aware it was morning and that she was in a strange place, in a strange bed. And then she felt the weight of Wolf Shadow's head on her shoulder, the warmth of his skin against her arm, and she knew what had awakened her.

Lying perfectly still so as not to disturb him, she glanced around the lodge, trying to ignore his nearness. She could hear Blackbird-in-the-Morning snoring softly across the way. The old woman was barely visible in the dim light filtering through the smoke hole.

Winter Rain's gaze was drawn back toward Wolf Shadow. She could feel his breath, warm against her neck. She felt her own breath catch in her throat as he rolled onto his side. His arm curled around her waist and now the full length of his body was pressed intimately against hers.

With a start, she realized he was awake and watching her. Heat flooded her cheeks.

"You all right?" he asked.

"Me?" Her voice came out in a squeak. "Why do you ask?"

"You look a little flushed." His voice was low and husky; his breath tickled her ear.

"I . . ."

Wolf Shadow's gaze moved to her mouth and lingered there. She felt the touch of his heated gaze as vividly as if he had kissed her. The flush in her cheeks intensified and spread downward, flooding her whole body with warmth. Her eyes widened as his arm tightened around her, drawing her body closer to his. There was no doubt that he was feeling better, she thought, no doubt at all. Just as there was no doubt that he was fully aroused.

She cleared her throat nervously. "Are you feeling better? Does your head still hurt?"

"I'm hurting in a lot of places," he muttered.

Her brow furrowed with concern. "Is there anything I can do?"

"Oh, yeah," he said with a wry grin. "But I doubt you'd be willing."

She looked at him blankly for a moment, and then her eyes widened as she realized what he meant.

Chance swore under his breath. She was a maiden, untouched, untutored in the ways of men and women, not some saloon tart he could bed and forget. She was a rich man's daughter, one who was worth fifteen grand to her old man, and he'd better remember that right quick. He was pretty sure old Bryant wouldn't want to find out his little girl had been seduced by the man sent to bring her back.

Muttering an oath, he lifted his arm from her waist and put some space between them. How the devil was he going to sleep beside her night after night and keep his hands off her? He hadn't wanted a woman this bad since he was a randy young buck.

He threw back the covers, took a deep breath, and stood up. Slipping on his moccasins, he left the lodge and headed for the river. Cold baths had never been among his favorite things, but this morning, it was just what he needed.

He was aware of being watched as he walked through the village toward the river. Warriors eyed him with suspicion, women and children with ill-disguised curiosity and distrust. He spotted several sentries keeping watch.

When he reached the river, he removed his clout and moccasins, took a deep breath, and plunged in. He swore as the cold water closed over him. But it was just what he needed.

Winter Rain breathed a sigh of relief when Wolf Shadow left the lodge. When he was near, she couldn't seem to think clearly. Her heartbeat quickened, and she felt nervous and excited, as if she were on the verge of some wondrous discovery. Sometimes it seemed as if she would jump right out of her skin. She felt her cheeks flush as she remembered the press of his body, hard and long and lean, against hers; the way he had looked at her, as if he were a hungry wolf and she a helpless fawn. She had been afraid he might kiss her again and was disappointed when he had not.

Where had he gone?

Rising, she pulled on her moccasins and combed her fingers through her hair. A glance at Blackbird-in-the-Morning showed her that the old woman was still sleeping soundly.

Moving quietly, Winter Rain stepped outside. It was

a clear crisp morning. Grabbing a waterskin, she headed for the river. The first task of the day was to draw fresh water for drinking and cooking; then she would gather wood for the fire.

But first, the river. She walked briskly, her gaze darting up and down the shore when she reached the water. Turning right, she passed several other women who had come down to draw water. She could have filled her waterskin anywhere, but she kept moving upriver. She told herself the reason she didn't stop where the Crow women were gathered was because she didn't want to suffer their cold looks or hear their cruel words, but the truth was, she was looking for Wolf Shadow, even though she was reluctant to admit it.

She found him a short time later, couldn't help grinning when she thought of how often she had found him standing naked in the river. This time he was hunkered down, submerged to midchest.

He didn't look happy to see her.

"What are you doing?" Moving upstream a little, she knelt at the river's edge to fill the waterskin.

"What does it look like?" he asked, his voice gruff.

She shrugged. "It looks like you're just sitting there. Are you not cold?"

"Not cold enough."

"I do not understand."

He scowled at her. "Don't I know it."

He sounded angry, though she did not know why. Perhaps it was merely that the cold water made his wounds ache, she mused, or perhaps he was upset at being a prisoner. It was not a fate a Lakota warrior could easily accept. Or maybe he was worried about facing the warrior who had captured him. She dismissed that thought as soon as it crossed her mind. When his wounds healed, Wolf Shadow would not be easily overcome.

"Why do you not come out?" she asked.

He looked down at himself, then back at her, one brow lifting in amusement. "I don't think that's a good idea."

"Why not?" she asked, and then, taking his meaning, she blushed to the roots of her hair. Rising quickly, she hurried back to the village.

"Finally, she gets it," he muttered irritably.

The morning meal was ready when Chance returned to Blackbird-in-the-Morning's lodge.

Winter Rain looked up when he stepped inside. She blushed when she met his gaze. Just looking at her made him hard and aching all over again. It was all too easy to remember how she had felt pressed against him that morning, to remember how ardently she had returned his kisses. Damn! He was going to be spending a lot of time in that river.

Sitting down, he glanced at Blackbird-in-the-Morning. Was she aware of the tension sparking between himself and Winter Rain? She couldn't miss it, he thought, looking back at Winter Rain. The attraction between the two of them was hot enough to set the lodge on fire.

When the meal was over, Winter Rain went outside. Aware of Blackbird-in-the-Morning's knowing look, he followed Winter Rain out of the lodge.

Finding a place in the shade, he watched her cut thin slices from the venison she had quartered the day before. The strips were about as long as her arm, perhaps three hands wide. When all the strips had been cut, she would arrange them over the drying rack beside the lodge. The rack was a long pole suspended on two sturdy forked poles that were high enough to prevent the dogs from jumping up and stealing the meat. Young boys sometimes grabbed a piece of meat and ran away with it. Chance remembered doing it himself a few times. He also remembered the day he'd been caught by one of the women. She had given him quite a thrashing, but it hadn't stopped him from doing it again. The women never had to worry about the girls. The girls knew what happened to the boys who got caught!

When the meat was thoroughly dried, it would be cut up and stored to be used as needed. Some of it would be pulverized, mixed with fat and made into pemmican. Dried cherries or grapes were often crushed, including pits and seeds, and added to the mix. It made a sweet treat.

Winter Rain bent over her task, all too aware that Wolf Shadow was watching her every move. What was he thinking? Why didn't he go away? His nearness and the heated look in his eyes made her nervous. The knife she held slipped and cut the side of her hand.

With a little yelp of pained surprise, she dropped the knife.

Wolf Shadow was at her side in an instant. "Here, let me take a look at that."

He picked up a waterskin lying nearby and rinsed away the blood, then dried her hand with a corner of his clout.

"Is it bad?" she asked, trying to see around him.

"No. Wait here."

He ducked inside Blackbird-in-the-Morning's lodge. After returning a moment later, he wrapped a strip of cloth around her hand and tied off the ends. "You'll be as good as new tomorrow."

She looked up at him, her gaze meeting his. There was no denying the attraction between them. It was always there, simmering just beneath the surface. He might have kissed her, and she might have let him, if Blackbird-in-the-Morning hadn't chosen that moment to step outside.

Wolf Shadow went back to sitting in the shade and

Winter Rain cut up the last pieces of venison and began hanging them on the rack to dry. Blackbird-in-the-Morning nodded approvingly, then found a place in the sun and sat down.

And now there were two people watching her. It made her self-conscious, but there was nothing she could do about it. She couldn't very well tell Wolf Shadow to go away, not with Blackbird-in-the-Morning sitting there, watching. After all, Wolf Shadow was supposed to be her husband.

Winter Rain placed another strip of venison on the rack, felt a sudden catch in her heart as she remembered all the times she had helped her mother do this very thing. It had not been work then, with the two of them sharing the task. Tears stung her eyes. She had to escape from this place, had to go back and find out if her mother and father had been killed.

She glanced over her shoulder at Wolf Shadow. The gash in his head was healing, as were the cuts the Crow had inflicted on him. In a day or two she would ask him to take her away from here. He wouldn't refuse; she was certain of that. If he stayed, he would have to fight Short Buffalo Horn. Surely he wouldn't want to take a chance on losing. Surely he was as anxious as she to get away from their enemies.

And then a new thought gave her pause. If they ran away from the Crow, there was nothing to stop him from taking her back to the *wasichu* who claimed to be her mother and father.

She reached for another strip of venison. She would take her chances with Wolf Shadow, she decided as she laid it over the rack. After all, she had a better chance of running away from him than from the Crow.

Smiling to herself, she finished her task. She would talk to him about it tonight, after Blackbird-in-the-Morning was asleep.

\*　　\*　　\*

Sitting back against one of the backrests he had made earlier that day, Chance watched Winter Rain move about the lodge. She had served them dinner, first the old woman and then him, before she filled a bowl for herself. She had glanced at him frequently while they ate, and almost dropped her bowl when Blackbird-in-the-Morning tapped her on the shoulder to ask for more. She was up to something, he thought, but what? And how was he going to get them both out of here? Blackbird-in-the-Morning was a decent sort, but he didn't want to be a prisoner—hers or anyone else's—nor did he want to fight Short Buffalo Horn to see whether he lived as a slave or died a nasty lingering death. Neither option was particularly appealing.

Feeling restless, he rose and left the lodge. While standing in the gathering dusk, he glanced around the village. Crow life was similar to that of the Lakota. If there was meat in abundance and a Crow warrior was not engaged in a war party or taking part in a ceremony, he would most likely be found in his lodge, perhaps repairing his weapons, perhaps merely sitting idle. In contrast, a Crow woman never seemed to have idle time. If she was not mending or making clothing or moccasins, gathering wood and water, or caring for her children, she was probably tanning a hide, drying meat, or making pemmican.

Like Lakota girls, Crow girls played with dolls, emulating their mothers; Crow boys played with toy bows and arrows. When they grew older, the girls cared for their younger siblings and learned housekeeping skills; the boys hunted rabbits and deer and buffalo, and learned the art of war. Sometimes a warrior would bring a buffalo calf back from a hunt and give it to his children, who would either pretend to hunt it, or ride it. Older boys sometimes went looking for orphaned calves after a hunt. They killed them with arrows, brought home the meat, and gave the skins to their girl playmates to use for coverings for their toy tipis or clothing for their dolls.

It seemed that, at least for the time being, the Crow were at peace. Chance wondered again how many Lakota had survived the attack. He wondered if there were enough warriors left to form a war party, wondered again if his cousin's family had survived the attack.

It was full dark now. Chance heard women calling their children to bed, saw small groups of men standing together, talking and smoking before they turned in for the night.

He was about to go back inside the old woman's lodge when he saw Short Buffalo Horn striding toward him. The warrior stopped a few paces away, his gaze moving over Chance the way a cowboy might look over a horse he was thinking about buying.

Tonight, Chance thought. If they were going to make a run for it, it would have to be tonight.

# Chapter 10

Chance took Winter Rain aside that evening after Blackbird-in-the-Morning had gone to bed. "Tonight," he said, careful to keep his voice pitched low. "We're leaving tonight."

"Tonight?" She looked up at him, her eyes wide. "But how? We have no horses, no food."

"Short Buffalo Horn gave me the once-over a while ago. He's tired of waiting. We're leaving tonight. Gather up whatever food you can find. I'll take care of getting the horses. Just be ready."

She started to say something, but he didn't give her time to argue. Instead, he left the lodge.

Standing in the shadows, he glanced up at the sky. Wakan Tanka was smiling down on him, he mused. Dark clouds were gathering overhead, shutting out the moon and stars. A good storm was just what they needed. There would be no moon to betray them; the rain would quickly wash out their tracks. With the inborn patience of a hunter, he squatted down on his heels and waited.

Winter Rain moved about the lodge, quietly packing one of the parfleches with pemmican and strips of dried venison. She rolled her sleeping robe into a tight cylinder and tied it closed with a strip of rawhide.

Winter Rain glanced around the dark lodge. Stealing from Blackbird-in-the-Morning made her feel guilty. The old woman might be the enemy, but she had been kind to her.

She glanced at the doorway, her head cocked to one side. Was it raining? She tiptoed to the doorway and drew back the flap, looking out. It was dark, so dark she couldn't even see the lodge across the way.

Ducking back inside, she sat down to wait for Wolf Shadow.

She didn't remember dozing, but she woke with a start, panic overtaking her when she felt a hand over her mouth.

"Shh, it's me."

Relief washed through her at the sound of his voice.

"Let's go," he whispered urgently.

Rising, she grabbed the parfleche, the waterskin, and her sleeping robe and followed him out of the lodge, her heart pounding wildly. What would the Crow do to them if they were caught trying to escape?

It was still raining, and so dark she could scarcely see Wolf Shadow even though he was right in front of her.

He led her through the sleeping camp, tossing bits of venison to the dogs they passed to keep them quiet.

There were two horses waiting for them when they reached the river. In a flash of lightning, she saw that Wolf Shadow had somehow managed to get not only his mare but his saddle and saddlebags, as well. A second flash of lightning showed a body sprawled face-down in the mud. One of the sentries, she thought as Wolf Shadow lifted her onto the back of the second horse.

"Wrap that robe around you," he said. "It might help to keep you dry."

He took the parfleche from her and tied it to the horn of his saddle, then swung onto his horse's back. "We're going to cross the river while we can," he said. "If the storm keeps up, we might not be able to cross it later. If we get separated, follow the river. Sooner or later, it will take you to a town. Understand?"

She nodded; then, realizing he couldn't see her, she said, "Yes, I understand."

"Let's go."

She glanced at the dead Crow as they rode by. She felt no pity for him. He might be one of the warriors who had attacked their village. She was glad he was dead.

Her horse followed Wolf Shadow's without any urging. Winter Rain huddled deeper into her sleeping robe. It did little to keep her dry, but it did protect her from the wind—all but her hands, which were soon numb with cold from holding on to the reins. She couldn't imagine how much colder Wolf Shadow must be, clad in nothing but his clout and moccasins.

They had ridden about two miles when the moon peeked through a break in the clouds and she saw the body of another Crow warrior lying in the mud. Had Wolf Shadow killed all the sentries? Or only those on this side of the village?

They rode steadily onward, always keeping the river, which was now a swirling mass of rushing water, on their right. From time to time, a flash of brilliant lightning illuminated their way, but there was nothing to see except tall prairie grass flattened by the storm and cottonwood trees swaying in the wind.

Winter Rain huddled deeper into her robe. She was cold, so cold. She thought fleetingly of the cozy fire in Blackbird-in-the-Morning's lodge, and for the briefest of moments, she was tempted to turn around and go back. But the moment of weakness passed quickly. She could endure the cold and the rain; she couldn't endure not knowing whether Mountain Sage and Eagle Lance were dead or alive.

They kept the horses at a steady walk all that night, stopping only briefly to let the animals rest.

It wasn't until late the next morning that Wolf Shadow judged it was safe to stop and make camp. The rain, which had lessened as the night wore on, had finally stopped. A short time later the sun burned away the last of the clouds.

Dismounting, Winter Rain leaned against her horse's shoulder. She was cold and wet and chilled to the bone. There was no dry wood to be found. Spreading her sleeping robe over a bush, she lifted her face up to the sun and let its warmth wash over her.

Wolf Shadow removed his rifle from the saddle boot. He had taken the weapon from one of the Crow sentries. Propping the rifle against a tree, he stripped the rigging from Smoke and spread the saddle blanket on the bush beside Winter Rain's sleeping robe.

"We'll rest here for the day." He thrust the parfleche into her hand, then took her horse's reins and led the horses a short distance away. Using a couple of pieces of rope he had pulled from his saddlebags, he fashioned two pairs of hobbles, then removed the bridles from the horses and left them to graze on the lush green grass.

Winter Rain sat down on a flat rock and rummaged through the parfleche, withdrawing jerky and pemmican. She handed a piece of each to Wolf Shadow, who accepted them with a grunt and sat down beside her. She glanced over at him. They had hardly spoken to each other since they left the Crow village.

Chance looked up and met her gaze. "What?"

"We are going back to our village, are we not?" she asked.

He nodded. Like Winter Rain, he was anxious to find out whether his loved ones had survived the Crow attack.

In spite of the sun, they were both shivering. Chance swallowed the last of his pemmican, then slid his arm around Winter Rain's shoulders.

She looked at him, her eyes wide. "What are you doing?"

"I don't know about you, but I'm colder than a witch's—" He checked himself. "Let's just say I'm mighty damn cold."

She stared at him a moment, then, noticing how much warmer she was where her body was pressed to his, she scooted a little closer, all too aware of the long muscular length of his leg against her own. Gradually, she grew warmer. He, too, was shivering less now. She lifted her cold, clammy skirt from her legs a little, thinking she would be warmer without her tunic but the thought of being naked in front of Wolf Shadow was more than she could bear. She was acutely conscious of his presence beside her. His slightest move set her nerves aflutter. There was a strength about him, an inner core of confidence and assurance that was exceptionally attractive, especially now, when her survival depended on him.

His hand on her shoulder was comforting.

His gaze, resting on her face, was disquieting.

"How long . . ." Her throat was suddenly dry. She swallowed and licked her lips. "How long until we get back home?"

"A few days. Don't worry. We'll make it."

Looking at him, at the determined set of his jaw, she didn't doubt him for a minute. Winter Rain allowed herself doze, her head resting against his shoulder.

Holding her, Cance felt a wave of protectiveness wash over him. She was so young, so innocent, so at home with the Lakota people. How would she react to life in San Francisco? Would she hate him for taking her back to her parents? The thought gave him pause, but in the end it didn't matter. He couldn't afford to worry about her feelings or what she wanted.

If he was going to save his ranch, he needed that ten grand and he needed it right quick!

She sighed and he tightened his arm around her shoulders.

She wasn't shivering anymore. Her skin was warm beneath his hand, her tunic was dry. Her hair was soft against his cheek. Damn. She smelled of rain and sunshine and woman. It was a potent combination and his body reacted automatically. He shifted uncomfortably, the nether parts of his body as hard as the rock they were sitting on.

She was sleeping soundly now. Her head lolled forward. Scooting over a little to give her more room, he eased her down until her head was resting on his thigh.

He shook his head, wondering why he had inflicted such torture on himself. Her eyelashes lay like thick black fans against her sun-kissed cheeks. Her lips, slightly parted, were as pink as the petals of the wild roses that grew along the river back at the ranch. His gaze was drawn to the slight rise and fall of her breasts. He clenched his hands to keep from touching her. Lust, he told himself. It was just lust, nothing more. It didn't matter that her eyes were as blue as a high mountain lake or that her skin was smooth and unblemished. And if her legs were long and shapely and her hair was as soft as silk beneath his hand, it didn't change a thing. It was still just lust, an itch that he could have scratched when he got back home.

But for now, he was content to sit there and watch her sleep.

*The little girl looked out the window, the wonder in her eyes turning to horror as screams and war cries filled the air. Dust clogged her nostrils; fear was a hard lump in her stomach. The girl clung to her mother,*

*cried out when an arrow hit her father. How had she
ever thought the Indians were beautiful or exciting? She
cried out when one of the warriors grabbed her and
pulled her out of her mother's arms and out of the
coach. . . .*

Winter Rain woke with a scream echoing in her
ears, only then realizing it had come from her own
throat.

Opening her eyes, she saw Wolf Shadow staring
down at her.

Shaken, she glanced around. Where was she? She
looked back at Wolf Shadow, and dissolved into tears.

"What is it, sweetheart?" He drew her into his arms
and patted her back.

"I . . . I remember." She sat up. Sobs racked her
body. "Iron Arrow shot my daddy. He pulled me out
of the coach and took me home with him." She took
a long shuddering breath. "I remember crying for my
mother while he carried me away."

So, he thought, after all these years, she finally remembered what had happened. That should make
things easier.

"I was so afraid. We rode for days before we
reached the village. When we got there, Eagle Lance
gave me to Mountain Sage. I remember that she cried
when she hugged me."

"The Bryants have been looking for you ever since
you were taken from them."

"They are well? Both of them?"

"Yes."

She stared into the distance, her thoughts obviously
turned inward. She didn't speak for several minutes,
and then she said, "I do not want to go back. Not
now. Not ever." She squared her shoulders and lifted
her chin defiantly. "And you cannot make me."

He could, he thought. He could take her back right
now. There was no one to stop him, but he wouldn't.

Not until they had gone back to the village. Winter Rain had a right to know whether Mountain Sage and Eagle Lance were still alive. And he couldn't go back to the ranch, not until he knew what had happened to Kills-Like-a-Hawk and his family.

With a shrug, Chance slid off the rock and stretched his arms and legs. "I don't know about you," he said, "but I could use something to eat."

She didn't say anything, but she went to the parfleche and pulled out a couple hunks of jerky. She handed him a piece, then sat down on the rock again.

Chance looked up at the sky, glad to see that it was clear. He ran his hand over Winter Rain's sleeping robe and his saddle blanket, then turned them both over. They would be fully dry by nightfall.

He glanced at their back trail, wondering if the Crow would come after them. He had killed three of their warriors. Would they decide to avenge their dead? Chance didn't think there was much to worry about. The storm would have washed out their tracks.

Swallowing the last of the jerky, he picked up the waterskin and took a drink, then went to check the hobbles on the horses.

Smoke whinnied softly as he approached, then rubbed her forehead against his chest.

"I wish all females were as easy to please as you are," he muttered as he obligingly scratched the mare's ears. He glanced over his shoulder at Winter Rain, who was taking a stroll beyond the rock. "What am I gonna do about that one?"

Smoke snorted softly and shook her head.

"Yeah, I don't know either. She's got me tied in knots, you know? Got me thinking about what it would be like to settle down . . ." He swore softly. "I must be getting soft in the head. I don't have time for a woman."

His gaze followed Winter Rain, resting on the sway

of her hips as she walked away. She stopped at a berry bush. He watched her bend over to pick a handful. His mouth watered as he watched her pop a few of the purple berries into her mouth. But it wasn't the fruit that made his mouth water, it was the way her tongue slid over her lips to lick up the juice. Damn!

Muttering an oath, he turned his back to her. Dammit, what *was* he going to do about Winter Rain? He hadn't been this attracted to a woman in years. Every time he looked at her, he felt like a kid with his first case of lust. Just looking at her made him ache with wanting her.

A few minutes later, he sensed her presence behind him.

"I found some berries," she said. "Do you want some?"

He turned to face her. She held out her hands, which were filled with the fat purple fruit. But it was her mouth that drew his attention. Her lips were red with juice.

"Thanks." His voice was gruff.

She watched him eat a few. "They are good, yes?"

"Yeah." He ate a few more, wondering what she would do if he kissed her, if his tongue licked at the juice in the corner of her mouth.

Her gaze met his. As if reading his mind, she took a step backward.

Chance was trying to decide whether to fish or cut bait when Smoke gave him a sharp push with her nose. He stumbled forward, his arms closing around Winter Rain to keep from knocking her to the ground. The last of the fruit tumbled from her hands as she clutched him to keeping from falling.

She looked up at him, her eyes wide, like a doe scenting danger on the evening breeze.

He told himself to let her go and back off. His life

was complicated enough without seducing a virgin. No woman was worth ten thousand dollars.

But her skin was soft and warm beneath his hands, her lips pink and far too tempting for any mortal man to resist once he had tasted their sweetness. He lowered his head slowly, giving her plenty of warning. Giving her plenty of time to back away.

And then it was too late. His mouth closed on hers as his arm tightened around her shoulders, until her upper body was pressed intimately against his.

He didn't close his eyes, and neither did she. For a moment she stood rigid in his embrace. Then, with a sigh, her eyelids fluttered down and she surrendered to the shivery sensations sweeping through her.

His hands moved slowly up and down her back, then slid lower to cup her buttocks, drawing her still closer, letting her feel his arousal. It excited her even as it sent tremors of uncertainty coursing through her. She knew she should tell him to stop, but when she opened her mouth to tell him so, his tongue slid inside, stealing the strength from her legs, robbing her of coherent thought.

Another minute, he thought, and she'd be flat on her back. He drew away. Hands clenched at his sides, he took a deep breath, held it for several seconds, then blew it out.

"We'd best get a move on," he said, his voice gruff. "No telling if they're after us, and I'd just as soon put a few more miles between us before tomorrow."

She didn't argue, merely looked up at him, her deep blue eyes mirroring the yearnings of his own heart before she turned away and began gathering up their meager belongings.

They rode all that night, stopping shortly before dawn to bed down in a clearing ringed by tall trees. Winter Rain was asleep almost as soon as she closed her eyes, but Chance lay awake a long time, his thoughts troubled by his growing need for the woman who slept beside him.

He wanted her, he thought, wanted her more than his next breath, but he had ten thousand good reasons to let her go.

# Chapter 11

The next morning dawned bright and clear. Breakfast was a quick meal of jerky and pemmican washed down by a drink of tepid water. Chance rinsed his mouth, thinking he'd give a dollar for a good cup of coffee.

Grabbing his saddle blanket, he smoothed it over Smoke's back, cinched the saddle in place, slid the rifle into the boot, and then removed the hobbles from the mare and from Winter Rain's gelding.

He kept his distance from Winter Rain. After the explosive kiss they had shared the day before, it seemed like the smart thing to do. From time to time, he caught her watching him surreptitiously, her expression wary and a little puzzled.

"Are you ready to go?" he asked.

She nodded.

Chance was wondering if he dared help her mount her horse when she took the reins from his hand and swung agilely onto the animal's back.

It was just as well. The thought of putting his hands on her was far too tempting. He wasn't a saint and he wasn't made out of stone, and as much as he needed that ten grand, he wasn't sure how many times he could touch her, kiss her, and still back off.

Smoke snorted and tossed her head as he climbed into the saddle. Feeling frisky, the mare humped her

back and crow-hopped before he pulled her down to
a walk.

Chance glanced over his shoulder to make sure
Winter Rain was behind him. And wished he hadn't.
She rode as confidently as any Lakota warrior, he
thought, but there was nothing remotely masculine
about her. Her hair shone blue-black in the early-
morning sun; her tunic rode up, revealing a good deal
of tanned skin. She had long shapely legs, legs he
could easily imagine wrapped around him.

Smoke bucked again and Chance gave the mare her
head, hoping a good run would help to shake the
image of Winter Rain from his mind.

He let the mare run until she slowed of her own
accord. Winter Rain drew up beside him a few moments later. She looked radiant. Her cheeks were
flushed, her eyes sparkled, her hair fell around her
shoulders in wild disarray that somehow made her
look more desirable than ever.

Damn, he had it bad!

In an effort to ignore the woman riding beside him,
he concentrated on the wild beauty of the land, the
verdant hills, the pair of red-tail hawks that wheeled
and soared effortlessly overhead, the way the grass
undulated like a vast green sea beneath the endless
blue vault of the sky. The land. It was in his blood,
as much a part of him as the color of his skin.

At midday he drew rein alongside a shallow stream.
Stepping from the saddle, he loosened the cinch and
let Smoke drink. From the corner of his eye, he
watched Winter Rein dismount and lead her horse
down to the stream. When her horse finished drinking,
Winter Rain knelt down and cupped her hands in the
water. Never had he seen anything more beautiful.
The sunlight glistened like golden dewdrops in her
hair and caressed her skin. Drops of water trickled

through her fingers, shining in the sun like liquid diamonds.

His gaze followed her as she rose lithely to her feet and moved behind some bushes for a few minutes' privacy.

Squatting on his heels, he stared across the stream. Damn, how had she gotten under his skin so fast? He was a man grown, not some kid looking to get laid for the first time, yet every time he looked at her, he felt like some randy youth.

The thought made him grin. Maybe that wasn't so bad after all.

He was tightening the cinch on his saddle when Winter Rain called his name, her voice high with excitement.

Following the sound of her voice, he found her kneeling beside a wild-eyed filly that was caught in a thicket. In her struggles to free herself, the filly had gotten badly tangled in the brush. Thorns had raked her hide, leaving dark brown splotches of blood on her golden coat. His gaze swept the ground, noting the prints of several wolves. But for the thorn bushes, she would have been easy prey.

Winter Rain looked up as he approached. "We must help her."

Chance grunted softly. The filly was lying on her side, too weak to do more than stare up at them. "There's a coil of rope in my saddlebag," he said. "Get it."

While Winter Rain went to retrieve the rope, Chance knelt at the filly's head. "Easy, girl," he murmured softly. "I'm not gonna hurt you. What the hell are you doing out here alone anyway? Easy now."

Still talking softly, he placed his hand on her neck. She jerked away, spooked by his touch.

"Hey, now, when we get to be friends, you'll be

sorry you did that. Where's your mama?'' he mused,
though he was pretty sure he knew the answer. The
mare would have wanted to stay with her foal, but the
stallion would have chased her back to the herd. Either that, or the filly was an orphan.

"Here." Winter Rain thrust the rope at him. "Will
she be all right?"

"Yeah, she's not badly hurt. Just scared." His gaze
ran over the filly. She looked to be about three
months old. "I don't think she's been without food or
water for more than a day or two at most. She's lucky
to be alive."

Talking softly to the filly, he fashioned a loop and
dropped it over her head, then carefully untangled her
legs from the thorny branches, incurring a good number of scratches on his arms and legs as he did so.

At last she was free. Scrambling to her feet, she
tried to run off, only to be brought up short by the
loop around her neck.

"Easy now," Chance said. Walking toward her, he
took up the slack.

The filly shook her head as he drew closer, stood
trembling all over as he gently stroked her neck.
"There now, darlin'. That doesn't hurt, does it?"

Winter Rain watched Wolf Shadow. His voice was
soft and low when he spoke to the filly, his touch light.
What would it be like to have him speak to her like
that, to feel his hand on her skin? The memory of his
kisses jumped to the forefront of her mind; her lips
tingled in remembrance.

He spoke to the filly for a long while, letting her
grow used to his voice and his touch. Now and then,
he breathed into her nostrils. When she stopped
trembling, he took a step forward, giving a gentle tug
on the rope. The filly immediately backed up and
shook her head, fighting the rope as it tightened
around her neck. Wolf Shadow eased up on the line.

He talked to the filly again, soothing her with his voice and his touch, and again gave a gentle tug on the rope. It took several tries, but eventually the filly learned to follow his lead and the three of them walked back to where they had left the horses.

"We'll have to take her with us," he said. "She's too young to be on her own."

Winter Rain looked up at him, her pleasure at his decision reflected in her smile and in her eyes.

"Come on, darlin'," Wolf Shadow said, speaking to the filly. "I'll bet you're thirsty."

Leading the filly down to the stream, he let her drink, but only a little. He walked her around for a short time, let her graze for a few minutes, then led her back to the stream and let her drink again.

Winter Rain's gaze never left him. She noted the effortless way Wolf Shadow moved, the gentleness of his touch. He was patient with the filly, never rushing her, never speaking harshly. He would be a good father, she thought, and wondered where that idea had come from.

But it wasn't only his voice and his manner she noticed. Just looking at him pleased something feminine deep within her. His shoulders were broad, his arms were long, his hands large and strong. The sun glinted in his hair. She watched the play of muscles in his back and shoulders as he moved. The scars on his back looked silver in the sunlight and she wondered again who had whipped him so cruelly and why. Perhaps someday she would ask him.

A short time later, they were riding again. The filly followed docilely behind Wolf Shadow's horse. Knowing the filly was still weak from her ordeal, he kept his mount at a walk so as not to tire her.

That, too, pleased Winter Rain immensely.

She rode a little behind him, careful not to let him see how she watched his every move. The way he held his horse's reins. The way he rode in the saddle, relaxed yet vigilant. The way he looked back every so often to make sure that she and the filly were all right.

Whatever else he might be, he was not only a brave warrior but a gentle man as well.

They rode until the filly was too tired to go on and then made camp in a tree-sheltered valley watered by a narrow stream that was so shallow Winter Rain was certain she could walk across it without getting her ankles wet.

It didn't take long to make camp. While Winter Rain gathered wood and dug a hole for the fire pit, Chance unsaddled and hobbled his horse, then hobbled Winter Rain's gelding. When that was done, he took the filly down to the stream and washed the blood from her coat, then spent a few minutes scratching her neck before turning her loose.

"Should we not keep her tied?" Winter Rain asked, coming up beside him.

Chance shook his head. "I don't think she'll go far, not with the other horses here."

Winter Rain smiled as the filly sidled up beside Wolf Shadow's mare and began chewing on her tail. Smoke's ears went back and she stamped her foot, warning the filly away.

Winter Rain laughed softly as the filly reared and spun around. She ran away, then trotted back to Smoke's side and began to graze.

"Horses need the company of other horses," Chance remarked. "She'll be as tame as a puppy pretty soon."

Winter Rain nodded. She was certain Wolf Shadow could tame any female, human or otherwise.

At dusk, Winter Rain lit the fire and they ate another meal of jerky and pemmican.

"I'm getting almighty tired of jerky," Chance said. "Tomorrow I'll see if I can get us some fresh meat."

"That would be good," Winter Rain agreed. She glanced over her shoulder, back the way they had come. "Do you think the Crow will follow us?"

"I sure as hell hope not," he muttered.

"What did you say?"

"Don't worry. I'm pretty sure the rain washed out our tracks."

"Yes, of course," she said, and he heard the relief in her voice.

Chance sat across the fire from her, aware of the attraction that hummed between them whenever she was near. He had known a lot of women in his time, some casually, a few intimately, but he'd never felt anything like this with any of them. He was aware of her every move, her every breath, the way her eyes sparkled as she watched the filly kick up her heels.

Leaning forward, he added a few pieces of wood to the fire. A faint breeze sent a flurry of embers shooting upward through the air like fireflies. He watched Winter Rain's gaze follow the sparks upward and then her gaze met his. Heat flared between them, hotter than the fire's flames.

Chance cleared his throat. "We'd better turn in," he said, his voice gruff. "I want to get an early start in the morning."

Winter Rain nodded, but she didn't move. And neither did he.

"We'll be home sometime tomorrow."

She nodded again, her eyes slowly widening as he gained his feet and moved around the fire toward her.

With every step, he told himself to turn around and go back but to no avail. She was too tempting and too damn close to ignore.

She stared up at him like a doe trapped by a cougar. He could see the pulse throbbing wildly in her throat. Her lips parted and the tip of her tongue moistened her lower lip. Just that simple act, nothing more, yet he was hard and aching.

He felt as though he were drowning in the deep blue depths of her eyes as he leaned toward her, his hands closing around her waist. Lifting her to her feet, he drew her up against him and held her tight.

"Rain . . ."

She looked up at him, speechless. Nervous, but not afraid.

He muttered an oath, then slanted his mouth over hers and kissed her. One of them was trembling, and he was pretty sure it wasn't her.

She surrendered to his touch with a sigh that aroused him still more. Her lips were warm and soft and sweetly yielding, parting willingly to allow him to explore the depths within.

It was a kiss that seemed to last forever and yet ended too soon.

His breathing was ragged when they drew apart. For a moment they stared at each other, and then he kissed her again, longer, deeper.

"Rain." He didn't seem to be able to say anything but her name. And then he was kissing her again.

Hardly aware of what he was doing, he drew her down on the ground until they were lying side by side, his hands molding her body to his while he scattered kisses on her cheeks, her lips, the tip of her nose. She moaned softly, a purely feminine sound that fanned the embers of his desire still more.

His hands slid up and down her back, cupped her buttocks to draw her more fully against his arousal. She clung to him, her hands as restless as his, if not as bold.

He closed his eyes, the better to lose himself in the

taste and the touch of her, only to open them again when she burst out laughing.

He was about to ask her what was so funny and then he saw the filly nibbling at a lock of Winter Rain's hair.

"Go on," Chance said, making a shooing motion with one hand. "Get out of here."

The filly backed off, only to sidle up to Winter Rain and begin nibbling on her hair again.

Winter Rain's laughter filled the air again as the filly's tongue tickled her neck.

Muttering an oath, Chance gained his feet, but he couldn't help laughing at the sight of Winter Rain trying to keep her hair out of the filly's mouth.

Winter Rain sat up. "Why is she doing that?"

"It's just something young horses do. You see a lot of dams with their tails chewed off. Some ranchers tie up their mares' tails until the foals are taken from their mothers."

Moving over to the fire, he added a few pieces of wood, then walked away from the camp. He didn't know about Winter Rain, but he needed a few minutes alone.

Dragging his hand across his jaw, he decided it was just as well that things had come to a halt when they had. Bedding Winter Rain would have been a big mistake, one he could ill afford, financially or emotionally. He needed that ten grand, not a shotgun wedding. But as he left the light of the fire behind, he was surprised to find that Edward Bryant's ten thousand dollars didn't seem as important as it once had.

Winter Rain watched Wolf Shadow leave the fire. Was he angry with her? As much as she had wanted his kisses, yearned for his touch, she couldn't help feeling the filly's intrusion had come at just the right time. She had been taught that chastity was a virtue and that she should stay a maiden until she married. She had never had trouble remembering that until she met Wolf Shadow. He had not spoken of loving her, only of wanting her.

Rising, she spread her bedroll beside the fire and slipped under the blankets, wondering if he would crawl in beside her to share the warmth.

She was still on edge, wondering about it, when she fell asleep.

# *Chapter 12*

The next day, the tension between them was palpable. Shivers of awareness rippled through Winter Rain whenever Wolf Shadow passed close by. They ate the morning meal in silence. She rolled her blankets into a tight cylinder while he readied the horses. A short time later, they were riding.

Winter Rain smiled at the antics of the filly. She ran ahead a short distance, then trotted back to nuzzle the other horses. She did this several times, pausing now and then to sniff at a bush or a rock. Sometimes she dashed ahead, rearing and bucking exuberantly.

Winter Rain slid a glance at Wolf Shadow to see if he was enjoying the filly's antics, but he seemed lost in thought.

"We should be there late this afternoon," Wolf Shadow remarked a short time later.

Winter Rain nodded, the thought of returning to their village filling her with anticipation and dread. What would they find there? Had anyone else survived the Crow attack?

Gradually the surrounding countryside grew familiar. They crossed a shallow stream and climbed up the opposite bank. The village lay ahead, just over the next small rise.

Unable to wait any longer, Winter Rain urged her horse into a lope and up the hill. She reined her horse to a halt at the top and stared down at the valley

below. The village was gone and in its place stood
the remains of scorched lodges. The grass had been
blackened by fire. There was no sign of life.

Heavyhearted, she urged her horse down the hill,
afraid of what she might find.

Chance followed Winter Rain, his gaze sweeping
the ruins of the village. The signs of battle were everywhere, from the churned-up ground to the charred
remains of the lodges. Bits of cloth, broken toys, ruined weapons, and scorched blankets littered the
ground.

Dismounting, he ground-reined Smoke, then walked
through the camp, now deserted. There were no bodies in evidence nor any sign that predators had
dragged any away, making him believe that at least a
few of the Lakota had survived the fight and come
back to bury their dead.

He walked toward Winter Rain, who was standing
in front of the burned-out remains of her mother's
lodge. She looked up as he approached, her eyes filled
with tears.

"They are dead, aren't they?" she asked, her voice
thick with grief.

"I don't know." Taking the reins from her hand, he
tied her horse to a clump of brush. Then he began to
walk around the outer circle of the camp, but the
ground was too badly chewed up for him to pick out
any tracks save those of the Crow war party heading
home.

His brow furrowed in thought, he made his way
back to Winter Rain, who was standing where he had
left her, looking as if her whole world had fallen apart.
Which, he supposed, it had. Still, she was luckier than
most. If it turned out that Mountain Sage and Eagle
Lance were dead, she still had people who loved her
and were waiting to take her in.

He clenched his hands at his sides to keep from

taking her in his arms. "If my cousin is still alive, he would have taken the people south to our winter camp. We'll go there."

Winter Rain nodded.

"No sense giving up hope until we know for sure."

She looked up at him, mute. If he had the sense God gave a goat, he'd take her to the Bryants now. But he couldn't go, not until he knew what had happened to Kills-Like-a-Hawk and his family.

"Rain, it'll be all right."

She took a step toward him and all his good intentions evaporated. She needed comforting and there was no one else to offer it. He held out his arms and she stepped into them. Her tears were warm where they fell on his chest.

He held her for several moments, forcing himself to remember she had come to him for solace and nothing more. But he couldn't keep his body from reacting to her nearness, and he turned sideways to keep her from noticing how her proximity affected him.

"Don't cry, sweetheart. You still have people who love you."

She jerked her head up, her gaze boring into his. "How can you speak to me of *them* when my parents may be dead?"

"Dammit, Rain, the Bryants *are* your parents."

"No!" She wrenched herself out of his arms. Head tilted to one side, she regarded him for a long moment. "What difference does it make to you whether I go back to them or not?"

Chance cleared his throat, somehow reluctant to tell her the truth. "I met your father. I told him I would try to find you. You're their only child. They miss you. They're worried about you."

"Go back to them. Tell them I am well. Tell them I am happy here."

"We need to go," he said, abruptly changing the

subject. He made a gesture that encompassed the village. "See if you can find anything we can use. I'm going hunting."

She glanced at the ruined lodges. He could tell she wasn't keen on the idea, but she didn't argue. Squaring her shoulders, she began to rummage through what was left of the lodge across from her mother's.

Taking up the reins of his horse, Chance swung into the saddle and rode toward the river. With any luck, he might be able to find a deer, or at least a rabbit.

It seemed unusually quiet as he approached the river. He glanced at the place where he had killed the first Crow warrior. There was no body, of course. The Crow would have carried their dead home.

With a shake of his head, Chance urged his horse upriver. He hadn't gone far when he spied a buck turning away from the water's edge. Lifting his rifle, Chance lined up his shot and curled his finger around the trigger. Steadying Smoke with his knees, he took a deep breath, let out half of it, and squeezed the trigger. The buck sprang forward, then dropped to the ground.

Dismounting, Chance gutted the deer, then draped the carcass over Smoke's withers. Swinging into the saddle, he rode back to where he had left Winter Rain.

He found her a good distance from the carnage, sorting through a small pile of goods she had retrieved. There wasn't much. Among other things, she'd found a waterskin, a trade blanket singed along one edge, a small cooking pot, a skinning knife, as well as a bowl and a spoon made of buffalo horn.

She looked up at his approach. "They left very little," she remarked, gesturing at what she had found.

Chance shrugged. "It's more than we had."

Dismounting, he lifted the buck from the back of

his horse and dropped it on the ground. "At least we'll have fresh meat for dinner."

He led the horses to a patch of grass. After stripping the rigging from Smoke, he hobbled his horse and Winter Rain's so they could graze. The filly nuzzled his arm and he spent a few minutes scratching her ears before going back to kneel beside Winter Rain. Butchering and skinning were women's work, but that didn't seem to matter just now.

They worked side by side, skinning the deer, cutting the meat into quarters and then into strips for drying. Winter Rain built a fire and spitted a couple of thick steaks.

Chance's mouth watered as the scent of roasting venison filled the air. When they finished skinning the deer, he found some branches and put together a drying rack. As tired as he was of jerked meat, there was no way to keep the rest of the venison fresh while they traveled.

They took a break to eat when the steaks were done. Chance stared into the distance. Unless he missed his guess, Kills-Like-a-Hawk would head for the Black Hills to hole up while the people nursed their wounds. There was food and shelter in the Hills. Game was plentiful. The people could hunt enough game to see them through the winter.

Chance shook his head. Damn, this couldn't have happened at a worse time. He needed to haul Winter Rain back to the Bryants, collect the rest of his reward, and hightail it to the bank. That was what he should do, he thought glumly, but he couldn't just ride off without knowing Kills-Like-a-Hawk's fate. Couldn't take Winter Rain kicking and screaming back to her parents. He didn't stop to wonder why. He had taken other women back home against their will.

He grunted softly. He had yet to find a kidnapped

white woman who wanted to go back to the white world after living with the Indians. He didn't know if it was because they were ashamed, or because they genuinely liked living with the Indians, but after a year or two of captivity, none of them were happy to be rescued. He had wondered, from time to time, how long it took them to readjust to civilization. He had rescued one woman who had been abducted from her home in New Mexico. She had borne a son to an Apache warrior. The boy was three when Chance found her. She had put up a hell of a fight when he took her back to her husband. She had run back to her Apache warrior three times before her husband stopped trying to get her back.

He couldn't fault the women for wanting to stay with the Indians. In spite of the hard work and grueling winters, it was a good way to live. Sometimes he wondered why he fought so hard to hang on to the ranch. It would be easier to let the bank have it and take up tipi living again. But some stubborn streak refused to let him just give up. The ranch had belonged to his old man. It had been the old man's dream and by damn, he intended to hang on to it.

He looked up to find Winter Rain watching him. "Think you could make me a shirt out of that hide?"

She nodded. "If you wish."

"Thanks."

They spent the next couple of days waiting for the meat to dry. Chance killed a couple of rabbits. Winter Rain gathered some wild vegetables and they had rabbit stew for dinner, along with some wild berries he had found. Winter Rain began the process of tanning the hide.

They spoke little. Chance had the feeling she was waiting for him to throw her on her horse and take her back to the Bryants. He had to admit the thought crossed his mind at least once a day. But his mind was more often occupied with thoughts of Winter Rain herself. Every time he looked at her, he was reminded of the way she felt in his arms, the sweet taste of her lips, the way her body felt against his.

He dreamed of her at night, erotic dreams that had him waking in the middle of the night, hard and aching.

Tonight was no different. Sitting up, he glanced over at the woman who occupied so much of his thoughts whether he was awake or asleep. She was sleeping soundly, her lips slightly parted, one hand tucked beneath her cheek. She looked young and vulnerable and so damned desirable it was all he could do to keep from crawling under the blanket beside her and taking her in his arms.

The worst of it was, he didn't think she would put up much of a fight.

Muttering an oath, he followed the moonlit trail down to the river. He dropped down on his belly and buried his face in the cold water, then took a long drink. It cooled his thirst but did little to cool his ardor.

Tomorrow, he thought. They would leave for the Black Hills tomorrow morning. The sooner they found out if Mountain Sage and Eagle Lance were alive, the sooner he could return Winter Rain to the Bryants and get on with his own life.

Sitting there, staring at the moonlight shimmering on the face of the water, he wondered why the thought of getting back home had suddenly lost its appeal.

# Chapter 13

Winter Rain felt a tremor of excitement when she saw the Paha Sapa rising in the distance. They had ridden hard for the last three days. In the evenings, she had worked on the shirt for Wolf Shadow. She had finished it last night. He wore it now. It gave her pleasure to know he was wearing something she had made with her own hands.

Winter Rain drank in the sight of the Black Hills. At last they had almost reached their destination. It was a place she had loved for as long as she could remember. Rising high about the plains, the Black Hills were the heart and soul of the Lakota people. Pines grew so thick on the hillsides that the sacred mountains looked black from a distance. She loved the deep green of the pines, the rust-red shale, the varied colors of clay and sandstone cliffs, loved to hear the songs of the pretty mountain bluebirds and the Western tanagers.

Mato Paha, Bear Butte, was located here, as was Mateo Teepee, the Devil's Tower, which rose thousands of feet above the surrounding prairie. It was here that Strong Elk had received his vision. A lump rose in her throat as she thought of him. Had he been killed by the Crow? And what of Dawn Song and Two Beavers and Pony Boy? What of all the other young men and women she had grown up with, worked and laughed with? Were they all dead?

The excitement she had experienced only moments ago quickly turned to dismay. What if they were all gone?

Unable to wait any longer, she urged her horse into a lope. She had to know if all those she loved were gone, though she didn't know what she would do if her worst fears proved true. She couldn't imagine her life without Mountain Sage and Eagle Lance, couldn't imagine living anywhere but here, in the Land of the Spotted Eagle.

Wolf Shadow called out to her to wait, but Winter Rain rode on, driven by her need to know. The filly tagged along behind, darting first one way and then the other.

Chance cursed softly as she raced away. Didn't she realize they had to proceed with caution? The Lakota were not the only people who sought shelter in the Black Hills. Too often of late, the Army had made its presence known. Miners were crossing the plains in search of gold and silver, settlers were looking for homesteads, missionaries were looking for converts, con men and easy women were chasing elusive dreams of easy money and easy living. He had met them all, saint and sinner alike.

He caught up with her as she reached the base of the Hills. Leaning out of the saddle, he grabbed hold of her horse's bridle and eased the horse to a stop.

"Let me go!"

"Just slow down, dammit. You can't go riding hell for leather like that. You don't know what you'll run into."

She glared at him, her anger slowly dissipating as she realized the truth of his words.

When he was sure she wouldn't take off like a jackrabbit with a fire under its tail, he urged his horse forward.

As always, he was immediately caught up in the grandeur and beauty of the Hills.

Like all Lakota, he had always had a reverence for the land, especially this land. To the Lakota, the Hills were the heart of everything that is.

The terrain within the Hills was wild and rugged, a land of lush grass and deep verdant valleys, gentle foothills and jagged rock formations, sandstone canyons and gulches, deep blue lakes and winding streams. There were scattered stands of aspen, birch, and oak. White-tailed deer, elk, and mule deer made their home in the Hills, as did mountain lions and bears. Coyotes could be heard yipping late at night. Goshawks and ospreys nested in the forest; bald eagles were often seen in the winter.

April was the Moon of the Birth of Calves. It was during the spring months that men and women tapped the box elders for the sweet sap within. Warriors began to break the young horses. Stallions not fit for breeding were castrated. It was also foaling season. The Lakota paid little attention to the mares, letting nature take its course. Women repaired their tipis or made new ones from the hides collected the winter before. Leggings and moccasins were made from the smoked tops of the old lodges. Young men went out to seek their visions.

In May, the Moon of Ripening Strawberries, the tribe moved from its winter quarters to higher ground, sometimes out of necessity, sometimes simply for the joy of moving to a new place.

Chance had always loved the summer. It was perhaps the busiest time of year. Families conducted hunts. Warriors went on raiding parties. Women were busy gathering early fruits and vegetables. Robes were painted while the weather was warm. Tribal hunts were organized whenever a herd of buffalo was found, but only a few animals were killed, as this was the time of year when the buffalo grew fat.

Summer was also the time for ceremonial affairs, a time of vision seeking and female virtue feasts. The Sun Dance, that most sacred ceremony, was held during the Cherry Ripening Moon. One of Chance's biggest regrets was that he had never participated in the Sun Dance, never sought a vision to guide him. At a time of life when he should have been pursuing a vision quest, he had been pursuing his mother's murderers.

In the autumn, women gathered nuts and vegetables and dried meat in preparation for the coming winter. Men went hunting more often to make sure there would be meat in their lodges. Sometimes the warriors burned the prairie grass to force the buffalo to come closer to the hunting camps.

Sometimes the young men planned war parties during hunting season. If the camp had to be moved before the hunters returned, a signpost, usually fashioned from the shoulder blade of a buffalo, was set up for them and pointed in the direction the tribe was moving. Hoofprints and a travois were drawn on the blade, along with the name of the chief. This not only told the hunters where the tribe had gone, but let other bands know as well.

At the first sign of winter, the People headed for the wooded hills and hollows of the Paha Sapa where there was an abundance of firewood. It was not winter now, but Chance was certain that if any of the People had survived the Crow attack they would come here to lick their wounds.

As they climbed upward, Chance took the lead. Kills-Like-a-Hawk's favorite campsite was located in a timbered hollow alongside a narrow winding river. As always, he had a sense of homecoming as he rode deeper into the heart of the Hills. This was where he had been born. This was where he had come to mourn when his grandfather passed away. This was where he had hoped to seek a vision.

He gazed up at the top of the Hills. Was he too old? Was it too late to follow that path, to seek out a vision to guide him? Had he been away from the People too long, spent too much time living in the white man's world?

He was still lost in thought when they reached Cottonwood Hollow. At first Chance didn't see any sign to indicate the hollow was occupied, and he feared that no one had survived or that, if they had, they had gone somewhere else, but then a trio of horses emerged from behind a stand of timber. Chance breathed a sigh of relief when he recognized Kills-Like-a-Hawk's rangy gray stallion.

He urged Smoke onward. Rounding a bend in the river, he saw thirteen brush huts that had been erected in the shelter of the pines. A large dog barked, its hackles rising, as they drew nearer.

Three warriors emerged from three of the huts, weapons in hand. They stared at Chance a moment, then lowered their weapons. Two of the men went back inside. The third stood, waiting while Chance dismounted.

*"Hou, cola,"* Chance said, grasping Crooked Lance's forearm.

Crooked Lance grasped Chance's arm in return. "We thought you had been killed."

"Not quite." Chance glanced at the huts. "What of my cousin?"

"He is alive, but badly hurt," Crooked Lance replied gravely. "His woman and son are dead, and so is his will to live."

Chance swore softly as he looked over his shoulder

to where Winter Rain waited. "What of Mountain Sage and Eagle Lance?"

"Mountain Sage lives."

At this news, Winter Rain slipped off her horse. "Where is my mother?"

Crooked Lance pointed at the hut nearest them. "She is there. My woman is with her."

*"Pilamaya,"* Winter Rain said, and hurried into the hut.

"How many survived?" Chance asked, staring after Winter Rain.

"I am not sure. Our number grows a few each day. After the battle, those who were not wounded went back and buried the dead."

Chance nodded. He had figured as much.

He noticed several women peering out of the huts. Recognizing Chance as one of them, they emerged from their dwellings and resumed the tasks his arrival had interrupted.

"Do you have sentries posted?"

*"Ai.* You passed one of them on your way in. There is another across the river. And one at the far end of the valley."

"How are you making out here?"

"The Crow took most of our horses and our stores for the winter. Our warriors take turns hunting while the women look after the injured. I fear Winter Rain's mother will not live much longer."

"And my cousin?"

Crooked Lance shrugged. "Perhaps knowing you survived will give him a reason to live."

"Where is Kills-Like-a-Hawk?"

"There." Crooked Lance pointed to the last hut. "I will look after your horses."

*"Pilamaya,"* Chance said, handing Smoke's reins to the warrior.

Kills-Like-a-Hawk would live, Chance thought as he walked toward his cousin's hut. Kills-Like-a-Hawk was the only family he had left, dammit. He wasn't going to lose him, too.

# Chapter 14

The hut was dimly lit by a small fire that burned in a shallow pit in the back. Chance paused in the entrance, letting his eyes adjust to the interior. He could make out the dark shape of his cousin lying on a deer hide near the fire. His cousin's breathing sounded labored.

There wasn't much in the lodge other than Kills-Like-a-Hawk's weapons, a waterskin, and Kills-Like-a-Hawk himself. The hut smelled of smoke, sweat, and sweet grass.

Chance crossed the short distance from the entrance to his cousin and hunkered down on his heels. He took a deep breath when he saw the numerous small cuts on his cousin's arms. He recognized them instantly for what they were: self-inflicted wounds of mourning.

"Kills-Like-a-Hawk?" he called softly. "Are you awake?"

His cousin stirred. In the faint light of the fire, Chance saw Kills-Like-a-Hawk's eyes open. "*Hau,* Tahunsa," he murmured. Hello, Cousin.

"How are you feeling?" Chance asked.

Kills-Like-a-Hawk grunted. "I think I will soon join my woman and my son."

"Like hell! Where are you hurt?"

Kills-Like-a-Hawk pulled a corner of the blanket back. A crude bandage was wrapped around his leg.

Moving carefully, Chance removed the bandage, revealing an ugly scabbed-over gash that ran from his cousin's knee to midthigh. The skin around the wound was discolored and swollen.

"It's infected," Chance remarked. Rising, he tossed a few sticks on the fire. "It needs to be lanced and drained."

"Leave it."

Chance stared at his cousin. "If that infection gets any worse, you'll lose that leg. Is that what you want?"

Kills-Like-a-Hawk shrugged. "I am ready to follow Wanagi Tacaka to Wanagi Yatu."

Chance withdrew his knife from the sheath at his side and held the blade over the flames. "Well, you may be ready to follow the Spirit Path to the Place of Souls," he muttered, turning the blade over, "but I'm not ready to let you go. Here," he said, picking up a stout stick, "bite down on this."

Kills-Like-a-Hawk stared at him a moment, his expression mutinous, making Chance wonder if he'd have to get a couple of the warriors in here to hold his cousin down, but in the end Kills-Like-a-Hawk clamped his teeth over the stick and closed his eyes.

Taking a deep breath, Chance slid the tip of the blade into the mass of swollen flesh. A horrible smell filled the hut as dark greenish yellow pus and blood so dark a red as to be almost black spurted from the wound.

Chance swore softly as he grabbed a bit of cloth and wiped the pus from his cousin's leg. Kills-Like-a-Hawk groaned softly as Chance pressed gently on the wound, forcing out more pus and dark red blood.

After several minutes, only bright red blood oozed from the wound.

Chance sat back, wiping the perspiration from his brow.

Kills-Like-a-Hawk opened his eyes and spat the

stick from between his teeth. "I am happy to see you, Tahunsa."

"I am happy to see you, too," Chance replied with a grin. Reaching for another bit of cloth, he dampened it with water from the waterskin and began to wash the blood and pus from his cousin's leg.

Kills-Like-a-Hawk winced as Chance began to rebandage his wound.

Chance sat back on his heels when he was done. "I am sorry about your loss, Tahunsa."

Kills-Like-a-Hawk looked away, his head bowed. "It is always hardest on those who are left behind."

Chance nodded. Slipping his arm under his cousin's shoulders, he lifted him up a little, then offered him a drink from the waterskin. Kills-Like-a-Hawk took a few swallows, then turned his head away, and Chance lowered him down on the hide once more.

"Get some rest now," Chance said, putting the waterskin aside. "I have some meat packed on my horse."

"I am not hungry."

"Maybe not," Chance replied with a wry grin, "but you are going to eat."

Silent tears trickled down Winter Rain's cheeks as she knelt at her mother's side. Mountain Sage was barely breathing. Her skin was cool, almost cold, to the touch.

Winter Rain looked up at Corn Woman. "How long has she been like this?"

"Since last night." Corn Woman shook her head sadly. "I am afraid she is dying," she said quietly.

"*Hiya! Ina? Ina,* can you hear me?" Winter Rain squeezed her mother's hand. "*Ina,* it is Winter Rain."

Her mother's eyelids fluttered open. "*Cunski?*"

"Yes, I am here."

Mountain Sage blinked several times, then lifted a

trembling hand to brush the tears from Winter Rain's cheek. *"Ceye sni yo,"* she murmured. Do not cry.

Winter Rain forced herself to smile. *"Ina . . ."*

*"Kokepe sni yo,"* Mountain Sage whispered. Do not be afraid.

*"Ina,"* she wailed softly. "Please, do not leave me!"

But her mother was looking past her, a faint smile curving her lips. The lines of pain seemed to fade from around her eyes and mouth. She held out her hand, as if reaching for someone. "Wapaha Wanbli," she murmured. She nodded, as if in reply to a question, then said, very clearly, *"Han, winyeya mankelo."* Yes, I am ready to go. She sighed and the light faded from her eyes. A moment later, her body went limp.

*"Ina!"* Winter Rain grabbed her mother's hand and held it to her breast. *"Ina,* do not leave me!"

But it was too late. She stared at her mother's body, her breath catching in her throat as she saw her mother's spirit float upward and disappear in a sliver of sunlight.

"I love you," she whispered, and ever so faintly she heard her mother's voice repeat the words.

Still holding her mother's hand, she bowed her head and let the tears flow.

Chance stood outside the hut where Winter Rain's mother was being cared for. He could hear Winter Rain crying, knew from the depths of grief evident in her sobs that her mother was dead. It was a sound that tore at his heart. He knew all too well what she was feeling.

He heard Corn Woman trying to comfort Winter Rain and suddenly he needed to be the one holding her. Ignoring tribal custom, he ducked inside without announcing his presence.

Corn Woman glanced over her shoulder. She frowned at him in silent reproach, then turned back to Winter Rain, who was rocking back and forth beside her mother's body.

Chance crossed the distance between them in two long strides. "Rain."

She looked up at him through red-rimmed eyes. Reaching down, he lifted her to her feet; then, holding her hand in his, he led her out of the hut and away from the camp.

Winter Rain followed Wolf Shadow blindly, her heart numb. Mountain Sage was dead and all the security in Winter Rain's world had died with her. She was hardly aware that Wolf Shadow had stopped walking until he drew her into his arms.

"I'm sorry, Rain," he said quietly. "I know how you loved her."

She nodded. "She was so good to me. She was always so gentle, so loving, no matter what I did, no matter how much I . . ." She stared up at him, her eyes wide. "No matter how many times I told her I hated her when I first came here. . . . It's true, isn't it? She wasn't my real mother."

It hurt to say the words aloud. She had known Mountain Sage wasn't her natural mother. Mountain Sage and Wolf Shadow had both told her that she had not been born Lakota, but she had refused to believe it, refused to accept it as the truth. But now, suddenly, she remembered everything she had blocked from her mind and heart.

"I remember," she whispered. "Eagle Lance and some of the other warriors attacked our coach. Iron Arrow wounded my . . . my *wasichu* father. Iron Arrow pulled me out of the coach and gave me to Eagle Lance, who took me home with him. Mountain Sage had lost a little girl and she was grieving. They adopted me as their own. They were so good to me, and now . . ." A fresh torrent of tears swept down her cheeks. "Now they're gone." She buried her face in Chance's shoulder. Her tears were warm against his chest.

Chance brushed his lips across the crown of her head. He wished he had some sage advice to offer her, some words of comfort that would ease her pain, but he knew only too well that at a time like this words were meaningless. All he could do was hold her while she cried. Time was the best healer of all.

He held her until her tears subsided, then led her over to a large flat rock. Sitting down, he drew her down beside him.

She sniffed, then wiped the last of her tears from her eyes with her fingertips before asking, "How is your cousin?"

"He's hurt pretty bad, but I . . . I think he'll recover."

"I'm glad."

"Rain . . ."

"Oh, Wolf Shadow, I'm going to miss her so!" she exclaimed softly, and dissolved into tears once more.

They buried Mountain Sage early the next morning. Winter Rain painted her mother's face for her journey into the Land of Many Lodges. It was there in the Land of Many Lodges that she would be reunited with Eagle Lance and her lost daughter, a place where there was no sorrow, a verdant land filled with all the good things of the earth.

At any other time, Mountain Sage would have been dressed in her best tunic. Her awl case and her sewing kit would have been placed at her side, and she would have been wrapped in a fine buffalo robe. Her favorite horse would have been killed and its tail placed on a pole. But her best tunic and all her belongings had been destroyed by the Crow. And the Lakota had no horses to spare.

Winter Rain, Corn Woman, Yellow Fawn, and Leaf

carried Mountain Sage's body out of the hut and placed it on the travois Chance had built. Followed by Chance and the others, Winter Rain led the travois pony away from the camp to a hill where Chance had erected a scaffold. They tied ropes around the body and then, as was custom, Winter Rain and Corn Woman climbed up on the scaffold and pulled the body up, while Yellow Fawn and Leaf pushed from below.

Chance stood nearby, watching—listening to the high-pitched keening that rose in the air as the women voiced their grief at the loss of their friend. He watched Winter Rain climb down from the scaffold, listened as she added her voice to the others. There were dark shadows under her eyes, fresh cuts on her forearms where she had expressed her grief.

While he watched, she cut off a lock of her hair and tied it to the burial scaffold, thereby leaving a part of herself behind. That one small act touched his heart as nothing else had.

Gradually the others returned to the camp, until only Chance and Winter Rain remained. Chance frowned thoughtfully as he looked at the blanket-wrapped body. Some believed that somewhere on the journey to the afterlife the spirit of the deceased had to pass by a woman whose name was Hihankara, the Owl Maker. It was Hihankara's job to examine each spirit for the proper tattoo marks that were to be found on the chin or the wrist or the forehead. If these marks that not found, the spirit would not be allowed into the afterworld. Instead, they were pushed off the Hanging Road and returned to earth where their spirits would wander for eternity. If a spirit made it past Hihankara, it was then judged by Tate, the Wind, before being judged by Skan, who ruled the sky.

Moving up beside Winter Rain, he took her hand in his. She looked at him through red-rimmed eyes and then she rested her head against his shoulder. With a sigh, he took her in his arms and held her close.

"You won't leave me, too, will you?" she asked in a small voice.

He hesitated only a moment before he answered, "No, sweetheart. I won't leave you."

# Chapter 15

The next few days passed quietly. Winter Rain continued to mourn for her mother.

Chance knew she also grieved for her friends, especially Dawn Song and Strong Elk, even though she continued to hope they might be alive. And there was always a chance, however slight, that they might have survived, that they might come riding into camp the way Pony Boy had. When Chance questioned him, Pony Boy said he had seen Strong Elk wounded in the battle and then had lost track of him. Chance figured Strong Elk was probably dead, but he kept his thoughts to himself. There was always a chance Strong Elk and Dawn Song and some of the others had survived the battle but were unable to make it to the Hills.

Chance left Rain alone when he thought she wanted solitude and tried to be there when she seemed to need comforting. Corn Woman had taken Winter Rain into her hut so that she had another woman for company; Chance had moved in with Kills-Like-a-Hawk.

Chance spent his days hunting or sitting at Kills-Like-a-Hawk's side, encouraging his cousin to eat, telling him that as shaman he was needed by the People now more than ever.

There were eleven men in the camp, fifteen women, and twenty-two children, all looking to Kills-Like-a-Hawk for guidance now that their chief was dead.

Four days after Chance had arrived in the Hills, he helped Kills-Like-a-Hawk outside for the first time. Kills-Like-a-Hawk looked gaunt and pale, his eyes sunken and filled with grief, but Chance knew his cousin had turned his back on death.

And life went on. One of the women whose husband had been killed by the Crow delivered a healthy baby boy and Kills-Like-a-Hawk decreed that they hold a feast in honor of a new life, a new warrior.

Hunting was good in the Hills. Chance killed a deer and asked Winter Rain to make him a new clout and a pair of leggings from the skin, not only because he needed them but because he thought it might help her to think of something besides her loss.

Pony Boy and Running Hawk killed a buffalo and the camp feasted on fresh tongue, hump, and ribs. Two days later, three Lakota warriors arrived in the camp, along with their wives and children. The next day, another warrior arrived, and Chance began to hope that their losses were not as severe as he had first thought and that more of the People had survived, that they were holed up somewhere waiting for their injuries to heal.

Now it was after midnight. The campfires were out, the people had gone to bed. Unable to sleep, Chance wandered down to the river. Standing at the river's edge, he stared across the slow-moving ribbon of black water. A faint wind stirred the leaves of the pines. The horse herd was a dark shifting shadow where it grazed a short distance away.

The faint rustle of a leaf drew his attention. He glanced over his shoulder to see Kills-Like-a-Hawk slowly making his way toward him. His cousin leaned heavily on a rough-hewn crutch Chance had fashioned for him earlier that day.

"*Hetayetu waste*, Tahunsa," Kills-Like-a-Hawk said. Good evening, Cousin.

*"Hetayetu,"* Chance replied, then gestured at the crutch. "That working all right for you?"

Kills-Like-a-Hawk nodded. *"Pilamaya."*

They stood there in silence for a moment, enjoying the quiet of the evening, before Kills-Like-a-Hawk spoke again.

"Something troubles you," Kills-Like-a-Hawk said. It was not a question, but a statement of fact.

Chance grunted softly.

Kills-Like-a-Hawk hobbled over to a fallen log and eased himself into a sitting position. "Do you wish to talk about it?"

Chance sat down beside his cousin. "Is it too late for me to seek a vision?" He grinned at the look of astonishment that spread over Kills-Like-a-Hawk's face. It wasn't often that he took his cousin by surprise.

"It is never too late, if it is what one truly desires. I will arrange it, if that is your wish."

"It is."

Kills-Like-a-Hawk nodded. "That is not all that troubles you."

"No," Chance admitted, "it's not."

"It is Winter Rain who keeps you from your bed."

Now it was Chance's turn to look astonished.

Kills-Like-a-Hawk laughed softly. "One does not have to be a shaman to see the way you look at her, or the way she looks at you. The air between you is hot with need. So, what is it about her that troubles you?"

"Many things," Chance said. "You know that her *wasichu* parents sent me here to find her and bring her home."

Kills-Like-a-Hawk nodded. "You remember what I told you before?"

"Yeah. You said I couldn't take her unless she wanted to go."

"That has not changed. She is one of us. If you take her against her will, you will be as our enemy."

"I understand."

"Has she refused to go with you?"

"I have not asked her since we came here."

Kills-Like-a-Hawk used his crutch to gain his feet. "Give her time," he advised.

"Time," Chance repeated as he watched his cousin make his way up the path to the camp. It was the one thing he couldn't spare. He stood up and began to pace as an idea popped into his mind. The more he thought about it, the better it sounded.

Whistling softly, he hurried after Kills-Like-a-Hawk.

"Leaving?" Winter Rain stared up at Wolf Shadow. "Where are you going?"

"I have some business to take care of." He tightened the cinch, picked up the reins.

Her thoughts in turmoil, Winter Rain glanced around the camp. How could Corn Woman and the other women be going about their duties as if this were just another day? Kills-Like-a-Hawk was sitting in the shade, smoking his pipe as if nothing had changed.

She looked back at Wolf Shadow. "Are you—" She bit down on her lower lip, stifling the sudden urge to cry. "Are you coming back?"

A faint smile tugged at the corners of Wolf Shadow's lips as he swung into the saddle. "I've got ten thousand good reasons to come back," he said, his smile widening.

She stared after him as he rode out of sight, unable to believe he had left. Only a few days earlier, he had promised not to leave her, and now he was gone. She had known him only a short time. In spite of the kisses they had shared, she wasn't sure how she felt about him.

Business, he had said. What kind of business? It suddenly occurred to her that she knew very little about Wolf Shadow. All she really knew was that he had come here to take her back to her *wasichu* parents.

Questions floated through her mind. Where did he live when he wasn't living with the People? Did he have a wife waiting for him at home? Children? How had he met her *wasichu* parents?

Turning away from the activity in the camp, she walked down to the river, surprised at how empty she felt inside now that Wolf Shadow was gone. How had he become so important to her so fast? From the first day she had seen him, he had never been far from her thoughts. His kisses had made her feel things she had never felt before, made her want things she didn't fully understand. He had rescued her from the Crow, comforted her when her mother died. . . . Sadness tugged at her heart.

Mountain Sage and Eagle Lance were dead. Wolf Shadow was gone, and she was alone, truly alone, for the first time in her life. She had no husband or father to hunt for her, to protect her. It was a sobering, frightening thought. What if Wolf Shadow never returned? Had she made a mistake in refusing to go with him? Would it have been so bad to meet her *wasichu* parents?

Sitting down on the bank, she tried again to remember her childhood in the *wasichu* world. Had it been so awful she had blocked it from her mind? Or had she blocked it because it had made it easier to adjust to her new life with the Lakota? If her *wasichu* parents had been looking for her all these years, they must have loved her, cared for her.

She had a sudden memory of her *wasichu* mother holding her, singing to her. . . . "Mama . . ."

The word, so long unsaid, whispered past her lips

and brought tears to her eyes. Had she made a mistake? But no, Wolf Shadow said he was coming back. He would take her home. Home. The image of a canopied bed jumped to the forefront of her mind. There was a pretty pink-and-white quilt on the bed, fluffy pillows, a doll with golden curls. . . .

She remembered then, remembered all of it—the big house on the hill, the wrought-iron fence, her dog, Heidi, and her pretty little pony, Snowflake. She remembered thinking her mother was the most beautiful woman in the world and wanting to marry her handsome daddy when she grew up. She remembered Mrs. Squires, the housekeeper, and Mrs. Rochefort, the plump French cook who had made her cookies shaped like trees and stars at Christmastime. Mrs. Rochefort had taught her to make gingerbread and had, on more than one occasion, snuck her treats before dinner. And there was Hart, the butler. And Marie Vachon, the pretty little French maid. She had caught Marie kissing Hans, the stableboy, in the barn one morning.

Teressa recalled her excitement when her father said he was taking a business trip and that she and Mama could go with him. They had ridden on a stagecoach and then a train. They had spent a month in New York City. Her mother had taken her sightseeing while her father took care of his business, whatever that might have been. At night, they had gone out to dinner in fancy restaurants. People had fussed over her wherever they went, complimenting her mother and father on having such a well-mannered little girl. She had basked in the attention. She had loved New York City, loved shopping in all the stores, loved the presents her father had bought her: a beautiful porcelain doll imported from France, complete with a crib and several changes of clothing, a dollhouse filled with cunningly made furniture, a hoopstick.

She remembered taking the train again, and then

the stage, remembered her excitement at seeing the Indians riding toward them, excitement that had soon turned to fear and then horror as the coach turned over.

Iron Arrow had grabbed her from her mother's arms and given her to Eagle Lance. And Eagle Lance had taken her home to Mountain Sage. She remembered it all now. She had been afraid at first, but not for very long. Mountain Sage had looked ill when Teressa first saw her. She had been scarecrow thin. Her cheeks had been hollow, her eyes filled with a deep sadness. Young as she was, Teressa had known somehow that it was her presence that had given Mountain Sage a reason to live and taken the sorrow from her eyes. The Indian couple had treated her kindly, giving her time to get used to living with them and with the Lakota.

Believing her natural parents dead, feeling guilty because of the love she felt for Mountain Sage and Eagle Lance, Teressa had blocked the memory of her parents and her other life from her mind.

A touch on her shoulder jerked her from the past. "You!" she exclaimed with a smile. "You startled me."

The filly tossed her head, then nuzzled Winter Rain's shoulder again.

Rising, Winter Rain stroked the filly's neck, then glanced at the trail leading away from the hollow.

"Do you think he'll really come back?" she wondered aloud. "And what will I do if he doesn't?"

Chance knew a moment of regret as he left the Lakota camp behind, but time was running out. His debt at the bank had to be paid before the end of the month or he would lose the ranch. In the meantime, the Lakota would spend the rest of the year in the Black Hills. Kills-Like-a-Hawk and Corn Woman would look after Winter Rain until he returned.

With an effort, he thrust everything from his mind but the peaceful beauty of the Hills. People lived and died, times changed, but the Paha Sapa, heart and soul of the Lakota nation, would endure forever. The Hills and the grasslands below housed a wealth of wildlife. Buffalo, deer, elk, wolves and coyotes, porcupines and beavers, ducks and magpies, hawks and badgers and skunks, all contributed something to the People, whether it was meat or hides or feathers. Fish and turtles were plentiful in the rivers.

Hunting was a serious and sacred business. The Lakota considered all life sacred; the animals were their brothers. They took no joy in killing, and hunting was a necessity, not a sport. Religious rites were held and a pipe was smoked before a hunt. When an animal was killed, the hunter said a prayer, thanking the animal for sacrificing its life. Later, when the meat was eaten, small pieces were set aside to be offered to the spirit, often accompanied by the words, "Acknowledge this so that I may become the owner of something good." Hunters sometimes sought a vision before undertaking a hunt, or asked for help from the tribal shaman.

Glancing up, Chance watched a spotted eagle soar high overhead, its powerful wings spread wide as it drifted effortlessly on the air currents. The sight filled his soul with a sense of peace, even though there could be no lasting peace for him so long as Jack Finch drew breath.

He shook the thought from his mind.

He would take care of his business with the bank and then he would return to his people, and to Winter Rain. He would seek a vision and hope that the Great Spirit would help him find that which he had sought for so long.

In the next few days, Winter Rain began to realize

just how much she had come to care about and rely on Wolf Shadow. She thought of him constantly, reliving every moment they had spent together. She had been happy living with the Lakota, had never realized what was missing from her life and her relationship with Strong Elk until Wolf Shadow's arrival. His presence had added a sense of anticipation to her life, a joy and excitement that had been missing before. Strong Elk had been a good man and she had been fond of him, but she had never cared for him the way she cared for Wolf Shadow. Was it possible she loved him? How was she to know? She had never been in love before, but surely it was love that made her yearn for Wolf Shadow's return, that made her long for the sound of his voice, ache for the touch of his hand.

She missed him desperately. As she went about her chores each day, she frequently found herself looking toward the trail, hoping for some sign of his return. At night she often huddled in her bed, weeping bitter tears—tears of grief for the loss of Mountain Sage and Eagle Lance, tears of loneliness and regret. Sometimes she went out to the horse herd to see the filly. Being with the horse made her feel closer to Wolf Shadow.

Corn Woman did her best to cheer her up, even though Corn Woman was grieving for her husband, who had been killed in the attack by the Crow. Yellow Fawn and Leaf, both mourning for members of their own families, also tried to distract Winter Rain. The three women, far older and wiser than Winter Rain, were accustomed to hardship and grief. As bitter as it was to bear, death was a part of life. They assured her that the pain would grow less each day. Winter Rain was grateful for their company and their advice, but deep inside, she didn't think the hurt would ever go away. Mountain Sage and Eagle Lance were dead, and a part of her had died with them.

# *Chapter 16*

Chance rode into Buffalo Springs just after noon. People stopped to stare at him as he made his way down Main Street. He guessed he couldn't blame them. Dressed as he was in buckskin shirt, clout, and moccasins, even people who knew him stopped to look twice. He nodded at Maisy Holbrook, who was sweeping the boardwalk in front of the bakery she ran with the help of her daughter, Alison. Old man Rumsfield was sitting in his usual place outside the barbershop, his head bent over a piece of whittling. He looked up, his eyebrows rising in surprise when he saw Chance ride by. The Wilsons' ten-year-old twins, Hester and Lester, grinned as they waved at him, then put their heads together, undoubtedly plotting mischief of some kind.

Chance reined his horse to a stop in front of the Buffalo Springs Hotel, which was where he normally stayed when he was in town. Dismounting, he dropped the reins over the hitch rack, pulled his rifle from the saddle boot, and climbed the stairs to the boardwalk.

Lyle Hunsacker, the hotel clerk, lifted a questioning brow as Chance approached the desk.

"I need a room," Chance said, "and a bath, right away."

"Yes," Hunsacker drawled. "I can see that."

"I'd be obliged if you'd send Billy over to Womack's to get me a change of clothes."

Hunsacker nodded. He was a tall middle-aged man with a mop of curly red hair and a pencil-thin mustache. Chance played poker with him from time to time.

Hunsacker pulled a key off the board behind the desk. "Number eight. I'll have some hot water sent up right away."

"Thanks."

"I'd like to hear the story behind that getup when you've got the time to tell it," Hunsacker remarked with a grin.

With a grunt, Chance took the key and went up the stairs. Number eight was his home away from home when it was available. It was a corner room overlooking the street. The double bed was comfortable, and there was a tub in one corner, an easy chair in another. A plain white bowl and pitcher sat atop a four-drawer mahogany chest. There were a couple of clean towels stacked on a shelf, along with a bar of soap.

Chance put his rifle across the foot of the bed, then sat down in the easy chair and pulled off his moccasins. Leaning back in the chair, he closed his eyes. As soon as he got cleaned up, he'd get Smoke settled in the livery and then take care of his business.

An hour later, bathed, shaved, and dressed in a pair of black whipcord trousers and a dark blue shirt, Chance knocked on Edward Bryant's door at the Windsor Hotel.

Rosalia Bryant opened it a moment later, her dark eyes widening in surprise when she saw him.

"Signore!" She leaned forward to look past him. "But . . . where is . . . ?" She looked up at him, a thousand questions in her eyes.

"May I come in?"

"Oh, *si*. Please, come in." She stood back to allow him entrance into the room.

"Rosa, who is it?"

"Eduardo, it is Signore McCloud."

"McCloud!" A door across the room opened and Edward Bryant emerged, leaning heavily on his cane. His gaze swept the room, his brow furrowing when he saw that Chance was alone.

"She's not here," Chance said.

Rosalia and Edward looked at each other, disappointment evident on their faces. Rosalia sat down on the sofa, her shoulders slumped.

Bryant cleared his throat. "She's not . . . ?"

Chance shook his head. "No, she's fine."

"Then where is she? Why didn't you bring her with you?"

"She didn't want to come."

Rosalia looked up, frowning. "I do not understand. She did not want to come home? But why not?"

Chance ran a hand through his hair. "I'm afraid she doesn't think of this as her home anymore, Mrs. Bryant."

Edward sat down on the sofa beside his wife, indicating that Chance should take the chair opposite the sofa.

Rosalia looked at her husband. "I do not understand."

"It's like this," Chance explained as he sat down. "She's been living with the Lakota for ten years. She's been happy there. The couple she lived with were good to her. They loved her and raised her like their own daughter. . . ."

"But she is our daughter!" Rosalia exclaimed.

Bryant took his wife's hand in his. "Go on, Mr. McCloud. Start at the beginning, please."

As succinctly as possible, Chance told them about Mountain Sage and Eagle Lance and how Teressa had spent the last ten years of her life. He told them about the attack by the Crow and how they had escaped and made their way to his people in the Black Hills. He told them everything, everything except what had passed between himself and their daughter.

Edward Bryant shook his head when Chance finished. "I cannot believe my daughter has been living like a savage. . . ." His face colored. "I meant no offense, Mr. McCloud."

"None taken."

"Well," Bryant said enthusiastically. "At least we know she's alive."

"I couldn't convince her to come back with me," Chance said, "and I couldn't take her by force, but . . ."

"Go on."

"What would you think about me taking you to her?"

Rosalia stared at him.

Bryant drummed his fingers on the table beside the sofa. "Go to her? But . . . is that wise?"

Rosalia stood up, her cheeks flushed. "Eduardo, we must go."

"Would it be safe for us?" Bryant asked. "For my wife?"

"I can't guarantee it," Chance replied honestly. "There's always a risk when you venture into Indian territory, and not just from the Indians. It's a wild land. Anything can happen."

"I do not care!" Rosalia said vehemently. "Eduardo, we must go. Now." She looked at Chance. "How soon can we leave?"

"That depends. I know the deal was for me to bring your daughter back here, but . . ."

"Ah, yes," Bryant said. "The reward. I believe I owe you ten thousand dollars."

"I was hoping you'd see it that way."

"I shall write you a check immediately."

"Much obliged."

After telling the Bryants to pack light and be ready

first thing in the morning, Chance's next stop was the Buffalo Springs Bank.

Harry Conreid couldn't hide his surprise, or his displeasure, when Chance announced he had come to pay off the loan on the Double C in full. The disappointment on old Harry's face was far more eloquent than words. No doubt Harry had been hoping to foreclose on the ranch. Hell, Chance thought irritably, it wouldn't have surprised him if Harry already had a buyer in mind.

Well, that was just too bad, Chance thought as he signed the necessary papers. The ranch was his and it was going to stay his.

He felt like the weight of the world had been lifted from his shoulders when he walked out of the bank, the deed to the ranch, stamped *Paid in Full*, in his hip pocket. His next stop was the telegraph office, where he sent a wire informing the owner of the bull that he had the money needed to purchase the animal. From there, he went to McMurty's Gun Shop and bought himself a new Colt and holster and several boxes of ammunition, and then he went to the saloon for a drink and to wait for a reply to his wire. It arrived an hour later.

After returning to his room, he sat down and wrote a letter to his foreman, telling him that the mortgage had been paid in full and that the bull he'd had his eye on for so long would be arriving at the railway station at the end of next week and that someone needed to be there to pick it up. He went on to explain that he was leaving town again and would return to the ranch as soon as possible.

Going downstairs, he gave the note to Hunsacker's teenage son, along with a dollar to take it out to the ranch.

That done, Chance went into the hotel dining room and ordered the biggest steak they had to offer, along with all the trimmings and a double helping of apple pie for dessert.

Later, sitting back in his chair sipping a second cup of coffee, he found himself thinking of Winter Rain, remembering the way she felt in his arms, the sweet innocence of her kisses, the sound of her laughter.

Muttering an oath, he shook her image from his mind. He had no time for a woman in his life, not now, not so long as Jack Finch walked the earth.

It didn't take long for Chance to realize it would have been a lot easier to bring Teressa to the Bryants than to take the Bryants to Teressa.

When he got to the hotel in the morning, he found that Rosalia had packed enough clothes, shoes, and hats to fill three large suitcases. By the time she pared her wardrobe down so that it would fit in a pair of saddlebags, half the day was gone.

Rosalia pulled on a pair of gloves as she followed Chance out of the hotel. "I thought we would be taking a carriage," she explained.

The next setback came when Chance learned, to his dismay, that Rosalia had never been on a horse and that Edward hadn't ridden since he'd taken that Indian arrow in his thigh.

Standing on the boardwalk in front of the hotel, Chance regarded the couple through narrowed eyes and then shook his head. "Listen, maybe we should just forget it. I'll go back to the Lakota and see if I can convince Teressa to come here."

"No!" Rosalia tugged on Chance's arm. "No, I have waited so long." She grabbed the reins to the chestnut gelding he had picked for her. "I will ride."

He had to admire the woman's determination even as he watched her struggle to put the wrong foot in the stirrup, a foot wearing a dainty pair of shoes that wouldn't last two minutes out on the trail.

An hour and a half later, after a hasty shopping trip to buy riding boots for both of the Bryants and a hat for Edward, and after a quick riding lesson for Rosalia, they were ready to go.

Chance took a deep breath and turned to check the load on the packhorse while Edward put his hands around his wife's waist and lifted her onto the back of her horse.

Certain he was making the biggest mistake of his life, Chance gathered the reins of the packhorse and swung into the saddle. After glancing over his shoulder to make sure Edward was mounted, Chance led the way out of town.

They made quite a sight, he mused ruefully. Rosalia wore a long-sleeved yellow silk shirt, a voluminous skirt that covered her legs and spread over the gelding's rump, a wide-brimmed straw hat adorned with pink and yellow streamers, and a pair of leather gloves. Edward wore a pair of striped trousers, a matching vest over a white linen shirt, and a ten-gallon hat straight out of the box. His cane was tied behind the cantle.

Blowing out a deep breath, Chance settled his hat on his head. It was going to be a hell of a long trip.

# Chapter 17

Winter Rain pressed a hand to her aching back. She was glad to have something to do even though tanning hides was not her favorite pastime. It was a long, hard process. Still, she wasn't about to complain. Helping Corn Woman was the least she could do in return for her friend's kindness in taking her in. If she had one complaint, it was that tanning didn't require much concentration and gave her far too much time to think, and as always, her thoughts were centered on Wolf Shadow. Where had he gone, and why had he left so abruptly? And when would he return? Would he return?

Kills-Like-a-Hawk seemed to think so. Wolf Shadow's cousin had recovered from his wounds. Now, whenever Kills-Like-a-Hawk went hunting, he always brought her a part of his kill so that there would be meat in Corn Woman's lodge. The hide she was tanning had been a gift from him, as well.

Winter Rain sat back on her heels and closed her eyes. And Wolf Shadow's image immediately sprang into her mind—smooth copper-hued skin stretched over a tall, muscular frame, hair as black as the berries that grew in the summer, eyes as gray as thunderclouds. Eyes that smiled at her, promising to reveal secrets she longed to know.

She lifted her fingertips to her lips, remembering how he had kissed her, the warmth of his breath, the exciting, frightening sensations he had aroused in her, feelings that invaded her dreams. Never before had she had such vivid dreams. Sometimes she woke in the middle of the night feeling hot and achy for the touch of his hand, yearning for the sound of his voice whispering her name.

"Winter Rain?"

She looked up, suddenly aware that Corn Woman had called her name several times.

The woman smiled a knowing smile. "He will come back."

"Who?" Winter Rain asked with feigned ignorance.

Corn Woman shook her head. "Wolf Shadow, of course."

Winter Rain shrugged, as if it made no difference to her whether he returned or not.

Laughing softly, Corn Woman knelt beside Winter Rain. She ran her hand over the hide pegged to the ground, nodding her approval. "Waiting is never easy, especially when one is young and eager."

"What will I do if he does not return?"

"You will find another."

"But I do not want another!" Winter Rain exclaimed, and in that moment she knew it was true.

"I have seen the way he looks at you," Corn Woman replied candidly. "He will return."

Winter Rain smiled, her heart feeling suddenly light and carefree for the first time in days, and then her mood grew sober once more. Mountain Sage and Eagle Lance were dead. She feared Strong Elk was dead, as well, along with so many others she had grown up with, boys and girls she had played with, elders who had taught her and told her stories, beautiful little dark-eyed babies she had held and fussed over. All gone.

She looked up at the touch of Corn Woman's hand on her shoulder.

"*Le mita cola*, do not dwell on the past," Corn
Woman said, her voice tinged with sadness. "*Hecheto
aloe.*" It is finished.

Winter Rain nodded. "I hear your words, but . . ."
A long, shuddering sigh escaped her. "I miss them
so!" She blinked rapidly, not wanting the other
woman to see her tears.

"Weep, child. You will feel better if you do."

Corn Woman's kindness, the understanding in her
voice, was Winter Rain's undoing. She had tried to be
brave for so long. Now she was suddenly overcome
with a sense of loss. Rising, she hurried into Corn
Woman's lodge. Dropping to her knees on her blankets, she rocked back and forth, her arms wrapped
around her waist, and let the tears flow.

After a time, exhaustion overcame her tears. Curling up on her blankets, she closed her eyes. Wolf
Shadow's image immediately rose in her mind. With
a sigh, she whispered his name, wondering if he was
lying in bed somewhere, thinking about her.

Chance banked the fire, then settled down on his
bedroll. He must have been out of his mind when he
decided to take the Bryants to Winter Rain. They
hadn't been on the trail more than an hour when Rosalia needed to stop for a moment of privacy. Thirty
minutes later, she needed to stretch her legs. An hour
later, Edward needed to take a break to rest his
wounded leg.

They hadn't gone more than another mile or two
when they came to a short, steep hill. Instead of leaning forward in the saddle, Rosalia leaned back. She
tumbled over her mount's rump with a shriek that
would have done a Lakota warrior proud, and sent
her horse bolting for cover.

Leaving Edward to look after his wife, Chance had
gone after her horse. By the time he caught the geld-

ing and made it back to where he had left the Bryants, the sun was setting and Chance decided they might as well stop for the night.

He shook his head. He figured they'd covered about nine miles. At this rate, it would be full on winter before they reached the Lakota camp.

Folding one arm under his head, he stared up at the stars scattered across the sky, shining like dewdrops at dawn, his thoughts turning, as they so often did, to Winter Rain.

"Teressa." He shared her name with the evening breeze, liking the way it sounded. Was she asleep? Or lying awake, restless and aching for his touch, as he was for hers?

He swore softly. He had to stop spending so much time thinking about her. She was too young, too innocent, for the likes of him. He had killed three men in cold blood, and even though they deserved to die, he had still done murder in the eyes of the law. And he wasn't done yet, wouldn't rest until the fourth man was dead.

Still, he couldn't keep her image from forming in his mind, couldn't stop remembering how good she felt in his arms. He closed his eyes, picturing her on the ranch, waiting for him at the end of the day, smiling at him from across the dinner table, sitting in the big old comfortable chair beside the fireplace, mending or sewing while he went over the ranch accounts, sleeping beside him at night, waking up beside him in the morning.

Damn! Where had *those* thoughts come from? He had never even considered getting married until he met Teressa Bryant. Even if he was crazy enough to ask her to marry him, even if she was crazy enough to say yes, he was pretty sure Edward Bryant would shoot him dead before he let his daughter—his only daughter—marry a half-breed cowboy. The Bryants were a high-class couple. No doubt they expected Teressa to marry a doctor or a lawyer and settle down in San Francisco. He was willing to bet the ranch that they expected her to do better than marry a cowboy who had been up to his ears in debt before her father came along.

Muttering an oath, he put everything from his mind but Teressa. She might never be his, he mused ruefully, but he would never forget her.

It took the Bryants a good hour to get ready the following morning. Since it only took Chance about twenty minutes to eat and saddle up when he was alone, he had a good deal of time to sit and wait. They both managed to look as clean and fresh as if they had just emerged from their hotel room. Edward had brushed the dust from his trousers and shined his boots; Rosalia had changed into a clean shirtwaist. This one was a yellow and green stripe. They ate breakfast as if they had all the time in the world. Watching them, it was obvious that even after many years of marriage they were still very much in love. Except for his own parents, Chance hadn't had much opportunity to be around married couples and it was interesting to watch the interplay between Edward and his wife, to notice how they smiled at each other, the way they stopped now and then to exchange a quick touch, a kiss.

Finally they were all saddled up and ready to go. Settling his hat on his head, Chance could only hope they'd make more miles today than they had yesterday.

"Oh, Eduardo, look!"

Chance glanced over his shoulder to see Rosalia pointing at a doe and her twin fawns, barely visible in a stand of timber several yards away.

"Are they not beautiful?" she murmured.

"Yes, indeed, my dear," Edward replied.

His voice, much louder than his wife's, spooked the doe. With a flick of her tail, the doe bounded away, the fawns at her heels.

Later that afternoon, Chance called a halt at the top of a rise. "Look there." He pointed westward, to where a small herd of buffalo was on the move.

Rosalia's eyes widened when she saw them. "*Buono cielo,* but they are very large, are they not?"

"Very," Chance agreed.

"I suppose you've hunted them, Mr. McCloud," Edward said, riding up alongside.

"Oh, yeah. They're mighty good eating."

"So I have heard. Perhaps we shall have the opportunity to taste some when we reach your camp."

"I wouldn't be surprised."

"Is there . . . that is, would I be allowed to join in a hunt?"

Chance resisted the urge to laugh out loud as he pictured Edward Bryant, all duded up in his striped trousers and fancy shirt, riding out with a handful of warriors clad in clouts and moccasins.

"I should love to give it a go," Edward remarked.

"Guess you'll just have to wait and see," Chance replied.

"I had no idea the country was so large," Rosalia said when they were riding again. "I have seen part of it from the train, of course, but it seems so much grander now."

They stopped again to watch a pair of eagles soaring overhead.

"*Quanto bello,*" Rosalia murmured. How beautiful. Edward nodded in agreement.

It was shortly after they had eaten the midday meal that the Indians found them. A dozen Cheyenne warriors.

Rosalia's face went pale. Edward's posture stiffened as he guided his horse alongside his wife's.

Chance frowned when he saw Edward reach inside his coat. "If that's a gun you're reaching for, leave it be."

Edward stared at him. "Surely you mean to fight?"

"Not if I don't have to. Just sit easy and keep your hands out where they can see them."

"Eduardo . . ." Rosalia looked at her husband, her eyes wide with fear.

"You're just gonna have to trust me on this," Chance said. "If you draw that weapon, we're as good as dead."

They were surrounded now. Chance forced himself to sit easy in the saddle. The Indians were Cheyenne, a hunting party from the looks of it. Chance raised his hand in the traditional sign of peace, careful to keep clear of his gun.

One of the Cheyenne warriors rode forward a little. He frowned as his gaze moved over Chance. "You are one of us," he said, speaking in Cheyenne and sign language, "yet you dress as our enemy." He looked at Rosalia and Edward. "You ride with our enemy."

"I am Wolf Shadow of the Lakota," Chance replied in halting Cheyenne. "These people have come to visit their daughter, who is also daughter to the Lakota."

The warrior grunted softly. "I am Chases Thunder of the Cheyenne."

Chance gestured at the packhorses, which were heavily laden with meat. "I see the hunting has been good."

Chases Thunder nodded. "Maheo has blessed us this day." Riding back toward the packhorses, he took the lead rope of the nearest one. Leading the animal toward Chance, he offered him the lead rope.

*"Hahoo,"* Chance said, taking the rope. Dis-

mounting, he went to his own packhorse and withdrew a pound of sugar and a sack of coffee, which he offered to Chases Thunder.

The warrior accepted the gifts with a nod. *"Hahoo,"* he said, and wheeling his horse around, he rode away, followed by the rest of the hunters.

Edward withdrew a snowy handkerchief from his inside coat pocket and wiped the sweat from his brow. Rosalia's shoulders slumped as she blew out a deep breath.

With a wry grin, Chance tied the Cheyenne pony's lead rope to the tail of his own pack horse, then swung into the saddle. "You two ready?"

Edward looked at his wife. "Are you ready, my dear?"

Rosalia looked at Chance. "Were they . . . friends of yours?"

"No, ma'am. Just some hunters on their way home. Thanks to them, we'll have fresh meat for dinner."

Rosalia glanced at the deer draped over the Cheyenne pony, her pale face growing even paler at the sight of the carcass slung over the horse's withers.

With a shake of his head, Chance clucked to his horse. The woman must have eaten meat before. Where did she think it came from?

He should have just kidnapped Winter Rain and worried about making things right with Kills-Like-a-Hawk and the People later. It would have been a hell of a lot easier, he mused with a wry grin. And a hell of a lot faster.

# Chapter 18

As the days turned to weeks, Winter Rain gave up hope that Wolf Shadow would return. She resigned herself to the fact that she would never see him again, told herself she didn't care.

And then, quite unexpectedly, she woke one morning certain that he was nearby. At first she told herself she was being foolish, that she only felt that way because she missed him so very very much.

But as the day progressed, the feeling grew stronger. There was no explanation for her feelings, but as dusk approached, she could no longer deny them, and even as she told herself she was being ridiculous, she was walking away from the camp toward the trail that led to the hollow.

She was out of breath when she reached the top of the rise. The setting sun cast a pale pink shadow over the grassland. Standing there, with one hand pressed to her side, she searched the narrow winding trail that led upward, looking for some sign of a rider. She saw squirrels running back and forth, chasing each other from tree to tree. She saw birds flitting from branch to branch. She saw a skunk delicately picking its way through the underbrush, but no sign of a tall man on a bay mare.

Heart heavy with disappointment, she was about to turn away when a rider wearing a long black coat and a black hat emerged from around a bend in the trail.

Winter Rain felt a shiver of excitement course through her. Though he was still too far away for her to see his face, her heart recognized him at once. Wolf Shadow had come back, just as Kills-Like-a-Hawk promised. Happiness blossomed inside her. He was here at last!

She frowned when she saw two other riders, a man and a woman, in the man's wake.

It couldn't be. She blinked at them and blinked again as they drew nearer. Could it be? Unable to believe her eyes, she moved farther down the trail, her gaze riveted on the woman's face. She was beautiful, so beautiful.

"Mama?"

She stood there, frozen, as the trio rode up the narrow trail to where she stood, her heart pounding with trepidation.

What should she say? What would her . . . her parents think when they saw her? Would they be disappointed?

And then, too soon, they were there.

Wolf Shadow drew his horse to a halt and her parents stopped behind him.

Leaning forward in the saddle, her mother started to say something to Wolf Shadow when she saw Winter Rain standing on the side of the trail. She stared at Winter Rain for several moments, and then Rosalia was off her horse and running toward Winter Rain, her arms outstretched, tears welling in her eyes.

*"Teressa! Mia bambina! Dio Di Elogio!"* Praise God!

Edward Bryant climbed out of the saddle and hurried after his wife. "Teressa! Is it really you?"

And then she was swallowed up in her parents' arms as they hugged and kissed her, both of them murmuring her name over and over again.

Tears filled Winter Rain's eyes as the warmth of

her parents' love surrounded her. Any doubts she'd had were swept away by a rush of memories—memories of her mother tucking her into bed at night, brushing her hair, reading to her, teaching her to do needlepoint; memories of her father taking her to the zoo, holding her hand as they crossed the street, teaching her to ride her first pony, listening to her prayers. How could she ever have forgotten them?

Chance leaned forward in the saddle, his arms crossed on the horn, watching the reunion. He felt a tug in the region of his heart as he watched Winter Rain embrace her mother. He would give up the ranch and everything else he held dear to be able to hold his own mother one more time. Grief rose within him and with it a fresh wave of determination to avenge her death. It took him a minute to realize Winter Rain and her parents were looking up at him expectantly.

He cleared his throat. "Did you say something, Rain?"

"I asked if you would give me a ride back to camp."

"Sure."

Reaching down, he took hold of her upper arm and lifted her up in front of him. He waited for Rosalia and Edward to mount their horses, then clucked to Smoke.

Winter Rain turned her head so she could see Wolf Shadow's face. "Thank you," she said quietly.

"You wouldn't go to them," Chance said with a negligent shrug. "What else could I do?"

"I am grateful. It was kind of you to go to so much trouble for us."

He wondered briefly what Winter Rain would think if she knew it hadn't been kindness at all that prompted him to bring her parents here.

Riding down the trail toward the camp, he was all too aware of the woman sitting in front of him. Her hair brushed against his cheek. Her scent filled his nostrils, her softly rounded bottom fit snugly between his thighs. He tried not to move, hoping she wouldn't notice the effect her nearness was having on him. She shifted her weight in the saddle and he almost groaned out loud. Damn!

Men and women stopped what they were doing as Chance and his companions rode into view. Since white people were rarely seen among the Lakota, they naturally drew a lot of curious looks, especially from the children.

Kills-Like-a-Hawk stepped outside just as Chance drew rein in front of his lodge. He looked up, his expression impassive as Chance lowered Winter Rain to the ground. Rosalia dismounted quickly, obviously eager to be near Winter Rain, and just as obviously unable to keep from touching the daughter she hadn't seen in ten years.

Edward Bryant dismounted with a low groan, one hand massaging his thigh.

Chance caught Winter Rain's gaze. "Why don't you introduce your folks to Kills-Like-a-Hawk?" he suggested. "I'll look after the horses."

Without giving her a chance to question him, he took up the reins of the other two horses and rode toward the herd. There was no way he could dismount now, not without everyone noticing his aroused state.

He was unsaddling Smoke when the filly trotted up to him. With a soft whinny, she rubbed her nose against his shoulder. He spent a few minutes stroking the filly's neck and scratching her ears, then stripped the rigging from the Bryants' horses and turned them loose with the rest of the herd.

Taking a deep breath, Chance picked up the Bryants' luggage and headed back to the village. There had been some changes while he'd been gone. The men had been busy hunting, as evidenced by the number of drying racks he saw. Several of the huts had been replaced by hide lodges.

Rosalia turned to look at him as he approached, visibly appalled by her surroundings. Her husband looked stunned. Winter Rain's smile looked forced as she told her parents that Kills-Like-a-Hawk had offered to let them have his lodge during their visit; he and Chance would stay in the lodge that had been set up for the single men.

"I . . . that is, I did not think we would stay here," Rosalia replied, glancing around uneasily.

Edward nodded. "I really need to get back to my business, Tessa. I've been gone far too long as it is."

Winter Rain looked at Wolf Shadow, and he knew that as happy as she was to see her parents, she wasn't quite ready to go back to civilization.

"Mrs. Bryant, I think maybe Winter . . . Teressa . . . would like you to meet her friends and get to know a little about the people she's been living with for so long. I think it might be a good idea. Might be good for all of you."

Chance looked at Bryant and grinned. "And you said you wanted to go on a hunt."

"Ah, yes," Edward said. "I had forgotten that. Do you think I can?"

"I'll arrange it."

"My dear, I think Mr. McCloud might be right." Bryant smiled at his daughter. "I don't suppose another few days will matter one way or the other."

"Thank you, Papa."

"I'll just put this stuff inside," Chance remarked, and ducked into Kills-Like-a-Hawk's lodge.

His cousin, who had gone inside to gather his belongings, looked up as Chance entered.

"So, Tahunsa, I see you found a way."

"Did you think I wouldn't?"

"No. If Winter Rain wishes to go with her *wasichu* parents, I cannot stop her."

"But you do not think she should go, or that I should take her from here."

"She has been one of us for many years. She will be missed."

"I am sorry you do not approve, Tahunsa."

Kills-Like-a-Hawk regarded him through narrowed eyes, his gaze seeming to penetrate into Chance's very soul. "Are you happy with your life, Wolf Shadow? Has revenge brought you that which you seek?"

"Do not worry about me. I am fine."

"Are you?"

Chance ran a hand through his hair. "Dammit, do not talk to me about revenge! Who is better at it than the Lakota?"

"Our People avenge their dead, yes, that is true. But it is more than the taking of a man's life that drives you. When you have killed the last of the *wasichu* who wronged your mother, you will still be empty inside. It is not the need for vengeance that consumes you. It is your own guilt. You must learn to forgive yourself for what happened. Only then will you find the peace you seek."

Chance stared at his cousin for stretched seconds, then, with a shake of his head, he turned and stalked out of the lodge.

Rosalia sat on a blanket inside the lodge that Teressa said was her home. It was a crude circular dwelling, completely lacking in any comforts other than a few furs and a few rustic cooking pots. There was no furniture to speak of other than two backrests fashioned from wood and covered with a hide. How had her daughter, who had spent her first formative years surrounded by the best of everything, survived ten years in this harsh environment?

Rosalia's gaze moved over her daughter. Teressa had grown into a lovely young woman. Her hair was thick and shiny, the same color as Rosalia's. Her skin was clear and unblemished. Her figure, though covered in a shapeless deerskin tunic, seemed slender but well rounded.

Rosalia felt another wave of regret for the years of her daughter's life that she had missed. She had missed the gangly years of adolescence, hadn't been there to watch Teressa blossom into the lovely woman she had become.

And Teressa! She, too, had missed out on so much. They had much to do when they returned home, and Teressa had much to learn, years of schooling to catch up on. They would have to buy her a new wardrobe, introduce her to society. No doubt living in the city would seem strange to her at first, perhaps even a little frightening.

Rosalia forced a timid smile as the Indian woman known as Corn Woman handed her a bowl and a spoon made of some kind of animal horn. Rosalia took it hesitantly, wondering what the contents of the bowl might be.

She glanced at Edward, who was sitting beside her. One look at his face told her he felt as out of place as she did, that he couldn't wait to take Teressa away from here.

Chance McCloud sat cross-legged on a fur on the other side of the fire pit, looking all too at home as he accepted a bowl and spoon from Winter Rain. Rosalia had not missed the way her daughter looked at Mr. McCloud, or the way Mr. McCloud looked at her daughter. She did not want to dwell on what might have happened between Teressa and McCloud. At any rate, whatever there was between the two of them would end as soon as Teressa was safely home again.

Teressa sat down beside McCloud and began to eat.

Rosalia dipped her spoon into the bowl, took a deep
breath, and swallowed a spoonful of what she thought
was beef stew. It definitely wasn't beef, she concluded.
The meat had a strong gamy taste and the broth was
thin. She thought it was flavored with sage and onion.
She ate it all because to put it aside would have been
impolite, and because she had no wish to hurt Teressa's feelings.

Beside her, Edward murmured, "Good Lord, what
is this?"

"It's venison stew."

Edward looked up, a flush spreading over his cheeks
as he met McCloud's gaze. "Oh." He cleared his
throat. "It is quite . . . ah . . . filling."

"I am sorry you do not like it," Teressa said.

"Did I say that, Tessa?" Edward asked quickly. "It
is just"—he cleared his throat again—"different from
anything I have ever tasted."

Chance grunted softly. That had to be the under-
statement of the century. Emptying his bowl, he put
it aside. "*Pilamaya,* Rain," he said, rising.

"Where are you going?" she asked.

He shrugged. "Nowhere. Just outside."

She watched him duck out of the lodge, wishing she
dared go with him.

"Teressa, dear?"

With a sigh, she turned back to her parents, but her
heart went outside with Wolf Shadow.

"Tessa?"

Winter Rain met her mother's gaze, wondering what
to call her. For the last ten years, she had thought
of Mountain Sage as her mother. It seemed disloyal,
somehow, to acknowledge another woman as her
mother.

"Have you been happy here with these people?"
Rosalia asked.

"Yes, very happy."

"They were good to you, then?"

Winter Rain nodded. "Yes, always."

"I am glad. At home, we read of terrible things in the newspapers."

"What kind of terrible things?" Winter Rain asked curiously.

"Atrocities," her father said. "Indian attacks on settlers and farmers. Men tortured and killed. Women and children taken captive and ra—"

"Eduardo!"

"What?" He glanced at Rosalia, and then noticed the shocked expression on Teressa's face. "Oh. Of course. Sorry."

"The people who raised me were very kind," Winter Rain said defensively. "I always had food, even when it was scarce. I always had the warmest blanket in winter."

Her parents exchanged a look she could not fathom, and then, apropos of nothing, her father asked, "And what of Mr. McCloud?"

Feeling the need for solitude, Chance walked away from the village. Having spent considerable time with Winter Rain's parents, he was more aware than ever of the vast gulf between himself and the Bryant family. Edward and Rosalia were cultured, wealthy people, accustomed to the best money could buy. They would want the same for Winter Rain. For Teressa, he amended. And who could blame them? She was a sweet-natured, beautiful young woman, one who deserved the best of everything. And the best thing he could do for her was get out of her life just as soon as possible. He would guide the Bryant family back to Buffalo Springs and then stop off at the ranch for a week or so. He'd check on the herd, see if the new bull had arrived, look into buying that land adjacent to the east pasture. Once he had made sure everything at the ranch was running smoothly, he would sniff around and see what he could find out about Jack Finch's whereabouts.

He was about to go back to the camp when he realized he was no longer alone.

"Mr. McCloud?"

He turned around and came face-to-face with Edward Bryant. "What can I do for you?"

"I know of no way to say this other than to just say it."

Chance raised one brow. "So say it."

"I want to know what there is between you and my daughter."

A dozen answers chased themselves through Chance's mind, most of them not very nice. "There's nothing between us," he replied at last. And it was the truth, and a lie.

Edward Bryant regarded him for several moments, then nodded curtly.

Chance muttered an oath under his breath as he watched Winter Rain's father walk away. The man hadn't said much, but the look in his eyes and the tone of his voice had said one thing clearly: Stay away from my daughter.

It was sound advice, Chance thought grimly, and hoped he was smart enough to take it.

# Chapter 19

A sigh whispered past Winter Rain's lips as she gazed up at the narrow slice of sky visible through the smoke hole of Kills-Like-a-Hawk's lodge. A single bright star winked down at her. *Star light, star bright, first star I see tonight . . .* The words she had often spoken in childhood tiptoed down the corridors of her mind. *Wish I may, wish I might . . .* If she knew her wish would come true, what would she wish for?

"Wolf Shadow."

His name came quickly to her lips. They'd had no time to be alone together since he had arrived with her parents three days ago. Was he avoiding her? She pushed that thought aside. There was no reason for him to do that. Was there?

She shook her head. She was just being foolish. She glanced across the lodge to where her parents were sleeping. She could hear the soft sound of her mother's breathing; an occasional snore from her father.

The last three days had passed amicably enough. She had felt the tension between her father and Wolf Shadow, though she didn't understand the reason for it. Her mother had listened with interest as Winter Rain explained the daily life of her people. The Lakota women had been just as interested in learning about Rosalia. They had gathered around her, marveling at the softness of her clothing, her underwear, her stockings, her boots, her soft leather riding gloves.

Her mother had been somewhat taken aback at first, but the warmth and openness of the Lakota women had quickly won her over.

Her father was more reserved, more ill at ease with the men of the tribe. Several of the warriors had invited him to go hunting with them, but Edward had refused, pleading his injured thigh as an excuse.

Tomorrow, she thought, one way or another, she would find a way to see Wolf Shadow alone. As soon as the thought crossed her mind, she knew why her father had stayed in camp.

Winter Rain rose early after a restless night. Dressing quickly, she made her way down to a quiet place past a bend in the river where the water ran still and not too deep. Undressing, she slipped into the pool, yelping softly as the cool water closed over her. During one of their talks, her mother had spent a few minutes refreshing Winter Rain's memory about life in the city. Three of the things her mother had mentioned were hot water to bathe in, scented soap to wash with, and soft toweling with which to dry oneself. Winter Rain was anxious to try all three, especially the hot water.

She closed her eyes, imagining herself sitting in an enameled tub, submerged in hot water and a froth of bubbles.

They would be leaving for her parents' home soon. She had mixed emotions at the thought of leaving the Lakota. She had been happy with the People, would have spent the rest of her life with them if Mountain Sage and Eagle Lance had not been killed. She didn't want to think about what she would have done if she had had to choose between her *wasichu* parents and her Lakota family. It would have been an impossible choice to make.

She opened her eyes abruptly, suddenly certain she was no longer alone.

Wolf Shadow stood on the bank, his arms folded over his chest. All too clearly she remembered a day near the river. *Tomorrow morning I'll try to get here earlier,* he had said, his gaze moving over her, as intimate as a caress. *Or maybe I'll come a little later and see what I can see.*

Well, he was certainly getting a good look now. Too late, she slid beneath the surface of the water and as she did so, she felt her cheeks grow hot as she recalled something else Wolf Shadow had said that day. He had predicted that the day would come when he would ask her to bathe with him and she wouldn't refuse.

She looked at him and felt a shiver of anticipation. Would he ask her to bathe with him today? What would she say if he did?

"You coming out anytime soon?" he asked.

"Maybe," she replied with a sauciness she had never felt before. "And maybe I am waiting for you to join me."

She stared at him, mortified by what she had said. She could see that he, too, was taken aback by her immodest words.

But only for a moment. The next thing she knew, he was peeling off his moccasins, stripping off his shirt, reaching for the cord that held his clout in place.

Heat suffused her body. She felt it climb up her neck, flood her face. Whatever had possessed her to say such a thing? And what should she do now?

Before she could think, before she could recall the words, he was naked and in the water moving toward her.

He didn't give her time to say she had made a mistake or ask her if she wanted to change her mind. One hand slid around her waist, the other cupped the back of her head, and then his mouth was on hers and he was kissing her.

It was like no other kiss they had shared. In spite of the cool water, her entire body seemed to be on fire and she pressed herself against him, wanting to be closer, closer. Never before had she felt anything as wonderful, as exciting, as the touch of his skin, warm and wet, against her own.

She knew it was wrong to let him hold her, touch her, but it didn't feel wrong. It felt wickedly, wonderfully right.

A low groan escaped his lips when he drew back. He gazed down at her, his eyes dark and hot as they moved over her, lingering on her lips, searing a path to her breasts.

"See here now! What's this?"

The sound of Edward Bryant's voice cooled the ardor between them like ice water thrown on a campfire. Chance thrust Winter Rain behind him, shielding her from her father's censuring gaze.

Bryant scowled at Chance, his brows rushing together in a look of supreme disapproval. "How long has this been going on?"

"There's nothing going on," Chance retorted. "The Lakota often bathe together."

"My daughter is not Lakota!" Bryant exclaimed, his voice rising. "And there was more going on here than bathing, sir!"

"Mr. Bryant, why don't you go on back to camp?" Chance suggested. "We'll be along in a few minutes."

Edward Bryant glared at Chance. "You expect me to leave my daughter here with you after what I saw?"

Chance returned Bryant's glare, his hands fisted at his sides.

"I'll expect you in five minutes, Teressa." Bryant spoke through clenched teeth, then turned on his heel and stalked back the way he had come, anger evident in the set of his shoulders, in every step he took.

Chance watched Bryant until he was out of sight before turning to face Winter Rain. "He's gone."

Winter Rain refused to meet his eyes. "I am so ashamed."

"Don't be. It was my fault."

She shook her head. "It was all my fault and you know it. I behaved shamelessly."

"Well, it's over and done with. Go get dressed. I'll walk you back to camp."

Still not meeting his eyes, she hurried out of the water. After grabbing her tunic and moccasins, she ducked behind a tree to dress.

Muttering an oath, Chance waded out of the river, shook the water from his hair, and pulled on his clout and moccasins. "You ready?" he called, draping his shirt over one shoulder.

"Yes." Her voice was subdued.

"Let's go. Waiting won't make it any easier."

Side by side, they walked up the path toward the camp.

"I tell you, Rosalia, if I had gotten there five minutes later, they would have been coupling in the water like seals."

"Eduardo, please, calm yourself."

"I am calm! Get our things together. We are leaving! Now! Today!"

"Very well, *inamorato*."

Edward paced the floor of the lodge, his anger building with every step. "To think I paid that scoundrel fifteen thousand dollars to find Tessa!"

"He did find her, Eduardo. And you cannot blame him for wanting to kiss her. She is *la bella donna*."

"No gentleman would take advantage of an innocent young woman!"

"You did not hire a gentleman," Rosalia reminded him quietly. "You hired a man who could find Tessa in this wild land."

Bryant took a deep breath. "You are right, as always, my dear. But we are still leaving."

Winter Rain stood outside Kills-Like-a-Hawk's lodge, her arms crossed over her breasts as she listened to her father and mother. She had known Wolf Shadow had come looking for her at her father's request, but for some reason she could not determine, it was painful to discover that Wolf Shadow had accepted money from her father. But even more painful was the sudden, overwhelming knowledge that her parents were taking her away from the People, away from the only life she really knew. She had known the day was coming when she would have to leave, but in the back of her mind she had hoped for a miracle, hoped that her parents would decide to stay here with her. She didn't want to leave the Lakota, didn't want to leave Corn Woman, Yellow Fawn, and Leaf, or any of the other people she loved and cared for. Even though she knew the Bryants were her true parents, even though she remembered her childhood with them, her mother and father were strangers to her now.

"Rain, what's wrong?"

"We are leaving today."

"Today? Who decided that?"

"My father. He is upset because of . . ." Her glance slid away from his in embarrassment.

"Because of what he saw at the river?"

"Yes."

Chance grunted softly. He couldn't blame Bryant. The man was only thinking of what was best for his daughter, and Chance knew he wasn't high on the man's list.

"I do not want to leave here."

"I'm sorry, sweetheart."

She looked up at him, her expression bleak, her eyes silently begging him to do something.

Chance took a step forward, then halted as Edward Bryant emerged from Kills-Like-a-Hawk's lodge.

"Ah, Mr. McCloud. Just the man I wish to see. We are leaving. Now. Please saddle our mounts."

"We won't get far today," Chance replied. "It's already past noon. By the time we're packed and ready to go, it'll be time to scout a place to spend the night."

Edward scowled at him and then, apparently seeing the wisdom in Chance's words, he nodded curtly. "Very well. We will leave tomorrow." He glanced at his daughter, then looked back at Chance. "Early."

"Yes, sir. I'll have your horses ready at first light," Chance replied curtly. Pivoting on his heel, he stalked away from the lodge.

Chance was getting ready to leave the single men's lodge when he heard a loud pounding on the door flap. He crossed the lodge floor and lifted the flap to find Edward Bryant standing outside.

"Is she here?"

"Who?" Chance asked. But in his gut he knew.

"Teressa. She is gone."

Chance swore a short, pithy oath. "She can't have gone far."

"You think she left on her own accord?"

"What do you think?"

"Some savage must have kidnapped her."

"I don't think so."

"What other explanation could there be?"

"Isn't it obvious? She doesn't want to leave here."

Chance could see that Bryant didn't want to believe that, but there was no other explanation for Teressa's disappearance. After grabbing his rifle, he stepped out of the lodge. Smoke whinnied softly as he took up the reins.

"Where are you going?" Bryant demanded.

"Where the hell do you think? I'm going after her."

"I will go with you," Bryant said, hurrying after him.

"I don't think so. The last thing I need is you out there slowing me down."

"But . . ."

"Forget it!" Chance paused in front of his cousin's lodge, his gaze searching the ground for signs of Winter Rain's tracks. It wasn't easy, picking one track out of dozens of others, but after a time he located Winter Rain's print.

He followed Rain's tracks to the horse herd. She had picked a horse, led it to a rock, pulled herself onto its back, and headed southward, deeper into the Hills.

Chance swore softly. Where the devil did she think she was going? He glanced over his shoulder, aware that Bryant was still following him.

"What are we supposed to do while you're gone?" Edward asked belligerently.

"Pray," Chance replied succinctly, and swinging onto Smoke's back, he followed Rain's trail.

Winter Rain eased back on the reins, bringing her horse to a stop. She wasn't sure now what foolishness had sent her running away from the village. But early this morning, after a sleepless night, running away had seemed like the only thing to do.

With a sigh, she reined her horse around and started back down the hill. She wasn't a child any longer. She couldn't run away and hide. What had she hoped to gain other than postponing the inevitable?

She hadn't gone far when she heard a low growl that caused a sudden sinking sensation in the pit of her stomach. She didn't waste any time looking up, just sank her heels in her mount's flanks. The gelding bolted down the hill.

Winter Rain clung to the reins with one hand and her horse's mane with the other, praying the horse wouldn't fall, praying they would make it safely down the hill.

She screamed as she felt a powerful blow to her left shoulder followed by a sharp burning sensation, and then she was tumbling off her horse, rolling over and over, to come to an abrupt halt in a thick stand of brush.

Breathless, her whole body aching from the fall, she could only lie there, her heart pounding in her ears as she waited for the mountain lion to attack her. She pressed her hands over her ears as a horrible scream filled the air, and she knew that the lion had caught up with her horse.

She closed her eyes, the image of the mountain lion's claws tearing into her horse's flesh making her sick to her stomach. With a sob, she turned her head to the side and retched. How could she have been so foolish as to leave the village alone? Grown warriors had been killed by mountain lions. What chance would she have had against a wild animal that not only weighed more than she did, but was armed with teeth and claws? Again, she thought of her horse, no doubt dead by now.

She was suddenly aware of a growing pain in her left arm. Afraid of what she might see, she slowly turned her head. The left side of her tunic was in shreds. Bile rose in her throat once again when she saw the blood that stained her dress. It flowed from four deep gashes in her left shoulder.

Trembling convulsively, she scooped up several handfuls of dirt and spread them over the wound to stop the bleeding. As the shock wore off, the pain grew worse. Tears welled in her eyes. What would she do if the mountain lion came back?

She pressed herself deeper into the brush. In spite of the heat of the day, she was shivering uncontrollably now, overcome by the pain in her shoulder. The blood seeping down her arm frightened her as did the realization that she might easily die out here. Even more frightening was the thought of predators finding her while she was alive but helpless.

She had to get back to the village, had to start now, before she lost any more blood and grew any weaker.

Biting down on her lower lip to keep from crying out, she crawled out from under the brush and looked around. There was no sight of the mountain lion or her horse. Had the gelding managed to get away? And where was the mountain lion?

Bracing her hand against a tree trunk, she gained her feet and stood there taking deep breaths while she waited for the world to stop spinning.

Which way was the camp? She looked around in an effort to get her bearings, then headed north, one slow step at a time, her gaze constantly moving back and forth. Where was the mountain lion?

Why, oh why, had she ever run away?

# Chapter 20

Chance urged Smoke into a trot, his gaze riveted to the ground, silently thanking Wakan Tanka that Winter Rain's trail was clear and easy to follow. Time and again he asked himself where the devil she was headed. There was nothing up this way but trees and more trees until at long last you reached a rocky summit. The Paha Sapa was not the place for a woman alone, and she had lived with the Lakota long enough to know it. It was a wild land, dangerous and unforgiving. She could fall prey to so many dangers: white hunters, the Cavalry, warriors from enemy tribes. Aside from the two-legged predators, there were bears and mountain lions and any number of other wild creatures. Her horse could step in a hole and break a leg. She could break a leg.

Muttering an oath, Chance leaned forward in the saddle as Smoke began climbing higher still. Gradually the trees grew taller and closer together, so thick in some places they shut out the sun. Pine needles muffled the sound of his horse's hooves.

A short time later, with a sharp snort and a toss of her head, the mare came to an abrupt halt in a small clearing.

Chance clucked to the mare, but she refused to move. Instead, she stood quivering beneath him, her ears nervously flicking back and forth.

"Come on," he said, digging his heels into the

mare's flanks. "I don't have time for any of your nonsense."

The mare shook her head and took a step backward.

And then he saw it, a patch of churned-up earth. Dismounting, he held tight to the reins with one hand while he drew his Colt with the other.

Smoke snorted and tossed her head as he moved slowly forward.

Chance studied the bloodstained ground. It was easy to see what had happened. A mountain lion had brought down Winter Rain's horse, killed it, and then dragged the carcass into the underbrush. He knew the mountain lion would return to feed on the carcass for several days.

But where was Winter Rain? "Rain." Her name whispered past his lips, and then unable to suppress the rising note of panic from his voice, he called her name again, louder this time. "Rain!"

He studied the ground again more closely, but there was no sign of footprints. Keeping his gun at hand, he backtracked the horse's trail, climbing steadily upward, until he came to the place where the lion had launched itself at the horse. And there, barely discernable in the dirt, he saw where she had landed, rolled, and gained her feet. He saw a bit of blood, too. Hers, or the horse's? There was no way to tell.

"Rain! Dammit, where are you?"

He followed the signs, saw where she had crawled into a dense thicket, then crawled out again and started walking. She couldn't be that far ahead of him. He holstered his weapon, then swung into the saddle.

"Hang on, sweetheart," he murmured. "I'm coming."

She wasn't going to make it. In spite of the dirt she had spread over the wound in her shoulder, blood continued to drip down her arm. Her vision was blurred, her legs were weak, she felt light-headed and dizzy.

With a low groan, she sank down on the ground and closed her eyes. *Help me, Wakan Tanka. I am so afraid.*

Sitting there, she lost track of time. Bits and pieces of her childhood flashed through her mind as she drifted between sleep and awareness—the rag doll her father had given her the Christmas she was six, the pretty white lace pinafore her mother had bought for her to wear for her seventh birthday party, the day she had taken Snowflake over a jump for the first time, the way Heidi used to curl up on her pillow at night. But mostly she thought of Wolf Shadow—the sound of his voice whispering in her ear, the touch of his hand in her hair, the shivery way it made her feel when he looked at her. Because of her foolishness, she might never see him again. . . .

She pulled the knife from the sheath at the back of her belt as she heard a rustle in the brush farther down the slope. Had the mountain lion come back? The very thought made her mouth go dry.

With an effort, she gained her feet. Her legs were shaking. Her hand was shaking. *Help me, Wakan Tanka. . . .*

The rustling grew louder. Whatever was coming was big. She stared ahead, resigned to her fate. She was too weak to fight, too weak to run.

Her eyes widened as a big bay horse emerged from the brush. Relief washed through her. The knife fell from her hand. The strength drained from her legs. She whispered his name, and then she fainted.

Chance was off his horse before Smoke came to a stop. "Rain!" Running forward, he gathered her into his arms, his gaze moving over her face, the blood that trickled down her arm, the ragged tears in the left shoulder of her tunic. It took but one glance to know that the mountain lion's claws had grazed her arm when it attacked her horse.

"Rain?" He kissed her lightly on the forehead. "Sweetheart, can you hear me?"

Her eyelids fluttered open. "Wolf Shadow."

"I'm here." Putting one arm around her shoulder and the other under her knees, he stood up and carried her to where Smoke waited. Settling Rain on the horse's back, he uncorked his canteen. "Here, drink this."

She hadn't realized how thirsty she was. Now she drank greedily.

"Take it easy, sweetheart."

Reaching around behind her, he untied her sash and wrapped it around her shoulder to stop the bleeding.

"Hang on to the horn," he said, placing her hands on the pommel.

When he was certain she was steady, he picked up her knife, sheathed it, and stuck it in his belt. Vaulting up behind her, he slipped one arm around her waist.

"Just relax," he said. "We'll be home soon."

She leaned back, her head nestled beneath his chin.

"That's right, honey," he murmured. "I've got you."

How was he ever going to let her go?

Edward and Rosalia were outside when he rode up to Kills-Like-a-Hawk's lodge.

Rosalia shrieked when she saw the blood that stained her daughter's tunic. "Teressa! *Mi bambina!*"

Corn Woman ran toward Chance and Winter Rain, followed by several of the other women.

Edward's face paled as he put his arm around his wife's shoulders. "Is she . . . ?"

"She'll be fine," Chance said. "Someone go find my cousin, quick!"

"I will go," Corn Woman said.

Dropping the reins, Chance stepped from the sad-

dle, then lifted Rain from the back of his horse and
carried her into Kills-Like-a-Hawk's lodge.

Rosalia hurried in after him. She spread one of the
bedrolls, then stood aside while Chance placed Rain on
the blankets and smoothed a lock of hair from her brow.

"Teressa?"

Her eyelids fluttered, but didn't open.

"Let her be," Chance said. "She's lost some blood.
She needs rest and . . ." He glanced over his shoulder
as Kills-Like-a-Hawk entered the lodge, followed by
Edward Bryant. From outside, he could hear the
hushed voices of Corn Woman and Leaf and some of
the other women.

"We need to get her to a doctor," Bryant said
brusquely.

"Kills-Like-a-Hawk is a doctor."

Bryant looked skeptical. "A witch doctor?"

"He's a shaman, one of the best. I suggest you and
Mrs. Bryant stand back and let him get to work."

Edward glared at Chance. "Now, see here—"

*"Eduardo, prego, venuto via . . ."* Taking her husband's hand, Rosalia moved to one side of the lodge.

Squatting on his heels, Kills-Like-a-Hawk stirred the
coals until he had a small fire burning. He picked up
a buckskin bag painted with colorful symbols and
sprinkled the contents into the fire. There was a gentle
hiss, followed by a wisp of blue smoke. Then he
reached into a larger bag and pulled out a handful of
white sage, which he place in the fire. In moments,
the scent of sweet sage filled the air.

Kills-Like-a-Hawk passed his hands through the
smoke, chanting softly as he drew the smoke over
Winter Rain. Moving to her side, he carefully unwrapped the sash from her arm. He ran his fingers
lightly over the wound, chanting all the while.

Next, he filled a bowl with water and gently washed
the dirt from the wound. She stirred but didn't wake.

Still chanting softly, Kills-Like-a-Hawk spread a layer of thick yellow salve over the gashes in her arm and shoulder, then covered the area with a piece of soft cloth. When that was done, he passed his hands through the smoke again, drawing it over her.

"What is he doing?" Bryant asked impatiently. "Dammit, this is a waste of time."

"Back off, Bryant," Chance said curtly. "He's saved a hell of a lot more lives than you have."

Muttering under his breath, Edward took a step backward.

Kills-Like-a-Hawk sat back on his heels. "She is not bad hurt, Tahunsa. She has lost some blood. The scratches are deep and will leave scars. But she will heal."

"*Pilamaya,* Tahunsa."

"She should rest now," Kills-Like-a-Hawk said.

With a nod, Chance gained his feet.

"I would like to stay with her," Rosalia said. "Would you ask Mr. Hawk if it is all right?"

"Of course it is," Chance said.

Kills-Like-a-Hawk handed Rosalia a waterskin. "She will be thirsty when she wakes."

"Thank you."

"How soon will she be able to travel?" Edward asked.

"A few days," Kills-Like-a-Hawk replied. "If the wounds do not become infected."

"Infected!" Rosalia exclaimed softly. "Oh, my."

"Barbaric country," Edward said. "Heathen medicine. No hospitals. I don't know how these people have survived."

Chance took a deep, calming breath. "Mr. Bryant, why don't you go outside?"

"See here—"

"No, you see here. You're a guest here. Your money and your social position don't mean a damn thing. My cousin knows what he's doing. If you can't respect him, at least keep your opinions to yourself. You got that?''

Bryant's face flushed a deep red; then, without a word, he stomped out of the lodge.

"I am sorry," Rosalia said. "My Eduardo does not handle these things well." She shrugged apologetically. "He does not mean to be unkind. It is just that he worries so."

Chance nodded. "I think I understand."

*"Grazie, Signore McCloud."* She offered him a faint smile, then moved to her daughter's side. Murmuring her name, Rosalia took Teressa's hand in hers.

Chance watched the two of them for a few minutes and then ducked out of the lodge.

Damn, why had he ever gotten mixed up in this mess? The answer came quickly enough—he'd had a fifteen-thousand-dollar incentive, and once he got shed of the Bryants and their all-too-tempting daughter, it would be worth it.

Teressa . . . He needed to get shed of her, too, the sooner the better. She was too big a distraction, too big a temptation, and he didn't need either one in his life, not now.

Winter Rain moved through a sea of pain and confusion toward his voice. Blinking, she glanced at her surroundings. She quickly recognized Kills-Like-a-Hawk's lodge though she had no recollection of the journey back to the village. Her mother sat beside her, her head bowed, her eyes closed, her rosary clasped in her hands.

"Wolf Shadow?"

"Teressa!" Rosalia's eyes flew open.

"Mama."

"Eduardo! She is awake."

A moment later, Edward Bryant burst into the

lodge, a huge grin spreading over his face when he saw that she had regained consciousness.

"Tessa!" He knelt beside her. "How are you feeling, baby?"

"Better." Her head hurt, her arm hurt, but she was glad to be alive. "Where is Wolf Shadow?"

Edward snorted softly. "He's gone hunting."

"Oh." She tried to keep the disappointment from her voice but knew by the expression on her mother's face that she had failed.

"We were worried about you." Rosalia brushed a wisp of hair from Teressa's brow, then placed her hand on her forehead, taking her temperature in the way of all mothers, red and white. She looked up at her husband. "Her fever has gone down," she said, obviously surprised. "Perhaps Mr. Hawk is a better doctor than we thought."

"Kills-Like-a-Hawk is not a doctor," Winter Rain said, struggling to sit up. "He's a shaman . . . a medicine man."

"Yes," Edward said dryly, "we know. Even though I didn't approve of his methods, I have no argument with the results." He grinned at her. "We'll be homeward bound in no time at all."

"Yes," Winter Rain murmured. "Home."

Chance stalked the deer on foot. He held Kills-Like-a-Hawk's bow in one hand, carried his cousin's quiver slung over his shoulder. It felt good to be alone in the Hills, surrounded by towering pines and birdcalls.

He tread softly, careful of where he placed his feet. He could see the buck just ahead, moving slowly in the cover of the forest, pausing now and then to nibble at the tender shoots of the trees.

Chance moved forward. His grandfather Buffalo Shield had taught him how to hunt with the bow. Buffalo Shield had been a wise and patient man. He had taught his grandson how to track, how to find his way across the plains using the sun by day and the moon and stars by night. He had taught him how to find water. Buffalo Shield had been killed in a battle with the Crow while Chance was hunting the men who had killed his mother. Even though he knew it was illogical, he had always blamed his mother's killers for his grandfather's death, as well. If he had been with the People at the time, he would have been in the battle. Perhaps if he had been there his grandfather would not have been killed.

Caught up in the past, he neglected to watch where he stepped; a twig snapped beneath his foot. That quickly, the buck was gone.

Chance blew out a breath of annoyance as he watched the buck disappear from sight. He would have to concentrate on the hunt if he didn't want to go back to camp empty-handed. As it was, he'd probably have to settle for something other than a deer. But it didn't really matter. He had taken to the Hills to take his mind off Winter Rain, and that wasn't working, either.

With luck, she would be ready to travel in a day or two.

It was late when he returned to the village. He had given up the hunt late in the afternoon and spent the rest of the day hiking in the Hills. It was dusk when he returned to where he had left Smoke. He looked after the mare, then built a small fire and cooked the rabbit he had killed earlier in the day. Hunkered down on his heels, he had kept his mind carefully blank while he ate his solitary meal.

And now he stood outside his cousin's lodge wondering how Rain had spent her day. Was she feeling better? He knew she was in good hands, what with Kills-Like-a-Hawk and her parents there, but he had a sudden, overpowering urge to see her for himself, to make sure she was all right.

Dropping Smoke's reins, Chance drew back the lodge flap and stepped inside. Light from the dying fire cast faint shadows on the lodge skins. He spared hardly a glance for Edward and Rosalia, who were sleeping soundly on the left side of the lodge. On silent feet, he moved around the fire pit to the right side of the lodge.

"Where were you all day?" Winter Rain asked in a soft whisper.

"What are you doing still awake?"

"I could not sleep."

He hunkered down on his ankles beside her. "How are you feeling?"

"Why did you leave?"

He shrugged. "I went hunting."

"Why are you avoiding me? Have I done something to displease you?"

"Of course not."

"I thought . . . you and I . . ." She took his hand in hers and placed it over her heart. "I thought you felt something for me, in here."

"I did. I do, but . . ."

"My heart beats fast whenever you are near. I thought it was the same for you."

"Rain . . . Teressa, once you get back home, you'll be so busy getting reacquainted with your parents and meeting new friends, you'll forget all about me."

"No! I will never forget you," she said, and he heard a catch in her voice that might have been a sob. "Will you forget me?"

"You know I won't."

She lifted her free hand and traced his lips with her fingertips. "Will you not kiss me again?"

"I don't think that's a good idea."

"You do not want to?"

He glanced over his shoulder to where her parents slept. "This isn't the time," he said dryly. "Or the place." Gently, he disentangled his hand from hers and drew the blanket up to her chin. "Get some sleep now."

With a nod, she watched him rise and pad quietly out of the lodge.

Before her parents took her home, she would find a time and a place.

# Chapter 21

The next few days were strained. Winter Rain stayed in bed most of the time, recovering from her wounds and trying to think of some way to catch Wolf Shadow alone. Her mother and father hovered over her as if they feared she would vanish again. They tried not to let her know how worried they were, but she could see it in their eyes. Occasionally at night she overheard them whispering together when they thought she was asleep. They talked about returning to San Francisco, about redecorating her room, about hiring a private tutor, about a coming-out party. Most frightening of all, she heard them discussing possible husbands. She wasn't even home yet, she thought, and they were already planning to marry her off!

She saw very little of Wolf Shadow. He stopped by to check on her each day, his manner cool and aloof. He spoke politely to her mother, avoided her father if possible, and never stayed more than a few minutes.

Her eyes devoured him whenever he was in the lodge. She couldn't stop thinking of him, dreaming of him. The accidental brush of his hand against hers sent waves of heat flooding through her. The sound of his voice awoke a thousand butterflies in her stomach. She often asked him foolish questions just to hear him talk, just to keep him with her a few minutes longer.

Today was no different. "Will we take the filly with

us when we leave?" she asked as he moved toward the door.

Wolf Shadow shook his head. "She'll be happier here," he answered, and stepped out of the lodge.

Winter Rain stared after him. "So will I," she murmured, but there was no one to hear her.

Corn Woman, Yellow Fawn, and Leaf came to visit her each day, as did several of the other women, both old and young. Kills-Like-a-Hawk also came by. On the third day, he pronounced her well enough to get up.

Her mother was at her side when she left the lodge. It felt good to be outside. She went for a short walk, then mentioned she would like to bathe. Her mother wouldn't hear of her bathing in the river, so they returned to the lodge and Rosalia filled a paunch with water. When it was hot, Winter Rain washed with warm water for the first time in ten years. There was no tub, of course, but her mother kept the hot water coming. They even managed to wash Winter Rain's hair.

Later, when her father came in, he announced they were leaving for home the following morning.

With that in mind, Winter Rain went from lodge to lodge to bid her friends good-bye. She managed to keep a brave face until she went to visit Corn Woman, and then she dissolved into tears.

"Ah, child," was all Corn Woman said. And then she put her arm around Winter Rain's shoulders and held her until her sobs subsided.

"What am I to do?" Winter Rain asked. "I do not want to leave this place."

"You will always have a home here with the People," Corn Woman reminded her with a gentle smile. "Perhaps there is a reason why you must return to the land of the *wasichu*."

"What reason?"

"Only the Great Spirit could tell you that."

"I will not know anyone there."

"You did not know anyone here when first you came to us." Corn Woman smiled kindly. "But you soon had friends here. I think it will be the same among the *wasichu*."

Winter Rain sighed heavily. What Corn Woman said was true, but she was still afraid to leave all that was familiar behind.

"In time, the path will be made clear to you." Corn Woman removed the beaded amulet from around her neck and handed it to Winter Rain. "Take this, so that you will always have something to remind you of this place and the people who love you."

Winter Rain's hand closed around the amulet. *"Pilamaya, kola."* Slipping the thong over her head, Winter Rain left Corn Woman's lodge.

Not wanting anyone to know she had been crying, she walked out to the horse herd. The filly ran toward her, then slid to a stop only a few feet away. Shaking her head, the filly rose on her hind legs, forelegs pawing the air before she dropped down on all fours again. Trotting forward, she nuzzled Winter Rain's arm.

"I will miss you, too," Winter Rain said, stroking the filly's neck.

She gazed at the quiet river, the pine-studded hills, the vast blue sky, the camp in the wooded hollow. This part of her life would soon be behind her. Tomorrow they would leave for the land of the *wasichu*.

Wrapping her arms around the filly's neck, she closed her eyes and wept.

They left early the following morning. Chance led the way out of the village with a packhorse in tow. Winter Rain and her mother came next, and her father, leading another packhorse, brought up the rear.

Winter Rain fought the urge to cry as they left the

village behind and began the descent out of the Hills. She wrapped one hand around the amulet Corn Woman had given her, a reminder of all she had left behind and all that would be waiting here when she returned. For she would return. She couldn't imagine being happy anywhere else. She would go home with her parents, spend time with them. She owed them that much. But next summer she would find a way to return to the Lakota.

She kept her gaze on Wolf Shadow's back. He had been her strength in these past weeks. No matter what happened in the future, she would never forget him. And she intended to make sure he didn't forget her, either. That thought warmed her and kept her company throughout the morning.

They stopped at midday to eat and rest the horses. Winter Rain hoped to find a few minutes alone with Wolf Shadow, but he didn't stay with them. Instead, he went ahead on foot. "Scouting around," he said, but she knew he was avoiding her again.

They traveled all that day. He kept the pace slow to accommodate her parents. Her father rode in stoic silence, his whole attitude one of impatience. Her mother, more relaxed, watched the passing countryside.

"It is so beautiful," she remarked. "So . . . so big. I am amazed that Signore McCloud can find his way without getting lost."

At dusk they stopped to water the horses and fill their waterskins, then moved on to make camp in the lee of a rocky crag. Winter Rain gathered wood for the fire and cooked the rabbits Wolf Shadow had killed earlier. Her father paced restlessly. Her mother hovered nearby.

"Is there anything I can do to help, Teressa *mia*?"

"No, Mama." Winter Rain smiled at her mother.

"I feel so helpless out here," Rosalia remarked.

"Why is Papa so restless?"

"He has business at home that needs his attention."

Winter Rain frowned. She knew her father worked, but she could not recall now what he did. "What business?"

"He owns the largest bank in San Francisco," Rosalia replied, pride evident in her voice.

Winter Rain nodded. A bank. Of course. She remembered her papa had left the house every morning to go to work at the bank. He had taken her with him a few times. The first time he had given her five dollars and showed her how to open a savings account. At birthdays and Christmas, he had given her money to add to her account.

The meal was ready when Wolf Shadow returned. It was a quiet meal. Her father had never been given to small talk at the table and it had been left to Winter Rain and her mother to fill the silence. But Rosalia was intimidated by Wolf Shadow's presence, and Winter Rain couldn't think of anything to say.

They went to bed after dinner, all but Wolf Shadow. She could see him now, standing a few feet away, staring off into the distance. She wondered what he was thinking about. Was he anxious to be rid of her and her parents so he could get back to his own life? Where did he live when he wasn't with the Lakota? What did he do?

She fell asleep wondering about the man who had stolen her heart.

The days and nights blurred together as they made their way across the vast grassy plains until, at last, they reached the first of the small towns that signaled the beginning of civilization. They passed through several such towns that were no more than a wide spot in the road lined by a few ramshackle buildings. Wolf

Shadow bought whatever supplies were available at each town.

A week later, they reached Buffalo Springs. It was a large town, much larger than any of the others she had seen along the way. The buildings—she counted over thirty—looked substantial, as if the town intended to be there for a long time. The streets were crowded with men and women. At one end of town was a big corral filled with cattle. She saw a building she recognized as a church and one she guessed was the schoolhouse. She remembered going to school, being eager to learn to read and write.

Riding down the street, she looked at the signs, silently sounding out the words. *Shoe-ma-ker. Den-tist. Bar-ber-shop. Sad-dle Ma-ker. Red Ace Sa-loon. Lil's Café. Post Off-ice. Sher-iff's Off-ice and Jail. The Cattle-men's Club. Rose's Di-ner.*

So many stores. So many people. She stared at the women. They wore brightly colored dresses with full skirts and long sleeves. Most wore bonnets. Some wore gloves. The men wore leggings, trousers they were called, like the ones Wolf Shadow wore and colorful shirts and big hats. And they all wore guns. Men and women alike turned to stare at her, and she bowed her head, suddenly self-conscious of her Lakota tunic and moccasins, which were covered with a fine coating of trail dust.

Wolf Shadow pulled up in front of a large building with big double doors and dark green shutters on the windows. The sign overhead read *Wind-sor Ho-tel.*

Wolf Shadow dismounted. He hesitated a moment, then moved to her side. Placing his hands on her waist, he lifted her from the saddle. As soon as her feet touched the ground, he turned to face her father.

"It's been nice doing business with you, Mr. Bryant."

The two men shook hands, then Wolf Shadow took up the reins of all four horses. He glanced briefly at Rosalia, and then his gaze rested on Winter Rain.

She looked back at him. Their time together was almost over, she thought desperately. There were a dozen questions she wanted to ask him, a dozen things she wanted to say, but not with her parents standing there, listening.

"Have a good trip home," he said quietly, and then he turned and headed down the street.

"All right, ladies," her father said briskly. "I'm going to the stage depot to see when the next coach leaves for Crooked River. Rosalia, have them send some hot water up to our rooms right away."

*"Si, Eduardo."*

Taking Winter Rain by the hand, Rosalia stepped up on the boardwalk and led the way into the hotel.

Winter Rain's gaze darted around the room. She remembered being in hotels before, most of them grander than this one, although this one was very nice. There were sofas and chairs covered in dark green velvet. Tables held pretty lamps with fringed shades. A large crystal chandelier hung from a thick gold chain.

She followed her mother across a patterned carpet to where a clerk stood behind a large desk. He smiled at her mother. "Mrs. Bryant. It's good to see you again," he said, and then paused, his gaze moving over Winter Rain. "I'm afraid we don't allow—"

"This is my daughter, Teressa," Rosalia interjected with a tight smile. "She will be staying with us."

"Yes, ma'am. Of course."

"We will need two rooms, adjoining. And please send up some hot water. We have had a difficult journey."

"Yes, ma'am. Right away, ma'am." Turning, the clerk plucked two keys off a board and handed them to her mother. "Rooms eight and ten."

"We left our luggage here during our last visit. Could you please have it sent up as soon as possible?"

"Right away, Mrs. Bryant."

"Thank you. Come, Tessa."

Feeling horribly out of place, Teressa followed her mother up a wide winding staircase, then down a well-lit corridor. Rosalia stopped in front of a door with a gold number eight on it. Turning the knob, she opened the door and stepped into the room.

It was a large corner room papered in pink cabbage roses. White curtains hung at the windows. There was a double bed topped by a white spread. A small chest of drawers, a comfortable-looking chair, a mirror on the wall. Peeking behind a flowered screen, she saw a bathtub.

Rosalia crossed the floor and opened the door that led into the next room.

Teressa trailed in her mother's wake.

Room number ten was a little larger than number eight. The same paper graced the walls.

"Your father and I will take this room," Rosalia said. "As soon as we get cleaned up, we'll go shopping. Would you like that?"

"Yes, Mama," Teressa replied.

Just then, the door opened and her father entered the room. "Unbelievable!" he muttered. "Simply unbelievable!"

"Eduardo, what is the matter?"

"It seems we just missed the stage going west."

"But there is another, is there not?"

He snorted. "Yes, of course, but the man at the stage office wasn't sure when it would arrive. He said there was some kind of trouble on the trail. A bridge is down or the trail washed away or something like that, and the stage has been delayed."

"For how long?"

"Possibily a week. Possibly as long as three weeks. Three weeks, can you believe that?"

"Perhaps it will not take that long."

"And what if it does?" He slammed his fist down on the top of the dresser. "Three weeks, Rosalia! What are we supposed to do here if it takes three weeks?"

Rosalia placed her hand on her husband's arm. "Calm down, Eduardo."

"I am calm!" He began to pace the floor, the color in his cheeks rising. "Three weeks!" He reached into his pocket and withdrew a sheet of yellow paper, which he waved in the air. "This arrived yesterday. It seems Cliff Vanderhyde is trying to weasel his way into a position on the Board of Directors at the bank. You know how I feel about that man! It is imperative that I get back there as soon as possible and put a stop to it. I can't wait three weeks!"

A knock at the door put an end to his tirade.

"That will be the boys with the water," Rosalia said.

Going to the door, she opened it to admit four boys each carrying two buckets of steaming water. She stepped back so they could enter the room, then asked one of the boys to fill the pitcher on the chest of drawers.

"So you can shave, Eduardo," she explained.

A moment later, two other boys entered the room carrying several large suitcases.

"Just put them on the bed, please," Rosalia directed.

Edward tipped each of the boys as they left the room. Rosalia stopped the last one. "The tub in room number eight needs to be filled as well."

"Yes, ma'am," he said politely. " Right away."

Teressa sat submerged as much as possible in the tub behind the screen. The warm water felt wonderful. The soap her mother had given her to bathe with smelled of lilacs.

Sitting there, her thoughts turned toward Wolf Shadow. Would she see him again? She couldn't believe he would ride out of her life without a word.

She stayed in the tub until the water grew cool. After drying with a towel, she pulled on her tunic and moccasins, then knocked on the door that adjoined her room with that of her parents.

Rosalia smiled as she opened the door. "Are you ready?"

"Yes, Mama."

"Eduardo, we will not be long."

He looked up from the paper he was reading. "Buy whatever you need."

Rosalia kissed him on the cheek. *"Grazie."*

Upon leaving the hotel, Rosalia stood on the boardwalk, looking up and down the street. "There," she said, and taking Teressa by the hand, she led her across the street and into Krause's Dry Goods Store.

Inside, Rosalia quickly picked out a modest ready-made dress of green-sprigged muslin, a cotton chemise and ruffled petticoat, and a pair of drawers. They also bought a pair of gloves, a straw hat that tied in a big bow under her chin, and several ribbons and a pair of pretty tortoiseshell combs for her hair.

From there, they went to Robison's Mercantile where Teressa picked out a comb and a hairbrush and a small reticule. Mama handed her several dollars, assuring her that a lady should always have a bit of money handy.

Their next stop was Clinger's Bootery where Teressa picked out a pair of soft leather half boots that weren't nearly as comfortable as her old moccasins.

Leaving the shoe shop, they returned to the hotel so Teressa could change.

Now, almost an hour later, she stared at herself in the mirror, thinking how very different she looked. Her mother had brushed her hair, then arranged it in a knot at her nape. With her hair done, and wearing her new clothes, Teressa hardly recognized the image in the mirror.

Where had Winter Rain gone? What would Wolf Shadow think if he could see her now?

*"Bella,"* Rosalia said, smiling. "When we get home, we will get you a whole new wardrobe."

Home. Teressa let out a sigh. Would this new world ever feel like home again?

"Come, Tessa. I saw a dressmaker's shop. Let us see what the seamstress in this Western town has to offer."

"But I have a dress."

Rosalia made a dismissive gesture with her hand. "One dress bought off the rack is not enough to last you until we get home. Come."

They walked down the street until they came to a store with a small sign in the window which read *Dressmaker. Mrs. Agnes Constantine, Proprietor and Seamstress.*

A tiny woman clad in a bright yellow dress greeted them with a smile almost as bright as her frock. "Welcome to my shop," she said. "I am Agnes Constantine. How may I help you, Mrs. . . ?"

"Bryant," Rosalia said, "and this is my daughter, Teressa. She has need of your services. We will need three dresses for every day, and one for evening, as well as petticoats and undergarments."

Agnes Constantine looked Teressa over with a knowing eye. "I have some patterns I think will suit." Turning, she moved toward a door in the back wall. "Come along, dear."

"Mama?"

"I will wait here while she measures you."

With a sigh, Teressa followed the seamstress into another room where the woman measured her from top to bottom.

"There," she said, dropping her tape measure into her pocket, "I think that does it."

Mrs. Constantine called Rosalia and the three of them went into another room where they spent an hour looking at patterns and fabric swatches.

Teressa was overwhelmed by the number of patterns and colors. There had been little variety in her clothing while living with the Indians. Most everything had been made of doeskin. Now, she would have full skirts made of colorful cotton and velvet and shirt-waists in all the colors of the rainbow and dresses with puffy sleeves edged in delicate lace. Once again, she wondered what Chance would think when he saw her in her new finery.

"How long will it take you to make up the dresses?" Rosalia asked.

"I can have one ready by tonight. The others will be ready day after tomorrow."

"*Grazie.* Come, Teressa."

Leaving the shop, they walked down the boardwalk to the hotel. Saddled horses were tied to hitching rails along the street. A wagon rumbled past, churning up a layer of thick yellow dust. A woman carrying a baby in one arm and holding a little girl by the hand smiled at Teressa as she passed by. From somewhere farther down the street came a sound that was vaguely familiar. It was a piano, she thought. Once, long ago, she had taken lessons.

When they returned to the hotel, Mama said it was time for supper. Feeling ill at ease in the presence of so many strangers, Teressa followed her mother into the hotel dining room. Teressa looked at the menu, but the words meant nothing to her and she let her mother order for her.

With her hands folded in her lap, she gazed around the room. Her lassitude vanished when she saw Wolf

Shadow sitting alone at a table near the window in the back.

Without thinking, she pushed away from the table and hurried toward him.

He looked up, his brows lifting in surprise. "Teressa, how pretty you look."

"Thank you." His compliment warmed her.

Rising, he pulled a chair out for her. "Sit down."

She did so, pleased and relieved that he had made her welcome. "I was afraid you would go away and I wouldn't see you again."

"I wouldn't have left town without telling you good-bye."

"You are leaving, then?"

"Tomorrow morning. I've been away long enough."

"Where will you go?"

"To my ranch."

"Is it close by?"

"About a day's ride to the west by wagon."

"I should like to see it sometime."

"Teressa, what are you doing?"

She looked up to find her father standing at her elbow, his face as dark as the storm clouds that gathered over the Black Hills in the winter. "Nothing, Papa, I was . . ."

"Come, Teressa, it is unseemly for you to sit at a table alone with a man."

"Yes, Papa." With an embarrassed glance at Wolf Shadow, Winter Rain followed her father back to the table where her mother waited.

Edward glanced over his shoulder to make sure Teressa was following him. When they reached their table, he held Teressa's chair for her, then sat down across from his wife.

"Rosalia, I have found a man who is going to Crooked River. He says we can go with him."

"Why would we want to go to Crooked River?" she asked.

"He says if we ride hard, we can get there in time to catch the train to San Francisco."

"Eduardo, I do not ever wish to sit on a horse again. Teressa and I will stay here and wait for the stage. You go on."

"Leave you here? Alone? The two of you . . ."

"We will be all right."

He shook his head. "No, I won't hear of it." He frowned a moment, then rose without a word and made his way back to Chance's table.

Chance sat back in his chair, his arms folded over his chest as he watched Teressa's father stride toward him. He grunted softly, wondering what the hell the man wanted now.

Without waiting for an invitation, Edward Bryant sat down. "I find I have need of your assistance once again."

"Is that right?"

"Yes. I have urgent business to attend to in San Francisco and I cannot wait here for the next stage. Mrs. Bryant does not wish to make the journey with me. I would like you to chaperone my family until the next stage arrives."

"I can't stay in town and look after your women," Chance said. "I've got a ranch to run and I've been away too long already."

Bryant reached into his coat pocket and withdrew his wallet. "How much do you want?"

"I don't need your money this time."

Bryant frowned thoughtfully. "Would you consider taking them to your ranch? I'll make it worth your while. You can name your own price."

Chance shook his head, yet even as he declined he was imagining Teressa at the ranch. He realized he

wanted her to show it to her even though he knew
her absence would haunt him long after she was gone.

"I don't have time to haggle, Mr. McCloud," Bryant
said imperiously.

"And I don't want your money," Chance retorted.
He held up a hand, silencing any further arguments
from Bryant. "I'll take Mrs. Bryant and Winter—Teressa out to my ranch. They can stay there until the
stage arrives."

Bryant considered the offer for a moment and
then nodded.

"I'll be leaving first thing in the morning. Tell them
to be ready."

"Yes, I will. And . . . thank you."

Chance nodded, knowing the man's thanks didn't
come easy.

He watched Bryant walk back to where Teressa and
Rosalia waited, then dropped a dollar on the table
and left the restaurant, wondering what the hell he'd
gotten himself into now.

# Chapter 22

Teressa couldn't stop smiling as she packed her few belongings, carefully folding her new dress. Wolf Shadow—she had to remember to call him Mr. McCloud now—was waiting for them downstairs. She and her mother were going to stay at the ranch until the next coach arrived.

Mr. McCloud was waiting in the lobby. Standing at the top of the stairs, her gaze swept over him. He wore a dark gray shirt, black trousers, and boots, all of which looked new. A black cowboy hat was pushed back on his head. A gun butt protruded from the holster strapped to his right thigh.

Clutching her bag in one hand, she hurried down the stairs, almost tripping on the hem of her skirt, which she had forgotten to lift out of the way.

He held out a steadying hand when she reached the bottom stair. "Careful, now."

Breathless, she gazed into his eyes, searching for some sign that he still cared, that she hadn't imagined the attraction between them.

She murmured, "Thank you, Mr. McCloud," as her mother joined them.

"Teressa, you must be more careful," Rosalia admonished. "Young ladies do not run down stairs."

"Yes, Mama."

Wolf Shadow squeezed her hand. "Are you two ready to go? I've got a buggy out front."

"Yes, thank you, Signore McCloud. Come, Tessa."

"What about the dresses we were supposed to pick up today?" Teressa asked as they left the hotel.

"I sent a message to Signora Constantine and asked her to send the dresses to Signore McCloud's ranch when they are ready."

A horse and buggy was tied up in front of the hotel. Teressa noticed that Wolf Shadow's horse was tied to the back of the conveyance. He stowed their bags under the seat, then handed them into the buggy.

He climbed in and released the brake. The seat was not very wide, and when he took up the reins, his shoulder brushed against hers. That slight contact sent a shiver of awareness through Teressa and made her acutely conscious of his nearness, and of his thigh pressed intimately against her own. She did not miss the look of disapproval on her mother's face, but she didn't care. She was sitting beside Wolf Shadow, her body bumping his with the buggy's every movement. She smiled inwardly, knowing he had lifted her into the buggy first just so they could sit side by side.

Several people turned to stare as they drove out of town.

"How far is it to your ranch, Signore McCloud?" Rosalia asked.

"About fifteen miles. We should be there before dark."

With a nod, Rosalia sat back, her hands folded in her lap.

"Are there many people there?" Teressa asked.

Chance shrugged. "Not many. I had a dozen cowhands and a cook working for me when I left."

Rosalia leaned forward so she could see his face. "Are there no women there?"

"Not the last time I looked."

"But . . . who looks after your house?"

"I do, when I'm there."

"You do your own laundry?"

"No. Cookie generally does it."

"Who is Cookie?" Teressa asked.

"The ranch cook. He cooks for the cowboys, and I usually eat with them." Chance looked at Rosalia. "I know you're used to having people around to wait on you, but while you're here, you'll be on your own most of the time and that will most likely include doing some of your own cooking. You can cook, can't you?"

"Yes, of course," Rosalia said without much enthusiasm. "Perhaps we should have stayed at the hotel."

Chance pulled back on the reins, bringing the horse to a halt. "I can take you back, if that's what you want."

"No, Mama!" Teressa exclaimed. "I want to see Mr. McCloud's ranch."

Rosalia regarded her for a long moment before she nodded. "Very well, Tessa."

Chance clucked to the horse, and the buggy lurched forward.

It was a long, silent ride. Chance wasn't given much to small talk and neither, apparently, were the two women. He was increasingly aware of Teressa's thigh pressed against his own. When the carriage hit a rut in the road, her breast bumped his arm. If he'd been smart, he would have put the mother in the middle but no one had ever accused him of being smart. Teressa. Her scent tickled his nostrils in spite of the dust stirred by the buggy's wheels. She was watching him. He could feel her gaze on his face, knew she was confused and hurt by his cool demeanor. He didn't want to hurt her, but it was best for both of them if he backed off now, while he still could, before things got out of hand.

At noon, he stopped the buggy and helped the

women alight. The cook at the hotel had packed them
a lunch. Chance had tossed a blanket under the seat.
He drew it out now and spread it out on a flat stretch
of ground. With all the grace of a queen, Rosalia sat
down and spread her skirts around her.

Teressa, less accustomed to high heels and full
skirts, lowered herself awkwardly onto the blanket.

Rosalia lifted the basket's lid. She handed each of
them a napkin, spread her own over her skirt. Teressa
did the same. The cook had packed enough food for
half a dozen people, along with plates, glasses, flatware, and a bottle of wine. Rosalia dished up fried
chicken, potato salad, sliced roast beef, and corn muf-
fins. Lastly, she withdrew a whole apple pie for dessert. She filled Chance's wineglass and, after a
moment, poured a small amount into Teressa's glass,
as well.

Chance sat cross-legged beside Teressa, careful to
remember his Sunday manners.

Teressa bit into a chicken leg. "Oh, this is very
good," she exclaimed. "What is it?"

"Fried chicken," Rosalia replied. "You must not eat
with your fingers, Tessa. It is not ladylike."

A flush climbed up her neck and flooded her
cheeks.

"The Lakota don't have forks, Mrs. Bryant,"
Chance said quietly. "They eat most of their food with
their fingers, or a knife."

"Yes, of course," ·Rosalia replied coolly. "But we
are not with the Lakota now. Teressa has much to
relearn. Much to remember."

The rest of the meal passed in almost total silence,
broken only when Rosalia asked if Chance would like
more wine. He declined, saying he had to look after
the horses.

Teressa stared after him as he led the horses toward
a water hole.

"Would you like a piece of pie?" Rosalia asked.

Teressa shook her head, her cheeks still burning from being corrected like a child in front of Chance.

"We would have been more comfortable in the hotel," Rosalia mused aloud. "I fear the conditions at Mr. McCloud's ranch are primitive."

Teressa turned and met her mother's gaze. "Primitive, Mama? More primitive than living with the Lakota?"

"I did not mean that, Tessa. Only that at the hotel we would not have to cook or clean up."

"I am not afraid of hard work."

Rosalia blew out a rather unladylike sigh of exasperation. "Tessa, I know you have lived under difficult conditions in the past. I, myself, did not come from a wealthy home, but it has been years since I have had to do menial tasks. It has been many years since I have had to cook or clean or do my own laundry. I am not sure I remember how; nor do I wish to. At home, your father and I have servants to do those things."

The discussion came to an end when Chance said it was time to go. Teressa felt a tingle of awareness as he lifted her onto the seat. He assisted her mother, then climbed up beside Teressa. Once again, she was aware of his nearness, of the solid muscle of his thigh pressed against her own as he leaned forward and took up the reins.

Teressa found herself thinking about her conversation with her mother as the wagon lurched forward. Rosalia was used to having servants to wait on her.

Teressa frowned. After being Blackbird-in-the-Morning's slave, she didn't think she wanted anything to do with servants, even though the ones at home had been well treated, with gifts at Christmas and time off on their birthdays.

*     *     *

She woke with a start to find her head pillowed on Chance's shoulder and Chance looking down at her. "Wake up, sleepyhead," he said, smiling. "We're here."

Teressa blinked up at him, momentarily disoriented. "Here?"

"My ranch."

"Oh!" Excitement swept the cobwebs from her mind and she sat up. The first thing she saw was the house. It was large and square and two stories high, with a verandah on the main floor that ran all the way around the house. Two rockers were situated on one side of the front door. The house was white, but the paint had faded to a dull gray. Several large trees grew on either side of the house, to the left was a large red-and-white barn, as well as a couple of peeled-pole corrals. One held several young calves, the other held a horse that paced restlessly from one end of the enclosure to the other. A long low building rose to the right of the house. Another corral held a half-dozen horses.

Low hills rose to the west. She could see cattle grazing in the distance. A large gray cat was stretched out on the verandah railing watching a hen cluck to a handful of yellow chicks. A pair of dogs crawled out from under the front steps and came forward, tongues lolling and tails wagging.

Chance climbed down from the buggy and came around to assist Rosalia to the ground. She settled her hat on her head, then shook the dust from her skirt while Chance helped Teressa out of the buggy.

"I could have climbed out by myself," she remarked, smoothing her skirt.

He smiled down at her. "I know." But then he would have had no excuse to put his hands on her, to span her tiny waist, to feel her breasts brush his chest as he lowered her feet to the ground.

She looked up at him, as if trying to read his mind, only to have her thoughts interrupted by her mother.

"Mr. McCloud?"

"Yes, Mrs. Bryant?"

"Would it be possible for us to wash up?"

"Of course." He tossed the reins over the hitch rail in front of the house. Reaching under the seats of the buggy, he lifted their valises and started up the steps.

"Come along, Tessa," Rosalia said. "Let us go and see what we've gotten ourselves into."

Teressa tried to take in everything at once as they entered the house. There was a small entryway; several brass hooks were on the wall to the left, and there was a hat rack in the corner beside the door.

The parlor was large and rectangular. The floor was of polished wood; a buffalo robe was spread in front of an enormous stone fireplace. There was a gun rack over the mantel. The furniture was large and dark and comfortable looking.

They walked down a narrow hallway to a set of stairs. A peek through the doorway on the left showed a kitchen.

She followed her mother and Chance up the stairs. Chance paused on the landing. "Do you want separate rooms?"

Teressa nodded; Rosalia said no.

"Well," Chance asked, looking from one woman to the other, "what's it to be?"

"I would like my own room, Mama. I have not had a room or a bed of my own in a very long time."

Rosalia regarded her daughter for a moment, then nodded. "Very well."

Chance opened the door to his left and stepped inside. "Mrs. Bryant, I trust you'll be comfortable here," he said, dropping her valise on the foot of the bed. "This was my father's room. Please, make yourself at home."

*"Grazie, Signore."*

"Teressa's room is next door," Chance said.

He left the room, smiling wryly as both women followed him. Apparently Mrs. Bryant didn't intend for her daughter to be alone with him if she had anything to do with it.

Teressa glanced around. This room was smaller than the previous one. A brass bed with a colorful quilt was located next to a large window. An oval mirror hung over a chest of drawers that looked as if it had been well used. There were a couple of rag rugs on the floor; a dream catcher hung on one wall alongside a feathered Lakota lance. She knew immediately that this was his room. He confirmed it a moment later when he opened the armoire and pulled out a pair of trousers, a shirt, and a pair of moccasins.

"I'll get Cookie to heat some water for the two of you," Chance said. "We've missed supper, but I reckon he'll throw something together for us. Come down when you're ready. The tub's in the last room at the end of the hall. There's clean towels and soap in the cupboard."

"Where are you going to sleep?" Teressa asked.

"Don't worry about me. I'll bed down on the sofa."

Rosalia followed him into the hall. She closed Teressa's door firmly, stood there like a mama grizzly guarding her cub.

Stifling the urge to grin, he walked toward the staircase. He could feel her gaze burning into his back and he couldn't help wondering if she intended to stand guard outside her daughter's door every night until the stage arrived.

Teressa walked slowly around the room, her hand moving over the quilt on the bed, the top of the chest of drawers. Knowing she had no business doing so, she opened the top drawer and peered inside. Kerchiefs, socks and hankies were thrown together, along with a pair of buckskin gloves and a single spur.

Her curiosity piqued, she opened the second drawer and found several pairs of long underwear, more socks, and the other spur.

The third drawer held a small rectangular box. Chewing on her lower lip, she lifted it from the drawer, placed it on top of the chest, and lifted the lid. Inside she found a man's gold pocket watch, a pair of wedding rings, a lady's handkerchief embroidered with pink and yellow flowers, a string of pearls, and a small tintype of a man and a woman on their wedding day. His parents?

Feeling suddenly guilty for prying, she closed the lid, replaced the box in the chest, and closed the drawer.

Moving to the bed, she unpacked her valise. She shook the wrinkles from her new dress, then looked around for a place to hang it. There was a small armoire in one corner. Opening the door, she saw several pairs of trousers, all dark colors, on hangers. A shelf held perhaps a dozen shirts, all neatly folded. The shelf above the shirts held a tan Stetson with a wide leather band. Three pairs of boots were on the bottom of the cabinet, along with a couple pairs of moccasins.

Finding an empty hanger, she hung her dress alongside his trousers, liking the way it looked there, as if they belonged together. The thought made her smile.

She moved the items from the top drawer to the second, her fingers lingering over each item. On impulse, she pressed a kerchief to her nose and took a deep breath, but all she smelled were soap and sunshine. When the drawer was empty, she placed her belongings in there, pleased, somehow, that her garments were now occupying a space where his had been.

Smiling, she closed the drawer, then twirled around the room. She had never felt like this before, giddy and excited and afraid all at once. With luck they would be here for almost a moon. Surely in that time she would find a way to get him alone.

Chance stood in the middle of the parlor, all too aware that for the first time in years he wasn't alone in the house. There would be someone sitting across from him at the dinner table and it wouldn't be Cookie or any of the ranch hands. Teressa. Beautiful, innocent Teressa with her beguiling smile and dark, trusting eyes. He had known from the moment he first set eyes on her that she would be his sooner or later. Why was he fighting it? He wanted her. She wanted him. He was here. She was here.

And her mother was here.

Remembering how Rosalia had stood outside Teressa's door, he had to grin. Men and women had been sneaking out from under watchful eyes for centuries. One frail woman wouldn't be a problem. Not when he felt his insides go up in flames every time Teressa's gaze met his. Not when the slightest touch of her hand had him in an agony of wanting. He had resisted what he wanted long enough.

Soon, perhaps tonight, she would be his.

The sun had set by the time Rosalia and Teressa bathed and dressed and made their way downstairs. They found Chance sitting at the kitchen table drinking a cup of coffee. A moment passed and then, as if remembering his manners, he gained his feet and held a chair for Rosalia.

"Would you like some coffee?"

*"Grazie."*

"Teressa?"

She shook her head. "I . . . I have never had any."

She sat down in the chair he held for her, shivered as his fingertips brushed her shoulder.

His gaze settled on her face, lingered on her lips. "Maybe it's time to try something new."

Her mouth went suddenly dry. She nodded, certain she wouldn't be able to speak.

She watched him pull a cup from the cupboard. His hands were large and capable, the fingers long and strong. He took a blue speckled coffeepot from the stove and filled the cup. After adding a spoonful of sugar and a hefty amount of cream, he offered it to her. His fingertips brushed against hers as she took the cup, and she shivered again, every nerve ending screaming for more.

He sat down at the table in the chair beside hers. She almost jumped when the toe of his moccasin slipped under her skirt to softly rub her calf.

"Dinner will be ready shortly." His voice was as calm as a summer day.

"*Grazie*. I find I am quite famished."

Chance smiled. "Well, it's just steak and eggs. It's filling but not fancy."

How could he behave so casually when his touch had her heart pounding like that of a stampeding buffalo?

A short time later a wizened old man with wispy white hair and bright blue eyes entered the kitchen. He placed the tray he was carrying on the table, plucked the cloth cover off, and jammed it in his pants pocket.

"Thanks, Cookie," Chance said.

The man grunted softly. "You gonna be taking your meals in here now?"

"For the next few weeks."

"Three meals?"

"That's right, Cookie. Think you can handle it?"

The old man glanced at the two women. Rosalia

returned his gaze without blinking an eye; Teressa smiled at him.

To Chance's astonishment, Cookie smiled back.

"That will not be necessary," Rosalia said.

Chance frowned at her. "Excuse me?"

"I will prepare our meals and look after the house."

Chance stared at her, thinking he wouldn't have been more surprised if she had declared she was going to share his bed.

Rosalia shrugged. "I will need something to occupy my time."

"Well, great."

"I will need some supplies from town."

Chance nodded. "Write out a list. I'll send one of the hands to pick it up." He looked at Cookie and shrugged. "I guess you're off the hook."

"Fine by me," Cookie muttered. He winked at Teressa, then shuffled out the back door.

"Well, dig in before it gets cold," Chance said.

The meal passed in relative silence. When it was over, Chance stood up. "I need to go out and check on a few things," he said. "You two make yourselves at home here. There's some books in the den if you're of a mind to read. If you go outside, stay close to the house."

"Can I go with you?" Teressa asked.

"I do not think that is a good idea, Tessa," Rosalia said.

"Why not, Mama? I want to see the ranch."

"Perhaps another day."

"There is nothing for me to do here," Teressa argued. "I want to go with Mr. McCloud."

"I said no, Tessa. And there will be plenty for you to do."

"Maybe another time," Chance said.

"We shall see," Rosalia replied.

Chance nodded. It would be a cold day in hell before Rosalia agreed to let Teressa be alone with him.

Grabbing his hat off the hook beside the back door, he left the house.

It was good to be back, he mused as he walked toward the barn. Opening one of the big double doors, he stepped inside, pleased to see that the men had taken care of patching the hole in the roof.

He spent a few minutes scratching Smoke's ears; then, moving toward the back of the barn, he slipped a bridle over the head of one of his favorite stock horses and led the animal out of the stall. He smoothed a blanket over the gelding's back, cinched a saddle in place, and led the horse outside.

"Hey, boss!"

Chance turned to see Roy DeYoung ambling toward him. Old Roy had been on the payroll as long as Chance could remember. Roy didn't spend many hours in the saddle anymore, but he was still a good hand.

"Howdy, Roy. Everything okay?"

"Sure, sure, never better. That bull you wanted arrived a couple days ago. We put him out in the north pasture, like you wanted."

"Obliged."

"Dave says we'll have a cash crop of calves come spring," DeYoung said, grinning. "That bull's been working overtime."

"He'd better be, for what I paid for him. Where is Dreesen?"

"Out on the south range."

"Tell him I want to see him when he comes in."

"Right. Oh, I almost forgot, Gideon's laid up. Busted his ankle day before yesterday."

"How the hell did he do that?"

"He was showing off. You know how he is. Thought

he could top that rank bronc. I told him not to try it,
but you know Gideon. He wouldn't listen."

Chance grunted. "We should probably just turn that
stud back out on the range before he kills someone."

DeYoung nodded. "Mebbe so."

"But not until I give it another try."

With a tsking sound, DeYoung headed for the
bunkhouse muttering, "Young'uns. Always gotta learn
the hard way."

With a grin, Chance swung into the saddle and
headed out to the north range to get a look at his
new bull.

Riding away, he realized that for the first time since
his father passed away, there would be someone waiting for him when he got home.

# Chapter 23

Teressa tiptoed out of the parlor and carefully opened the front door. She paused on the veranda, grateful to be outside, grateful to be out from under her mother's probing gaze. Grabbing a minute here and there, she had managed to explore the other ranch buildings. The bunkhouse where the cowboys lived was long and low. Bunks lined both walls. There were hooks on the walls to hold jackets or hats. Each man had a trunk at the end of his bed. The one thing that stood out in her mind was the atrocious smell that had assaulted her nostrils when she peeked inside. It seemed to be a combination of sweaty men, cow manure, tobacco, smelly boots, and smoke from the lamps that hung from the ceiling. She had seen several decks of playing cards, a couple of well-read dime novels. A worn Bible. A breezeway connected the bunkhouse to the cookhouse. Saddles, bridles, and ropes hung from pegs along the breezeway.

They had been at the ranch for a little over a week now and she loved it. Too often, she found herself pretending she lived here and that Chance was her husband.

To Teressa's astonishment, her mother had quickly taken over the running of the house. To her dismay, Rosalia had insisted that Teressa pitch in and help. After all, her mother explained, it was good for a woman, even a wealthy young woman, to know how to cook and clean and run a household. How else was one to know if one's servants were doing things correctly?

Tessa had to admit that once she got the hang of it, cooking on the white man's stove was easier than cooking over an open fire, and while she didn't particularly care for cooking, she loved baking. Mama had taught her to bake fluffy rolls, carrot cake, and apple pie. To Tessa's delight, Chance had praised her efforts, declaring he had never tasted anything better.

But she didn't want to bake now. Mama had fallen asleep over a bit of mending and Teressa escaped out the front door, eager to explore the outside.

Descending the steps, she walked toward the nearest corrals. The calves were cute, but it was the horse that drew her attention. It was big and black with one white stocking on its left foreleg. The stallion stopped its restless pacing as she approached. Ears back, it watched her suspiciously.

Teressa held out her hand. "Hello, handsome one."

At the sound of her voice, the stallion snorted and backed away.

"Are you afraid of me?" she asked.

The stallion shook its head.

"Good. Come here." Stepping up on the bottom rail, she held out her hand again. "I will not hurt you."

Snuffling softly, the stallion took a tentative step forward.

"Come on," she coaxed softly. "Come to me."

The stallion took another step forward, and then another, and then he was close enough to touch. Moving slowly so as not to spook him, she lifted her hand and stroked his neck. The stallion quivered at her touch, but didn't run away. Instead, he lowered his head, as if asking her to scratch between his ears. Laughing softly, she did so.

Riding into the yard, Chance swore under his breath

when he saw Teressa petting the stallion. Was she out of her mind? That horse was wild. Yet even as he watched, Teressa was stroking the stud's neck, scratching its ears. Unbelievable.

Dismounting near the house, he threw Smoke's reins over the hitch rail, then walked slowly toward the corral. As soon as he drew near, the stallion tossed its head and pranced to the far side of the corral.

Teressa glanced over her shoulder to see what had spooked the stallion and smiled when she saw Wolf Shadow walking toward her.

"Sorry," he said. Moving up beside Teressa, he draped his arms over the top rail. "You're the first one he's let get close."

"He is beautiful."

"Yeah. But he's a bad one."

"He does not seem bad to me."

"Honey, you could sweet talk a snake out of its skin."

She frowned at him a moment, her expression so serious it was almost funny. "Why would I want to?"

"Never mind." Chance looked at the stallion for a moment. "Do you think you could get a hackamore on him?"

"I can try."

"Wait here."

Chance walked back to the house and untied his horse. He led Smoke into the barn, unsaddled her, gave her a quick rubdown, and put the horse in her stall. Removing the hackamore, he carried it to the corral and handed it to Teressa.

"Be careful."

She nodded.

"You're not afraid, are you? If you are, you don't have to do it."

"I am not afraid." Ducking through the rails, she walked slowly toward the stallion.

The stallion snorted but didn't back away.

Chance watched the horse carefully. He didn't know the stallion's history. They'd caught the horse off the range just before he went looking for Teressa. Chance didn't think the horse had been born wild. He had the look of a horse with some good bloodlines. Good conformation. Wide, intelligent eyes. But he wouldn't let any of the men get near him. Chance was pretty sure the stallion had been abused by a previous owner.

Teressa was at the stallion's head now. She was speaking to it quietly. Chance could hear the sound of her voice, though he couldn't make out the words.

A moment later, she slid the hackamore over the horse's head and fastened it in place. Taking up the reins, she led the horse around the corral. It followed her, docile as a puppy.

Chance grunted softly. "Do you think you can ride him?"

"I can try."

"Do you want a saddle?"

"No."

It was a silly question. She'd been riding bareback for years.

His fingers curled around the fence rail as she grabbed hold of the stallion's mane and vaulted onto its back. The horse shook its head but didn't buck.

Teressa stroked the stallion's neck, speaking softly all the while. Lifting the reins, she touched her heels to the horse's flanks and after a moment it moved out, smooth as you please.

"Well, I'll be damned," Chance muttered. "That bronc has thrown every man on the place, including me."

Teressa smiled at him as she passed by, her eyes alight with pleasure.

They made a pretty sight, Chance thought. Mighty pretty indeed.

"Teressa Elizabeth Bryant, what are you doing?"

Chance glanced up at the house to see Rosalia standing on the porch, one hand pressed to her heart.

Flying down the stairs, Rosalia ran toward the corral. "Get down from there this instant!"

Rosalia's words brought the desired effect. Spooked by the woman's shout, the stallion reared. With a squeal of surprise, Teressa slid over the stallion's rump and landed on her backside in the dirt.

Rosalia screamed. And screamed again.

Chance grabbed her by the arm. "Mrs. Bryant, shut up!"

She stared at him, stunned into silence at the tone of his voice.

Chance looked over his shoulder. "Teressa, are you all right?"

"Yes." Gaining her feet, she walked slowly toward the stallion. "Come," she said, extending her hand. "Come to me."

The stallion eyed her warily for a moment, then reached out to nuzzle her hand.

Smiling, Teressa caught the reins.

Rosalia glared at Chance. "How dare you speak to me like that!"

"Lady, you could have gotten her killed. Is that what you want?"

"Of course not!" She twisted free of his grasp. "Teressa, come out of there this instant. Well-bred young ladies do not ride astride."

Teressa looked at her mother a moment and then started laughing.

Rosalia gaped at her.

Chance grinned.

Teressa laughed until there were tears in her eyes, tears of merriment that abruptly turned to tears of sorrow as she remembered riding across the plains with Dawn Song on the way to a new campsite. They had always dressed in their best because it was a time when the young men liked to show off for the maidens. The unmarried warriors dressed in their best, too. Mounted on their finest horses, they rode up and down the line, showing off their riding skills, flirting with the maidens.

"Tessa?" Rosalia took a tentative step forward, but fear of the horse kept her from entering the corral.

"Go back to the house," Chance said. "I'll take care of this."

"I will not! I am her mother. She needs me."

"Just go up to the house and wait. I'll bring her along in a minute."

With a look of disapproval, Rosalia turned on her heel and walked away.

Muttering an oath, Chance ducked into the corral. The stallion snorted at his approach.

"Easy, fella. I'm not gonna hurt you," Chance said. Taking the reins from Teressa's hand, he unfastened the bridle and slid it over the horse's head. Freed of the restraint, the stallion bolted across the corral.

"Come on, Teressa." Taking her by the hand, he led her out of the corral.

"What is it, honey?" he asked gently.

She shook her head. Tears continued to pour down her checks.

With a sigh, Chance drew her into his arms. "Was it something your mother said?"

"Y-yes . . . n-no."

"You can tell me."

"It was just . . . what she said . . . about well-bred young ladies riding . . . It reminded me of Dawn Song . . . and . . . and my mother." She sniffed. "My other mother. I miss them so."

"Go on and cry, honey," he said, stroking her hair. "You deserve it."

And cry she did, until she had no tears left, until

she stood quiet in the circle of his arms, content to
be there.

"I'm sorry," she murmured, her voice muffled
against his shirtfront.

"No charge."

She looked up at him and frowned. Her eyes were
red and swollen, but it was her lips that tempted his
gaze. Ripe and pink and slightly parted.

Chance cleared his throat. "You can cry on my
shoulder anytime, sweetheart; that's all I meant."

"Oh."

He blew out a breath. Dammit. If she kept looking
at him like that, he wouldn't be responsible for his
actions. Fortunately, Rosalia Bryant was waiting for
them in the house, and he didn't think she was likely
to wait much longer before she came bursting through
the door to see what was taking them so long.

"Come on," he said, taking her by the hand. "Your
mother's waiting."

Chance stared at the embers in the hearth. He'd
been lying there on the sofa for hours trying to get
some sleep, but it was impossible. His hearing seemed
to have grown more acute since Teressa moved in. He
was aware of her every footstep, had been able to
close his eyes and follow her progress through the
rooms upstairs, had felt his body harden as he imagined her sitting in his bathtub covered with lather and,
later, getting ready for bed.

Damn!

More than once, he'd started for the stairs. In spite
of his earlier vow to pursue her, some innate sense of
honor he hadn't known he possessed kept him from
going to her room.

He bolted upright and glanced over his shoulder at
the sound of a light tread on the stairs.

"Please . . ." He whispered the word like a prayer,

wondering as he did so what he was asking for. Let it be her? Don't let it be her?

She padded toward him, her bare feet peeking out from beneath a long white cotton nightgown. Her hair, thick and rich and looking black in the dim light, trailed down her back and fell over her shoulders. He had an overwhelming need to bury his hands in the wealth of her hair, to bury his face in it, to hold her close and never let her go.

"I did not mean to wake you," she said ever so softly.

"You didn't."

"I . . ." She licked her lips, her gaze sliding away from his.

"Did you want something? A drink?"

"I do want something . . ." She took a deep breath, and then said it all in a rush. "I wanted to be with you. Everything here is so strange. The food. The clothes. I miss being with the People. I miss hearing their language. They don't feel so far away when I'm with you. . . ."

"Come here, sweetheart."

She practically ran to him. He lifted the blanket and she slid in beside him. He knew what she was feeling. He had felt it himself.

"Comfortable?" he asked.

She nodded, but didn't meet his gaze.

Embarrassed, he wondered, or afraid she might see her own longing mirrored in his eyes.

The silence between them grew taut. He was aware of her every move, could feel the warmth of her thigh against his own, smell the warm womanly scent of her with every breath he took. Lord, but he wanted her.

He tried to think of something to say, some words of reassurance, but he couldn't think, not with her sitting so close, couldn't think of anything but the need burning through him.

"Chance."

"What is it, honey?"

"Nothing. I . . . I never said your *wasichu* name before."

"I like the way you say it."

"Will you take me back home?"

"Teressa . . ."

"Please."

She was looking at him now, her eyes silently pleading with him. Lord, how could he refuse her when she looked at him like that?

"They'll just come after you again," he said. "They know where to look now."

"We could go live with the Cheyenne until they stop looking."

"Running away never solved anything," he said. And drawing her into his arms, he stopped running away from what he wanted and kissed her.

Her lips were soft, so soft, and sweetly yielding. She moaned softly and then she was sitting sideways on his lap, her arms locked around his neck as she kissed him back, kissed him so there could be no mistaking that she wanted his kisses as badly as he wanted hers.

He slid one hand up her neck into her hair while his other hand moved restlessly over her back. She pressed herself against him, her breasts warm and soft against his bare chest. He was glad he'd decided to sleep in jeans, though at the moment they were feeling mighty snug.

They were both breathing hard when the kiss ended. She drew back a little, her hands cupping his cheeks, her gaze moving over his face.

"You do care for me, don't you?" she asked.

"More than you know."

"Do you love me?"

"Since the first time I saw you."

Warmth flooded her being only to be washed away

by confusion. "I do not understand. Why have you been so . . . so . . ."

"Distant?"

"Yes."

He took her hands in his and kissed one and then the other. "It's a long story."

"Will you not tell me?"

"It's an ugly story, Teressa."

"Is it about the man who whipped you?"

"Yeah."

"I would like to know."

He took a deep breath. Only Kills-Like-a-Hawk and a few others knew how his mother had died, or of his long search to avenge her death.

Putting his arm around her shoulder, he drew her closer. He stared into the hearth, watching the last embers wink out.

"It happened the summer I was sixteen," he began. "My mother wanted to visit her cousin who lived with the Cheyenne. My father was away, so she asked me to go with her. We had made camp for the night when four men rode up. . . ."

Teressa listened with growing horror as he told her what had happened. His words painted an image so sharp, so vivid, she saw it as if it were happening all over again. She saw how valiantly he fought them as they tied him up, felt his rage and helplessness when they took turns violating his mother.

He went on, relating how he had worked his way free and managed to kill one of the men, how the other three had tied him to a tree, then taken turns whipping him until he was unconscious.

Tears burned her eyes as he told her how his mother had crawled toward him on her hands and knees, concerned for his welfare even though she was slowly bleeding to death. She wept as she saw him cradling his mother in his arms, shared his grief when he knew she was dead.

His voice turned cold and flat as he told how he had hunted down the men who had killed his mother, how he had made sure they knew who he was and why he was there. He had killed three of them and now only one remained.

"I am so sorry," she whispered. "So very sorry."

"So were they, when I caught up with them." He shook his head, as if clearing the memory from his mind. "You'd better go on back to bed."

"Chance . . ."

He shook his head. "Maybe when this is over. . . ."

She wanted to argue with him. She wanted to beg him to give up the search for the last man, to go back to the People with her, or let her stay on the ranch with him.

But she said nothing. He had made a warrior's vow, and she knew he would not rest until it had been fulfilled. Leaning forward, she kissed his cheek, then slid off the sofa and left the room.

Chance listened to her footsteps, each one growing fainter as she climbed the stairs. Why had he told her? Why had he sent her away? She had left the room and it was as if she had taken his heart and soul with her, leaving behind nothing but an empty husk fueled by an insatiable need for vengeance.

He ran his hands through his hair. He had to find the last man. He had sworn a blood oath to avenge his mother's death and he would not, could not, rest as long as Jack Finch still lived.

# *Chapter 24*

Teressa woke early after a sleepless night. Rising, she dressed quickly and left the house. Standing on the edge of the porch, she watched the activity near the barn as the ranch hands saddled their horses. She saw Cookie hauling water from the well. One of the men was forking hay to the calves in the pen. A dozen chickens scratched in the dirt, digging up worms and grubs for the countless baby chicks that followed them. Several cats prowled near the chickens. A rooster strutted back and forth on the top rail of one of the corrals. A faint breeze stirred the weathervane on top of the barn.

It was going to be another beautiful day, she mused. Or would be, if it weren't wash day. She didn't mind cooking, though she preferred baking. She didn't mind dusting and waxing the furniture, or shaking out the rugs, or making the beds, or washing and drying the dishes. But she hated doing the laundry. There were washtubs to fill, clothes to scrub and rinse and hang on the line out back. It was a job that took all day and left her back aching when it was over. And after wash day, came ironing day, which was almost as bad.

But that was later. For now, she was content to watch the men mount up and ride out. And then she saw Chance leading Smoke out of the barn. He paused to speak to Cookie, then swung effortlessly into the saddle.

Her gaze moved over him. He looked handsome and rugged in a dark blue shirt, leather vest, Levi's, chaps, and scuffed boots.

He was settling his hat on his head when he saw her. He said something else to Cookie, then rode toward her.

"Morning, Teressa," he said. "You're up early."

"I couldn't sleep. What are you doing today?"

"Riding out to look for strays."

"I wish I could go with you."

"Do you think your mother would approve?"

"Probably not. But I could ask her."

"Go ahead. I'll wait."

The sun had nothing on the smile she flashed him, Chance thought. He had enjoyed having Teressa here more than he would have thought possible. She ran out to meet him each evening, anxious to hear about his day, eager to tell him all about hers. He had been afraid her constant chatter would start to annoy him, but he found himself looking forward to seeing her at the end of a hard day on the range. He was even getting used to having Rosalia around. He had to admit the house had never looked better. The furniture gleamed. The windows sparkled. There wasn't a speck of dirt or dust to be found. And he had never eaten better in his life.

It came as somewhat of a shock to realize he was going to miss them, both of them, when they were gone.

Teressa burst through the doorway a few moments later, grinning from ear to ear. "I can go!" she exclaimed.

Chance grinned back at her. "Come on, let's find you a horse."

Gripping her forearm, he swung her up behind him and rode to the barn. He then dismounted and lifted her from the back of his horse, and they went into the barn. Chance moved down the center aisle, stopping when he came to a stall near the back.

"This here's Daisy Blue," he said, patting the neck of a pretty little dun-colored mare. "She's trail wise, not easily spooked, and has a nice gait."

Smiling, Teressa patted the mare's shoulder, then stepped aside as Chance bridled the mare and led her out of the stall.

Moments later, the mare was saddled and ready. Chance lifted Teressa onto the horse's back.

"Comfortable?" he asked, looking up at her.

"I guess so." The saddle felt odd, hard and cold when compared to sitting on a horse's bare back.

"I think those stirrups are a little too long," Chance remarked. He shortened the length a little, then slipped her foot into the stirrup. "Is that better?"

"Yes, thank you."

"Let's go, then." Turning, he walked out of the barn.

Taking up the reins, Teressa clucked to the horse and followed Chance outside, found herself admiring the easy way he moved as he took up the reins of his own mount and swung into the saddle.

"You should have a hat," Chance remarked. "Here, wear mine."

She settled his hat on her head, liking the feel of it, the fact that it was his. "What about you?" she asked.

"I'll be all right. You ready?"

She nodded eagerly.

"Let's go."

It wasn't long until the ranch house was out of sight and there was nothing to see but rolling grass, scattered stands of pines and cottonwood, and a seemingly endless blue sky.

"Is all this land yours?" Teressa asked.

"Yep."

She frowned, trying to comprehend the fact that he owned the land. The Lakota did not claim to own the land. The earth was their mother, and the People treated her with reverence and respect. Sometimes, when you walked the land, you could feel her heartbeat beneath your feet. Mother Earth provided food and shelter and when life was over, she cradled the dead in her arms.

Chance watched the play of emotions over her face. He knew that owning the land was a hard concept for his people to accept. At one time, it had been difficult for him to understand, as well, but no more. Right or wrong, like it or not, it was the white man's way to claim the land for his own and Chance intended to hang on to this piece of ground, to pass it on to his son, should he have one.

As much as he loved living with the Lakota, loved their wandering way of life, he knew it couldn't last much longer. More and more whites were leaving the East, lured westward by the promise of getting rich quick. Encounters between the Indians and the whites were growing less friendly, more aggressive. White hunters were killing the buffalo. Farmers were plowing the land, cutting the timber for fences, damming the rivers. In retaliation, the Indians were attacking the hunters and farmers, who then went to the Army demanding protection against the Indians.

Chance shook his head. Though he hated to admit it, he knew that in the long run the Indians could not win the fight.

Now and then they passed small bunches of cattle. Chance was pleased to note that most of the cows had calves at their sides.

"You like it here, don't you?" Teressa asked.

"Yeah."

"Did you always want to be a cowboy?"

"No, it just sort of got under my skin. It's a hell of a life. Cows have got to be the dumbest creatures on God's green earth."

It was no easy task, being a cowboy. There was range to ride, fence to mend. In the spring, the men spent a good deal of their time pulling cows out of bogs. In the summer, there was always danger of fire. Wintertime was mostly spent on maintenance and repairs and gathering firewood. From time to time, some of the men had to ride out to make sure the cattle weren't starving or freezing to death. Cattle had a tendency to stand in deep snow and freeze to death rather than try to find food. It was also necessary to chop through the ice so the cattle could drink from the rivers and water holes. Another winter assignment, one the men vied for, was wolf hunting. When the pickings among their natural prey were slim, wolves often stalked cattle. Moving in packs, they would surround a cow, disable it by severing a hamstring and then move in for the kill. Some ranches hired men to hunt wolves, offering them a five dollar bounty for each hide, but Chance didn't like that practice. He believed, as all Lakota did, that everything living was related. It was one thing to kill an animal because you needed the meat or the hide and another to destroy it for no better reason than it was trying to survive.

Riding the line was another dreary task. Line shacks were located every seven or eight miles around the outer edge of the ranch's range. In the winter, the men were posted there to keep an eye on the weaker stock and to make sure the herd didn't drift with the storm and wander off the range.

There was the spring roundup, when the calves were brought in and branded, and another roundup in the fall when the cows that were going to be sent to market were gathered. At this time, any calves that had been born after the spring roundup, or that were missed previously, were branded.

Cowboys were a breed apart; there was no doubt about that. They lived by their own code and for the most part were loyal to the brand they rode for. No cowboy worth his salt ever borrowed a horse from another man's string without asking for permission first. You didn't whip or kick a borrowed horse. You didn't wave at an oncoming rider, knowing such a move might spook the horse. A man on foot didn't grab the bridle of a mounted man's horse. A man was expected to close a corral or pasture gate behind him and to remove his spurs when he entered the boss's house. A man might get by with rustling a few head of cattle, but stealing a horse was a hanging offense.

"Look!"

Roused from his reverie, Chance looked to where Teressa pointed and saw a mother skunk walking along a stream bank, followed by two striped babies.

"Real cute," he muttered, reining his horse away from the stream. "Come on."

Giving the smelly little family a wide berth, Chance urged his horse into an easy lope. It was a beautiful day for a ride. The sky was a bright, clear blue and the air was warm but not hot.

He let his horse run until it slowed and stopped of its own accord. Dismounting, he watched Teressa pull up beside him. She looked beautiful, with her cheeks flushed pink and her blue eyes sparkling like sapphires. His hat had blown off her head and hung by its thong down her back.

"That was wonderful!" she exclaimed as he lifted her from the back of her horse.

He let her body slide down the front of his, his hands lingering at her waist longer that was necessary. He knew he should let her go, put some distance between them before it was too late. And then, as she leaned in to him, he knew it was already too late.

Muttering an oath, he pulled her closer. "Teressa."

She looked up at him through smoky blue eyes, her lips slightly parted.

"Tell me to stop."

Instead, she slipped her arms around his waist. "Don't stop."

Even as he lowered his head and claimed her lips with his own, he was telling himself all the reasons why it wouldn't work, but none of them seemed to matter, not now, not when he could feel the soft sweet length of her body pressed intimately against his, not when she was kissing him back, the tip of her tongue exploring his lower lip, not when her hands were slipping under his shirt, sliding over the bare skin of his back.

He groaned low in his throat. "I don't want to hurt you."

"You won't." Her nails raked his back ever so lightly. "You won't."

"Teressa . . ." How many nights had he dreamed of this, ached for this, burned for this moment? Since the first time he had seen her by the river, he had wanted her, needed her with an intensity that was undeniable. He had fought against it, telling himself she was too young, that he had no time for a woman in his life, that he had a blood vow to fulfill, but none of that seemed to matter now, not when Teressa was in his arms, her breasts crushed against his chest, her kisses searing a path to his soul.

He lifted his hat over her head and flung it aside, his fingers delving into the wealth of her hair, loving the way it curled around his fingers. He rained kisses over her cheeks, her eyelids, the tip of her nose. Her lips. Ah, sweet, so sweet, filled with secrets he yearned to savor.

Somehow they were lying on the grass wrapped in each other's arms, their bodies entwined, straining to be closer, though he wasn't sure that was possible.

She kissed him greedily, her hands restless and arousing as they moved up and down his back and arms, slid over his chest, caressed his cheek. And then she took his hand and pressed it over her breast, and he was lost.

His hands were trembling as he undressed her, his breath catching in his throat as her body was bared to his gaze. She was unbelievably beautiful, her skin clear and unblemished, her figure slender and perfect.

She flushed under his gaze but didn't look away, didn't try to shield herself from his eyes. "You are pleased?" she asked.

"You're beautiful, Teressa. More beautiful than anything I've ever seen."

She smiled with pleasure, and then she began to undress him. He noted that her hands, too, were trembling as she slid his shirt off his shoulders and somehow that made it all seem right.

He tugged off his boots and socks, lifted his hips so she could slide his jeans and long handles down his hips.

And then there was nothing between them but desire.

For a moment, his gaze moved over her, unable to believe she was there, his for the taking, and yet deep inside he had known from the moment he first saw her that this moment was inevitable.

He cupped her cheek. "Tessa . . ."

She smiled at him, her eyes glowing as she drew him down beside her. "Love me, Wolf Shadow," she murmured.

"I do," he replied, his voice husky with desire.

"Then show me. Show me now."

Gathering her in his arms, he kissed her, worship-

ping her with his hands, his lips, his voice. She was
fire and honey in his arms, warm and willing as she
teased and tempted him, her hands learning the con-
tours of his body, her teeth nipping at him. She purred
with pleasure as his hands moved over her. She loved
his hands, big and brown and ever so gentle as they
glided over her skin, arousing her until she was mind-
less, breathless.

"Now," she whispered, her voice ragged. "Now,
Wolf Shadow."

With a low growl, he rose over her. She gasped with
mingled pleasure and pain as his body became a part
of hers. And then she was lost in a dizzying world of
sensation as he began to move deep within her. She
clutched at his shoulders, reaching for something elusive, afraid she wouldn't find it.

"It's all right, honey," he murmured. "I know the
way. Just follow me and let yourself go."

Clinging to his shoulders, her legs locked around his
waist, she closed her eyes and followed him over the
edge of the abyss into paradise. . . .

Chance brushed a lock of hair from Teressa's face.
"You all right?"

She looked up at him, her eyes cloudy with spent
passion, her lips slightly swollen from his kisses, her
expression that of a woman who had been well and
truly pleasured.

And then she laughed softly. "I am better than all
right."

He couldn't help it. He laughed out loud. And then
he drew her into his arms and hugged her tight. Lord,
but it felt good to laugh.

"Wolf Shadow?"

He drew back, frowning at the hesitant note in
her voice.

"What is it, honey?"

"Have you . . . ?" Her cheeks turned rosy as she cleared her throat. "Have you done this with many women?"

"Not many."

"More than one?"

"Tessa . . ."

Her gaze slid away from his but not before he saw the hurt in her eyes.

Chance swore under his breath. How could he make her understand that none of them had meant anything to him? Would she believe him if he tried? Dammit, he had to do something to wipe that look from her eyes.

"Tessa, those other women, they didn't mean anything. I never really knew what making love was all about until today. Making love to you was like making love for the first time."

She looked at him, her eyes wide with hope. "Truly?"

"Truly." He stroked his knuckles over her cheek. "You've ruined me for all other women."

She smiled at him. It was a decidedly feminine smile, filled with just a hint of self-satisfaction.

"From now on it's just you and me, darlin'," he murmured.

And then he kissed her, aware that this kiss was vastly different from all the others he had showered on her. They had been filled with passion and excitement; this one was a mark of possession, a brand. She was his now, and it changed everything.

# Chapter 25

They bathed in the stream, splashing and laughing like a couple of kids playing hooky, and then, submerged in the shallow water, they made love again. She had no words to describe how it felt to experience his body sliding against hers while the water eddied and flowed around them. If the first time had been ecstasy, the second time bordered on sheer rapture. She cried his name aloud as, with one last thrust, he carried them both over the edge.

Happiness bubbled up inside Teressa, burst forth in a wave of laughter when she looked up and saw a squirrel staring down at them.

"What's so funny?" Chance asked, and then, following her gaze, he laughed, too, laughed until he was breathless. It was cleansing, somehow, to lie there in the water with Teressa and laugh.

And when the laughter died away, he drew her into his arms. Holding her close, he felt all his hatred melt away, and with it the relentless need for vengeance that had driven him for the last nine years of his life. In the back of his mind, he heard the voice of Kills-Like-a-Hawk. *You will never find the peace you are seeking until you put your hatred behind you.*

"Wolf Shadow?" Teressa stroked his back. "Is something wrong?"

He shook his head. "Not anymore, sweetheart. For the first time in years, everything is just right."

"We didn't find any stray cattle," Teressa mused later, as they dressed.

Leaning forward, Chance stroked her cheek. "I found something much better."

It was near dusk when they returned to the ranch. Rosalia was standing out on the front porch when they rode into the yard.

Rosalia's gaze rested on Teressa's face for a long moment. Then, her lips tightening, she looked at Chance. A last glance at Teressa and then she turned and went back into the house.

Teressa turned anguished eyes in Chance's direction. "She knows. How can she know?"

"She doesn't know anything," Chance said, but they both knew he was lying.

Dinner was a strained and silent affair. Troubled by her mother's silent disapproval, Teressa went up to bed immediately after dinner.

Chance was sitting in his office, going over some papers, when Rosalia entered the room and closed the door behind her.

"I know my daughter thinks she loves you," Rosalia said, getting right to the point. "Perhaps you think you love her."

When he started to speak, she silenced him with a wave of her hand.

"Teressa is very young. Until today, she was an innocent. I want you to leave my daughter alone, Signore McCloud. Her father and I have plans for her future. Soon we will be on our way home. Do not fill her heart and mind with empty promises."

"And what if she doesn't want to go with you? What if she has plans of her own?"

Rosalia lifted her chin and squared her shoulders. "I am her mother. Teressa will do as she is told. I am warning you for the last time. Leave my daughter alone."

She eyed him for a moment, then opened the door and swept regally out of the room.

Muttering an oath, Chance sat back in his chair, wondering how to play the hand Teressa's mother had dealt him. Should he respect Rosalia's wishes or follow the urgings of his own heart?

He rose and paced the floor. Time and again he headed toward the stairs and time and again he turned away. Tomorrow, he thought, he would talk to Rosalia tomorrow when they'd both had a chance to cool off.

Chance ate breakfast with the hands the next morning, then rode out with Dreesen to check on the river that ran through the east pasture. A tree had fallen across the river, blocking the water's flow. He sent Dreesen back to the ranch to get a couple of men to drag the tree out of the way and cut it for firewood; then he rode out to line shack number six to look in on the men. They were running low on supplies and he made a note to restock their larder.

It was near dark when he returned to the ranch. He dismounted in front of the barn and removed the saddle and blanket from his horse. Then he checked the gelding's feet, gave the animal a good brushing, and led the horse into the barn and into a clean stall.

Outside, Chance spent a few minutes watching the stallion prance back and forth. He shook his head, remembering how easily Teressa had charmed the wild stud. Tomorrow he would try his hand at breaking the stud one more time, and if he didn't have better luck than he'd had in the past, he would turn the horse loose.

Walking up to the house, he realized for the first

time that there were no lights burning. No smoke rose from the chimney. Worried now, he ran up the walkway to the porch. He took the steps two at a time and flung open the door.

"Teressa?" Standing there, listening to his voice echoing off the walls, he knew the house was empty.

Muttering an oath, he climbed the stairs and pushed open the door to her room. Even in the dim light, he could see it was empty.

"Damn. Damn, damn, damn!" Removing his hat, he ran his hand through his hair, resettled his hat on his head, and went back downstairs.

Going out the back door, he crossed the yard to the cookhouse. "Cookie?"

"Yeah, boss?" Cookie looked up from the dough he was kneading for tomorrow's bread.

"The women . . ."

Cookie punched his fist in the dough. "They lit out this morning, right after you did."

"Thanks, Cookie."

"I reckon you'll be taking your meals with the men again."

"Reckon so."

With a nod, Cookie covered the ball of dough and began punching up another one.

Chance stared at him for a moment, then went back to the house. So, he mused as he paced the floor. That was that. Rosalia Bryant had packed up and quit the field.

He ran a hand over his jaw. "Oh, hell," he muttered. Maybe it was for the best.

"Best for who?" he muttered. Rosalia? Teressa? It certainly wasn't the best for him. Dammit, the house had never felt so empty.

A short time later, Cookie rang the dinner bell, but Chance had no appetite and no inclination to sit around making small talk with the men. Instead he went into his den and sat down at his desk, trying to go over the ranch accounts, but for the first time in his life he couldn't summon any interest in the ranch.

Closing the books, he went to stand at the window. The bills were paid. They'd had a successful calving season. The new bull was everything he had hoped it would be. The stock was healthy. The rivers and water holes were full; there was plenty of grass and hay enough to see them through the winter.

He grunted softly. Now would be the perfect time to resume his search for Finch, but even bringing the last of his mother's killers to justice failed to spark his interest. His every thought was for Teressa. He had been determined to keep her at arm's length, determined not to let her get under his skin, yet she had done just that. He had told himself he didn't have time for a woman, that he had nothing to offer her, that she was too young, too innocent. All in vain. He had been lost from the first moment he'd seen her, and now, thanks to her mother, it seemed she was really lost to him.

Moving away from the window, he went outside. For a moment he stood on the porch and then he descended the stairs and made his way toward the corral that held the wild stallion.

As he drew near, the horse snorted and bolted to the far side of the corral. With a shake of his head, Chance folded his arms across the top rail and watched the stallion prance back and forth, foxlike ears twitching, nostrils flaring to test the wind as though searching for Teressa's scent.

"Yeah," Chance said ruefully. "I miss her, too." Lifting the latch, Chance opened the gate wide. "Go on. Get out of here."

The stallion stared at him, then pawed the ground. Striding into the corral, Chance approached the horse. "Go on," he said, making a shooing motion with one hand. "Get before I change my mind!"

With a toss of its head, the stallion pranced toward the gate, then bolted out of the corral. A moment later, the horse was swallowed up by the darkness.

"What the hell," Chance muttered as he returned to the house. "At least one of us will be happy."

Teressa clung to the side of the wagon seat, unable to believe that her mother had practically dragged her out of Wolf Shadow's house, or that they were now on their way to Crooked River to wait for the train that would take them to San Francisco. She had cried all the way from the ranch into town, had begged her mother to turn around, to let her say good-bye or at least leave him a note, but Rosalia had been adamant. They were leaving first thing in the morning and nothing Teressa had said would change her mother's mind.

She groaned as the wagon lurched over another rut in the road. She was beginning to think the man her mother had hired to take them to Crooked River was deliberately looking for ruts. Given a choice, she would have preferred riding a horse to riding in the wagon.

The road, such as it was, stretched out for miles and miles ahead of them. Teressa stared out at the ocean of tall grass that surrounded them on all sides. A few trees were scattered here and there as well as occasional outcroppings of rock. The driver—Jacko Kilkenny—had told them it would take four days to reach Crooked River. Four days of this, she thought, and her backside would be black and blue! It was a good thing their belongings were tied down in the back, else they would have bounced out long ago.

She slid a glance at her mother, who sat between Teressa and the driver. Rosalia stared straight ahead, one white-gloved hand clutching the edge of the seat, the other hand holding her floppy-brimmed hat in place. In spite of the dust and the wind and the bumpy road, Rosalia looked serene and unruffled.

Teressa looked out at the countryside again. What had Wolf Shadow thought when he returned home and found them gone without a word? Tears stung her eyes as she recalled the day they had made love. She had on occasion overheard Eagle Lance and Mountain Sage being intimate late at night. She had sometimes wondered at the muted sounds she had heard. Now she understood the soft expression in her mother's eyes the following morning, the smile that always teased her father's lips, the way they had looked at each other, the little touches they had exchanged.

She closed her eyes, remembering the wonder of Wolf Shadow's kisses, the tingling excitement of his touches, the way her whole body had come alive when he caressed her.

She had tingled all over when she touched him, as well. She had explored every inch of him, reveling in the way his muscles quivered beneath her fingertips, the way his body had moved, lithe and sensuous. She had delighted in the hard planes of his chest, the ridged muscles in his flat belly, the latent strength in his broad back and shoulders. He had treated her so gently, so tenderly. He could have crushed her with one hand, yet she had never been afraid, not for a moment. She had known he would never knowingly hurt her, had done everything in his power to make her first time as wonderful as she had hoped it would be. She smiled a secret smile. The second time had been even more wonderful.

And now she was miles away from him. What must he think? Surely he would know she hadn't left him because she wanted to. Hope burst within her as a new thought occurred to her. He would come after her. He had to. He loved her. He had told her so in every way possible.

At dusk, Jacko pulled into a stagecoach way station for the night. It was a ramshackle building, long and low, with a flat roof and a chimney that listed decidedly to the left.

"Will we be welcome here, Signore Kilkenny?" Rosalia asked dubiously.

"Sure. Long as your money's good." In spite of his bulk, he jumped lightly to the ground. Tossing the reins over the hitch rack, he turned to offer Teressa his hand.

She wished fleetingly that she had taken her mother's advice and worn gloves as she placed her hand in his sweaty, grimy one.

She glanced around as Kilkenny assisted her mother from the wagon. In addition to the long, low building, there was a corral filled with horses, and a large barn. A third building, large and square, stood behind the barn.

Rosalia was trying to shake the dust from her skirts when the door of the way station opened and a woman peered out.

"Land sakes," she exclaimed. "I thought I heard horses. I told Jed we had comp'ny but he said no, the stage ain't due for another two weeks." She hurried out of the building, one hand extended. "I'm Mrs. Morganstern. Me and the mister run this place." She stared openly at Rosalia and Teressa. "My, I ain't seen such pretty clothes in a month of Sundays. Come on inside. You two must be about wore out, riding in that wagon."

Smiling broadly, she ushered them inside. "Sit down. Make yourselves at home."

Rosalia took a place on one of the benches. Removing her gloves, she placed them in her skirt pocket, then unpinned her hat and placed it on the table.

Teressa sat down on the opposite bench and stared out the window.

"Can I get you some cold buttermilk?" Mrs. Morganstern asked.

"Yes, thank you," Rosalia replied politely.

Teressa shook her head.

"How about a sarsaparilla?" Mrs. Morganstern offered.

"I . . . I don't know what that is."

"Land sakes, child, you'll love it."

The woman hurried off, only to return a moment later with two mugs.

Teressa accepted the mug the woman offered and took a small sip of the contents. She smiled, pleased by the faintly sweet taste.

Mrs. Morganstern beamed at her. "I reckon you ladies are right hungry. Well, supper's just about ready. You rest yourselves, and I'll be back directly."

And so saying, she disappeared through a doorway that Teressa guessed led to the kitchen.

She glanced around the room. There wasn't much to see. A long plank table with wooden benches on either side. A well-worn overstuffed chair covered by a faded blanket, a lumpy sofa. A rifle hung over the fireplace mantel. There was a small picture of some flowers tacked to one wall. A pair of oil lamps hung from the ceiling. Dusty yellow curtains covered the single window.

With a sigh, she ran her hand over her hair, then took another sip of her drink, wondering if they had sarsaparilla in San Francisco. A short time later Mrs. Morganstern reentered the room carrying a tray laden with chipped, mismatched dishes, mugs, and flatware. She smiled at Teressa as she set the table, then went back into the kitchen. Several more trips put dinner on the table.

Mrs. Morganstern stepped outside and rang the dinner bell. Minutes later, Jacko entered the station followed by a tall, skinny man wearing a pair of baggy overalls over a chambray shirt.

Mrs. Morganstern introduced her husband and then they all took their places at the table. Mr. Morganstern said grace, then dug into the bowls placed in the center of the table.

Dinner was roast beef, potatoes, tinned peaches, and biscuits hot from the oven.

Jacko and Mr. Morganstern ate with a great deal of gusto. Mrs. Morganstern's manners were considerably better. She made small talk during the meal, remarking on the weather and how difficult it was to keep the house clean with all the dust in the air.

Rosalia made polite replies. Jacko and Mr. Morganstern grunted from time to time.

Teressa paid no attention to the conversation at the table. Keeping her gaze on her plate, she ate in silence, her thoughts centered on Wolf Shadow. She couldn't shake off her disappointment that he hadn't come after her. Doubts plagued her. Maybe he didn't love her. Maybe she had misunderstood what happened between them. Maybe it had meant more to her than to him.

It was that depressing thought that followed her to sleep that night.

They reached Crooked River three days later. It was a large town, larger than Buffalo Springs, but getting there had been the longest, most uncomfortable journey of Teressa's life. Long days on bumpy roads. Long nights spent in crude way stations. She was glad that that part of the journey was over.

When they went to the station to buy tickets, they learned the train had been delayed a day due to a tree that had fallen on the tracks. Looking at the train schedule, Teressa noted that if the train had not been

delayed, they would have missed it altogether. Had
that happened, they would have had to wait two weeks
for the next one. Teressa was glad for the delay. It
meant being able to bathe in a tub, being able to sleep
in a real bed. It meant one more day to hope that by
some miracle Wolf Shadow would arrive.

Teressa glanced over her shoulder one last time before boarding the train. She had been so sure Wolf
Shadow would come for her. So sure. Though it had
taken them four days by wagon to reach Crooked
River, she knew he could have made it sooner on
horseback.

"Come, Tessa."

"Yes, Mama."

With a sigh of resignation, Teressa climbed the last
step into the passenger car and followed her mother
down the narrow aisle to a pair of vacant seats near
the rear of the car.

Teressa sat down near the window and stared out,
a tiny part of her still hoping that Chance would ride
up and steal her away. She searched the faces of the
people gathered on the platform to bid good-bye to
friends and loved ones, but she didn't see a tall man
with long black hair and copper-hued skin.

"We'll be there soon," Rosalia said, taking the seat
across from Teressa. She smoothed her skirt, patted
her hair. "It will be wonderful to be home again, to
be back among civilized people."

Teressa said nothing, just stared out the window.
The people in San Francisco wouldn't think she was
civilized. She didn't remember any of the things she
had learned in school, but her mother had assured her
that didn't matter. Once they returned home, a private
tutor would be hired for her. She would have a new
wardrobe; they would redecorate her bedroom and
introduce her to polite society.

The fact that Teressa had no interest in any of those things mattered not one whit. She was the daughter of a wealthy businessman; she was expected to be a credit to her family, to marry well and raise a family. Her father had already picked out a number of men he considered worthy suitors.

With a sigh, Teressa pressed her hand to her stomach. She could be pregnant, even now. Closing her eyes, she imagined a baby growing inside her. Wolf Shadow's baby. None of the suitors her father thought so highly of would want to marry her if she was carrying another man's baby, especially if that man was half Indian.

Her eyes flew open as a shrill whistle pierced the air and then, with a great grinding of wheels, the train lurched forward.

People on the platform waved to their friends. Horses snorted and shied as the train moved down the track, picking up speed as it went.

Teressa glanced back one last time, felt the hot sting of tears in her eyes as the platform, swathed in a great cloud of hazy gray smoke, slowly faded from view.

# Chapter 26

Teressa stared at the huge three-story house located at the top of a high hill. She counted five chimneys as the buggy carried them ever closer to their destination.

Tall trees lined both sides of the winding road that led up to the house. The sight stirred memories. Once, she had pretended that the tree-lined road was a path to an enchanted kingdom where a wicked witch kept her imprisoned, waiting for a handsome prince to come rescue her.

Teressa sighed. Her fairy tale hadn't ended the way she had planned. Instead of rescuing her from a wicked witch, her handsome prince had taken her away from the only life she truly remembered. Who would rescue her this time?

The carriage halted and the driver opened the door and handed Rosalia out of the carriage. Teressa offered him a shy smile and a word of thanks as he helped her alight. For a moment she could only stare at the house as memories flooded her mind. She recalled her last Christmas here. Mama had given a party and the house had been ablaze with lights and people and presents. She wondered if her pony was still alive, if Mrs. Rochefort still made gingerbread men, if fish still swam in the pond in the backyard, if her runaway kitten had ever come home.

She smiled faintly as she followed her mother up

the wide stone steps. Such childish thoughts and memories, but then, she had been a child when she lived here before.

The massive front door opened and Hart stood there, looking much as Teressa remembered him, except that his hair was gray and he seemed shorter and heavier than she recalled.

"Miss Teressa!" A huge smile of welcome spread over his face. "Welcome home!"

"Thank you, Hart."

He beamed at her and then, to her complete surprise, he embraced her. Moments later, Mrs. Squires, Mrs. Rochefort, and Marie were there, too.

"My dear, oh my dear," Mrs. Rochefort murmured as she gave her a hug. "How beautiful you are!"

Marie kissed her on the cheek. "Welcome home, mademoiselle."

Tears rolled down Teressa's cheeks as she hugged them all in return. "I missed you," she said. "All of you."

"Tonight, all your favorite foods," Mrs. Rochefort said, and then looked over at Rosalia to make sure it was all right.

Rosalia nodded. "That is a wonderful idea, Mrs. Rochefort. Would you please heat some water? I should like to bathe, and I am sure Tessa would also like to clean up after our journey."

"Yes, ma'am," Mrs. Rochefort said.

"Marie, please light the fires in the bedrooms. There's a bit of a chill in the air."

*"Oui, madam."*

"Come, Tessa." Rosalia moved toward the wide curving staircase that led to the upper floors.

Teressa followed her mother up the stairs. Ten years since she had been in the house, she thought, and yet it was all so familiar. How could she ever have forgotten this place? Her mother turned left at the top of the stairs. Teressa smiled as they passed the tiny alcove where she used to hide from her father.

She took a deep breath when they reached her room, and then she opened the door. Her room was just as she had left it.

"We will have to buy you a new bed," Rosalia remarked, entering the room behind her.

Teressa smiled faintly as she looked at the narrow bed she had once slept in, with its frilly pink canopy and matching spread.

"We shall go shopping tomorrow," Rosalia said. "Tonight you can sleep in one of the guest rooms. I will have Marie make up the bed for you."

"Yes, Mama."

Rosalia came up behind her and gave her a hug. "I am so glad you are back home, *la mia piccola ragazza.*"

Teressa wandered around the room after her mother left for her own chambers. Everything a little girl could have desired was in this room—no doubt she'd had every toy, doll, and game known to man.

She ran her fingertips over the spread, smiled at a doll that had once been her favorite, ran her hand over the back of the small rocking chair in the corner, picked up a favorite picture book.

She paused at the window that looked out over the backyard. She wasn't sure what she had expected to feel when she got here, and was surprised to find that she had missed the house and its people. Yet even amid a sense of homecoming, she was lonely for Wolf Shadow, for the vast rolling plains, for the smell of smoke and sage, the sound of the Lakota language in her ears.

She didn't know if Wolf Shadow would come for her or not, but she knew she wouldn't stay in San Francisco long. She would be eighteen soon, old enough to do as she wished. Her parents couldn't force her to stay here if she chose to leave. Even if she didn't go back to the Lakota to stay, she would go back. She had roots there, too, deeper in some ways, than the ones she had here.

A knock at the door scattered her thoughts. "Yes?"

The door opened and Marie stepped into the room. "Your bath is ready, mademoiselle."

"Thank you, Marie."

With a smile and a curtsy, the maid left the room.

Teressa glanced around the room. She was home again, in her own room again. And all she wanted to do was cry.

# Chapter 27

Chance tossed his hat on the rack, shrugged out of his jacket, and ran a hand through his hair. He'd spent the last ten hours in the saddle and he was tired and hungry and angry enough to drive his fist through the wall.

He had spent the last two and a half weeks trying to talk himself out of going after Teressa and into going after Finch. Finally, three days ago, he had decided he couldn't live without her. His decision made, he had been getting ready to go when Dreesen had come in with a report that two hundred head of cattle had been rustled off the east range.

He had taken Dreesen and four of the ranch hands and ridden out to the east range. At first glance, it looked like the cattle had been stolen by Indians. Had that been the case, Chance would have let the matter drop. Granted, losing two hundred head would have cost him a good deal, but he couldn't blame the Indians. Thanks to white hunters, the buffalo weren't as numerous as they had been.

Chance had been about to turn back when some inner prompting urged him to follow the trail a little further. They had ridden about five miles when he found it, a Bull Durham sack, the remains of a hand-rolled cigarette, and the imprint of a boot heel. It wasn't much in the way of evidence. Indians liked tobacco, too, and there were a dozen ways some warrior could have gotten hold of a sack of tobacco or a pair of boots, but deep in his gut Chance knew it wasn't Indians who had stolen his cattle.

Chance and his men had ridden hard. Slowed by the herd, it hadn't been hard to overtake the rustlers. They had waited until nightfall, taken out the nighthawk, then thrown down on the four men huddled around the campfire. All the rustlers must have had loved ones waiting for them because they surrendered without a fight.

Dreesen had been all for hanging the lot of them on the spot. Chance had to admit the idea was tempting, but in the end he had sent Dreesen and the rest of the hands back to the ranch with the cattle and he had taken the rustlers into town.

After dropping the rustlers off at the jail and signing the necessary papers, he had stopped by the hotel, only to find out that Rosalia and Teressa weren't registered there. He knew they hadn't left town by coach, since the next stage wasn't due for another couple of days.

It had been Sorenson over at the livery who had told him that they'd hired a rig and driver and left town, headed west.

Chance shook his head. He'd bet his last dollar they'd lit out for Crooked River to catch the next train west. Damn. Why had he waited so long to go after her? By the time he made it to Crooked River, they'd be long gone.

Dammit!

Feeling like an old man, he climbed the stairs to his room, opened the door, and stepped inside. He closed his eyes and took a deep breath. Was it his imagination, or could he still smell her scent? Murmuring her name, he recalled the hours they had spent in each other's arms a few weeks ago. He knew he was no good for her, but she was sure as hell good for him.

She had made him laugh again, made him dream again, made him long for a life he had turned his back on.

"Teressa."

She would be in San Francisco now, living in her old man's fancy house, being waited on by servants, wearing expensive clothes, eating lavish meals, having her every wish fulfilled, her every need met. Hell, why would she want to come back here? But one way or another, he had to see her again.

He shed his clothing and washed off in the water Cookie had heated for him, then pulled on a clean pair of long handles. After blowing out the lamp, he crawled into bed. She had slept here. The thought of her in his bed left him hard and aching. Murmuring her name, he buried his face in his pillow. Sleep was a long time coming, and when slumber finally claimed him, his dreams were filled with images that did nothing to ease his longing for a dark-haired beauty with deep blue eyes.

Chance woke at first light, reluctant to leave behind the dream he'd been having. Rising, he dressed quickly and went down to breakfast with the men. After issuing the day's orders, he took his foreman aside.

"I'll be riding out as soon as I saddle up," he informed Dreesen. "When I get to 'Friso, I'll let you know where I'm staying. Have some of the men stick close to the east range, and send McCarthy and Boyd up to the number four line shack to relieve Farrell and Ackerman."

"Right, boss. Anything else?"

"That's all I can think of right now."

"I caught Henley out behind the barn last night. He was dead drunk. You want I should fire him?"

"Yeah. I've warned him three times. Take his pay out of the cash drawer in my office."

Dreesen nodded. "That's gonna leave us a man short."

"Put out the word we're hiring. I'll leave it up to you."

"How long you think you'll be gone?"

"I'm not sure. I hate to leave again so soon, but it can't be helped."

"Don't worry about it. Except for those rustlers, things have been mighty quiet."

"Thanks, Dave." He clapped his foreman on the shoulder, then headed for the barn.

Thirty minutes later, he was riding hard for Crooked River.

He reached the town three days later. He had ridden hard and fast and his first stop was the livery. Once he'd made certain his horse would be well cared for, he went to the train depot. As luck would have it, the next westbound train was scheduled to leave town the day after tomorrow at noon, and he intended to be on it.

Leaving the train depot, he strolled down the boardwalk. Crooked River was a good-size town, bigger and more settled than Buffalo Springs. He passed by a Chinese laundry, a couple of saloons in full swing, a fancy restaurant, a soda shop, another restaurant, a millinery shop, a general store, a barbershop.

Chance ran a hand over his jaw, thinking a shave and a haircut probably wouldn't hurt. He paused outside a saloon. Peering over the batwing doors, he glanced around the room. It was obviously an establishment for serious gamblers. There were no doves in cheap, low-cut outfits to distract a man. He stood there a minute, wondering whether he should go in and idle away a few hours playing cards or just go find a hotel room. In the end, the whisper of cards being dealt and the prospect of a quiet drink drew him inside.

He stood there a moment, getting a feel for the place, his gaze wandering from one table to the next, before he made his way toward a table near the back of the room.

"Evenin', gents," he drawled. "Mind if I sit in for a few hands?"

The four men sitting at the table looked up, each one taking his measure before inviting him to sit down. They introduced themselves as Mort Warner, Axle Foley, Bob Sunderland, and Jules Sturgeon.

Chance sat down in the vacant chair and bought his way into the game. Warner was dealing a new hand when Sunderland removed his jacket. It was then that Chance saw the star pinned to his vest.

Sunderland caught his gaze. "Hope you don't have any qualms about playing poker with a lawman."

"Not at all," Chance said with a wry grin. "I reckon it assures an honest cut and an honest deal."

Sunderland grinned wryly. "Reckon so."

Chance picked up the hand he was dealt and for the next hour or so, lost himself in the pleasure of playing cards with four men who appreciated a good game. From time to time, one of the men bought a round of drinks, and Chance took his turn.

The conversation was sporadic. Warner talked about falling beef prices, Foley complained about lack of rain, Sturgeon expressed some concern about the new store opening across the street from his own.

Chance was thinking of calling it a night when Sunderland mentioned Jack Finch. Chance sat up, suddenly wide-awake.

"Was anyone killed?" Sturgeon asked.

"He killed the shotgun guard and one of the passengers who tried to stop him."

"What happened?" Chance asked, trying to keep the excitement out of his voice.

Sunderland's sharp brown eyes rested on Chance's face. "Coach was robbed outside of Deadwood."

"That's pretty far from here," Warner remarked. "You think he's headed this way?"

"He was, last I heard," Sunderland replied, his gaze still on Chance.

"How long ago was the holdup?" Chance asked.

"Day before yesterday. You know Finch?"

Chance hesitated, debating between the truth and a lie. At the moment, the truth seemed wiser. "I met him once."

"Is that right?"

Chance nodded curtly.

The two men stared at each other for stretched seconds, then Sunderland shrugged. "No law against knowing a man."

"Reckon not." Gathering his winnings, Chance pushed his chair away from the table and stood. "Thanks for the game."

Chance left the saloon and stood on the boardwalk. Jack Finch was headed this way. There weren't that many towns between here and Deadwood. There was a good chance Finch would come here. It was the first solid clue he'd had to the man's whereabouts in five years.

He gazed out into the darkness, torn between the need to wait here and see if Finch showed up and his yearning to see Teressa again.

Muttering an oath, he crossed the street to the hotel and checked in. The room at the top of the stairs was small but clean. Pulling back the covers, he sank down on the mattress, one arm folded behind his head, and

stared up at the ceiling. He had vowed a blood oath
to avenge his mother. He had promised Teressa that
he would not leave her, had taken her innocence, told
her he loved her.

How could he turn his back on his vow?

How could he turn his back on Teressa?

Torn by indecision, he closed his eyes and in the
back of his mind heard his mother's dying words. *Be
happy, my son.*

But how could he live with himself if he let Finch
get away with what he'd done?

# Chapter 28

The following morning, Chance bought a ticket to San Francisco for himself and made arrangements for Smoke to travel in the stock car.

Leaving the depot, he wandered aimlessly through the town, pausing when he came to a shop that sold men's clothing. Looking down at his plaid shirt and jeans, he entered the store. When he left an hour later, he had a couple of new shirts and a new pair of wool trousers. He made two more stops, purchasing a new hat and a new pair of boots.

After dropping off his packages in his hotel room, he went to the livery, saddled Smoke, and rode away from the town.

Once clear of the town, he gave the mare her head. It felt good to ride across the plains, to have a day to himself, a day with no responsibilities. Such days had been rare since his father died, what with trying to run the ranch, pay off the old man's debts, and get a line on Finch's whereabouts.

Finch. With a shake of his head, Chance put the man out of his mind, determined not to spoil the day with thoughts of the last of the low-down scum that had killed his mother.

He would think of Teressa instead. His mood lightened immediately as her image sprang to mind. Whether dressed in a simple Lakota tunic with her hair falling over her shoulder or in a demure gown cut in the latest style with her hair piled atop her head, she was the loveliest, sweetest, most desirable woman he had ever known. Since the first moment he had seen her, she had filled his thoughts and his heart. He would not lose her now.

He rode until dusk, then returned to Crooked River. After cleaning up, he went to the hotel dining room for supper, then moseyed down to the saloon where he had played cards the night before. Warner, Foley, and Sturgeon were sitting at the same table as the previous night. When they saw Chance, they waved him over. The fourth man at the table eyed Chance suspiciously as he sat down.

"You're an Injun, ain't ya?" the man asked, his tone surly.

"That's right," Chance replied, his hand resting on the butt of his Colt. "You got a problem with that?"

"Leave him be, Moss," Sturgeon said. "He's all right."

"Is that so? I ain't never met an honest Injun."

A muscle worked in Chance's jaw as he met Moss's gaze head-on. After a moment, the other man looked away.

Chance glanced at the other three men. "I'm not looking for any trouble. Maybe it would be best if I found another game."

Warner fixed Moss with a hard look. "There won't be any trouble, will there, Eli?"

Moss cleared his throat. "Not from me."

"Let's play cards, then," Foley said. Picking up the deck, he shuffled the cards, offered Sturgeon the cut, and dealt a new hand.

The play passed peacefully for the next hour. Lady Luck smiled on Chance as she was wont to do and he won more than he lost. With each hand he won, Moss's frown deepened.

"All right," Moss said as he tossed his last raise into

the pot. "Let's see you beat this!" One by one, he turned his cards over, revealing a full house, queens over threes.

"Beats me," Sturgeon said, tossing in his hand.

"Me, too," Warner said.

"Damn!" Foley turned his cards over; another full house, nines over sixes.

Grinning, Moss reached for the pot.

"Hold on there," Chance said. "The pot's mine."

Eyes narrowed, Moss looked up as Chance spread his cards on the table. Four sevens.

Moss spat an obscenity. "You're mighty lucky, mister."

With a nod, Chance raked in the pot.

"Too lucky."

"Back off, Moss," Foley warned. "You're drunk."

"I say he's cheatin'," Moss said loudly. "No one's that lucky."

At Moss's accusation, the men at the surrounding tables turned to see what was going on until gradually all eyes in the place were focused on Chance and Eli Moss.

Slowly, Chance pushed away from the table. "Don't do it."

"Won't be no trouble so long as you admit you're cheatin' and the pot's mine. Go on, say it."

Foley, Sturgeon, and Warner exchanged worried looks.

Chance kept his gaze on Moss. He knew the exact moment the man decided to reach for his gun. Muttering an oath, Chance dove across the table, his shoulder slamming into Moss's chest. Greenbacks and coins went flying. Moss's chair skittered backward, then tipped over and they both hit the floor. Men at nearby tables scrambled to their feet to get out of the way.

Chance grunted as Moss's fist connected with his

jaw, knew a moment of satisfaction as he drove his own fist into the other man's face. Blood spurted from Moss's nose.

"All right! That's enough!"

Bob Sunderland's voice cut across the din.

Chance gained his feet. Breathing heavily, he lifted a hand to his jaw.

"What the hell's going on here?" Sunderland demanded.

"He was cheatin', Sheriff," Moss said, jabbing a finger in Chance's direction. "I called him on it and he hit me."

Sunderland looked at Chance. "Is that right?"

"Not quite."

"We can sort this out in my office," Sunderland said. "I'll take that iron. Yours, too, Eli."

Chance glared at the sheriff. "Am I under arrest?"

"Reckon so."

Chance swore as he handed the sheriff his Colt.

Sunderland jerked a thumb toward the door. "Let's go."

"Don't worry about your stake, McCloud," Foley said. "I'll hang on to it for you."

"Obliged," Chance muttered.

Sullen-faced, Eli Moss picked up his hat and strode out of the saloon. Grabbing his own hat, Chance followed him. Damn and double damn.

The sheriff's office was a large square brick building located at the end of Main Street. Sunderland unlocked the door and motioned Moss and Chance inside. Opening a drawer in his desk, the Sheriff dropped Moss's Remington and Chance's Colt inside, locked the drawer, then gestured at a pair of cells.

"Listen, Sheriff . . ."

"Not now, McCloud."

Chance swore. "I wasn't cheating."

"I'll take your statement in a few minutes. Inside."

Jaw clenched, Chance stepped into the cell. He flinched as the door swung shut behind him, glared at Moss as the sheriff locked him up.

Sunderland pulled a couple of forms out of the top drawer of his desk, picked up a pen, dipped it in the inkwell in the corner. His lips moved as he filled out the form.

"This is the fourth time I've had you in here in the last month, Eli," he remarked.

Moss grimaced, but said nothing.

"Gonna cost you ten days in the lockup this time and a twenty-dollar fine for being drunk and disorderly in public."

Muttering an oath, Moss dropped down on the cot in the corner and pulled his hat down over his eyes.

Chance gripped the bars in his hands, his eyes narrowed as he watched the lawman.

Feeling his gaze, Sunderland looked up. "First offense, two days and two dollars."

"I'm leaving town tomorrow afternoon."

" 'Fraid not."

"Dammit, I've already bought my ticket."

"I'll have my deputy exchange it for you."

Chance pressed his forehead against the bars. If he missed the train tomorrow, he'd have to wait another two weeks for the next one. Dammit!

# Chapter 29

The next few days passed quickly. As a child, Teressa had never really understood or appreciated what it meant to be rich, but the benefits of being wealthy were soon evident.

They spent a day at the dressmaker, and the following afternoon she had three fashionable new dresses that turned heads wherever she went. New hats, new shoes, new gloves. She had only to remark that she liked something and it was hers. Painters were hired to repaint her bedroom. She had a new suite of furniture, new carpets and lamps.

To her chagrin, she found she enjoyed being waited on. Marie brought her hot cocoa and scones in the morning; lunch was anything she desired, and dinner was always an elaborate meal. Oftentimes, one or more of her father's business acquaintances joined them at the table.

The only thing she didn't like was the way people sometimes looked at her. It seemed everyone she met knew she had been kidnapped by the Lakota, but they were too well-bred, too polite, to question her about her past. But she could see the speculation in their eyes, knew they were wondering what her life had been like among the Indians. There were always stories in the newspapers about Indian attacks, about captives being abused and tortured, about women who had been brutally raped. Men looked at her and wondered.

Her days and evenings were never dull. They went to the theater and the opera; girls who had been her friends when she was a child came to visit. They were all grown up now, virtual strangers to Teressa, as she was to them. A few came to call and never returned. The rest seemed willing to renew their acquaintance, especially Cynthia Witherspoon. Teressa remembered Cynthia. As children, they had been best friends, spending the night at each other's homes, sharing secrets, playing house. They had taken piano lessons together, sat side by side in church. Their friendship was quickly renewed. It was Cynthia who made the parties and the outings bearable.

Cynthia was the only one Teressa dared talk to about Wolf Shadow. It was so good to have someone she could confide in, someone who didn't think she was awful for loving a half-breed.

"It sounds like he loves you, too, Tess," Cynthia had said. "And if he doesn't come for you, then it's his loss." Cynthia had tossed her hair over her shoulder in a gesture Teressa remembered from childhood. "Just remember, there are lots of handsome men who would love to court you."

But she didn't want another man. She wanted Wolf Shadow. At night, alone in her room, her thoughts always turned to him, to the kisses they had shared, the night they had made love. He had been so tender; she had been certain he loved her as much as she loved him.

Every night she sent the same prayer toward heaven. *Please, Wakan Tanka, help him find the path that will lead him back to me. . . .* And with the passage of each new day, she grew more convinced that he wasn't coming after her.

At first she had made excuses for him—he'd had business to take care of at the ranch; he missed the train; he lost his ticket; the train was delayed, held up, attacked by Indians. But as the days turned to weeks, she forced herself to admit the truth. He wasn't coming. They had shared something wonderful, something beautiful, but it was over.

Now she stood in front of the full-length mirror in her newly remodeled bedroom and studied her reflection. Today was her eighteenth birthday and her parents were having a dinner party to celebrate, even though Teressa didn't feel like celebrating.

If only Wolf Shadow were there with her. What would he think if he could see her now? Her dress was a muted shade of mauve with a square neck, long fitted sleeves, and a full skirt over a modest bustle. She wore matching slippers on her feet. Her hair was arranged in loose curls atop her head, with a few strands left loose to fall over her shoulders. A slender gold chain circled her throat.

Marie knocked at the door. "Your mother wishes you to join them downstairs, mademoiselle. The guests are beginning to arrive."

"Thank you, Marie. I'll be right down."

With one last look at her reflection, Teressa picked up her fan and left the room. No doubt her mother had invited dozens of eligible young men. She could have told her parents they were wasting their time. She had met countless young men since she arrived in San Francisco. None of them interested her in the least. They were handsome. They were charming. They were polite and rich and amusing. But they weren't Wolf Shadow.

Fixing a smile on her face, she made her way down the stairs. She was the guest of honor, after all.

\*　　\*　　\*

Chance paced the floor of his cell, his frustration rising with every passing moment. He glanced at the clock again. Two more hours and he'd be free.

Dammit. He hated being locked up. Hated small enclosed spaces. Hated the man snoring in the next cell. Damn Moss!

He pivoted on his heel as Sunderland opened the cell door.

"Go on, get out of here," the sheriff said, handing him his Colt. "Your pacing is driving me crazy."

He didn't need to be told twice. Muttering a heartfelt "obliged," Chance grabbed his holster from the end of the bed, shoved his Colt into the leather, and left the jail.

Outside, he strapped on his gunbelt, then took a deep breath. No more saloons; no more poker. He wasn't going to miss that damn train again. No, sir! Even if he had to hole up in his room until it was time to leave town.

Eleven days later Chance led Smoke up the ramp and into the stock car, made sure the mare had feed and water, and then climbed into the passenger car. He walked through several cars until he found one that wasn't too crowded. Locating an empty seat, he tossed his saddlebags on the overhead rack and sat down next to the window. Not long ago, it had taken six months to cross the country; now a man could go from New York City to San Francisco in six days.

Leaning back, he pulled his hat down low, stretched his legs out in front of him, and closed his eyes.

Twenty minutes later, amid a long piercing whistle, the grinding of wheels, and a spurt of steam, the train was in motion.

Chance pushed his hat back and glanced out the window. He'd never been on a train before, and as the engine picked up speed, he found it rather exhilarating in spite of the noise and the occasional cinders that blew through the open windows.

As they left the town behind, there was nothing but miles and miles of grassland as far as the eye could see. Now and then he spied a stand of tall timber. Rivers cut narrow swaths of blue through an ocean of grass.

As the train moved deeper into the plains, he spotted a few head of buffalo, and a short while later, he saw a dozen warriors. He'd heard of whites shooting both buffalo and Indians from fast-moving trains and he noticed that the warriors were careful to stay out of rifle range of the iron horse.

Tugging his hat down again, he closed his eyes. "San Francisco, here I come," he muttered.

The trip was unremarkable. Chance spent a good part of it just staring out the window, watching the scenery flash by. Once, the land had belonged to the Sioux and the Cheyenne, the Comanche and the Arapaho. Now, more and more of it was being fenced off. Houses and barns sprouted like mushrooms. Sheets flapped on clotheslines. Windmills raised their arms toward the sky. Small towns that owed their very existence to the iron horse lined the tracks.

He felt a rush of excitement as San Francisco came into view. Though he had never been here before, he had heard a lot about the town from a California cowboy who had worked on the ranch one summer. The city had drawn people from many different countries and from all walks of life, the cowboy had told him. Teachers and hucksters, bankers and whores, artists and whiskey peddlers, business men and con men, miners and millionaires, all had come to the coast looking to start a new life.

After disembarking from the train, Chance collected

his horse and his luggage. He saddled Smoke, tied his gear behind the cantle, and swung into the saddle.

The streets were crowded with men, many wearing the clothes of their native lands. He heard men speaking in Italian and French and in languages he couldn't begin to recognize.

The people of San Francisco were nothing if not inventive. He'd heard that in some places two different companies managed to conduct business in the same building simply by switching workers and signs.

From what he saw, it looked like the Chinese had dug in their heels and intended to stay. They resided in a mysterious, noisy section of town that was brightly decorated with calligraphy, colored ribbons, and shops crammed with exotic foods, Oriental paraphernalia, and countless laundries, as well as half a dozen pharmacies, a Chinese theater, and several restaurants that were frequented by many non-Asian citizens.

He'd been told that most of the Negro population lived west of Montgomery Street, and that the majority of the men worked as laborers, mechanics, waiters, porters, barbers, and businessmen.

Then there was the infamous Barbary Coast, a place Chance had often heard of but had no intention of visiting. It was said that any man who risked walking near the waterfront risked being shanghaied. More than one man had ventured into a bawdy house for a few hours of pleasure and woke in the hold of a ship bound for the Orient. Women were a minority in 'Frisco. Young men, eager to seek their fortune, made up the bulk of the population. Still, like women everywhere, they had managed to make their presence and their influence known. One of the first things they had done was see that gambling on Sunday was outlawed. But that was only one day of the week. Men with money in their pockets and time on their hands were eager for any diversion they could find. Horse races, cockfights, and bullfights were popular, along with drinking and whoring.

Like any big city, there was an area where the wealthy lived and entertained. Chance had no trouble finding the rich section of town, or finding out which of the houses belonged to Edward Bryant and his family.

As he had suspected, the Bryants lived in one of the biggest houses on one of the biggest lots in the city.

Reining Smoke to a halt in front of the fence that surrounded the property, Chance stared up at the place that could only be called a mansion. Damn, he'd known the Bryants had money, but he had never expected anything like this.

He watched the house for half an hour or so, but no one came out and no one one went in. He was debating the wisdom of riding up to the front door and demanding to see Teressa when a closed carriage approached the gate. A liveried driver halted the team. He looked down his nose at Chance, jumped lightly to the ground, and opened the gate. Regaining his seat, he picked up the reins and clucked to the horses, and the carriage moved forward. When it was inside the gate, the driver halted the carriage, hopped down, and closed the gate with a flourish.

Chance stared after the carriage as it rolled up the long winding drive. He was pretty sure his presence would not be welcome here. If he decided to call on Teressa, would common courtesy dictate that the Bryants make him welcome, or would Edward have him thrown out on his ear? Perhaps before he approached the Bryants he should find a way to speak to Teressa alone and find out if her feelings for him had changed.

He glanced up at the house again. He would never be able to offer her anything like this. Now that she was home again, now that she'd had a taste of the high life, she might not be so anxious to leave. With that in mind, he reined Smoke around and rode down the hill. He had some hard thinking to do.

After settling the mare in a livery barn, Chance got a room at the nearest hotel, then dropped off his luggage. Too restless to sit still, he left the hotel and made his way to the saloon across the street.

He crossed the polished hardwood floor to the bar, ordered a beer from a florid-faced man in a crisp white apron, then contemplated his reflection in the mirror behind the counter. How would he ever manage to get Teressa alone? He could send her a note asking her to meet him, but there was always a chance her mother would intercept it. He could wait outside the gate, but he was pretty sure well-bred young ladies didn't leave home unchaperoned.

Damn.

He glanced around the saloon, only then noticing that the place seemed to cater to wealthy, well-dressed men clad in expensive city suits. There was no sawdust on the floor, no women in evidence, no paintings of voluptuous females behind the bar riddled with bullet holes from rowdy cowboys.

He was sipping his brew when two men moved up to stand beside him. They nodded at him politely before ordering drinks. Chance couldn't help hearing their conversation.

"I hear it's going to be quite a blowout," the first man said. "Buffet supper, dancing, cake, and champagne."

"I don't mind that, Dupre, but a fancy costume ball?" The second man shook his head. "The wife is all aflutter, but I don't much cotton to the idea of parading around in some ridiculous outfit."

"I'd parade around naked for a chance to meet Bryant's daughter. Have you seen her? She's a beauty."

The second man snorted. "That's fine for you. You don't have a wife and three kids."

Dupre laughed. "She could change all that, if she'll have me."

"I don't imagine old man Bryant is all that anxious to marry her off. After all, they've only just got her back."

"So, will I see you tomorrow, Hamilton?"

Hamilton sighed heavily. "Likely you will."

"The wife's talked of nothing else for days."

Chance drained his glass and left the saloon. A costume ball at the Bryants' tomorrow night. He grinned into the gathering darkness as he headed for the hotel. As always, Lady Luck was smiling on him.

Music from the second floor wafted upward as Teressa smoothed a hand over her skirt. Didn't her mother ever get tired of parties? Surely she could find something more productive to do with her time. Sometimes Teressa felt guilty for the life she was living. With the Lakota, there had been little time to laze about. There had been wood and water to collect, food to prepare, clothes to make or repair, hides to tan, meat to dry. So many tasks, all of them necessary for survival. Here, life seemed to be nothing but a never-ending round of shopping and visiting, dining and dancing.

She took a last look in the mirror, then, with a sigh, she left her bedroom and walked down the hallway to the stairs that led to the second-floor ballroom. She had been opposed to a costume ball at first, but now, dressed in an elaborate gown with her hair tucked up inside a wig and hiding behind a jeweled mask that covered most of her face, she found herself looking forward to it. She doubted if anyone would recognize her and found the idea freeing somehow.

The ballroom was already crowded. A king danced with a unicorn, a queen waltzed by on the arm of a friar, a courtesan laughed behind her fan at something a knave had said, a bear danced with a fairy queen, a clown partnered a red-haired angel.

The air was filled with music and laughter. People crowded around the buffet table, or sat at the small round tables scattered around the edge of the dance floor.

The next hour passed in a blur as she danced with one partner after another. She was pleased that no one guessed her identity. As the evening wore on, she became aware that someone was watching her, someone wearing the guise of a musketeer. Whether she was at the buffet table, being twirled around the floor, or sipping a glass of champagne, she had only to turn her head to find him nearby. It was disturbing and yet somehow exciting at the same time.

It was near midnight when she slipped out onto the veranda for a bit of air. She heard no sound, and yet she knew that the man who had been watching her was standing behind her.

Pulse racing, she slowly turned to face him. A large hat with a curling brim and a feather sat atop his head at a rakish angle. There was a sword at his side, boots upon his feet.

He took a step toward her. "May I have this dance?"

His voice was little more than a whisper, but she recognized it instantly. "Wolf Shadow! What are you doing here?"

"What do you think?" He held out his hand. "Dance with me?"

Feeling as though she were in a dream, she moved into his arms, let him guide her in the steps of a waltz. He held her far closer than was proper, but she didn't care. It felt so good to be in his embrace, to know that he was there. Happiness bubbled up inside her. He had come for her! He did care.

The music ended, but he didn't release her. She

looked up at him as he drew her closer, felt her heart-beat increase as he removed his mask and then hers and placed them on the railing.

He whispered her name and then he lowered his head and claimed her lips with his own.

Her eyelids fluttered down and she leaned into him, hungry for the feel of his body pressed against hers, eager for his kisses, desperate for his touch. His fingers splayed over her back, drawing her closer still, letting her feel the evidence of his desire.

His tongue slid over her lower lip, dipped inside to slide over the silky softness within.

Heat flared deep within her, sizzling along her nerve endings until she was quivering with need. Her moan was swallowed by his kisses.

"Is there some place where we can be alone?" he asked, his voice husky.

"Not here. Not tonight."

"Where?" He feathered kisses over her eyelids, her cheeks, the sensitive place behind her ear. "When?"

"Tomorrow. I'm . . ." It was hard to think, hard to speak, with him kissing her so intimately. "I'm sup-posed to visit . . . an acquaintance."

"Go on." He pressed a kiss to her breast.

Heat spiraled through her. "Wait for me . . . at the bottom . . . Oh, Wolf Shadow." She wrapped her arms around his neck, afraid her legs would no longer sup-port her.

"The bottom of what?"

"The hill. I'll be in the . . . the carriage. Follow me to her house."

He kissed her again, then moved away at the sound of voices.

Teressa stared up at him.

"We're no longer alone," he said quietly.

"Oh!" She pressed a hand to her heated cheeks, then quickly replaced her mask.

Chance slipped his mask over his face as well. "What time tomorrow?"

"Two o'clock."

"I'll be there," he promised.

Taking a deep breath, she returned to the ballroom.

# Chapter 30

Teressa slept late the next morning. She dressed quickly and hurried down to breakfast to find her parents already seated at the table.

"Good morning, Mama," she said, kissing her mother on the cheek. "Papa." She kissed the top of his head, then took her place at the table. "Isn't it a lovely day?"

Her father looked at her over the top of his newspaper. "You seem unusually cheerful this morning," he remarked. "Can this mean you're finally beginning to like it here?"

"I like it here very much," she replied. Who wouldn't like San Francisco? Even though she longed to be back with the Lakota, she had to admit that San Francisco was an exciting place to live. It was, after all, the tenth largest city in the United States, with an abundance of things to see and do. There were plush hotels, fancy restaurants, parks, churches, synagogues, schools, and libraries. She smiled inwardly. The city was even more exciting, now that Wolf Shadow was here.

Her parents exchanged glances. "I see," her father said. He looked at her thoughtfully for a moment. "Does this have something to do with the dance last night?"

Before Teressa could answer, Mrs. Rochefort entered the room, bringing Teressa a cup of hot chocolate. Chocolate was one thing Teressa couldn't seem to get enough of.

Teressa smiled at the cook. "Good morning, Mrs. Rochefort," she said. "I'm not very hungry today. Could you please bring me some buttered toast and a glass of orange juice?"

"Right away, miss."

Rosalia waited until the cook left the room before leaning forward, her gaze intent upon Teressa's face. "Did one of the young men at the ball catch your eye?"

Teressa's smile widened. "Yes. One did."

"Well," her father asked rather gruffly, "might we know his name?"

"Not right now, Papa."

"And just why not? I know all the young men who were present last evening. They were all invited in hopes you would find one to your liking. If one pleased you, I should very much like to know who it was."

"All in good time," Teressa said. She placed her napkin in her lap as the cook set a plate in front of her. "Thank you, Mrs. Rochefort."

"Will there be anything else, miss?"

"Not right now."

With a nod, the cook left the room.

"I do not like this secrecy, Tessa," her mother said sternly.

"I'm sorry, Mama. I'll tell you soon, both of you. I promise." She spread some strawberry marmalade on a triangle of toast and took a bite, then sipped her juice.

Her parents looked at each other, disapproval evident in their expressions, but they said no more about it.

Teressa looked up as the clock chimed the hour. Eleven-thirty. Two and a half hours until she saw him again. Just thinking about it made her stomach flutter with excitement, and she pushed her plate away, too nervous to eat.

Her parents made small talk as they lingered over breakfast. Teressa listened quietly, her thoughts on her coming meeting with Wolf Shadow. She shook her head. She would have to call him Chance here in the city, she thought, though he would always be Wolf Shadow as far as she was concerned.

"Teressa?"

She looked up, aware that her mother had said something to her.

"I'm sorry, Mama, I wasn't listening. What did you say?"

"I asked if you are going to visit Cynthia today," her mother repeated.

"Yes. We're going shopping. I'm to be there at two."

"I'll have Mason bring the carriage around," her father said, rising. "I'll see you both at dinner."

He paused beside Teressa's chair and squeezed her shoulder. "Have a good day, my dear."

"Thank you, Papa."

Teressa rose from the table while her father kissed her mother good-bye. She didn't want to be left alone with Rosalia, not now.

Edward leaned down and kissed Rosalia's cheek. "I may be late."

"We will wait for you, Eduardo."

"I'll walk you to the door, Papa," Teressa said, and linked her arm with his.

She bid her father good-bye, then hurried up to her room and closed the door.

Only two hours to get ready! Whatever would she wear?


Chance spent the early part of the afternoon satisfying his curiosity about the Barbary Coast. He had been warned by the clerk at the hotel to avoid the place at night, when the jayhawkers, short-card sharps, rounders, pickpockets, prostitutes and their assistants were out and about, but he figured he'd be safe enough during the day.

Strolling through the area bounded by Montgomery, Stockton, Washington, and Broadway streets, one hand resting lightly on the butt of his gun, Chance got a glimpse of what the area was like after dark. Here and there, frowsy, overblown women stared at him from their seats just inside open doorways, an invitation in their eyes. Chance had been warned to avoid these "deadfalls" as they were called, places where the bar stocked drugged whiskey. Beyond the open doorways, tawdry red and white curtains hung over arched doorways into back rooms he had no desire to see.

He passed Chinese "coolies" carrying bamboo poles balanced on their shoulders at every turn. He saw a number of Chinese women, as well, and couldn't help staring at their odd clothing—loose blue or black cotton trousers and straight-cut sacques of broadcloth, satin, or cotton. The wealthier ones wore fancy satin slippers and gold or silver bracelets.

He watched a couple of small black-skinned men with straight black hair and sharp black eyes carrying huge baskets on their heads. He had never seen black men before and he stared at them curiously, and grinned when they stared back. Equally curious, perhaps?

It seemed every other building was a saloon, none of which seemed to be doing any business in the light of day. He glanced at the names as he passed by. *The Roaring Gimlet, The Bull's Run, The Cock of the Walk, Star of the Union, Every Man Is Welcome.*

The only life in the place seemed to come from a Chinese gambling house where loud music drifted out the door. He saw several rows of Chinese men sitting on long low benches in a basement, all of them busily engaged in rolling cigars. The sign over the doorway proclaimed they were *Choice Brands of Havana and Domestic Cigars.*

Chance shook his head as he left the area. He'd been in some tough towns—Dodge, Kansas City, Hays, Deadwood, but the Barbary Coast beat them all.

After swinging onto Smoke's back, he left the Coast behind. It was one-thirty, and he didn't want to be late.

Teressa sat close to the carriage window, her heart pounding. Would he be there? She leaned out the window as they reached the bottom of the hill. Was he here? She felt the first stirrings of disappointment stir within her, and then he rode out of the shadows between two buildings, a tall handsome man astride a big bay mare.

As he left the alley, she saw that he was wearing a pair of brown whipcord trousers, boots, and a dark green shirt. A black hat was pulled low on his forehead, and his holster was strapped around his lean waist. He looked dark and dangerous and more handsome than ever.

Teressa smiled and settled back in the seat as Chance fell in behind the carriage. Soon, she thought, soon she would be in his arms again.

A short time later the carriage drew up in front of Cynthia Witherspoon's house. Teressa alighted as soon as Mason opened the door and lowered the step.

"Thank you, Mason."

"Shall I wait, miss?"

"That won't be necessary. Take the day off, if you like. Just be back before dinner, say six o'clock?"

"Yes, miss. Thank you, miss."

She opened the gate and started up the walk. Pausing, she glanced over her shoulder to make sure the carriage was gone, then hurried back down the walk to where Chance was holding the gate open for her.

She looked up at him and smiled. "Hello."

"Hello, yourself," he murmured, and pulled her into his arms.

For a moment she surrendered to his kiss; then, mindful of being out in the open, she drew away. "Not here."

"Where, then?"

"I don't know." She bit down on her lower lip, her brow furrowed thoughtfully. "I have to go explain to Cynthia. She's waiting for me. I'll be right back."

Chance watched her hurry up the steps to the front door, noting the gentle sway of her hips. She wore a pale blue dress that he guessed probably cost more than he paid his cowhands in a year, and a small white hat with blue feathers.

A butler answered the door and Teressa disappeared inside. The man stared at Chance with disdain, then closed the door.

Chance glanced up and down the street. The houses were all large and well kept, the grounds impeccable, a sharp contrast to the seedier side of the city he had visited earlier, where harlots waited in shadowed alleyways and men sought forgetfulness in smoke-filled opium dens.

He glanced up at the house, wondering what was taking Teressa so long.

Cynthia Witherspoon swept into the front parlor in a brown-and-yellow-striped dress dripping lace at the collar and cuffs. She was a tall girl, with light brown hair, hazel eyes, and a determined chin. A dimple winked in her cheek when she smiled at her guest.

"Tess! You're right on time. Come in and sit down. Helga made the most divine tea cakes. I can't wait for you to try one."

"Not now, Cyn. I know we were supposed to spend the day together, but something's come up."

"Is something wrong?"

"No, nothing like that." Teressa took Cynthia's hands in hers. "He's here, Cyn. Wolf Shadow is in San Francisco."

"He is! When can I meet him?"

"Soon. He's waiting for me outside."

"He's here now? Where?" Cynthia hurried to the window in the front parlor and pulled back the edge of the curtain. "Oh! Is that him? The man standing by the horse?"

"Yes."

"He's very handsome, isn't he?"

"I told you he was. Anyway, I want to spend the day with him."

"Of course you do. Where are the two of you going?"

"Just somewhere where we can be alone."

Cynthia's eyes lit up. "That's so romantic! But do be careful. I can't imagine what your mother would say."

"I can, but it doesn't matter. Oh, Cyn, I love him so much."

Cynthia hugged her. "I was the one who always wanted to go and have adventures, remember? You were the one who wanted to stay at home. Life just isn't fair." She loosed a dramatic sigh. "You'd better not keep him waiting any longer. What time will you be back?"

"Sometime before dinner."

"All right." Cynthia's expression sobered. "Do be careful, Tess."

"I will." Teressa hugged her friend, then hurried out of the house and down the steps.

"Ready?" Chance asked.

"Yes."

He lifted her up on Smoke's back, then vaulted up behind her. Taking up the reins, he clucked to the mare.

"Where are we going?" she asked.

"I found a place on the outskirts of town where we can be alone."

"What kind of place?"

His lips brushed her hair. "You'll see."

Content to go wherever he wanted, she leaned back against him, happier than she had been in weeks.

He took her to the back of a park located near the outskirts of the city. Dismounting, he lifted her from Smoke's back, unsaddled and hobbled the horse, and then took her in his arms.

She hugged him tight. "I missed you so much! I didn't think you were coming."

His gazed burned into hers. "How could you think that?"

"I was afraid," she admitted. "Afraid you didn't love me the way I love you."

"Don't ever be afraid again," he admonished, his voice husky.

She cupped his cheek in the palm of her hand. "I still can't believe you're here."

"Maybe this will convince you," he said, and claimed her lips with his own.

A slow fire spread through her, engulfing her, warming the cold, empty places his absence had left deep inside her.

His tongue slid over her lower lip, dipped inside to engage in a sensual mating dance with her own.

She moaned softly, her fingers digging into his back

to draw him closer, closer. She gasped, "I love you," when he lifted his head, and then he was kissing her again, harder, deeper, his hands gliding over her body until she was shivering with desire, aching with need.

Chance swore softly as they parted, both out of breath.

Teressa looked up at him. "Wolf . . ."

"I know, sweetheart." He glanced around. He couldn't make love to her, not here. This was a public place and even though it was deserted now, that didn't mean it would stay that way. "How do you feel about going to a hotel?"

"Together?" Her eyes widened. "In broad daylight?" Though she had only been back home for a few weeks, her mother had already made certain she understood how important it was to comport herself in a ladylike manner at all times. An unmarried woman's reputation must be above reproach.

He shrugged. "Not a very good idea, I guess."

"I don't care! I want you so badly. Let's go somewhere. Hurry!"

Minutes later, Smoke was saddled and they were riding back toward the city.

Chance drew rein in front of the first hotel they came to. Dismounting, he tossed the reins over the hitching post, then lifted Teressa from the back of the mare. Taking her hand, he led the way into the hotel.

It was small and clean. Chance asked for a room, signed the register, and picked up the key.

Teressa's heart was pounding as they made their way up the staircase and down the hall to their room. Chance opened the door, swung her into his arms, carried her across the threshold, and closed the door with his foot. Then he took off his hat and tossed it on the chair.

Teressa glanced at their surroundings. It was a pretty room, done in dusty rose and white. But it was the bed that caught her eye. A big brass bed with a cherry-colored spread. The sight of it, and what they would be doing in it, made her heart pound with anticipation.

Chance followed her gaze. "We don't have to make love if you'd rather not," he said. "We can just talk."

A faint blush pinked her cheeks. "I haven't changed my mind."

He kissed her as he lowered her feet to the floor, his body reacting immediately to the feel of her body sliding against his. "You're sure?"

She wrapped her arms around his waist. "Very," she replied, and then looked up at him, her eyes narrowed. "You haven't changed your mind, have you?"

He put his hands over her buttocks and drew her hips closer, letting her feel his arousal. "No, ma'am."

Chance took a few steps backward, drawing her with him, and then fell back on the bed.

"Wolf Shadow, my hat! You'll crush it."

"Sorry, sweetheart."

She quickly removed the pin that held it in place and set it on the table beside the bed, then, laughing softly, she bent down to drop butterfly kisses on his cheeks, his nose, his jaw.

When he reached for her, she batted away his hands. Sitting up, she straddled his hips and then began to unbutton his shirt. He lifted up a little so she could slide it off his shoulders. She dropped his shirt on the floor, paused a moment to admire the width of his shoulders, the broad expanse of his chest, his hard, flat stomach, then reached for the buckle of his gunbelt. He obligingly lifted his hips so she could remove it, sucked in a breath when she unfastened his belt buckle, unbuttoned his fly.

"Hold on a minute," he said. "It's my turn."

Holding her gaze with his own, he unfastened the long row of tiny cloth-covered buttons that fastened her gown down the front. He drew the bodice slowly over her shoulders and down her arms, slipped the straps of her chemise down, baring her breasts to his gaze.

"Beautiful," he murmured. "So beautiful."

Gathering her skirts in his hands, he lifted her dress and petticoats over her head and tossed them aside, leaving her clad in only her shoes, stockings, and drawers.

She ran her hands over his chest.

He caressed her breasts.

She pulled off his boots and his socks.

He removed her shoes, slid his hands over the smooth curve of her thighs before removing her stockings.

She dragged his trousers over his lean hips and down his legs and tossed them on the floor in a heap.

He peeled off her drawers, plucked the pins from her hair until it fell like a dark brown waterfall over her shoulders, and then tugged her down beside him, crushing her breasts against his chest while his hands drifted lazily over the smooth skin of her back.

"How soon do you have to be home?" he asked.

"Not for hours."

A slow smile spread over his face. "Hours to make love to you."

She smiled back at him, her fingertips playing in the hair on his chest, sliding over his belly, teasing the inside of his thigh.

"Keep that up and it won't take hours," he drawled.

Happy laughter rose in her throat as she locked her arms around his neck. "I'm sure we'll be able to find a way to fill the time."

"Got any ideas?"

"We could do this." She nibbled on his earlobe. "Or this." Her tongue slid across his lower lip.

"Or this," he said, and deftly tucking her beneath

him, he kissed her, his tongue plundering the warm depths of her mouth, his hands playing over her body. He was the bow and she was the violin, and his touch was the touch of the master's hand, playing notes only he would ever hear.

She quivered beneath him as his body merged with hers, giving him everything she had to give, reveling in every kiss, every caress, until her body arched with pleasure, her hands clutching at his shoulders as ripples of pleasure spread through her.

He cried her name as her body convulsed around him. With one last thrust, he followed her over the edge.

He rolled onto his side, drawing her with him, their bodies still joined, while the sweat cooled on their skin and their breathing returned to normal.

Her eyes were closed, and his gaze moved over her face, noting the sweep of her lashes on her cheeks, the smile on her face that said she had been well and truly pleasured, the curve of her cheek, still faintly flushed with passion.

Leaning forward, he brushed a kiss across her lips.

She moaned softly and opened her eyes, her smile widening. "I love you."

Her words sank deep into his soul, wrapped around his heart like fine silken threads, forever binding his heart to hers.

"Teressa . . . sweetheart."

"Tell me," she whispered.

"I love you," he said, his voice rough with emotion, yet the words seemed inadequate to convey the depth of his love, to express the way she made him feel, the things she made him want. For the first time since his mother died, he wanted more than revenge. He wanted a real home, a wife, a family.

She gazed into his eyes, hers glowing with love.

"Marry me, Tessa."

"All right."

"Just like that?" he asked, chuckling.

"Just like that."

"Are you sure? Your folks won't like it. They might even disown you."

She threw her arms around his neck. "I don't care."

"Brave girl. I always said you had the heart of a warrior."

"When?" she asked, dropping kisses on his cheeks, his brow, the tip of his chin.

"That's up to you."

"I'll have to tell my parents."

Chance nodded. "Do you want me to be there?"

She nodded, grateful that he had offered. She would need his strength because her mother and father were going to be furious when they found out. But she didn't want to think about that now. All she wanted was to be in Wolf Shadow's arms.

It was what he wanted too, and he spent the next two hours telling her and showing her how much he loved her in every way he could think of.


Teressa sighed. "I wish we could stay here forever."

They were lying on the bed, facing each other, arms and legs entwined. Chance gave her shoulder a squeeze. "We could stay and live on room service."

She grinned and then grew sober. "My parents will never approve of our marriage. Maybe we should just run away."

"Is that what you want to do? If it is, just say so."

"I don't know." Her finger made lazy circles on his chest. "They really have been good to me since we got here. I know they love me. I hate to hurt them. . . ."

His hand caressed her cheek. "Just tell me what you want to do, sweetheart."

"Maybe we should tell them and see what happens. We can always run away if they put up a big fuss."

"All right. That's what we'll do." He glanced out the window. "We'd better go. It's getting late."

Rising, they filled the basin on the highboy with water from the pitcher and took turns washing each other and then drying each other off.

When they were dressed, Chance drew Teressa into his arms for one more hug, one more kiss, and then reluctantly released her. "When do you want to talk to your folks?"

"Tomorrow's Sunday. Papa will be home all day. Can you come by after lunch, say about one-thirty?"

Chance plucked his hat from the chair and settled it on his head. "I'll be there."

Standing up on her tiptoes, she kissed his cheek, then took his hand and they left the hotel.

Outside, Chance paused on the boardwalk, his glance sweeping up one side of the street and down the other.

"Is something wrong?" Teressa asked.

"I don't know. I have the feeling we're being watched."

# Chapter 31

Teressa glanced up and down the street. The board-walk was crowded as usual. Well-dressed women could be seen browsing in shop windows or standing in the shade, visiting. Several young boys were rolling hoops down the alley across the street; there were a number of men hurrying to and fro. A man in a straw hat was unloading crates from a large wagon.

"I don't see anyone who seems to be watching us," she said, alarmed by Wolf Shadow's tone. "Do you?"

He shook his head. "No. It's just a feeling." A feeling that had saved his life on more than one occasion. "Come on. Let's get out of here."

He lifted her onto Smoke's back, took up the reins, and swung up behind her. Clucking to the mare, he rode away from the hotel, a furious itching between his shoulder blades.

They made good time back to the Witherspoon house. Chance dismounted and lifted Teressa from the saddle. He glanced up and down the street; seeing no one, he drew her into his arms and gave her a quick kiss. "I love you, sweetheart."

"I love you more."

"Impossible." He kissed the tip of her nose. "I'll see you tomorrow," he promised.

She nodded. Lifting the hem of her skirt, she turned and hurried up the path to the house.

Cynthia was waiting for her in the front parlor. "Well," she said, putting aside the book she had been reading. "I don't have to ask if you had a good time."

Teressa felt her cheeks grow hot. "What do you mean?"

"I mean it's written all over your face. You're practically glowing." Cynthia patted the seat beside her. "Come here and tell me everything."

Teressa sat down beside her friend and folded her hands in her lap.

"So, tell me. What did you do? Where did you go?"

"We spent the whole day in a hotel room."

"A hotel!" Cynthia exclaimed, looking mortified. "What were you thinking? What if your parents find out?"

Teressa shrugged as if it didn't matter, although the very thought filled her with dread. "I don't care. I love him, Cyn. I love him so much it hurts."

"What was it like? Weren't you embarrassed? Was he gentle? Did you see him without . . . well, you know . . . naked?"

"Cynthia!" Teressa stared at her friend in shock.

"He's very handsome." Cynthia tugged on Teressa's sleeve. "Come on, 'fess up, Tess. What was it like? I've always heard it's painful the first time. Was it?"

"It wasn't the first time, and it was wonderful, Cyn. You can't imagine."

Cynthia stared at her wide-eyed. "You've done it before? With him?"

"Of course with him!" Teressa closed her eyes a moment, then smiled at her friend. "He asked me to marry him."

"Marry him!" Cynthia squealed. "But he's—"

She broke off as Teressa's eyes narrowed ominously. "He's what?"

"He's gorgeous, Tess, but he *is* part Indian. And it

doesn't look like he has much money. And you said he
lives on a ranch." She said the last with an aggrieved
expression. "A ranch, Tess. Is that what you want?"

"I'd live in a mud hut with him if he asked me."

Cynthia blinked at her. "I think you mean that."

"I do."

Cynthia stared at her in disbelief. "But Tess . . . have
you thought about what you'd be giving up? And what
about your parents? You know they'll never approve."

"I know. We're going to talk to them tomorrow
after church. If they won't give us their blessing"—
she shrugged—"we're going to run away."

"On, Tessa, that would be so romantic, but are you
sure you know what you're doing?"

"I'm sure. I've never been surer of anything in my
life."

Some of her courage faltered when Mason arrived
to take her home. It was easy to be brave with Wolf
Shadow and Cynthia, but alone in the carriage doubts
assailed her. Her father was accustomed to having
things his way; as far as he was concerned, his way
was the only way! She didn't want to argue with him.
Even though she hadn't lived under his roof for ten
years, she remembered how much she had loved him
when she was a little girl. She still loved him, even
though at times he seemed stricter and more rigid than
she recalled. She didn't want to hurt his feelings, nor
did she want to spend the rest of her life in San Francisco. She missed Wolf Shadow. She missed his ranch,
the vast countryside uncluttered by buildings and people, the vast blue sky, the quiet nights.

She sat up straight and squared her shoulders. She
was a big girl now, old enough to make her own deci-
sions, old enough to choose her own husband and decide where and how she would live.

Smiling faintly, she gazed out the carriage window. Everything would work out somehow. It just had to.

As it turned out, she was the one who was late for dinner. Hart gave her a disapproving look when he opened the door.

"Your parents have already sat down to dinner, miss," he said.

"Thank you, Hart." Removing her hat, she handed it to him, then hurried into the dining room.

Her father pulled his watch from his pocket, looked at it, then looked up at her, one brow arched.

Teressa slid into her chair, unfolded her napkin, and placed it across her lap. "I'm sorry I'm late."

Rosalia picked up the tiny silver bell beside her plate and rang it. Moments later, Mrs. Rochefort set a plate before Teressa.

"How is Cynthia?" Rosalia asked.

"She's well."

Her father's gaze locked with hers. "Did you have a pleasant day together?"

Something in her father's tone made Teressa suddenly uneasy. "Yes, of course."

"Just the two of you?"

Teressa nodded. "Her parents are out of town, you know, visiting Cyn's brother in Sacramento."

"Alfred is doing very well, I hear," Rosalia remarked.

"Yes," Teressa said. "Cynthia said they're going to make him a partner in the law firm."

"Alfred is a good man," her father remarked. "A credit to his family."

"Yes, indeed," Teressa agreed. She was relieved when her father changed the subject.

Keeping her gaze on her plate, she paid little attention to her parents' conversation. She had a horrible feeling that her father knew where she had spent the day, but that was impossible. Wasn't it?

She excused herself from the table as soon as the meal was over. Upstairs in her room, she paced the floor. Wolf Shadow had remarked that he felt as though they were being watched. Had someone seen her coming out of the hotel with him and reported it to her father? The very idea was appalling.

Going to the window, she stared into the distance. Surely if her father suspected something he would have remarked on it at dinner. Patience was one virtue her father lacked. When he was upset, everyone knew it.

Taking a deep breath, she told herself there was nothing to worry about.

She was still telling herself that when she went to bed that night.


After saying good-bye to Teressa, Chance left Smoke at the livery, then stopped in the hotel dining room for dinner. Sitting there, eating fried steak and potatoes, he couldn't help smiling as his thoughts turned toward Teressa and the day they had spent together. She was everything he had ever dreamed of and never hoped to have. Warm, caring, giving, with more passion than any other woman he had ever known. It was incredible that she loved him, that she was willing to give up a life of ease and refinement to marry him. He only hoped that after a month or two of living on the ranch, she wouldn't regret it.

He left the dining room and stood on the boardwalk for a few minutes, then made his way to the saloon across the street. It didn't take long to find a vacant place at one of the poker tables, and he settled back in his chair, glad to have a way to pass the time for the next few hours.

The men at the table were all strangers to each

other, which kept small talk at a minimum and suited Chance just fine. He won several hands and bought a round of drinks.

He had just picked up a fresh hand when he felt that warning tingle on the back of his neck. He tossed a dollar into the pot, put his cards facedown on the table, then glanced toward the bar, as if he were looking for the bartender. His gaze moved over the faces of the men standing at the rail. No one seemed to be paying him any attention; none of the men avoided his glance, but he couldn't shake the feeling that he was being watched.

He lost the next two hands, threw in the third and left the saloon. He ducked into the doorway of the building at the end of the boardwalk, listening for the sound of footsteps following him, laughed softly when he heard nothing.

Emerging from the shadows, he started across the street.

The faint creak of a footfall behind him was his only warning. He started to turn when white-hot pain exploded across the back of his head and then the world went black.

"So, Tess, what are your plans for the day?" Edward asked as they sat down to lunch on Sunday afternoon.

She unfolded her napkin, then folded it again. "I'm expecting company."

"Company?" Rosalia asked. "Is Cynthia coming over? Why didn't she come home with us after church?"

"It's not Cynthia."

"Did you invite this mysterious person to lunch?" her mother asked. "Should we wait?"

"No."

Rosalia rang the bell; a few moments later, Marie served the afternoon meal.

"So," her father said, "who is this mysterious guest?"

Teressa glanced from her mother to her father. "Mr. McCloud."

Her father lifted one brow. "Indeed?"

"Yes. He's here in San Francisco."

"How do you know that?" her mother asked.

"I . . . I saw him on the street the other day, when I went to Cynthia's, and I asked him to come over today after church. I knew you'd both want to see him again," she said, her words running together in her haste to get them out. "After all, if it weren't for him, I wouldn't be here now."

"Yes, of course," Edward said. "We owe him a great deal."

Teressa breathed a sigh of relief that they hadn't questioned her further. Soon. He would be here soon. A million butterflies seemed to be racing around her stomach at the thought of telling her parents she planned to marry Wolf Shadow. She pushed her food around on her plate, too nervous to eat.

"Was the meal not to your liking, Miss Teressa?" Marie asked when she came in to see if anything else was needed. "Shall I ask Mrs. Rochefort to prepare you something else?"

"No, thank you, Marie. I'm just not very hungry."

With a nod, the maid left the room.

Rosalia placed her napkin on the table and Edward immediately rose to pull her chair out for her. Teressa rose, also. Excusing herself, she hurried up to her room to freshen up. Wolf Shadow would be here soon.

She was downstairs, sitting in the front parlor, when the clock chimed the half hour. Her excitement grew as the minutes passed.

Five minutes.

Ten.

Fifteen.

Rising, she walked to the window, drew back the curtains, and peered outside. No sign of a tall man on a bay horse.

Where was he?

Two o'clock came and went.

Her father strolled into the parlor. He stopped at the hearth and withdrew a cigar from a box on the mantel. He cut off the end, struck a match, and lit the cigar.

"He's late," Teressa remarked inanely.

"Perhaps he was detained," her father said. "Or perhaps he was called back to his ranch on business."

"He would have told me."

"Indeed?" Her father's gaze bored into her, hard and unblinking. "Why would he do that?"

"Because it would have been the polite thing to do, since he knew I was expecting him."

She flinched as the clock struck the quarter hour.

"Polite. Yes, though I do not recall Mr. McCloud as being particularly polite. Do you?"

"He was always kind to me."

"He is not coming, Teressa," Edward said.

She looked up at her father, her heart pounding, a sudden sinking sensation in the pit of her stomach. "What have you done to him?"

"I?" He puffed on his cigar, then shook his head. "I have done nothing to him."

Teressa stared at her father and knew in that instant that he was lying to her.

# Chapter 32

Chance groaned softly as he opened his eyes to blackness as thick as a grave. What happened? And where the hell was he?

His head throbbed with every breath. The floor beneath him seemed to be moving and he closed his eyes again. When he tried to lift his hand to explore the back of his head, he discovered his arms were bound behind his back; his feet were tied at his ankles. The familiar weight of his Colt was missing.

Dammit.

Ignoring the pounding in his head, he opened his eyes again. He couldn't see a thing except for a narrow strip of light beneath what he assumed was a door. There didn't seem to be any windows.

The air was filled with the sharp tangy scent of the ocean; he could hear the faint lapping of waves, the creak of timbers. Fear spiraled through him when he realized he was on a ship.

Cursing softly, he closed his eyes again. It didn't take a genius to figure out who was behind this. It was obvious that Bryant had somehow learned of his meeting with Teressa. There remained only the question of what Bryant's next move would be.

Chance wasn't sure he wanted to know the answer. He never would have guessed her old man would go this far to keep them apart.

The hours passed slowly. He dozed and woke and

dozed again. When next he woke, the light under the door had disappeared.

How long had he been here? His head throbbed; his mouth was dry. He wondered what Teressa was thinking. Was she worried, or angry?

He sat up a little straighter when he heard footsteps outside the door.

There was a faint creak as the door opened. A man stood silhouetted in the opening.

Chance grunted softly. "Bryant."

Edward stepped inside. Drawing a match from his pocket, he lit the lantern hanging on a hook to the left of the doorway, then closed the door behind him. "Mr. McCloud. What am I to do with you?"

"You could find a doctor to stitch up the cut in my head, unless you plan to pitch me into the bay."

"Nothing so barbaric as that."

"Just gonna shanghai me?"

"Would you rather be dead?"

There was no answer to that. Instead he asked, "Will you let me write a letter to my foreman?"

Bryant considered that a moment, then nodded. "I'll have one of the men bring you paper and pen. The ship sets sail at dawn. If you ever make your way back to this part of the world, stay away from my daughter else a worse fate befalls you."

And so saying, Bryant snuffed out the lantern and left the room, leaving Chance staring into the darkness.

Chance dozed again, lulled to sleep by the gentle rocking motion of the ship.

He woke with a start when he heard the door open. A sailor who didn't look old enough to shave entered the room carrying a lantern, a sheet of paper, a bottle of ink, a pen, and a hogleg that was almost bigger than he was.

He placed the paper, bottle, and pen on the floor beside Chance. Pulling a knife from inside his boot, he cut Chance free, then leveled the pistol at him. "Bryant said to let you write a letter," he said, taking a step backward. "See that's all you do."

Shaking the rope off his wrists, Chance uncapped the bottle of ink and dipped the pen in the bottle. Writing slowly, he began to set down instructions to his foreman, his mind racing. He had to get out of here before the ship set sail.

He glanced up at the sailor. The kid had lowered the gun, but he was watching him intently.

Chance took a deep breath. He was only going to get one chance to make a break for it.

Shifting his position, he made as though he was going to dip the pen again. Instead, he grabbed the bottle and flung the contents into the kid's face. Lunging forward, he grabbed the kid around the knees and jerked backward. The kid landed hard on his butt, the back of his head hitting the floor with a satisfying thud. The gun fell from his hand and went skittering across the floor.

The kid sat up, dazed, black ink dripping down his cheeks.

Chance drew back his fist and launched a haymaker. With a grunt, the kid's eyes rolled up in his head and he went limp. Pulling the knife from the sailor's boot, Chance cut his feet free, picked up the kid's gun, and lurched to his feet. He lifted his free hand, exploring a lump on the back of his head. His hair was stiff with dried blood.

"That's one I owe you, Bryant," he muttered.

Chance blew out a deep breath, waited until his feet were steady under him, then peered out of the open doorway. The passageway ahead of him was empty. Moving slowly and cautiously, he headed toward the ladder that led to the upper deck.

The ship was quiet under a full moon. Holstering

the gun, he climbed up on deck. He made his way toward the rear of the ship, keeping to the shadows.

"You there! Stop!"

He didn't wait to see if they were talking to him or someone else. He climbed up on the rail and dove over the side.

Bryant slammed his fist on the desk. "What do you mean, he got away?"

The young sailor shifted nervously from one foot to the other, then cleared his throat. "I . . . uh . . ."

Bryant jabbed a finger in the boy's direction. "What's that all over your face?"

A tide of red washed into the kid's cheeks. "Ink, sir. He threw it in my face, then hit me when I was down."

Bryant jerked his head toward the door. "Go on, get out of here. And tell Twist I want my money back."

The kid nodded sharply and hurried out of the room.

Bryant muttered an oath. Damn. Why hadn't McCloud stayed back on his ranch where he belonged?

Teressa was coming down the stairs from her bedroom when she saw a young man leave her father's office. Whether it was impulse or inspiration, she didn't know, but she followed the sailor out of the house and down the driveway.

"Wait, please."

He stopped, started to turn, and then kept going.

"Please, wait!"

He stopped this time, his expression guarded as he turned to face her.

"What did you see my father about?"

"Business."

"What kind of business? Did it have anything to do with a man? A man named McCloud?"

The young man's eyes widened, and then he shook his head.

"It did, didn't it?" Teressa asked insistently. "Do you know where he is? Is he . . . Oh, Lord, he isn't . . . ?" She couldn't say the word.

The young man rubbed his jaw. "He's alive and well, miss. That's all I can tell you."

Relief washed through her. "Thank you."

Turning, she hurried back into the house and up to her room. Whatever her father had planned had obviously failed. She had to find Wolf Shadow, but how? He wouldn't come here again; she was sure of that.

She paced the floor, then went to the window and stared out into the darkness.

If he wanted to get in touch with her, what would he do?

Of course! He would leave a message for her with Cynthia.

Feeling better, she put on her nightgown and went to bed. The sooner she got to sleep, the sooner tomorrow would come.

The sun had barely cleared the horizon when she woke the following morning. Dressing quickly, she tiptoed down the hall and out of the house. Hurrying to the barn, she roused Mason from bed, waited impatiently while he harnessed a horse to the carriage.

"Are you sure about this, miss?" Mason asked as he handed her into the carriage.

"Your father didn't say anything about your going anywhere this morning."

"He must have forgotten," Teressa said imperiously. "Please hurry. I don't want to be late."

Mason looked at her speculatively for a moment,

then, with a shrug, he closed the door and took his seat on the box.

Teressa spread a lap robe over her legs as the carriage lurched forward. Her parents would be furious when they learned she had gone out without telling them, but she would deal with them later. Right now, she had to know that Wolf Shadow was all right.

The Witherspoons' butler was not happy to see her so early in the morning. "Miss Cynthia is still abed." His expression said that was where she should be, too.

"I must see her right away, Manly. Please tell her I'm here."

"Very well, miss. Come in." Manly stepped back so she could enter the foyer.

Teressa stepped over the threshold and followed Manly into the parlor. "Sit down, please."

She did as he asked, only to gain her feet again as soon as he left the room. She was too agitated to sit still. It was a large room with high ceilings and green-and-gold-striped wallpaper. Windows overlooked the street and the side yard. Lamps with fancy fringed shades were set on the tables. A thick carpet covered the floor.

She turned quickly at the sound of footsteps.

"Tess, what on earth are you doing here at this time of the morning?" Cynthia asked. She smothered a yawn behind her hand. "Do you know what time it is?"

"Has Wolf Shadow been here? Did he leave any message for me?"

"Yes, he did. He came by late last night and gave me a letter and asked if I'd give it to you today. How did you know? My father was very upset that I had a male caller at such an hour."

"I'm sorry to cause you trouble, Cyn. Where's the letter?"

Cynthia waved at one of the chairs. "Sit down." She smothered another yawn. "I'll get it."

Teressa was too excited to sit. She walked to the window, looked out, walked back to the center of the room.

Cynthia returned a few minutes later. "Here." She extended a white envelope. "What does he say?"

Teressa's fingers were shaking as she opened the envelope and withdrew a single sheet of paper. She read the words quickly.

> *Teressa, I'm sorry about yesterday. I was detained. If you can get away, meet me at the hotel where we met before. I'll wait until midnight. Chance."*

"Well," Cynthia said, "what does it say?"

"He wants me to meet him at the hotel today."

"What time?"

"Anytime. He said he'll wait until tonight."

Cynthia sighed, her hands clutched to her breasts. "That's so romantic. Just like Romeo and Juliet."

"Who are they? Romeo and Juliet?"

"It's a play by Shakespeare about a boy and girl who fall in love. But their families are enemies and refuse to let them be married. Anyway, it has a very unhappy ending."

"What happened to them?"

"They died."

"Oh!"

"Let's hope your romance has a happier ending," Cynthia said, giving her a hug. "Just be careful."

"I will."

Returning home, Teressa was relieved to find that her parents were still abed. She tiptoed up the back stairs and entered her bedroom, closing the door behind her; then she took Wolf Shadow's note from her pocket and read it again. Detained? Though he hadn't said so, she was certain her father had something to do with that. But what?

After changing into her nightgown, she slipped back into bed and drew the covers up to her chin. She hadn't intended to go back to sleep, but she woke with a start when Marie came in to light the fire and lay out her clothes for the day.

A short time later, clad in a clean dress, her hair in a long braid down her back, Teressa went downstairs to breakfast.

"Good morning," her mother said, smiling.

"Good morning, Mama. Papa."

Her father lowered his morning paper and smiled at her. "You slept late," he remarked.

Teressa shrugged as she slid into her chair. Lifting the cover on the tray in the center of the table, she helped herself to ham and eggs and biscuits.

"Have you any plans for this afternoon?" her father asked.

"I thought I might go shopping with Cynthia. Why?"

"No reason. You'd better finish your breakfast. Mr. Russell will be here for your lesson shortly."

Teressa nodded. Mr. Russell was her tutor. He said she was making remarkable progress. Even Teressa was surprised at how quickly things came back to her.

They were almost finished with the meal when the butler entered the room.

"What is it, Hart?" her father asked.

"There is a gentleman to see you, sir."

"Take him into the library. I'll join him there in a few minutes."

"Very good, sir."

"Business at home so early in the morning, Eduardo?" Rosalia inquired.

"Yes, my dear." He finished his coffee, wiped his mouth, and laid the napkin aside. "Forgive me."

Rosalia smiled up at him. "Of course."

Teressa waited until her father had left the room, then rose. "I need to get my books," she said. "Mr. Russell will be here. I don't want to keep him waiting."

Rosalia nodded.

Teressa left the room. Her mother wouldn't leave the dining room until she'd had another cup of tea.

As stealthily as she could, Teressa made her way toward the library, located at the far end of the house. The door was closed, but not latched. Leaning closer, she heard a voice she didn't recognize.

". . . followed him to the hotel where they met before."

"He's there now?"

"Yes, sir. Shall we take him?"

Her father didn't answer right away, and then he said, "Not yet. But if my daughter arrives, you are to intercept her and bring her home."

"And McCloud?"

"Have someone watch him. And this time, don't let him get away!"

"Yes, sir."

At the sound of footsteps, she turned and hurried up the stairs to her room. Stunned by what she had heard, she closed the door, then leaned back against it, more certain than ever that her father had somehow kept Chance from coming to the house on Sunday. What kind of game was her father playing? And if he knew she was seeing Chance, why didn't he say so?

Grabbing her books, she went downstairs. Mr. Russell arrived moments later. Try as she might, she couldn't concentrate on her lessons, couldn't think of anything but Wolf Shadow. Was his life in danger because of her? More than once, Mr. Russell asked her where her mind was. At last, the two hours were up and Mr. Russell took his leave, saying that he hoped she would be more attentive next time.

She was glad her father hadn't come home for lunch. She didn't think she could sit through a meal with him and not demand to know what he had done to Wolf Shadow. Her mother chatted about a birthday party one of her friends was giving for a mutual acquaintance, which relieved Teressa of having to make small talk.

When the meal was over, she called for the carriage. Twenty minutes later she was sitting at a small round table with Cynthia in Cynthia's sitting room.

"I need your help, Cyn."

"Does it have anything to do with that gorgeous man?"

"Yes."

"What can I do?"

"I want you to go to the hotel and meet him. My father is having Wolf Shadow followed, so I can't go."

Cynthia's face lit up. "Oh, this is so exciting! I feel like a spy. What should I tell him?"

"Tell him he's being watched and . . ." Teressa frowned. "I don't know! If he's being followed, there's no way for us to meet."

Cynthia tapped her fingers on the table. "Maybe he needs a disguise."

"A disguise?"

"Of course! Let's see. What about one of my father's suits? Oh! Even better. What about one of Helga's dresses? He could wear one of her big hats, too, to hide his face. She has one with a black veil that she wears to church."

"Wolf Shadow? In a dress?" Teressa burst out laughing.

"They're about the same size," Cynthia said, giggling. "He could even wear her dress over his own clothes."

"It's worth a try. If he's willing, tell him to meet us at St. Mathias at two o'clock."

"Us?"

"Of course. No one will suspect three women going to church."

Cynthia grinned. "Are you going to wait for me here?"

"No. Someone might be watching me, too. I'll have Mason drive me to town and drop me off at Lawson's. I'll go out the back door and meet you at the church. Are you sure you want to do this, Cyn?" Teressa asked. "After all, your reputation . . ."

"Fiddlesticks! You're my best friend." Cynthia said, patting Teressa's shoulder. "I'll see you at St. Mathias at two."

# Chapter 33

Chance paced the floor of his hotel room, wondering if Teressa had received his message, wondering if she would come.

He lifted a hand to his head. He had taken the time to stop and see a doctor the night before. The sawbones had cleaned the wound, remarking that Chance was lucky he had such a hard head.

The clock had just struck the quarter hour when there was a knock at the door. Bless the girl. She was here.

Her name was on his lips as he opened the door, but it wasn't Teressa. It was her friend, carrying a wrapped parcel in a large string bag.

"What are you doing here?" he asked, frowning.

"May I come in? I have a message from Tessa."

Chance stepped back to allow her into the room, closed the door behind her.

He listened somewhat skeptically as Cynthia told him their plan. When she finished, he eyed the parcel she had placed on the bed.

"Hurry," she said. "It's almost two."

Chance opened the package to reveal a dark brown and green dress and a large, floppy-brimmed hat with a veil. "You want me to wear this?"

Cynthia nodded. "No one will recognize you."

Chance grunted. That was for damn sure. "What about shoes?"

"I can't help you there. Helga has very small feet, but I think the dress will cover your boots."

Chance shook his head, then reached for the dress, pulled it over his head, and shoved his arms into the sleeves.

"It fits," Cynthia exclaimed. Moving around behind him, she began to button up the back. "Your gun makes a large lump on your hip. Maybe you'd better take it off."

"I don't think that's a good idea."

"You can wrap it up in paper and I can carry it in my bag."

Chance considered that for a moment, then nodded. Reaching under the skirt, he removed his gunbelt and wrapped it in brown paper, then put it in the bag.

Cynthia put the hat on his head and dropped the veil in place. "Your long hair adds the perfect touch," she remarked. "Let me see you walk."

"Walk?"

She nodded and made a get-along motion with her hand.

Chance walked across the floor.

"No, no, no," Cynthia said. "You have to take much smaller steps, and try to move your hips a little. Like this." She walked to the window and back. "See?"

With a shake of his head, Chance tried again.

"That's a little better. Try again."

With an aggrieved sigh, Chance shortened his stride and tried to put a sway in his walk.

Ten minutes later, Cynthia was of the opinion that he was as good as he was going to get.

"Let's go." She picked up her bag, a small gasp of surprise issuing from her lips. "How do you wear this thing? It's so heavy."

Chance shrugged.

"Remember," she said, opening the door, "small steps. And keep your head down."

Feeling like a fool, Chance followed Cynthia down the stairway and out of the hotel. She had a carriage waiting out front. He watched her climb in. She was all grace and elegance. Following her inside, he was certain he looked anything but graceful.

Once the carriage was on its way, he glanced out the window. No one seemed to be following them.

St. Mathias was located on the corner of a quiet intersection. When the carriage came to a halt, the driver hopped down from the box to open the door.

Chance put his hand on Cynthia's arm to stay her. "Wait a minute," he said quietly.

"Thank you, Parker. I believe we'll just sit here a moment."

"Yes, ma'am," the driver replied, and moved away from the carriage.

"What are we waiting for?" Cynthia asked.

"To see if anyone comes up behind us."

They sat there for perhaps five minutes before Chance deemed it safe to enter the church.

Teressa was waiting for them on the back pew. There was no one else in the church save for an elderly woman kneeling at the altar in the front of the church.

Chance slid into the pew beside Teressa, and Cynthia slid in beside him.

Teressa looked at him and burst out laughing. She clapped her hand over her mouth when the elderly woman turned to stare at her.

"I overheard my father talking this morning," Teressa said, her voice low. "What did he do to you?"

"He tried to shanghai me."

Her eyes widened in disbelief. "He wouldn't!"

"Well, he did."

"Were you scared?"

He took her hand in his and gave it a squeeze. "I was afraid I'd never see you again."

"Are you all right?" she asked anxiously.

"I'm fine."

"What are we going to do now?"

"What do you want to do?"

"I want to be with you."

"Are you ready to go?" he asked.

"Now?" She had nothing but the clothes on her back and her reticule, which held only a few dollars and a lace handkerchief.

"Right now. There's a train leaving in about thirty minutes."

She didn't hesitate. "Let's go."

He squeezed her hand. "That's my girl. I'll leave first. Cynthia, can you take her to the station?"

"Of course." Cynthia pressed one hand to her heart. "Oh, this is so romantic!"

Chance grinned at the girl's theatrics. "Tessa, I'll see you at the train." He squeezed her hand again. "Be sure to bring Cynthia's bag with you," he said, and slid out of the pew.

Cynthia moved closer to Teressa. "I'll miss you," she said woefully.

"I'll write to you," Teressa said. "And you can come visit us."

Cynthia brightened. "Oh, that would be so exciting! What shall I tell your parents when they come looking for you?"

"Just tell them I've gone home."

Thirty minutes later, Teressa was sitting beside Chance, who was still in disguise. "What about Smoke?" she asked, dropping Cynthia's bag on the floor. "Are you just going to leave her here?"

"No. I asked the livery man to have her loaded on the next train."

"Why didn't you bring her on this one?"

"I didn't want to arouse any suspicion, in case your father's having the livery watched, too."

"Oh. I still can't believe he tried to shanghai you." The very thought sent chills down her spine. Men who were shanghaied were rarely seen or heard from again.

With a shrill whistle and a grinding of wheels, the engine set into motion. Teressa glanced out the window. She couldn't help feeling a moment of regret at not being able to tell her mother and father good-bye and yet, if it weren't for her father, she wouldn't be running away.

With a sigh, she settled back in her seat once more. "Are we going to the ranch?"

"Yeah." If Bryant came after him again, he wanted to be on his own land.

She was quiet a moment before she said, "Do you think my father will come after us?"

"What do you think?" He shifted on the seat. "I feel as if I'm smothering in this thing," he said, brushing at the veil that covered his face.

Teressa grinned at him. "I guess you could take it off."

"Good idea."

The train wasn't too crowded; there were only a few other people in the car, most of them looking out the window. A woman was crooning softly to the baby in her arms. A man in a suit and tie was reading the newspaper.

For all that he'd thought no one was paying any attention, all eyes seemed to be on him as he jerked the hat from his head and tossed it on the floor, then turned his back toward Teressa so she could unbutton the dress.

Chance hadn't known too many embarrassing moments in his life, but this one topped them all. Rising, he stepped out of the dress and shoved it under the seat, along with the hat. Picking up the string bag, he unwrapped his gun belt and holster and strapped it on. The familiar weight of the Colt against his hip was reassuring.

He ran a hand through his hair, wishing he hadn't left his own hat at the hotel.

Teressa grinned at him. "Welcome back, Mr. McCloud."

"Very funny," he muttered.

"It was a good idea, though," she said.

He nodded. "Was it yours?"

"No, Cynthia gets all the credit."

"Smart girl."

"Yes. I'm going to miss her."

He slid his arm around her shoulders. "Are you sure about this?"

She snuggled against him. "I'm sure."

"I'd like us to get married as soon as we get back to the ranch. How do you feel about that?"

She looked up at him, her eyes filled with love. "Wonderful."

He kissed her lightly. "We'll talk to the preacher as soon as we get to Buffalo Springs."


The trip to Crooked River was uneventful. After disembarking from the train, they went directly to the stage depot. The next stage to Buffalo Springs wasn't due until the following afternoon. Chance bought two tickets, and then they walked down the dusty street toward the center of town.

Crooked River was booming, Chance thought, glancing around. There were new buildings going up on both sides of the street. Several others wore new coats of paint.

Teressa tugged on his arm and he turned to see her looking in the window of the Bon Ton Millinery Shoppe.

"Look," she said, pointing at a white straw hat bedecked with colorful ribbons.

"It's pretty." He ran a hand through his hair, wishing again that he hadn't left his hat back in 'Frisco.

"Do you think I could try it on?"

"Sure, honey. I'll wait for you out here."

With a smile, she opened the door and stepped inside.

Chance watched Teressa sit down on a small stool while a gray-haired lady in a dark blue dress handed her the bonnet. Teressa put it on, deftly tied the ribbons beneath her chin, then turned toward the window. She tilted her head to one side, a smile on her face.

Chance nodded his approval.

She spoke to the clerk, then pulled two dollars from her bag and handed it to the woman. A moment later, she stepped out onto the boardwalk.

"Do you like it?" she asked.

He nodded. "Very much." He ran his hand through his hair again. "I need a new hat, too."

"There's a shop over there," Teressa said, pointing across the street.

She entered the store with him, stood quietly while he tried on a black hat with a rolled brim.

He turned to face her. "What do you think?"

"I like the tan one."

Chance plucked another hat off the shelf. "This one?"

Teressa nodded.

Removing the black hat, he tried on the tan one. "All right, the tan one it is." He paid for the hat, grateful that the men who had shanghaied him hadn't robbed him as well, although he imagined they would have thought of it sooner or later.

They left the store and continued down the street to the hotel, where Chance secured a room for the two of them.

Teressa couldn't help blushing when the clerk's gaze settled on her left hand, obviously looking for a wedding ring. Squaring her shoulders, she met his smirk with an aloof expression.

The clerk slid a key across the desk. "Room twenty-three."

"We'd like some hot water sent up for a bath," Chance said, picking up the key.

"Yes, sir."

Taking Teressa by the hand, Chance headed for the staircase.

Room twenty-three was located at the end of the hall. It was a large corner room with one window overlooking Main Street and another overlooking an alley. Starched white curtains hung at the windows. The bed was large, covered with a blue and beige spread. A large cherrywood chest with an oval mirror stood against one wall. A comfortable-looking overstuffed chair stood in the corner. There was a zinc tub partially hidden behind a screen.

Chance tossed the key on top of the dresser, then drew Teressa into his arms. With a sigh, she rested her cheek against his chest. His lips brushed the crown of her head as his arms tightened around her.

"Tell me no one will ever separate us again," Teressa said, clinging to him.

"No one will ever take you from me again. I can promise you that."

She smiled up at him. "I love you, Wolf Shadow."

He arched one brow. "Wolf Shadow?"

She shrugged. "That's how I always think of you. Would you rather I called you Chance?"

He chuckled softly. "Sweetheart, you can call me anything you want."

Rising on tiptoes, she locked her hands at his nape and pressed her lips to his, only to pull away when there was a knock at the door. "That didn't take long," she remarked.

"Not long enough," Chance muttered as he opened the door to admit two young men carrying buckets of hot water.

They filled the tub, nodded at Teressa, and left the room.

"Too bad the tub's not bigger," Chance mused as he closed and locked the door.

Teressa looked at him, a teasing smile curving her lips. "And why do we need a bigger tub? This one looks plenty big enough to me."

"Big enough for you, maybe. But not for the two of us."

"The two of us?"

He pointed at her, then at himself. "You. Me. Two."

She gave him a little push. "Ladies first."

"Can I watch?"

She looked at him in mock horror. "No!"

"I'll wash your back," he murmured suggestively.

"I remember the first time you offered to do that," she said.

He put his hand on her shoulder, let it slide slowly down her arm. "And do you remember what else I said?"

She felt her cheeks flush. "You said 'One of these days, I'll ask you to bathe with me and you won't refuse.' But the tub is still too small. Besides, we did bathe together."

"That was in a river. Come on, the water's getting cold."

She wouldn't have believed they could both fit in the tub, which just proved how wrong she could be, and how stubborn he could be.

He got in first and she settled herself between his thighs, her knees bent, her back to his chest. Picking up the soap, Wolf Shadow washed her back and her shoulders, reached around to wash her belly. She was tingling with anticipation as his hands moved upward, shivered with pleasure as his soapy hands slid over her body.

Growing up, she had never dreamed that falling in love would be like this, that any man could become such an intimate and important part of her life.

With a great deal of effort and splashing, she managed to turn around in the tub so they were face-to-face.

"My turn," she said, and taking the soap from his hand, she washed his broad shoulders and muscular chest. It was amazingly erotic to run her hands over his soapy body, to hear the growl of pleasure that rumbled in his throat, to know that her touch aroused him so quickly.

The water was growing cold when Chance lifted her from the tub, quickly dried them both, and carried her to bed.

It was a long time later when they went downstairs for supper.

They boarded the stagecoach a little after noon the next day. The window shades, meant to keep out dust, sun, and rain, were up. Teressa sighed as she glanced out the window. The journey to San Francisco was still fresh in her mind, and she wasn't looking forward to spending another four days bouncing around inside a dusty coach. It was not the most comfortable way to travel. The stage she and her mother had taken to Crooked River had stopped every twenty miles or so to change horses and twice a day to eat. The food along the way had usually consisted of boiled beans, salted meat, hardtack, and coffee, and cost a dollar a plate. The worst part was that the passengers had been given only seven minutes to eat it. Sometimes dinner had consisted of tough beefsteak, boiled potatoes, stewed beans, and dried apple pie. She didn't know which menu was worse.

But she wasn't complaining. She was with Wolf Shadow and that was all that mattered. She glanced at the other passengers in the coach. A red-haired man sat on Wolf's left side. A minister in collar and frock coat sat across from her. A young couple sat beside him. Somewhat shyly, they introduced themselves as Joseph and Emily Thompson. They had been married a month earlier and were returning home from their honeymoon. Teressa was glad no one was sitting on the narrow bench in the center of the coach.

A short time later she felt the coach sway as the driver and guard took their places topside. A sharp crack split the air as the driver snapped the whip and the horses leaned into the traces.

Teressa looked at Wolf Shadow and smiled as he took her hand and gave it a squeeze.

She smiled back, excitement fluttering in her stomach. Soon they would be back at Wolf Shadow's ranch; soon she would be his wife. "Do you think we can go visit the Lakota in the spring?"

"Sure, sweetheart. If that's what you want."

"Lakota?" the florid-faced man exclaimed. "You want to visit Indians? Haven't you heard? They attacked the last stage that went out. Killed three people."

Teressa looked at Wolf Shadow, waiting to see what he would say.

"We have family there," Chance said, his unblinking gaze focused on the other man's face. "You got a problem with that?"

The red-haired man swallowed hard. "I . . . uh . . . No, sir."

Chance's gaze flicked over the faces of the other passengers. "Anybody else?"

There were murmured denials, and suddenly everyone in the coach was looking everywhere and anywhere except at Chance.

Teressa thought he looked a trifle self-satisfied as he leaned back in his seat and slid his arm around her shoulders.

# Chapter 34

Rosalia Bryant entered her husband's study, her eyes filled with worry. "Where can she be, Eduardo? It will be dark soon and she is not yet home."

Edward Bryant shook his head. "I don't know where she is, but I have a pretty good idea."

"What do you mean?"

Rising, he drummed his fingers on the top of his desk. "I think she's run off."

Rosalia's eyes widened. "Run off? You mean eloped? With McCloud?"

"That is exactly what I mean. Damn the man! I had him, but he got away. He's as slippery as an eel."

Sitting in the chair in front of her husband's desk, Rosalia folded her hands in her lap. "What are you not telling me?"

Edward muttered an oath and dropped back in his chair. "I think he was at the masquerade. I happened to see the two of them together the next day when Tessa was supposed to be visiting with Cynthia. They went to the Royal Arms that afternoon and didn't leave until hours later. You can imagine what they were doing there."

Rosalia shook her head. "No, not Teressa."

Edward grunted softly. "I thought I had the problem solved, but the bastard managed to escape. He didn't go back to his hotel. I don't know where he holed up, or where he is now."

Rising, he rounded the desk and began to pace the floor. "I don't think he's gone far," he said, thinking aloud. "His horse is still at the livery, but wherever he is, you can be sure Teressa is with him."

"What are we going to do?"

"I'm going to see Cynthia Witherspoon. I think she knows where they are, and I, by damn, intend to find out."

# Chapter 35

They were about an hour away from Buffalo Springs when the coach came to a halt.

"What is it? What's happening?"

The question came from Emily Thompson. Her husband shook his head. "I don't know, dear."

"It's a holdup," Chance said. "Just do what they say. Give them whatever they ask for."

"Now see here . . ." the florid-faced man sputtered.

"I doubt if anything you have is worth your life," Chance said curtly.

"Joseph, I'm scared."

Joseph Thompson put his arm around his wife and held her close, though he looked just as frightened as she did.

The minister closed his eyes. Teressa assumed he was praying for deliverance.

Outside, one of the robbers hollered for the driver to throw down the strongbox. A shot was fired, someone yelped in pain, something heavy hit the ground with a sharp thud. She hoped it was the money box and not the driver.

More voices, and then a man wearing a kerchief over the lower half of his face opened the door and ordered them outside.

Chance was the last one out of the coach. There were three men, all masked. Chance raised his hands over his head as ordered, stood mute as one of the bandits relieved him of his Colt and carelessly tossed it aside. A second outlaw stood a little apart from the other two, covering the passengers with a rifle while his companions moved among the passengers, taking cash and whatever else caught their fancy.

"No!" Emily cried. "Please don't take my wedding ring!"

"Give it to him," Joseph said. "I'll buy you another one."

"But I want this one!"

The bandit grabbed Emily's hand, intent on taking the ring. She jerked her hand away from him. Angry now, the bandit slapped her. She reeled back, the man's handprint already showing as a dark bruise on her pale skin.

"There's no call for that," Chance said, taking a step forward.

The outlaw turned his gun on Chance. "Mind your own business!"

Chance stared at the man, the muscles in his back twitching. He'd been sixteen the last time he heard that voice. "Finch."

The bandit's eyes widened in surprise. "You know me?"

"I know you're a cold-blooded murderer."

"I never murdered anybody who didn't have it coming." Finch took a step forward. "Who the hell are you?" he demanded. "And how the hell do you know who I am?" He stared at Chance for several moments, his brow furrowed.

Chance could almost see the man's mind turning, trying to place him. He knew the exact moment when Finch realized who he was.

Finch's eyes widened in disbelief. "No, it can't be!"

"Remember me now, do you?"

"I remember your mother," Finch said with a leer. "How is she?"

"She died after what you did to her."

Finch swore. "I should have known. It was you, wasn't it? You're the one who killed Weston and Hicks?"

Chance nodded, his hands clenched at his sides. "And I aim to take you out the same way."

"I don't think so."

Chance tensed as Finch's finger curled around the trigger. He was about to tackle Finch in a last desperate play when Teressa cried, "No!" and threw herself in front of Chance as the outlaw fired.

Her harsh cry was swallowed up in the report of Finch's pistol as he squeezed the trigger.

The next few minutes seemed to pass in slow motion.

A bright crimson stain spread over the front of Teressa's bodice.

Lowering his gun hand, Finch stared at Teressa as her knees gave way and she dropped to the ground. The other two bandits both stopped what they were doing and turned in the direction of the gunshot.

Chance dove for his Colt. He rolled to the right as his hand closed over the walnut grips of the gun.

Finch was the first of the outlaws to move. He pivoted on his heel, his gun tracking Chance's movements. Chance quickly rolled to the left and fired. The two men fired within seconds of each other. Chance's bullet found its mark, but Finch's shot went wild.

The remaining outlaws were moving, too, but it was too late. Chance rolled to the left once again. Sprawled on his stomach, he fired at the two bandits.

There was a sudden silence, punctuated by Emily's high-pitched wail.

After making sure all three outlaws were dead, Chance hurried to Teressa's side. Her bodice was soaked with blood; her face was pale.

"She's dead, isn't she?" Emily wailed.

"No!" She couldn't be dead. He wouldn't let her be dead. He lifted her carefully so he could check her back, relieved to see that the bullet had gone through. Relieved that the wound was in her shoulder and not in her chest, as he had feared at first.

He looked up at Emily Thompson, who was hovering nearby, her face streaked with tears. "Tear off a strip of your petticoat," he said brusquely.

She stared at him a moment, then quickly tore off the bottom ruffle and thrust it into his hand.

Chance ripped the material in thirds. He made two thick pads that he placed over the wounds, front and back, then used the third strip to hold them in place.

"Teressa? Teressa!"

Whimpering softly, she opened her eyes. "Are you all right?"

"You damn fool. I'm fine. What were you thinking to jump in front of a bullet like that?"

"I couldn't let him shoot you."

He gathered her gently into his arms. "Dammit, Tessa, don't you ever do anything like that again."

"Is he dead?"

Chance glanced at Finch's body. "Yeah, he's dead."

So was the shotgun guard. They wrapped his body in one of the lap robes and tied him onto the roof of the coach.

"What about the others?" the minister asked. "Shouldn't we bury them?"

"Let the coyotes have 'em," the stagecoach driver said.

"It's our Christian duty," the minister said.

"I'm not feeling very Christian right now," the driver retorted. "They killed a friend of mine." He spat a stream of tobacco in the dirt. "As far as I'm concerned, they can rot."

"If you have a shovel . . ."

"Parson, this stage is leaving in about two minutes," the driver said. "With you or without you."

"At least give me time to pray for them."

"Make it short."

They reached Buffalo Springs just over three hours later. Under other circumstances, they would have covered the distance in far less time, but mindful of his wounded passenger, the driver kept the horses at a walk.

As soon as they reached town, Chance carried Teressa to the doctor's office. The doctor cleaned the wounds, applied disinfectant and clean bandages, then put her arm in a sling and advised her to stay in bed for a couple of weeks.

"Give her plenty of liquids," the doctor told Chance. "Make sure she gets lots of rest. The bullet went clean through. She'll be as good as new in no time."

Chance thanked the doctor, then lifted Teressa into his arms and carried her out of the office and across the street.

"Where are we going?"

"To the hotel."

"I can walk," she protested, aware of the curious stares of passersby, but Chance ignored her. "And why are we going to the hotel?"

"You've been bounced around enough for one day. I want you to rest, like the doctor said."

Lyle Hunsacker looked a trifle surprised to see Chance enter the hotel with Teressa in his arms. Mindful of Teressa's reputation, Chance asked for two rooms.

Hunsacker handed Chance two keys. "I'll sign the register for you, Mr. McCloud."

"Obliged."

Opening the door to the first room, Chance carried Teressa inside. Drawing back the covers, he settled her in bed, then sat down beside her.

"You scared the hell out of me," he said, brushing a lock of hair from her brow. "Don't you ever do anything like that again, you hear?"

"He might have killed you."

"Better me than you. Are you all right? Do you want anything?"

"Just you," she murmured fervently, "here beside me."

In spite of her insistance that she felt perfectly fine, Teressa slept most of the day. Chance had their dinner sent up from the hotel dining room. She had little appetite and after eating only about half of her dinner, she fell asleep again.

Chance sat in the chair beside the bed, watching her, thinking how close he had come to losing her.

They left for the ranch the next morning after breakfast. Chance insisted she spend the rest of the day in bed, threatening to tie her to the bedpost if she so much as thought about getting up.

"The doctor said two days' rest," he said firmly. "And two days is what you're getting."

Her protests fell on deaf ears.

"You promised to marry me as soon as we got here," she said. "You haven't changed your mind, have you?"

Mindful of her injured shoulder, he drew her carefully into his arms. "Of course not. Name the day."

"Two weeks from tomorrow will be fine."

"Two weeks! You don't mean it!"

"I'm sorry, darlin'."

"But I don't want to wait two weeks," she wailed.

"Me, either, but you heard the doc."

"Oh, you," she said sulkily and then frowned.

"What's wrong now?" he asked.

"I don't have a dress to wear. I don't have any clothes at all except the ones I'm wearing."

"We'll go into town as soon as you're back on your feet. You can buy all the clothes you need while I talk to the preacher and take care of a few things. We can be married two weeks from today. How does that sound?"

"Tomorrow would be better," she said stubbornly.

As promised, Chance took Teressa into town as soon as she was on her feet again. He kept the team at a walk so as not to cause Teressa any undue pain.

When they reached town, he dropped her off at the dress shop, promising to pick her up in front of the hotel in two hours to take her to lunch.

"Better make it three," she said, and with a wave and a smile, she went into the shop. She hadn't expected to find much of a selection, but to her surprise, the store carried a number of dresses suitable for a wedding.

She chose a pale pink gown with a fitted bodice and a slim skirt, pleased that it didn't need any alterations. She bought several other dresses for everyday use, as well as undergarments, a robe, and a nightgown. She paid for her purchases with money Chance had given her and left the shop.

She browsed in several other stores, buying a new pair of boots for everyday wear on the ranch, a pair of dainty shoes to wear with her wedding dress, and a pair of house slippers. She bought a simple white hat for church, wondering as she did so if Chance even went to church. She picked out a delicate confection of lace and flowers to wear at the wedding, and a floppy-brimmed sunbonnet for daily use. At the mercantile, she bought soap, a brush, a comb, and pins for her hair.

She reached the hotel just as Chance pulled up in the wagon.

He whistled softly when he saw her. "Did you buy out every store in town?"

"Almost," she replied.

Taking the packages from her hands, he loaded them into the back of the wagon.

"Are you ready for lunch?"

She nodded and placed her hand on his arm and they went into the hotel. He held her chair for her, then took a seat across from her.

"Find everything you wanted?" he asked.

"Yes. Did you talk to the preacher?"

"Yeah. Everything's all set for tomorrow afternoon at one. I thought we'd spend the night here at the hotel, if that's all right with you."

"Of course."

She was surprised when she discovered he'd gotten two rooms, touched when he told her he didn't want any hint of scandal damaging her reputation. "We'll be living here a long time," he told her, "and the people hereabouts have long memories."

She laughed softly, touched by his concern. "This is the last night you'll be sleeping alone, Mr. McCloud."

"You don't know how glad I am to hear you say that," he replied, grinning. "And I intend to hold you to it."

Their wedding day dawned bright and clear. They ate breakfast in the hotel dining room, then went upstairs to dress for the wedding.

At twelve forty-five, Chance knocked on her hotel room door. She opened it a moment later, a smile lighting her face.

She was radiant, Chance thought, from the crown of her hat to the soles of her feet. Her dress, though modest, flattered every curve.

"Chance?"

He blinked at the sound of her voice, only then

realizing that he had been staring at her like a man seeing a woman for the first time.

"You're beautiful," he murmured.

"Thank you." Her gaze moved over him. "You're looking very handsome yourself."

He had bought a new suit of clothes. His black coat and white shirt were the perfect complement to his copper-hued skin and dark hair and eyes. He looked tall and lean and good enough to eat. The thought brought a rush of heat to her cheeks.

"Shall we?" he asked, offering her his arm.

Smiling happily, she placed her hand on his arm and they walked down the street to the church.

The minister was waiting for them inside. A elderly man and woman who would be their witnesses stood beside him. He introduced them as Mr. and Mrs. Browne.

Chance took Teressa's hand in his as the minister began to speak. She gazed up at Chance. Lost in the love she saw in his eyes, she was hardly aware of the words that were spoken until the minister said, "You may kiss the bride."

Chance drew her into his arms. "I love you," he said, and lowering his head, he kissed her for the first time as her husband.

"Stop!"

Teressa jerked out of Chance's arms at the sound of her father's voice. "Papa! Mama! What are you doing here? How did you know . . . ?" Her voice trailed off. Of course. Her father had spoken to Cynthia.

"This wedding will not take place," Edward Bryant said. He hurried down the aisle, closely followed by his wife.

"I'm afraid you're too late," Chance said, holding tight to Teressa's hand. "It's already done."

"I will have it annulled! Today!"

"No you won't, Papa," Teressa said. "It's already been consummated."

Bryant's eyes widened, then narrowed ominously as he glared at Chance. "You bas—"

"Sir, I would remind you that you're in the house of the Lord," the minister said, cutting him off.

"Teressa, let's go."

"No, Papa. I'm Chance's wife now."

"The marriage will be annulled!"

"Papa, I don't think that's a good idea," Teressa said calmly. "Unless you want your first grandchild to be illegitimate."

Edward gaped at her.

Rosalia dropped down on the front pew, looking aghast.

"You're pregnant!" Her father spoke the words with the same horror he might have used if she had told him she had the plague.

"Yes. And I'm Wolf Shadow's wife, so you may as well get used to the idea."

"There's cake and champagne waiting for us at the hotel," Chance said, grinning. "We'd love to have you join us."

Edward turned to look at his wife. She stood, her face pale, and held out her hand. "Come, Eduardo," she said, forcing a smile. "Let us celebrate our daughter's marriage."

Teressa looked up at Chance and grinned. "Welcome to my family, Mr. McCloud."

The celebration didn't last long. The Bryants toasted the happy couple. They ate cake and drank champagne, but through it all they looked as though they were in a daze. It would be a while, Chance mused, before they fully accepted the fact that their daughter had married a half-breed rancher.

After her parents bid them good-bye, with the

promise they would see them the following morning, Chance carried his bride up the stairs to their hotel room. Opening the door, he carried her inside, kicked the door shut with his heel.

"A baby?" he asked, still holding her in his arms.

"I had to say something to make them stop talking about an annulment," she said, grinning at him.

"So it's not true?"

"It could be." She wrapped her arms around his neck. "But just in case I'm not . . ."

He grinned at her. "I get your drift, Mrs. McCloud, and I'll do my best to make sure you're in the family way just as soon as possible. Starting right now," he promised, and carrying her to bed, he made love to her as thoroughly and tenderly as ever a man had loved a woman.

And nine months later, his wife's little white lie turned out to be a nine-pound baby boy.

# *Epilogue*

Teressa sat in the shade of a huge old cottonwood, her four-month-old son sleeping peacefully on a buffalo hide beside her as she watched her husband put a handsome buckskin stallion through its paces. The horse was fresh off the range, still green broke and rough around the edges, but it was quick to learn and Wolf Shadow—she never did learn to call him Chance—had hopes that the stallion would make a good cutting horse.

She smiled and waved as Wolf Shadow looked in her direction. Life had never been better. Their child was healthy and happy, the ranch was prospering, and her parents had finally given them their blessing.

She glanced fondly at her son. They had named him Luke, after Wolf Shadow's father. Soon, they would go to visit the People so that Wolf Shadow could seek a vision. And while they were there, they would have a feast to honor their son and Wolf Shadow would proclaim that their son would be known as Snow Wolf among the People.

She knew Wolf Shadow was looking forward to seeing Kills-Like-a-Hawk again. She, too, was eager to return to the Black Hills, to show off her handsome son to Corn Woman and Yellow Fawn and Leaf, to hear the Lakota language, to lie inside a snug lodge and listen to the wind whisper against the lodgeskins.

Her heart swelled with love and peace as she watched Wolf Shadow dismount and walk toward her. She glanced down at her son and then back to her husband. At long last, she knew where she belonged.

*Dear Reader:*

*I hope you enjoyed reading the story of Wolf Shadow and Teressa as much as I enjoyed writing it. I always fall in love with my hero, and I hope you did, too.*

*I can't believe this is my thirty-seventh book. I remember when I was writing stories and hiding them under the bed! For those of you who have dreams of being published, hang on to that dream and make it come true.*

*I want to thank all of you for your letters and support. I love it when I get a letter from someone who tells me they hated reading until they picked up one of my books. I've always loved to read, and it makes me feel good to know that one of my books helped someone else discover the joy of reading.*

*God bless you all. God bless America.*

*Madeline*
*www.madelinebaker.net*